The
JEWEL
BOX

C. MICHELLE MCCARTY

All the best!

Michelle McCarty

ISBN: 1481107151
ISBN 13: 9781481107150

Library of Congress Control Number: 2012922853
CreateSpace Independent Publishing Platform
North Charleston, South Carolina

For my compass and shining star, my daughter Kim

~In loving memory of Jack Mynier

"We dance round in a ring and suppose, but the Secret sits in the middle and knows."

~ Robert Frost

1

A wise man once told me the universe drops bizarre beings into our lives for the purpose of developing our souls. Apparently the cosmos deems my soul a work in progress, because here comes another dose of crazy.

I looked past my customer and onto the Strand, watching Delilah Carlino speed walk toward my antique shop. Despite living two hours from Galveston, my warped friend episodically drops into my world, hoping to create havoc. Her lunacy lost me a couple of sales over the past decade, so I wrapped and rang Sunday's final transaction in record time.

"Looks like your shipment of knockoffs finally got here from Taiwan," Delilah shouted over the soft tingling of bells as she bolted through the front door.

Ignoring her attempt to take center stage and disrupt business, I thanked my customer, ushered him out, flipped my "Closed" sign, and locked the dead bolt. Only days from Halloween and Delilah's fiftieth birthday, she still wore the same garb she donned during the Sixties—jean shorts and captioned T-shirt. Unfortunately these days said T-shirts express her personal and often R-rated opinions, accentuated with her Bedazzle gun. I'm not one to criticize how people choose to present themselves, but her rhinestone revelations could use some censorship.

"So, what time are they delivering that old bar?"

"They promised to have it here before six." Wishing I hadn't answered her call this morning, much less mentioned the delivery, I reached over and

1

gave her a quick hug. Speedy hugs were crucial with Delilah; otherwise one could be overcome by her fragrant salute to Oscar de la Renta. Today she was saturated bangs to bunions with *Intrusion*. "Jeez, Delilah, are you shooting perfume intravenously?"

"Guess I went overboard soaking my short and curlies in concentrated oil this morning."

Nowadays most people respect those with allergies and refrain from basting their bodies in fragrance. Not Delilah. "Why marinade in perfume for a trek down to Galveston?"

"Ya never know when I might run across some handsome hunk." She dramatically shook her chin length, bobbed hair, revealing silver streaks. In her youth, beauty queen Delilah sported shimmering blue-black hair that fell below her waist and swung from side to side as she walked, leaving hordes of men with dangling tongues. She still possessed a perfect nose, flawless skin, and big baby blues she flamboyantly framed with midnight black eyeliner that extended to the corner of her eyes into butterfly wings. "I'm not a willowy blonde like you, so I have to woo men with my scent."

"You don't need to be wooing anyone, Delilah."

"Yes I do. If Eric doesn't stop asking for tush ten times a week, he's gonna be out on his Bill O'Reilly-watching-ass." She opened a jumbo pack of cinnamon gum.

"Still not smoking?" I segued.

"Almost a year now, but I dream about sucking sticks every single night."

"Well, I'm proud of you."

"At least someone cares. Eric says my nicotine cravings are making me even more frigid."

I never lend credence to comments incapable of sustaining a shelf life of more than ten seconds. Fabricating stories about her hubby became Delilah's source of entertainment after Caller ID technology put the brakes on her ridiculous routine of crank calling old boyfriends.

"BTW I told my sex fiend husband to microwave dinner without me, 'cause we're looking for treasures in the sand this evening."

"NFW," I responded. Acronyms are synonymous with electronic communication, but face to face they're about as charming as conversational burping.

"No friggin' way? Why not?" She propped her elbows on my satinwood Pembroke table, fashioning her hands under her chin in supplication. "Pretty please?"

"Beg till you're blue in the face, but those treasure hunting days are over."

"Dang it, Shaaareee." Delilah intentionally inflated my name with country twang. "Why can't we use that contraption to find metal on the beach? Is the moon in Uranus again?"

"Lovely. I encourage you to watch one PBS special on the big bang theory, and now you're spouting childish clichés. My attempts to enlighten you have once again backfired."

"Hey, I learned about dependent opposites who can't live without each other. You know, the yin and yang thang."

"Ah, yin and yang." I slipped out of my heels and wiggled my toes.

"Yeah. You guys have it out the wazoo and Eric and I will never have anything remotely close." Delilah likes to theorize all marriages are superior to hers. "Why couldn't I have had a fantasy love affair like yours?" She revved into action.

"Fantasy? What kind of fantasy involves anguish like we've gone through?"

"Anguish aside, you're definitely the Yin to his Yang. The Cleopatra to his Marc Antony." She paused before loudly belting into suggestive song. "The *Magic* to his Johnson."

"I like your last analogy, but please lower your voice. Shops are closing and people passing by can hear you." I waved at my neighboring kite store owner.

"Okay." Delilah dropped her volume about half a decibel. "But only if we can drag that silver detector along the shore to scoop up coins for me a boob job. No sense in Dolly having all the fun."

"Stop asking." I shot her a stern look. Sharing my sentimental gift from Beau was not an option. "Besides, you've never missed out on fun, so don't mess with what Ma Nature blessed."

"I'm not gonna. It's a little late for me to be enhancing my mini-melons, and after all these years I'm not sure I could maneuver anything bigger than my B cups." She rambunctiously began to shimmy her bosom.

3

"Behave." I placed my hands cease-and-desist fashion on her shoulders when I noticed the souvenir shop owner slowing her pace to stare inside my window. Irritating everyone in our interplanetary system has long been Delilah's *raison d'être,* yet she wonders why our friendship waned. Some thirty-odd years ago, Delilah literally crashed into my world by ramming her '68 Camaro into the back bumper of my new 1970 Mustang. She was frazzled over a recent job loss. I was frazzled in general. Married young, divorced before my daughter Nikki turned two, and one hell of a mess at twenty-three, I foolishly hired Delilah as an evening babysitter. Still, despite opposing viewpoints on almost everything, our alliance is sealed by a sacred bond. Delilah knows a shameful secret from my past. I don't want it broadcast across Texas.

"Cherie, they're here!" Delilah tapped the window, signaling the truck driver to the back.

I rushed to open the receiving entrance and greeted a somewhat pale but powerfully built, twenty-something guy. Delilah leaned against an oak armoire and was spraying on her third or fourth layer of *Intrusion* when in walks another mover.

"Whoa," Delilah said before making a beeline toward the incoming hunk.

This second "Body-by-Adonis" was sun-bronzed and slightly older than the first. "Where you want this monster, ma'am?" he nodded my way, recognizing me as the one in charge.

"In this corner by the window, please." I motioned.

"Texas sure grows some fine looking movers." Delilah invaded his personal space and tugged her tank top downward to cleavage view level. Known for flirting with every three-legged man who crosses her path, she amplified her Mae West tramp act for this duo.

The muscular men gingerly situated my bar in its window view for passersby, even with Delilah slithering so close I worried rape charges might get filed. I finally unglued her from their chest hairs and gave them their tip while offering an apologetic smile. "Thanks for skillfully maneuvering the bar around my unexpected obstacle."

"I'll escort 'em out." Delilah ignored my barb and latched onto their arms. "I need to buy some wine."

"Better hurry. They close in ten minutes." I attempted to expedite matters so the guys could breathe fresh, less perfumed air. As the trio left, Delilah threatened to follow them home, but scooted off in the opposite direction after blowing a few farewell air kisses their way.

The historic downtown Strand is only blocks from Galveston's waterfront, and consists of unique shops, eateries, museums, live music venues, and horse drawn carriages to delight visitors during December's "Dickens on The Strand" event. Unfortunately almost every shop but the liquor store closes at six. I optimistically hoped Delilah would find a better caliber of grapes than those fermented into Boone's Farm—her staple wine of the Seventies. She returned in speedy fashion, flaunting the surprisingly decent bottle of wine she scored.

"Cherie, get some wine glasses and sit down so we can celebrate your finding this bar."

"As long as we keep the celebration to one drink." I grabbed glasses from a China hutch. "I'm in a crunch for time, but I'll crank up the oldies. Gotta have Sixties music." I turned on KLDE, escorted our wine glasses to a settee and motioned her to join me. My favorite disc jockey, Colonel St. James was hawking good times and great oldies, and promising to play *Treat Her Right* by Houstonian, Roy Head.

"He can still do the alligator." Delilah popped a huge gum bubble. She knew Roy back in the Seventies when she was recycling bass players. "So how the heck did you stumble across this bar?" She clutched the bottle of Ruffino while digging through her purse for a corkscrew.

"At an antique shop in Warrenton that Nikki insisted we visit, despite our aching feet."

"You're so lucky." Delilah lifted the cork with the agility of a professional wine steward.

"It was kismet." I smiled.

"And there's Beau's old metal detector." She pointed to a wall near the bar.

"We encased it last weekend. Don't you love the glass and mahogany display box?"

"Now remind me how you wound up working for Beau," Delilah dug for facts I had never divulged. She tossed her gum into the trash, plopped beside me on the settee, and snuggled into a cushion with the insouciance of someone intent on making an ass groove. "And why the hell he changed your name from Jill to Cherie." She paused to fill my glass with wine.

Only my mother still calls me by my given name, so hearing "Jill" spoken by anyone else always sounds off mark.

"Some other time," I fibbed. Exactly how I met Beau was one detail she didn't need for her diary. "I don't mean to be rude Delilah, but one glass of wine truly is my limit. I've got a special evening planned and need to freshen up."

"I'd like to have a special evening just once in my life before I die." She guzzled half a glass of wine and poured herself a refill as *Sugar Sugar* by The Archies played on my radio.

"You've enjoyed countless special times with your nice husband, Delilah."

"My perpetually horny husband?" she asked in incredulous tone.

"Pleeease!" I released two hair pins from my ballerina twist, letting my hair fall onto my shoulders. "Considering some of the scoundrels you dated during our younger years, you should be thrilled to have a decent man."

"At least the bad boys were exciting." She swirled her glass of Ruffino. "I liked the good old days, back when you were wild and crazy like me. Before you got all sophisticated."

"Sophisticated? Puh-leeeze, Delilah, I'm still gauche as all get out. And my wild and crazy days were riddled with idiotic behavior I'd rather not relive. Talk about hard-earned lessons."

She sipped her wine without responding, seemingly preoccupied by something complex, like what effect quantum mechanics have on particles near a black hole or how to persuade scientists to invent Limpdix—a pill identical in appearance to Viagra but with opposite effect.

The phone rang and I got up to answer Ellen's customary check-up call. Albeit I've matured into a responsible adult post my "stupid is as stupid does" years, my older sister still worries about me. As she talked about Thanksgiving plans, her loving tone warmed my soul. If it weren't for decades of Ellen's guidance, I might be pondering the perfect lipstick shade to match my bright orange jumpsuit about now.

My sister and I were raised in Lake Jackson, Texas, a sleepy little town sixty miles south of Houston. Ellen won homemaking awards. I won running medals. Ellen was quiet like our mother. I was mouthy like Dad. Ellen: calm, confident, respectful. Me: anxious, insecure, cheeky. My sister adored our family and seemed content with small town living. I never connected with either parent and dreamed about escaping to an exciting, big city life. Our timid, meticulous mother softly spouted quotes in lieu of discussing subjects necessary for maturing girls. A gracious woman of virtue, my mother Lynn regarded men as sole financial supporters in proper families and placed major stress on being chaste as though virginity resulted in eternal love with Prince Charming—or one of his well-heeled cousins. The word "virgin" got mega air time in our home, yet requests for in depth details about sex turned Mother's face beet red as she fidgeted with her pearl necklace. After constant explanations filled with Mother's indecipherable quotes, we finally stopped asking.

At the opposite side of the spectrum was our dad, George, a six-foot, fun loving extrovert whose jovial comments and high-spirited harmonica tunes resonated throughout our otherwise quiet home. Dad worked Dow Chemical's evening shift, so his sightings were rare but never dull. Occasionally Dad's cheerful temperament changed to wrath, and he walked around ranting and spewing expletives. Mother countered his cursing by running our noisy vacuum or floor buffer to shield our genteel ears. Her attempts to hide his erratic nature were futile, and by my teens it was obvious my parents got their spiritual enlightenment from differing sources. Mother's straight from Betty Crocker and Dad's straight from Jack Daniels.

The sound of pouring wine and clinking glass interrupted my childhood mind drift. "I'm sorry, Ellen. Delilah's here funneling wine down her gullet and if I don't intervene it might take the Jaws-of-Life to detach her from my settee."

"Get to it, then. I've gotta slap on some dye to combat gray hairs invading my crown. You're lucky you got Mother's champagne blonde hair color. I'm stuck with Dad's dark brown shade that shows every new tiny strand of gray."

"But you've got his big brown eyes to distract from those incoming enemies."

"Ha! You got Mother's unique kiwi green eye color. And what did I get? Her short physique. Meanwhile you get Dad's height."

7

"You're five foot three and I'm five seven. I thought you'd be over this gene jealousy by now."

"I am. Mainly 'cause I'm the brainy one."

"Love you, sis. Let's chat tomorrow." I hung up and headed over to take charge of Delilah's wine situation. No more vino for Mrs. Carlino. The time to end our visit had commenced.

"Thanks for the wine, Delilah, but I really need you out of here so I can get my butt in gear." Being blunt was mandatory once wine hit her system.

"I know, I know." Delilah stood to leave. "What the heck is this?" She pulled a *Jack of Clubs* card from between the settee cushions.

I grabbed the thin rectangular piece of plastic from her. "Just one lost from its deck." I momentarily placed the card against my heart.

"Oh." She seemed oblivious to my trembling hand as she flung her purse over her shoulder. "Well, good thing you're booting me out cuz if I'm not home by nine, Eric starts dialing those 900 sex numbers."

"You're bent beyond repair, Delilah." I corked the remaining wine and walked her to the door. "And thanks again for the surprise drop by. Seeing you is always my distinct pleasure."

She hugged me before heading out the door. "Give Nikki my love," she yelled.

I nodded, thinking how after three decades, my daughter barely knew Delilah. After all, she only babysat Nikki briefly in 1970. It seemed so long ago, yet like only the blink of an eye.

Bliss comes from unusual sources, and suddenly *my* bar caused tears of happiness to well. I walked over, placed the *Jack of Clubs* card front and center, picked up Delilah's abandoned pack of cinnamon gum, and ran my fingers across the bar's surface, sentimentally touching every little groove. I slid a stick of gum into my mouth while sliding onto one of four barstools I'd moved alongside the bar earlier. Delilah's curiosity about my working for Beau left me with wide ranging emotions. Vexation. My friend knows too much of my personal business and teases about dragging skeletons from my closet for entertainment purposes. Details. In a few decades my grandchildren will be asking that same question, and unlike Delilah they deserve an answer. Truth. Nothing sets the heart free like revealing secrets that can haunt your soul and govern your life.

8

2

I glanced out my window into the skies over the Gulf, recalling my trajectory toward Beau. Late in 1968, I divorced my husband who reciprocated by vanishing to a foreign country and leaving our toddler without child support. Trying to put cornflakes on the table for my daughter Nikki propelled me into survival mode. I couldn't travel back in time, otherwise I would've heeded Mother's "Look before you leap!" adage, instead of rushing into marriage with Jethro Bodine's mirror image. Kent Novak never had anything original to say, but I fell for his light blue eyes, dark wavy hair, and muscular butt. The guy was eager to take me away from Lake Jackson—so what if we didn't know squat about each other? And thanks to my "Gracious ladies sit with legs crossed at the ankles while knees are kindly kept together" mother, I wed as a virgin. An awful awakening for me when the mind-blowing passion I'd read about in romance novels failed to visit our bridal suite. At least our wedding night served as my introduction to liquor.

We moved to the big city of Houston, but life with Kent remained dreadfully dull. Especially in the bedroom. Sex proved perfunctorily uneventful, although occasionally if I knocked back enough vodka to accommodate adequate visual delusions, I could somewhat imagine Kent bumping and grinding. A rock-hard ass does not a great lover make.

Mr. Boring insisted I be a housewife, so when Ellen and her husband Charles started a lathe business, I jumped at the chance to tend my four-year-old nephew, Jimmy. With bright, smiling eyes, blond curly hair, mischievous sense of humor and brains beyond his age, this preschooler brightened my dull life. Hell, he was ten times more interesting than Kent.

Still, after a year of humdrum living, about once a week I contemplated sticking my head inside our gas oven. Until the morning I awoke with nausea accompanied by vomiting. I stayed on my knees so often, Jimmy and Kent thought I had converted to Catholicism. Hail Mary and *inanimate* conception, I was pregnant!

Jacy Nicole's birth was the most exciting day of my life, and our instant mother-daughter bond gave me reason to exist. Nikki brought such happiness, I wrote elaborate notes about her every move, visualizing its evolution into a great children's book. Then my little princess got colic. Hello cranky baby, goodbye journalism fantasy. Jimmy helped me through baby blues and other rough toddler times before splitting for Pre-K, but his departure left me facing reality. Reading nursery rhymes and playing kid games had become the highlight of my existence. Naturally, I pondered said existence.

"Never marry a stranger," I advised my sixteen-month-old as we crafted macaroni art.

"Go bye-bye." Nikki swept elbow pieces and glue into her painted box.

It was kismet. I packed our bags.

Leaving behind almost everything, I waved goodbye to Kent as we passed in the doorway when he came home from work. He looked so sad and bewildered, for a minute I felt like a real jerk for my inconsiderate exit from the black and white dullness of our life. Sixty-one seconds later, I'd hopped in my Corvair Coupe, turned the radio full blast and was singing along with Steppenwolf's *Born to Be Wild* while driving Nikki away from our first home.

Shortly after Nikki and I arrived at my parent's home, I learned Kent remarried before the ink dried on our divorce decree. Men sure don't stay sad long. His newlywed butt soon got drafted and shortly after he shipped overseas, I found out nice guy Kent deceitfully filled out military paperwork. Claiming his new wife as his only dependent meant no child support. Fine. He could evaporate for all I cared. I was hell-bent on getting by without his financial aid.

I enrolled at community college and got a part-time evening job as office assistant, which prompted quotes from Mother. "A woman's place is in the home!" *In one ear and out the other, Lynn!* Morning classes revitalized my stale brain, and working at a fast paced marketing firm fueled my hyperactive nature. Employees stayed super busy, thanks to our thirty-something tall, lanky boss with piercing raven eyes, slick black hair, and a villainous look that intimidated most. Not me. I found Wesley's tailored suits and smug poise alluring in a John Dillinger sort of way.

But I didn't do well at balancing employment, education, and motherhood. My behavior slipped into back sassing, dish throwing, door slamming, tears flowing, mood swings. Mother spouted self help quotes for a while, then next thing I knew my erratic behind was parked in a psychologist's chair. Well, general practitioner slash psychologist. Dual practice was common in Lake Jackson, where I suspected one could go to the proctologist and flip over for a pelvic exam. The doctor/therapist prescribed an antidepressant to help ease my confusion.

After two *Tofranil* filled weeks my disposition went on the upswing.

"Hey Jill," Wesley shouted as we worked late one evening. "Wanna go over projected sales before heading out?"

Hmmm. Hang with suave guy or head home for an earful of Mother's quotes? I bolted down the hall and into his office.

"What can I get you to drink?"

"Orange juice," I answered, knowing Lake Jackson was in a dry county.

"With what?" Wesley opened a cabinet that could have passed as a Spec's Mini Mart.

"Gotta pass on the liquor. Mother forbids drinking in her house."

"Well, I hate drinking alone, this isn't your mother's house, and I won't tell if you don't."

"I'm taking medication and my doc said not to mix it with alcohol."

My excuse was still hanging in mid-air when Wesley jumped from behind his desk and walked around to my chair. "Let me see your prescription," he insisted.

I handed him my bottle of Tofranil. "These damn quacks!" he said angrily and looked into my eyes. "You don't need to be popping pills and your daughter certainly doesn't need her mom hooked on tranquil-izers." Boom! He took my vial of capsules to the bathroom and began flushing.

Years of inconsistency in my home life made me in awe of such asser-tiveness. When Wesley returned, he handed me a large drink. Sipping on my tequila and orange juice for over an hour, I listened to the man in the Brooks Brother's shirt who got more attractive by the minute.

Wasn't long before I dropped out of college to become office manager, and also became charmed by my boss. Wesley drove a cherry red Lincoln Continental convertible, which fueled my daydreams into thoughts of romantic deeds with this fiery guy. What a disappointment when my fantasy finally came to life. Our liaison evolved after a stressful day amplified into an evening of nonstop tequila shots, so it didn't rate high on the romance scale. Future "romantic" deeds always included alcohol and always transpired on the office sofa. I wasn't exactly qualified to rate sex, but considered Wesley eighty percent better than inert Kent. Experienced Wesley taught me Sex Ed 101, albeit carnal encounters failed to arouse—much less satisfy me. Within weeks Wesley's behavior began to parallel my dad's. I foolishly presumed his moodiness would end once we left Lake Jackson, so before you could say two-neurotics-in-transit, Wesley hooked a tow bar to his convertible for dragging my car to El Paso, his assigned city to establish a company branch. My virtuous mother accepted my lie about us living in separate housing, likely because she couldn't fathom her daughter shacking up with the second guy who came along.

Traveling to El Paso included a stop in Houston. Wesley had a business meeting. Nikki was begging to spend time with Cousin Jimmy. And yours truly had to see my gynecologist about an overwhelming pain that parked in my grassy knoll and refused to leave. I also squeezed in a visit with my best friend from high school. Katie entered my life during sophomore year when her family transferred to Texas from Michigan. Her tales of life out-side southern boundaries captivated me, but her uninhibited persona drew me to her. She mimicked my odd habit of walking on my tip toes. I mocked her excessive eyelash fluttering. By the summer of '63 we were inseparable. Although we talked occasionally after high school, I hadn't seen Kat since Nikki's birth. My doctor was near her apartment, so she insisted I bring my bikini to sunbathe at her pool and catch up on lost time.

The girl hadn't changed a bit. Thin, leggy Katie, whose thick, curly, auburn hair almost overshadowed her oval face and ski shaped nose, possessed huge hazel eyes and a fetching way of looking at people that made her seem prettier than she was. Incredibly stylish (she could pin a dead cockroach in her hair and start a trend), Kat possessed such effervescence I worried she might internally combust. Flattery was her forte. She was rattling on about my recent short hair cut enhancing my green eyes when I noticed rumpled twenty dollar bills scattered around her living room. Kat took two pink cans of Tab from the fridge, placed them on folded twenties to use as coasters, sat beside me, and insisted I brief her on my sex life since we both left high school as virgins. "Start talking," she commanded with gusto.

I leaned against the luxurious cushions of her sofa and elaborated on my two vastly different sexual experiences. Then she told me about her sex-capades! During her demonstration of Kama Sutra positions, I noticed a giant bowl filled with about a zillion quarters sitting beside a Tiffany lamp on top of her expensive TV. "For the laundromat," she said, following my gaze.

"Pleeease." I stood for a closer look at her coin mountain. "There's at least two hundred bucks in this bowl. And more twenty dollar bills in this room than I've ever seen. What's up?"

Kat motioned me to her bedroom, pranced over to the closet, pulled out a small duffel bag, threw it across her bed, and opened it. Small sequined underwear and other glittery items tumbled out, along with greenbacks of all denominations. "I'm making the money, cutie." She winked. "I'm working as a waitress and part-time dancer in a darling little club near downtown called the Jewel Box."

"God, Katie!"

"It's not so bad, Jill. I mainly wait tables and only dance a couple times a night when the club's short on dancers." She shook her bountiful booty. "It's really kinda groovy. My family thinks I work in a restaurant and I go by the name Laura, so they'll never find out."

"You always had a wild streak, but God." I slipped into my blue cro-chet bikini wondering how my friend got involved in such a job, and trying to stop reiterating "God."

"So, Jill. What did doc say about those spasms in your tulip garden?"

"It's a cyst that's fortunately shrinking, but he prescribed Phenaphen for my pain. He also said my severely tilted uterus makes my chances of getting pregnant about one in a million."

"Weird diagnosis." Kat pulled her bouncy red curls into a loose ponytail.

"Makes me triply glad I have Nikki, but you gotta love those pregnancy odds, eh?"

When we got to the pool she spilled more details about her job. "On rare times that I dance, I play *Fever* by Peggy Lee and move as slow and enticingly as the law allows."

I'd always admired the way Kat exuded naughtiness in our private con-versations, but this public declaration was worlds apart from two teenagers talking trash behind closed doors.

"Or I play *Shake a Tail Feather*, and turn my fanny to the crowd and shimmy wildly." She offered a provocative sample.

I felt slightly embarrassed, and happy we were alone at the pool.

Kat's laid back attitude about her bizarre job baffled me. I left her apartment feeling my world had gone topsy turvy, and tried to embrace Mother's quote: "To each his own" as I got in my car. After all, Kat seemed happy. And she was making a buttload of money.

When I walked into Ellen's house Nikki rushed to me, so I grabbed her right arm and leg, giving her an extra long jet twirl. She squealed in delight. All was right in my world again.

"Wesley called. He's running a little late," Ellen shouted from the kitchen.

"No surprise," I responded. "More airplane," Nikki requested. We negotiated a flight tower position instead and she climbed on my shoulders to ride into the kitchen to help Ellen.

Wesley arrived discourteously late for dinner. I took advantage of his social blunder. "Kat wants to meet us at Brennan's tomorrow before we leave town, and I said we would." He agreed—with zero enthusiasm.

Charles shot him a look that had "rude jackass" written all over it. Wesley made a hasty exit for the hotel room he'd rented for the night.

༄

Wesley's chances of winning a Mr. Congeniality award dwindled drastically as he sipped whiskey and made no effort to hide his bored shitless look while Kat and I reminisced over wine. Ignoring him, Kat pinched off an end slice of French bread, popped it into her mouth, rolled her eyes as if to emphasize how tasty it was, and then knocked back her third glass of Rothschild like it was iced tea. By the time she finished her fourth glass she began discussing her job. Wesley suddenly got real interested. I couldn't believe my ears when he said me working with Kat would be the perfect opportunity for *us* to earn quick money and start our own marketing firm. "Right on!" Kat squeezed my arm. "The owner's been saying we should hire another waitress to keep up with booming business. And you'll rake in the tips with your curvy body, cutie."

I took a pain med and chased it with wine.

Maybe it was the combination of Phenaphen and Rothschild, Kat's assurance the job wasn't as horrible as it sounded, or my emotional instability and Wesley's cunning, but before the bill arrived, I had acquiesced. Apparently, virtue is not matrilineal. As Kat patted my trembling hand, Wesley volunteered to delay leaving for El Paso so he could oversee my first few nights. By the time we left the restaurant, my sweet friend had convinced me working together would be a total blast and I would get hip to the topless club scene. I didn't want to seem "square." Wesley checked out of La Quinta and into the swanky Carousel Motel off the Gulf Freeway, closer to Kat's apartment.

Kat called the following morning to say the job was mine. She also said Texas law prohibited dancing topless without complete coverage of the nipple and suggested we meet downtown at Southern Importers to buy pasties to cover said nipples. What the hell were pasties?

We walked into the shop on San Jacinto where Kat guided me through the phenomenal supply of novelty fabric, party props, theatrical makeup, costumes and accessories. When we got to a corner near the back of the store, she opened drawers of a nondescript cabinet and removed various small, cone shaped objects, some plain, some sequined, and some sporting tassels. Bubbling with enthusiasm and making light of the whole situation, Kat placed two tasseled pasties over her blouse (tit-level), then tried a few circular swings before placing an unadorned one over her eye, monocle fashion. "Jill, my little chickadee." Kat raised her perfectly plucked eyebrows mischievously, à la W.C. Fields. "I insist you stay at my villa on the south side instead of driving across town at three in the morning."

"Okay, I'll stay with you awhile," I agreed just to get her way-too-happy ass out of there. I kept my eyes lowered as we stood at the register, and my cheeks felt flush long after we reached our prospective cars and left Southern Importers.

I returned to my sister's house and held Nikki against me like we were still connected at the umbilical cord. "You're suffocating me!" She fled my grip.

"I've decided to take that new restaurant job I mentioned," I lied to Ellen. "Could you possibly keep Nikki, since you're doing books for the business at home now?"

"Sure. What's your schedule?"

"Hectic, long hours. I thought I'd stay with Kat during the week and spend every Sunday and Monday here."

Ellen agreed. Jimmy cheered. Nikki squealed. My brother-in-law stared at the girls of *Petticoat Junction*. Wesley remained at his hotel, where I'd gone earlier in the day and interrupted his watching bootleg films of women impaling themselves on cucumbers and whatnot. No doubt his evening wasn't nearly as innocent as Charles checking out Hooterville hotties.

3

My first day at the Jewel Box didn't exactly turn into the total blast Kat had predicted. Having been inside a bar only twice before, I was terrified about going to a topless club and anticipatory anxiety caused me to vomit during the ride from Kat's apartment. So much for Wesley's custom eggshell leather interior—I'll spare you further details. Located on the east side of Holcombe Boulevard between the prestigious Medical Center and the predominately Jewish, upscale McGregor area, the white stucco building was barely discernible except for its red door. Hanging above the door from a black wrought iron fixture was a small white octagonal sign with "Jewel Box" embossed in exquisite red lettering. Just below the club's name "Topless Go-Go" was written in subtle black calligraphy so small I almost didn't see it. My nausea intensified.

Wesley and Katie practically dragged me to the front door, with him firmly reminding me this job was vital to our future, thus the sooner I settled my queasy stomach and started making cash, the sooner we'd leave Houston. I wanted to throw up on him. My IQ was nowhere near Mensa requirements, so like a cow being herded to slaughter, I let Wesley steer me inside.

In the entryway stood an antique treasure chest lined in red satin and filled with replicas of glass jewels illuminated by incoming sunlight when the door opened and by soft recessed lights when it closed. I stepped onto plush red carpet, looking at the lower level packed with small round tables and skirted Parson chairs. Then I glanced along the left wall and saw a tiny, round dance stage with red velvet drapes cascading from a mirror behind it. Only a stone's throw away stood a colorful jukebox against the club's back wall. "You've gotta meet Beau. He burns cool." Kat grabbed my hand and dragged me to the upper level. Wesley stood by the chest, eyeballing jewels.

A scattering of tables shared the area with a long, crescent shaped mahogany bar, polished to an incredible shine and softly reflecting overhead twinkling of dimly lit chandeliers. Maybe two months of this wouldn't be so bad, after all.

"This is Beauregard Phillipe Duvalé," Kat introduced. "We call him Beau."

Towering behind the bar, looking like Clark Gable's twin with smaller ears, the impeccably dressed, handsome owner smiled broadly, his stunning steel-grey eyes sparkling. "Welcome to the Jewel Box." Beau graciously extended his hand.

"Pardon my wet glove," I mumbled.

"What?" A puzzled look replaced his broad smile as he straightened his black tie.

"It's just something she says when she's nervous." Kat rubbed my back.

"Dorothy Parkerisms." I scraped fingernail polish, relaxing slightly.

"Dorothy Parker had legendary wit," Beau said, his demeanor comforting.

"She's like heroin." I massaged my upper arm.

"You mean she's your heroine?" he gently inquired.

"No, I meant heroin."

"You do narcotics?" Beau asked in stern tone.

"No, but thanks for asking." I nodded as though he had offered candy.

Kat thumped my arm. "She's messin' with your melon, Beau."

"So we got us a pretty girl with kooky wit, do we?" He snapped a bar towel near me.

I flinched, but quickly regrouped and grabbed my nose. "Lysol your linens, man."

I wasn't sure what Kat meant by "burns cool," but Beau seemed nicer than I'd presumed anyone running such a club would be. His eyes reflected warmth and kindness and the timbre of his voice was bass, yet gentle. Beau suggested Kat seat Wesley while he and I got acquainted. Saying he sensed my uneasiness, Beau told me about his French heritage, and I admitted my longing to visit Paris, especially Sylvia Beach's bookshop once frequented by literary greats such as Joyce, Fitzgerald, Thurber, and Hemingway. As I momentarily envisioned the '20's era in Paris, Beau suggested I go by "Cherie" a name of French origin. It sounded enchanting flowing from his lips. I repeated the name, attempting to enunciate it as well as Beau. *Cherie* was perfect!

Unfortunately, walking through the door and assuming an alias was the easy part. Kat (aka Laura) whisked me away to the dressing room, found me a locker, and taught me the art of gluing on pasties while reminding me that complete coverage of areola was strictly enforced in our great Lone Star State. I nervously slipped my sheer lingerie top over my pasties and panties, before sitting on a red leather vanity bench to await Kat's Maybelline makeover on me.

While slapping enough makeup on my face to cover anything from warts to war wounds, Kat went over her personal conduct rules for wait-ressing in the Jewel Box. "You'll get great tips if you bat your eyelashes and smile." She offered an example by tilting her head slightly, smiling brightly, and batting her Bambi-like eyelashes excessively. Kat rambled on about thanking men for tips, seemingly oblivious to my onset of panic.

"Oh, and never. . . I repeat, *never*, let anyone kiss you on the lips. Just turn your head to the side then rush away with their order, or drop your chin so they end up kissing your forehead. Any major problems, Beau'll bolt from behind that bar like thunderous Thor to save our butts."

"Beau seems really nice." My voice trembled.

"Ole Hawk Eye is the greatest." She flashed a big, sincere smile. "Okay, cutie, don't forget to call me Laura and I'll work at calling you Cherie."

Paralyzed with fear, I couldn't find the nerve to move my scantily clad body out of the dressing room. Mother spent years instilling the proper dress code for ladies, and trust me, it was nothing like the skimpy clothing clinging to my body. Kat finally noticed me shaking and tried to relax me by saying we had to put red tablecloths and candles on all tables. I went into freeze frame against the wall. She prodded. "C'mon, we're the only girls here. Dancers don't show up til two or three in the afternoon."

My paralysis turned into full-on body tremors. Then Wesley came knocking.

19

"Here's something for your nerves." He handed me a shot of tequila via Kat who had propped her foot against the dressing room door, barely allowing room for his large hand.

"I just took a pain pill and shouldn't drink," I protested.

"It's not going to kill you, Jill. Just chug it. Don't let me down tonight." Wesley's voice faded as he walked away. "Soon this'll all seem like a figment of your imagination."

A figment? No. This was real, and I was the half-naked one living it!

"Cutie, I don't know about this guy." Kat frowned and handed me the tequila, before questioning the number of pain meds I used. I lied to my best friend. I was taking more than the recommended daily dose. After downing my tequila, I slipped out of the dressing room and somehow endured the embarrassing walk to the waitress station, wishing the dim lights were dimmer so the sheerness of my top would be less conspicuous. Wesley met me with another shot of tequila.

"There's hardly any customers, so lemme show you the dance routine." Kat grabbed the back of my top, pulling me through the club. She set her tray on a table, plugged quarters into the jukebox, and stepped onto the tiny, round stage to begin dancing. Choosing *Backfield in Motion* for obvious reasons, Katie as "Laura" gyrated her shapely derriere at the few men present, then turned and gazed into their eyes, rolling her shoulders provocatively. As the song ended, she shook her ample chest before bending over to flaunt her fanny. I felt embarrassed to the core of my being as I watched her dancing almost naked in front of these guys. She stepped off the stage without a modicum of modesty, and shouted my direction. "Go wait tables while I freshen up, cutie." I momentarily lost my ability to breathe. I self-consciously walked around the small club checking for drink orders, but if customers attempted small talk, response of any sort failed to cross my lips as my brain inked their beverage choices. I waited nervously at the waitress station until Kat came back. "You need to get on the stage and practice dancing before the club gets busy."

"Oh no, I can't!" My head shook a frantic "No" as the rest of me stood petrified.

"C'mon, cutie. Go-go dancing is nothing compared to what strippers have to do. Those girls wear elaborate getups and undress down to the bare essentials by ripping off long gloves with their teeth and such. And they dance about ten minutes. We just have to jiggle around on that little stage for one song."

Wesley rushed over and compassionately poured two more shots of tequila down me.

"This is it girl." Kat plugged quarters in the jukebox, selected *I Heard It Through the Grapevine* by Marvin Gaye, and shoved me onto the stage.

Nightmare! Phenaphen, tequila and frazzled nerves had my head spinning, and my rubbery legs barely made contact with the little stage before I fainted. Kat fanned my face. Wesley ordered me to try again. Beau showed concern, saying I could just wait tables since more dancers were traipsing in. I thanked him, and vowed to make it through the dreadful night. How would I ever "get hip" to this scene?

Wesley stayed the entire evening, constantly bugging me by asking how much I was making. I had turned tons of bills into twenties, but was amazed at closing when I counted two hundred and forty dollars. "Talk about the inequities in life," I said to Beau. "Education certainly isn't necessary for making money in this place. My last job didn't pay this much a month."

"Don't you know the world is a glass dictionary?" he asked.

"Ah, a man who quotes philosophy is usually sincere."

"Nay, nay young child." Beau offered a quick wink. "Even the devil can quote texts."

"Pleeease, Beau. . . don't shatter my dreams about poetic men."

"I'm just quoting Emerson. Translated it means if you open your eyes and pay attention, you'll always learn something new. Educate yourself." He flipped on the overhead lights, revealing a slightly stained carpet and other flaws previously hidden by soft lighting.

"Jeez, Beau." I covered my eyes. "Next time warn me before you turn on the bright lights. I prefer illusions."

৵৹

By my third day things were getting easier, but nowhere near good—much less great. Wesley's hotel room wasn't far from Kat's, but I spent more time with her and only saw him midway through my work shift. On our fourth day of hanging out, Kat persuaded me to lighten my champagne blonde hair to a chalk white color. I hated it. With ice hair and separation anxiety over Nikki, my minor relief came from seeing Beau's face light up when Kat and I walked through the door. His tall stature and GQ looks made me feel I was in the presence of a suave Hollywood star, but his poetic aura and innate charm couldn't be duplicated by any actor. Dressed in a tux style suit with white ribbed shirt, red suspenders and black tie, Beau always stood behind the bar shuffling cards or counting money. His bar-back cleaned while Beau handled all financial aspects, claiming "too many hands in a register, a sure fire way to go broke."

Kat and I usually arrived early so she could play with her hair and makeup, but after getting dressed I always rushed to the bar to chat with Beau and listen to the great music playing nonstop on the jukebox. He generously shared his time with me between welcoming early customers with news of the day and jokes. Beau kept several packs of playing cards under the bar, and frequently performed a magic trick that resulted in a disappearing *Jack of Clubs* card. We never figured out how he made it vanish then later reappear in a shoe, purse, and even once inside my cherished and tattered coming-of-age book from the early Sixties, *A Wrinkle in Time*.

"Isn't that an adolescent read, baby?" Beau asked when I returned his card.

"Guess I still haven't grown up. It's geared to teens, but everyone should read it."

"What's your favorite genre?"

"Humorous, romantic fiction. I love Jane Austen, especially after my prim and proper Mother limited romance novels while pushing books on housekeeping and such."

"What a loss."

"Actually, I tucked favorite novels inside my clothes hamper. A great hiding place since Ellen and I were assigned laundry duty once we were tall enough to reach the Maytag."

Beau chuckled.

"I rushed through Saturday chores so I could read novels and myths that delighted my soul, instead of reading *Good Housekeeping* or Biblical folklore, which dampened my spirits."

"Well, baby, I'm glad you were resourceful. Your essence is indeed spirited!"

"Much more so when Nikki's by my side."

"Since you enjoy books," Beau paused and reached under the bar. "Here's something for you to read in the dressing room when you feel downhearted."

He handed me Emerson's *Twelve Essential Essays,* which didn't look like my cup of tea, but I thanked him, hoping it would prove interesting enough to relax me. Beau never used vulgar language and chastised Kat when she did, albeit he occasionally uttered damn or hell. He was comforting in a gentle, protective way. Still, every time I had to go on that little stage and dance, I fell apart.

On my first weekend at the Jewel Box, I learned Beau hired off-duty policemen to oversee crowd control and men behaving badly. Their presence helped calm my nerves, until one officer became a tad too frisky. Naturally it was the hairy cop. Each time Katie-Laura or I walked past Zane he commented in carnal undertones about our bodies. If murmuring was his attempt to convey sexiness, he should have waxed before leaving home. Back hair creeping up a neck collar cancels any chance of seduction. Zane stood at the only entrance to our waitress station, grinning as though an amorous snail had slithered into his padded cod piece or whatever tighty-whities he wore to compress excess butt hair. After his first beer, he took to touching our bums every time we entered and left the waitress post with our trays.

I told Beau about Zane. He parked him at the front door with orders to keep his hairy hands off all girls. Zane pouted until walleyed Wendy, whose uncontrollable peepers flew down to men's private parts, started hanging with him. Beau didn't care since she rarely sold cocktails. Wendy's money came on stage, thanks to cups that runneth over, and long, wavy brown hair she flung wildly to cover her eye during dances.

My first Friday night netted me three hundred dollars. Wesley kindly allowed me to buy some totally groovy, inexpensive white go-go boots to wear on my second Saturday night, which is when I raked in over four hundred bucks. That same night, Wesley drank himself into a stupor and called me vile names. I told him to hit the door and go to hell! A bold statement for someone who'd had subservience drilled into her brain since birth. I wasn't sure which persona initiated it, but Jill aka Cherie, suddenly felt liberated.

In the wee hours of morning as we sat at the bar counting money and unwinding, Kat and Beau seemed happy about my sending Wesley away.

"How'd you meet this guy?" Beau locked his cash pouch and pulled out a deck of cards.

"He was my boss, and seemed decent enough. I was in emotional turmoil and under the influence of prescription drugs when he tossed out my meds and offered a shoulder to lean on."

"Shoulder!" Kat snapped. "Now Sir Galahad expects you to kiss his horse's behind."

"Well, baby, I don't know him, but he seems a bit pushy." Beau shuffled cards. "Especially when it comes to money you're making and he's taking."

"It was for us to start a legitimate company. He has experience and connections—we just need cash to get it off the ground."

"I've never taken a nickel from a woman, and would shovel sewers before letting a female support me. But I'm old-fashioned, I guess."

"You're such a gentleman, Beau. Nothing like I presumed, since I was expecting a lecherous swine libidinously groping his bevy of wayward girls."

Beau shook his head. "It's almost the other way around, baby. You've likely seen some of these girls offering me sexual favors."

"Which you diplomatically decline." I let my high heels drop against the bar rail.

"I have morals and I love my wife." He adjusted his red suspenders. "Even though we only see each other in the mornings and early afternoons between tending our businesses."

"So you've never been tempted by any of these chicks?" Kat winked at him.

"Not even slightly."

"Ouch! That kinda makes Cherie and me feel terribly unsexy," she teased.

"Save your flirting for customers. But feel sexy about you two being smarter than average. The majority of dancers who drift through this joint barely have functioning frontal lobes, and most customers check their brains at the front door."

"Nice back paddle, man." Kat shot me a sweet smile. "Cherie, in case Beau didn't lecture you on club clientele, he says just because a guy blows a ton of money in here doesn't mean he's wealthy. One customer spends hundreds every week, but Beau says he lives in a shabby apartment and sleeps on an army cot. Then there's old fat ass Murray who comes in night after night, stands at the bar trying to manhandle every girl who walks by, but won't fork over one thin dime. And he's filthy rich. Right, Beau?"

"He's from money, and also invented some surgical device they utilize down the street."

"Can't believe we're only blocks from the world's largest hospital complex." I flexed my toes.

"Texas Medical Center is the biggest in the *world?*" Kat asked.

"You bet," Beau confirmed. "That's what I love about Texas. The state does everything big. Some are successes and some aren't. You girls are too young to remember Galveston's glitzy gambling days with its Balinese Room where legendary acts like Burns & Allen, Frank Sinatra, Jack Benny, and others entertained. Illicit action ran rampant on that Pleasure Pier."

"I love that the Flagship Hotel is the only hotel built entirely over water." Kat bragged.

"Well, my sweet friend, Texas has five thousand square miles of inland waterways, which is more than Florida and Minnesota—the Land of Lakes. Most Americans still think of Texas as a dry and dusty state."

"While we're talking Texas history, I've got some Larry McMurtry books you two might like to read." Beau placed a 7 Up on my coaster and a Coke on Katie-Laura's. "His storytelling is predominately set in either the old West or contemporary Texas, and he's a damn good writer."

"Whatcha got?" I stretched my upper body to try and relax my stiff shoulders.

"*Leaving Cheyenne* and *The Last Picture Show.* Both books are being made into films. Wanna read 'em?"

"Sure." I blinked tired eyes. "I've never read anything by him."

"Okay, baby!" Beau seemed thrilled by my acceptance. "He's a native Texan. I'm not, but I love the old West and always felt like I was born a hundred years too late."

Kat grimaced and reached behind her back with a stir straw. "Frontier stories aren't my bag. I dig trashy romance paperbacks. Jill . . . oops I meant *Cherie,* can you reach my itch? It's down below my shoulder blades but not quite to my butt crack."

"Lovely." I made a moue. Scratching her bronzed skin reminded me of our teenage years spent lounging on Surfside beach flirting with out-of-town guys. Kat always coated me with Coppertone so I wouldn't burn my fair skin, while her olive skin darkened without lotion. On rainy weekends we stretched across her lilac lace bedspread reading novels and sharing every dream and fantasy while others did whatever it was they did in Lake Jackson for fun. Occasionally we hitched rides to Houston with her older sister to see French films, which spiraled our desires to depart Dullsville. And here we sat. Nothing dull about this place. Except a carpet due for its weekly steam-cleaning along with the Parson chairs on Monday.

"Okay, baby." Beau nodded at me. "Shuffle these cards. I don't trust Laura anymore."

Katie yanked the deck from his hand. "Let's play something other than Blackjack. And no tricks this time."

"Cards with. . .with. . . without sleight of hand?" Beau stuttered and threw his fist against his forehead like he was having a brain hemorrhage. "There's no damn fun in that. Hell, I might as well teach you the British version of Black Jack."

"You must be off your trolley to think we fancy learning a game created by those bloody awful blokes across the pond who believe all Americans are turnips," Kat said with a fairly decent Cockney accent. "Go ahead and give us the rundown. Just don't plan on conning this bird out of me hard earned quid."

Beau grinned at her cute attempt at British slang. "It's for two or more players with a sole aim of discarding all cards to win."

"Boring," I interrupted. "Why don't you try Tarot readings? Seems more exciting."

"You two girls always talk about excitement, but won't do much about it. Just put all the suits together in this deck and verify the *Jack of Clubs* is intact." Beau handed me the cards.

"What's the significance of that card again?" Kat asked with a yawn.

"The dark-haired man represents different things—from a secret admirer to an obliging helper, but I prefer its definition as a playful prankster."

"It's two-thirty in the morning, Beau." I split the deck, knowing which card would vanish about twenty seconds after it fell into his hand.

26

Bam! Someone pounded the club door. Kat stiffened. "Saturday nights lead to weird Sunday mornings when drunks and people of bad intent ramble along streets and businesses looking for trouble," she whispered.

My belly did flipflops.

Beau pulled his .44 Magnum from under the bar. "You and Kat stay seated and out of view," he said quietly before walking to the locked door. "Who are you and what do you need?" Beau demanded in threatening tone.

"It's Wesley."

"Creepy jackass!" Kat scrunched her nose, making a sour face.

"So what?" Beau broadcast, this time with less intimidation.

"Well, I'd like to talk to Jill." Wesley's voice echoed through the heavy door. "Apologize. If she'll let me."

Beau looked over at me. "Come back in twenty minutes!" he said to Wesley, apparently reading doubt on my face. Beau then went back behind the bar, put away his Magnum and the playing cards, allowing me quiet time to mull over my situation.

"Whatever drew you to him, cutie?" Kat stood in her chair to stretch across the bar and retrieve her hidden pint of Bacardi from a shelf.

"Jeez, I don't know. I'm insecure and he's not. Opposites attract. I don't know. Wesley perceives himself as Eros and talks incessantly about taking me down transplendent rivers of love, but his drunken forcefulness makes me feel like I'm up bleak creek without a paddle."

"Transplendent rivers of love?" Beau let go a hearty laugh. "You read that in some romance novel didn't you?"

"I did." I nodded my head while meeting Beau's eyes.

"Why don't you ditch this character?" Kat poured rum into her Coke.

"It's crossed my mind. But I'm incredibly insecure these days."

"No way!" Kat stirred her drink. "You've always radiated confidence."

"False bravado," I admitted.

"That's bound to backfire on you one of these days, baby."

Next thing I knew, I was making excuses for Wesley, saying his behavior was triggered by this shameful job. Beau didn't look pleased, but listened patiently to my rambling. "I just can't do this. It's not for me and would kill my mother if she found out. Well, maybe not." My chin trembled. "She'd probably refuse to believe her daughter could deviate from such strong

Southern upbringing into this sinful job. Or she'd spend the rest of her life praying for my soul."

Kat reached over and gently rubbed my shoulders. "Cutie, I'm sorry for bringing you here. It took me a while to get over my guilt, but the money sure helps."

I looked across the bar at Beau, who had been unusually quiet. "Sorry, Beau. This is my last night. It was nice meeting you, but I have to say it's hard for a small town girl like me to understand a person like you owning such an immoral establishment."

Kat moaned as Beau leaned across the bar, looking like Rhett Butler mildly irritated by Miss Scarlett's commentary. His stunning steel-grey eyes weren't twinkling as usual. "Are you finished talking?"

"Yes. Sir."

"Then do me a favor and listen for a minute, before you leave this *immoral* establishment." Beau's emphasis on the word immoral seemed a tad scornful.

Knowing Beau well enough to know he needed more than a minute to make any statement, I placed my duffel bag on the bar thinking it would make a nice pillow if he got too long winded.

"Baby, if you act like a lady, you'll be treated like a lady."

"Oh pleeease." My pulse rose. "That's ludicrous! A *lady* working in a topless club?"

"What's wrong with making a living by putting a smile on someone's face? Men come in this club for many different reasons, ranging from those wanting to deviate from the norm to the curious, lonely, bored, and voyeuristic ones. Believe it or not, we occasionally get some nice, decent men in here. Some just need to be touched and a simple pat on the shoulder after seating them pacifies most and makes them less likely to touch or grab you. I'm not always nearby to defend, so if anyone touches you inappropriately, smack the crap out of them. And if they speak vulgar to you or any dancers, remind them obnoxious behavior is not tolerated in the Jewel Box. To sum it up, if men get offensive, try handling it in ladylike fashion. Don't let them talk down to you, touch you inappropriately, and for God's sake, never let them kiss your lips."

"Let me get this straight. I can parade around half naked in front of these guys, wallop a punch when necessary, tell them to go to hell if I don't like what they say, but a kiss on the lips is incontrovertibly taboo." I shook my head. "I'm sorry Beau, but this job goes against my upbringing." I struggled to force my aching, swollen feet back into my high heels.

"Well, I hate to see you go, baby." Understanding filled his face.

Moments later Wesley rapped on the door. Kat made another hateful face, but Beau gave me a sincere, almost fatherly smile as he took the keys to allow Wesley back inside the club.

Wesley thanked Beau, and apologized profusely to me, before making a solemn promise to stop drinking. He tried to humor Kat, but she wasn't having any of it. Then Wesley urged me to come to El Paso with him the following week, bring Nikki, and forget this club situation ever happened. Kat hugged me so tight I thought she was trying to paralyze me so I couldn't walk. But being with Nikki and heading west with Wesley seemed preferable to spending another night walking around in pasties and panties. I left with the man in the pinstriped suit.

4

I stretched across my precious bar to look up into the skies over the Gulf where a smattering of stars blessed the sky with light. Flipping back in time triggered tiny spasms in my neck as visions of arriving in El Paso with Wesley surfaced. The only pleasant memory of that West Texas town was finding a *Jack of Clubs* card at the bottom of my purse the night we arrived. Wesley leased a big house and hired a woman to cook and clean, but the transformation I'd hoped for never materialized as the previously charming guy got more irrational by the hour.

We hired a bi-lingual lady to care for Nikki five hours a day while I worked at the office. She taught Nikki Spanish phrases as they played games or frequented nearby parks, but within weeks our life began a downward spiral. Wesley's moods fluctuated something fierce as he took control of everything, down to monitoring my soda intake. "Water's free, hon." He often stayed late at the office drinking himself comatose, and I soon learned liquor served as a chaser for any drugs he could find. Epiphany, Jill! The damn Tofranil he so valiantly saved me from "getting hooked on" months earlier had gone down his esophagus—not the toilet.

Wesley spent a small fortune on liquor and narcotics, and then insisted we be financially sensible and maintain only one car. Yep. His Lincoln remained and I never saw a penny from the sale of my Corvair. Totally dependent on His *high*ness for transportation, my optimism vanished as rapidly as my part-time income.

Mother always disregarded friction with my dad by simply ignoring him, but I lacked her knack for staying silent and composed. One night Wesley came home obnoxiously drunk, and began cussing everything, including characters on Mayberry R.F.D. "Aunt Bee's a fucking magpie."

"Shut it!" I shouted, appalled at his vulgarities entering my daughter's ears.

A vase flew past my head and shattered against the fireplace. "You shut up!" his tone, crazy belligerent. "Bitches don't back talk."

"Please," I begged.

Nikki started crying. Wesley got angrier. I got a fist in the face.

"You sorry SOB," I said as blood dripped from my mouth. "You sorry SOB!" I ramped up my volume.

Wham! Wesley slammed me into the wall. Nikki started screaming at the top of her lungs. I suddenly understood Mother's "Silence is golden" quote and inched away from Wesley. In a whisper, I begged my horrified little girl to stop crying. She intuitively understood my pleas and walked wordlessly to her room. Wesley's rage ended abruptly with him passing out on the sofa as his grand finale.

The following morning when Wesley saw my body blanketed with bruises, and my right eye severely swollen and clotted with blood, he suggested I stay home from work. The moment Mr. Thoughtful walked out the door, I phoned Ellen, told her things weren't working out, and asked her to wire money so I could return to Houston. Not only did she agree, she asked no questions. Unlike me, Ellen had absorbed Mother's quote: "Ask me no questions and I'll tell you no lies." I had always been the family question asker. And the vain one who practically lived in front of a mirror, but I disregarded my appearance and walked four miles to Western Union, lugging Nikki on my hip most of the way. Two days later when Wesley left for work, Nikki and I packed our belongings and took a cab to the bus station, leaving the psychopath and El Paso.

It was my first and last bus trip, but that Greyhound ride felt wonderful. I stroked sleeping Nikki's hair while allowing Sixties music to flow privately in my head, even though The Beatles *Lady Madonna* seemed to be on endless loop. By the time we arrived in Houston my black eye was less obvious, but Ellen never asked one question when I asked her to watch Nikki and loan me her car for a few days. I headed straight to the Jewel Box.

I walked through the door with the same apprehension I'd felt months before. Thankfully Kat met me with a big hug and we walked arm in arm to the bar.

"Baby," Beau said warmly. "It's great to see you."

His calling me baby in such sincere and caring tone, almost brought tears to my eyes. "I just dropped in to see if anyone's filled my white go-go boots."

"I'd love to have you back, but you've got to stay longer than two weeks."

"I promise, Beau. And unlike Wesley, I keep my word. The maniac sold my car, so it'll take me a while to buy some wheels. Guess you could say I got myself into a worse predicament than waitressing in a topless club."

"You're a hard working girl. Welcome back. This is a strange business, but you'll earn a nice sum of money and maybe become a pretty good judge of men along the way."

"Cutie, you might even meet the man of your dreams here." Kat batted her lashes.

"Pleeease! What a revolting thought. The last place I'd consider looking for love is here. No offense Beau."

"None taken." He wiped down the bar.

"Really, Kat. Would you date any of the misfits who stray into this joint?"

"Never in a million years. I'm just here for the money."

"Baby, Laura told me about your problems with Wesley, and I say you're better off here. Any man who strikes a woman is a savage, and even if he says it won't happen again, it will. Now you've learned expensive clothing doesn't make a man Prince Charming."

"Well, Prince Charming, a.k.a. Marquis de Sade."

"Life is an education, so take notes and you might learn more than you'd ever imagined working here. See you tomorrow night, baby."

The year was 1969. Nightly newscasts flashed shocking photos depicting the war in Vietnam, angry protestors, men burning draft notices, and a growing divide in our country. Meanwhile thousands indulged in psychedelic experiences with pot, LSD, and other mind altering chemicals. In May the X-rated movie *Midnight Cowboy* debuted to record crowds.

In June the musical *Hair* opened yet another simultaneous production in Paris, France, and at month's end, the Stonewall riots in New York City marked the beginning of America's Gay Rights movement. In early July, scientists discovered the chemical structure of antibodies, and on July 20th "Houston" was the first word spoken from the moon by Neil Armstrong. Civil rights activists were making marginal progress after Martin Luther King's death. Then came Woodstock. That's the month I returned to the Jewel Box with a different attitude. A somewhat schizoid "I am woman hear me roar/please God, don't let my family and friends find out what I'm doing" attitude.

My garrulous nature blended with anxiety and generated ceaseless babble as I moved through the crowd hustling quarters by asking, "Got a dollar for the jukebox?" I always got at least ten bucks. Maybe it was just the eagerness of the men to get the music going and another half naked girl dancing, but not once did I hear any complaints about the jukebox costing a dollar a song. Jeez, back in Lake Jackson you could get six plays for a quarter.

As I danced (if you could call it that), I simply absorbed the music and stared dreamily into the crowd of faceless men, thinking anything other than where I was or what I was doing. Listening to *I Heard It Through The Grapevine*, I often transposed the motley crue into Twain, Whitman, Frost, Burns, and even Anaïs Nin, as I recited "Life has no plot," while turning in circles on the tiny stage waiting for Marvin's last line. People say "What doesn't kill you will make you stronger," but every time I stepped down and slithered into the dressing room, I thanked God I was a full-time waitress and only danced occasionally. Dancers were a different breed altogether, which Beau explained ranged from aspiring Penthouse Pets who had recently left their job slinging hash, to college girls from assorted backgrounds supporting their education, and tattooed motorcycle mamas supporting their old men and drug habits. Beau rarely turned down unattractive dancers, letting them stay to make enough money to move on, which he expedited by padding their nightly pay with twenty dollars more in drink sales than they sold. He said without dancers he'd have no Jewel Box, so he never made them adhere to a schedule like us waitresses. But he kept a vigil watch over them, and fired those caught soliciting prostitution.

34

"Amazing Paulette," Beau said with a hint of intrigue as he watched a gorgeous dancer work the crowd.

I refreshed my pastel pink lipstick. "I can't believe that drop-dead beauty is leaving for Copenhagen soon. She sells tons of cocktails and always reminds men to tip us."

Beau nodded as Kat leaned toward me. "Paulette's real name is Paul. Our only dancer with fake boobs is going through steps to become a woman," Kat whispered. "I don't know where he hides his jewels since Beau labeled our dressing room off limits and he shows up in work attire, but he/she does it well."

"Oh my God!" I bit my tongue in disbelief.

"Keep mute about it," Beau requested. "The transgender process has been around for a couple of decades in other countries. Germany and Denmark, mostly. I ran into a few guys awaiting feminization surgery in Vegas, but never one anywhere near this passable. Hell, he's more feminine than most women."

I stood stunned, likely with mouth wide open. Paulette was about five foot two, small boned, and spoke in such girly tones I couldn't believe she was a he. Men practically drooled over her while digging cash from their wallets.

"Wipe that shocked look off your face," Kat said. "And let's go make the most of her last week here. She's the prettiest, sweetest, best smelling dancer on board right now!"

"And my least problematic," Beau added as Kat dragged me away by my hair.

During the following week, I scrutinized Paulette for signs of Paul, to no avail. Silky smooth legs led to nothing discernable under the sequined bikini bottoms all employees wore. Kat presumed Paul had never been blessed with a sizable penis. Beau figured duct tape. I envied his delicate beauty, and was bewildered by his almost invisible Adam's apple.

I'd earned nearly enough to buy a used car for getting back and forth to Ellen's so I could sleep with Nikki, but my second stint at the Jewel Box wasn't going much better than my first. And men like "Slick" didn't make things any easier. The young, brawny biker-type wore his jet black hair slicked down with grease and dressed head to toe in black leather accessorized with garish chains. This thug who claimed he was a Mafia hit man, always sat at the end of the bar by the waitress station, laying on the charm while asking me or Kat to go out with him. When we refused his advances, he became obnoxious. "Slick's the kind of guy who could probably spread vaginal diseases just by standing too close," Kat warned me. Beau occasionally booted his odious butt out the door. Slick usually left growling about us now being on "the list" while slowly caressing his boot at ankle level, as though his hidden Luger would someday settle the issue.

On the flip side, we had Gabe and Al. These business partners called themselves "trim men," and Kat and I called them our "Nicer than nicest, nice guys," because these repeat customers were extremely generous with their money and never tried to cop a feel like most men who came in. But they were hardly saints. With the exception of me and Kat, Gabe immediately attached an unpleasant nickname to every girl in the house, regardless of her chosen alias. The two married men wore T-shirts and faded blue jeans, but in spite of their clothing and slight sawdust smell, they always seemed exceptionally clean from face to fingernails.

Al was forty-something, super polite and friendly. Elfin-like and slightly graying, he had mischievous eyes, a fuzzy worm-looking moustache on his rubicund face, and cheeks that begged to be pinched. After a couple of beers, his voice jumped an octave, his nose reddened to match his cheeks, and he grinned from ear to ear as his eyes darted from dancer to dancer. The girls loved his amenable behavior and extravagant spending, and Al loved the girl's attention. So much so that he fell in love every time the moon changed. Many dancers counted on him for a profitable evening and took advantage of his generosity—until Gabe intervened, spoiling everyone's fun. Most nights when the partners left the club, an excessively maudlin, slightly stumbling Al was calmly guided out by Gabe, who often shook his head and rendered the same expression exasperated parents make when trying to control their unruly kids. One night as Gabe did his ushering bit, he turned to me as the door closed and grumbled, "Everyone knows old men are twice boys."

"Was he quoting Aristophanes?" I asked Kat as she flew by.

"Who cares? He just took his forty-year-old son home, not to mention our tips." She frowned. "We could make Al spend every cent in his pocket, if that damn stingy, stick-in-the-mud didn't always tag along and oversee his spending."

Gabe might have been a pain in the ass, but stingy was hardly the adjective I'd attach to anyone who dropped as much money on our tip trays as he did.

Gabe was twenty-something, quiet, and enigmatic. Of average height and slim build, he walked with a slow, confident stride, standing straight with his head slightly tilted back as if to say, "Bite my ass." He drank slowly and spoke only when a grunt wouldn't serve as suitable answer. When he did speak, an urbane vocabulary embroidered his adopted Texas drawl, which he incorporated into his extremely rare, yet sometimes profound and frequently crude comments.

Gabe's short blond hair was layered, and swept horizontally across his forehead onto skin tanned from the sun. His flaxen hair was in sharp contrast to his dark, short and well groomed moustache that stood guard over ruby red lips, and his strong, decisive nose amplified his masculinity. Gabe's handsome looks caused most dancers to come to his table, but wordlessly, his pale blue eyes exuded frigid indifference and the girls swiftly turned their attention to Al. Gabe sat at the table like a bear with a burr up his butt, looking thoroughly irritated as he and Al alternated paying for drinks. Unlike his partner, Gabe never got drunk, but everyone knew to disregard the guy dubbed "arrogant asshole" until his mood got slightly altered by a few beers.

The first time I waited on their table, Al enthusiastically interrogated, "Aren't you new here? Where'd you work before? Is your name Sherry or Cherry?"

"Oh, pleeeease! My name is pronounced Sha-Ree like Little Stevie Wonder's new song, *My Cherie Amour.* It's French, ya know. And yes, I'm new here. I'm a recently divorced mom with no prior work experience of this nature." I flashed a big smile and awaited my tip. Gabe stared absently into the smoke filled room as Al and I continued blabbing while he placed money on my tray. Being my nervous but talkative self, I turned to Gabe. "Don't you ever talk?"

Without changing his gaze, Gabe drew deeply on a cigarette, and then issued a stream of smoke into the air. "Don't you ever *not* talk?" he replied icily.

What a jerk! I rushed away, determined not to let the rude asshole dampen my karma.

Nights later while serving beer to the partners, I remained void of comment to Gabe, but cheerful as always to Al, even though he wasn't reaching into his pocket for money fast enough to suit me. Al started singing *My Cherie Amour, lovely as a summer day.* I was accustomed to hearing the song customers seemed compelled to sing after hearing my name, but lingering too long at a table meant lost tips elsewhere. I tapped my tip tray on the table. Gabe slowly slid three dollars on it. "Wow, thanks!" I smiled.

With his usual benign expression, he dryly remarked, "I'd do just about anything for a piece of ass."

Al laughed as though his partner was George Carlin. A curious triumph coarsened Gabe's face. "You uncouth jerk." I shot Gabe a censorious gaze.

The young one leaned back in his chair and in most derisive tone, retorted, "Well, aren't we the sanctimonious one?"

How dare he make a lascivious remark and then speak condescendingly to me. I lifted my chin, stormed away, and told Kat I wasn't waiting on the heathens again, despite their generous tips. She dashed to their table and began saying something, which didn't look like the reprimand I'd hoped, seeing as how her face was framed in sunshine the entire time. Eventually she twisted her butt back to the waitress area. "They both apologized and promise to behave. Gabe even grinned and said something about you being the most *prolix* person he's ever met. What the heck does prolix mean, cutie?"

"It means excessively wordy. But I'd rather be talkative than be a laconic jerk like him."

"Don't know what laconic means either, but lighten up and stop being such a square. Gabe's a decent enough guy, he just likes trying to get a rise out of people."

It was impossible to avoid Gabe and Al's table on busy nights, but I took their orders and delivered in speedy fashion. Gabe seemed to delight in getting my reaction to his flat-out vulgarities or phrases filled with *double entendre.* I frowned, but kept my cool and their tips. On an extremely slow evening as the old one sucked suds, my innate need to chatter kicked in as I turned to the young one. "So, what does 'trim men' mean?"

38

Looking as though talking to me a dreadful chore, Gabe curtly said, "We're custom carpenters who specialize in spiral staircases."

"I read Walt Whitman's father was a carpenter," I continued in spite of his terse tone.

My comment was apparently amusing to Gabe who shot a look across the table to Al, indicating my IQ less than Lucy and Ethel's combined, chuckled, threw his head back, swallowed a long drink of Budweiser, then turned his eyes to me. "Yeaaah," he mocked, "we're just a couple of worthless, ole carpenters."

I didn't consider my remark rude, and didn't like the way he elongated yeah in arrogant tone. "I never realized using the words carpenter and Whitman in the same sentence could offend anyone." I scanned the room. "But then, I failed to consider subliterate barflies."

The words barely fluttered from my mouth before I realized I had committed a major topless club *faux pas*. Never insult those attached to the hands that toss out the tips that are the paycheck. I attempted a save. "I'm sorry if I offended. I must've taken a tiny vacation and left my bitch personality in charge. I've been trying to enroll her in a Dale Carnegie course."

"That's okay." Al unleashed a goofy ass grin as he cut his eyes toward Gabe. "Here Cherie, take our last three dollars for your tip. We'll go without dinner."

"Thank you so much Al, at least I won't go without pastie glue. You are the God of generosity, no matter what Greek legends say," I said sweetly, walking away.

Although Gabe remained reserved, occasionally after a few beers he would casually blurt, "You know I'd do anything for a piece of ass, don't you?" I learned to ignore his comments and simply move onto the next table, but one night he became difficult, holding my tip tray while slowly singing, "Myyyyyy Cheeeeeeeeerie Amour."

The guy was starting to crawl up my nerves. "Gabe, please just give me my tray so I can work." I looked around at lost tips.

"You gonna give me a piece of ass, if I do?" he asked in exaggerated Texas drawl.

"Pleeease stop spouting that stupid line. You need shock therapy or something."

"I'll bet shock therapy couldn't be as electrifying as a piece of ass from you." He slapped a five dollar tip on my tray.

Okay. The tip momentarily numbed my tongue. But not my desire to beat him at his little game of verbal insolence. "Maybe a cattle prod would get my point across."

"Whoa, a cattle prod! I grew up on a farm and. . ."

"So did Robert Burns. But you're hardly poetic. In fact, I think you're the sort of man who gets excited by a cattle prod and aroused by livestock."

"Nice return, Blondie."

"Blondie?"

"Yeaaah, you remind me of that ditzy Goldie chick on *Laugh In*."

"Ditzy!? Well, you remind me of something my dad once coughed up during a nasty illness." I grabbed my tip tray and walked away.

"Hey, I think Goldie's cute and just pretends to be ditzy," he shouted as my white go-go boots kept walking. "And maybe I'm the one who needs that Dale Carnegie course."

I relayed mine and Gabe's encounter to Beau while placing my drink order. Only semi-amused, he took on a stern, fatherly look. "Baby." He turned his head to hide a little grin, "That phlegm bit wasn't exactly ladylike verbiage."

From day one, I sensed Beau was trying to pull a Professor Higgins on me, but I wasn't a quick study like Eliza Doolittle. "Well pardon me." I fluttered my eyelashes Katie-Laura fashion, "I didn't realize your rules for 'ladylike verbiage' were written in Sanskrit. But I'll bet Gabe thinks twice before he spouts off to me again."

"Maybe, maybe not." Beau shook his head as though talking to me somewhat hopeless. "And you're one to talk about spouting off. Stop wasting time and losing money by debating customers. Hell, you're longer winded than Pentecostal preachers speaking in tongues."

I attempted a Pentecostal chant before grabbing my drink tray to head back into the crowd. I adored Beau, but didn't think my recurring repartee with Gabe a waste of time, and actually enjoyed the challenging diversion, which established an understanding of sorts between the so-called "arrogant asshole" and me. Even though Gabe usually reigned triumphant, I suspected his public performance failed to correspond with the man inside.

5

The day after I spent three thousand bucks on a used Chevy Nova, Wesley called the Jewel Box alternating threatening messages with pleas for reuniting. Making foolish mistakes was customary for me, but having the crap beat out of me wasn't. When the psycho said he was on his way to Houston, I slammed the phone in his ear and told Beau I had to quit.

"I've got a plan," my surrogate father said. "Angel's pregnant and swelling up like a dirigible. Instead of dancing I'll have her wait tables until she moves back to Maine. Meanwhile, you lay low."

"But. . ."

"No buts. Just lease an apartment for you and Nikki, stay away from your usual hangouts including the club, Kat, and Ellen's house for a couple of weeks."

I sighed. Buying the Nova left me with less than two hundred bucks.

"Here, baby." Beau handed me a thousand dollars to prepay rent, buy a bed, and other necessities. "You can pay me back a little each night."

"You burn cool!" I kissed his cheek.

"Paying several months rent in advance should placate managers enough to let you lease under an alias without questions."

"And temporary vanishing will hopefully make Wesley vanish forever."

"Just choose a simple name like Bertha Smith or Carol Wood."

The look on Beau's face was so sincere, I respectfully opted for Carol. "Good Lord, Beau. Bertha?"

He chuckled. The Jewel Box was Beau's first venture in the topless business, although he had owned various clubs in Dallas and Houston after

41

moving to Texas from Nevada, where he had managed several casinos. His wife Celeste owned an exclusive boutique near River Oaks, Houston's most affluent neighborhood, thus left management of the Jewel Box to Beau. She preferred not to be seen anywhere near the place.

After moving into an apartment as Carol Wood, I spent two wonderful weeks with Nikki. Beau came by for quick visits and taught Nikki card games, while offering me Larry McMurtry novels. Emerson was too esoteric, so I was diggin' McMurtry. Beau also introduced us to Nora, an older lady who occasionally babysat his son, Gilles. Beau worshipped that boy, so I knew Nikki would be in competent hands. We went through trial runs, and as much as my daughter liked Nora, a day didn't pass without her pleading to stay with Jimmy again. I finally gave in and took my unrelenting child to see her cousin the weekend before my scheduled return to work. Praying Wesley wasn't lurking about, I crept through my sister's neighborhood, eyes peeled for his red convertible. Despite my fears, bruiser Wesley never materialized and the cousins laughed nonstop for two days.

Although Nikki was developing quite the melodramatic personality, she surprised me by not throwing a tantrum when I parked her with sixty-year-old sitter, Nora. After three weeks at work, I repaid Beau, bought nicer furniture, and put money aside for replacing my used car with a new one. But Saturday night of my fourth week dampened my spirits when I only made a hundred dollars. I needed a dependable car for driving late at night.

With a sleeping Nikki sprawled across my shoulder, I was struggling to open my apartment door when Wesley came up behind me and shoved us inside, instantly waking Nikki. The creep had followed me from the Jewel Box to Nora's, and then to my place. Nikki didn't scream. She just clung tightly to me, watching Wesley's every move. He spent a few minutes begging me to come back to him and ignoring my polite refusal, until I picked up a note pad by the phone and used Nikki's red crayon to write capital N, capital O, exclamation point! He responded by ripping my phone from the wall, then holding a gun at my throat until I promised to accompany him back to El Paso. And marry him. Who could turn down that proposal? On Sunday Wesley used Nikki as hostage, making me pack belongings while he sat on my sofa watching sitcoms.

Love American Style, indeed. Wherever he went, he kept Nikki within reach. Shortly after my Nova keys went missing on Monday, Wesley forced me to close my bank account. Guns are highly persuasive. When he took Nikki along to rent a U-Haul, I briefly attempted to reconnect my ripped phone cord before running to a nearby pay phone. Ellen wasn't home, so I called Mother collect.

A.J. Foyt would've been impressed. Mother made the hour drive in forty-five minutes. When she knocked at my door and shouted my name, Nikki bolted from Wesley's side. He grabbed me. I broke from his grasp, pushed Nikki into the bathroom and ordered her to lock the door. Instead of calling my name, Mother began a loud countdown threatening to call the police when she reached five. On her count of three Wesley opened the door, and she rushed inside displaying a forceful demeanor I had never seen in her. Wesley fell back on his acting career. So ingratiating he could've persuaded a Mormon to drink coffee with whiskey and denounce Joseph Smith, Wesley laughed as he told us there were no bullets in the gun. Then he audaciously attempted to convince Mother that he and I belonged together. Okay. Maybe I was a bit emotionally unstable, but this guy was every psychiatrist's wet dream.

"Unearth her car keys!" My meek, docile, mother interrupted his diatribe.

Wesley dragged my keys from his pants pocket. Mother yanked them from his hand. "We're heading to Lake Jackson and if you ever come near this family again, you'd better have bullets in your gun. Because I'll have 'em in mine, and I'll blow your brains across Texas."

You can't buy memories like that! I gained new respect for my mild-mannered mother who'd turned Superwoman before my eyes.

Nikki and I spent a week in Lake Jackson before heading back to Houston to meet movers who would put our belongings in storage, while we resumed life with Ellen. Being alone was not an option. When I opened the door to an empty apartment, Nikki shrieked and I almost lost my lunch. The psychopath had taken everything we owned, from our sofa to my sweet baby girl's hair ribbons. Materialistic things meant nothing, but losing Nikki's favorite doll and irreplaceable baby photos crushed me. I held Nikki in my arms as we sat on the floor and cried.

After a month of turning down minimum wage jobs, I rang Kat. She couldn't contain her excitement when I asked about returning to the Jewel Box. "Beau's gonna be tickled."

Ellen didn't seem anywhere near tickled, but agreed to watch Nikki when I told her about returning to my *restaurant* gig. "I'll only stay overnight with Kat until I can make enough money to buy a better car," I promised my sister while kissing Nikki's cheek.

"You're the best mommy ever." Nikki stuck her gooey lollipop in my mouth.

Toddlers are so naïve.

☙

Four nights and nine hundred bucks later, I hoped the weekend crowd would propel me closer to the driver's seat of a Ford Mustang. Next goal was to sock away enough money to support us through our future, which I dreamed, included owning a home, continued education, and my own business. As in childhood years, I dreamed often, choosing fantasy over reality. Escapism helped me make it through some awful nights. Kat continually assured me things would get easier and I would adjust, but I couldn't calm down. Thank heaven for Phenaphen. My pain had lost intensity, but I appreciated the dream-state offered by my meds. The Jewel Box unnerved me, especially when a shortage of dancers meant removing my sheer lingerie top, stepping onto the round stage and attempting to dance. I felt sure everyone could hear the fierce pounding of my heart—even over the blaring jukebox.

"Thank you Mr. Gaye," I mumbled as Marvin sang *Grapevine's* ending line. I then scurried to the dressing room with sweat pouring profusely from every pore of my body, trickling into the glue now barely holding pasties over my nipples. Blotting perspiration with a clean, damp bar towel, I was reapplying glue when Kat rushed in.

"C'mon, cutie. Three dancers just walked in followed by Al and Gabe. I told 'em you're back and those guys are dying to see you."

"Hallelujah!" I checked myself in the wall-to-wall mirror before following Kat out. Through a packed house, I could hear Al calling my name from across the room. I looked upward into the noisy crowd of

Friday night customers and saw my favorite guys sitting at their usual table. Kat delivered their drinks as I bounced up the two steps to the elevated area near the bar to say hello. It had been weeks since I last saw them and I actually missed these partners.

Smiling and standing up, Al exclaimed in high nasal pitch, "It's good to have you back. We sure missed you!" Then he reached out and gave me a hug and quick kiss on the cheek. Al had given me pecks on the cheek before, but tonight it felt especially comforting. "Your hair has really grown," he commented with a grin. "You look great!"

"Thank you." I patted Al's shoulder. In spite of the surroundings and our bad start, these two guys always made me feel at ease. It was going to be a good night.

Not frowning, but not beaming like his partner, Gabe stood awaiting his obligatory hug, then pleasantly said, "Welcome back, Blondie," while reaching forward. As he leaned forward and as I turned, somehow instead of his lips touching my cheek, they were against my mouth. Ohmigod! We were touching lips! The cardinal sin Kat and Beau warned me against was echoing in my head: "Never, never let men kiss you on the lips."

Too late. Our lips were together. His lips felt wonderfully soft against mine and the gentleness of his kiss went everywhere, making me weak and breathless. My body seemed to be floating in mid-air in some strange, sort of dreamlike state; weightless, formless, yet fully aware of my being. Gabe ended the kiss and opened his eyes as I opened mine. We stood staring at each other, not saying a word.

"Huh hummmm." Al loudly cleared his throat, evidently noticing our mouth-to-mouth. Gabe hurriedly pulled out a chair, and somewhat shyly, asked me to join them.

I sat down, trembling. I had never felt so odd.

"You okay?" Gabe asked, The Chi-Lites crooning *Oh Girl* in the background.

My head nodded yes as I lowered my eyes and noticed every hair on my arms standing on end.

"So you ran off to places unknown," Al interjected, noticing the awkwardness between Gabe and me.

"Uh, yes. But I'm back for good and won't be leaving again anytime soon." I swallowed, attempting to continue, "Uuh. . . can I get you guys another drink?" Looking at their full beers, I felt slightly foolish and for the first time in years, completing a sentence was difficult. I looked at Gabe and felt discernible panic brewing. Did he notice my reaction to his kiss? Did he feel what I felt? Why had I felt anything? And why with this guy, of all people?

"You can't be our waitress tonight," Gabe said softly, raking hair from his forehead with his hand. "Laura's going to wait on us and you're going to sit and drink cocktails. If you'd like."

"Oh," I muttered, feeling dazed.

Interpreting my open syllable as acceptance, Gabe began rambling about my being a vagabond voyager or something. My head was spinning as though I'd taken one Phenaphen too many, but tonight I hadn't taken any. What was happening here? The loquacious one was fumbling for words, while Gabe the mute was suddenly talking a blue streak.

"Katie. . . oops sorry. *Laura.*" I touched her arm. "Please tell Beau I'd like a real cocktail, not a Kool-Aid one. Gabriel wants me to sit for a minute."

She raised an eyebrow at my request, and then echoed, "Gabriel?"

I hadn't realized I'd called Gabe, Gabriel and words escaped me as I scraped away a coat of cherry blossom pink polish from my thumbnail.

"We're paying Blondie to sit here," Gabriel said calmly, apparently detecting my inability to speak.

"Well, only for a few minutes." Laura batted her lashes and smiled brightly. "Then I'll need her help. In case no one's noticed, this joint's jumping!"

Sitting quietly in a semi-cognizant state, I watched Gabriel douse another cigarette as Al sat flapping his moustache to some dancer he asked to join our table. The dancers made tips while dancing and profits from cocktails bought by customers. "Men gladly pay a buck and a half for a few minutes of company," Beau told me on my first day. The tiny drinks were served in "mock crystal" martini glasses and consisted of nothing stronger than Kool-Aid. "The bar keeps fifty cents from each cocktail, the girls keep a dollar, and General Foods gets richer. I rarely serve liquor to girls 'cause I have to watch their consumption. I don't need drunk dancers passing out or puking in their purses instead of selling cocktails." Beau also launched my love of peppermint schnapps and 7 Up, a refreshing girlie toddy that gave me minty breath throughout the evening as I sipped a short one for hours. Hard liquor slowed me and affected my tips, so I usually abstained. If a customer offered, I thanked him, took my Kool-Aid cocktail tableside, knocked it back while placing my hand on his shoulder, and left to make more tips. Easy way to add fifty bucks to my nightly take.

The smidgen of schnapps in my cocktail did little to relax me, yet Gabriel seemed calm as ever. Although he usually made rude remarks about the ignorance of dancers Al invited to their table, tonight he seemed oblivious to any conversations around us, asking me all sorts of questions. Even listening as I told him more than he needed to know about Nikki. I briefed him on my ordeal with Wesley and mentioned using a phony identity in my attempt to hide from the lunatic. Gabriel repeated the name "Carol Wood," then told me a joke about a hare-lipped woman and a man with a wooden eye: Physical impairments caused insecurities and shyness in both, but after finally getting the nerve to talk, the man with the wooden eye asked the hare-lipped woman if she'd like to have dinner with him. She replied, "Would I!" But being overly sensitive, the man with the wooden eye misinterpreted and angrily snapped back, "Harelip! Harelip!" then stormed away. Apparently I went overboard in the laughter department, because for the remainder of the night, Gabe answered questions such as, "Would you like another drink," with "Wood eye!"

"You're being so nice." I sipped my cocktail. "I'm beginning to think a human being is hiding under that gruff exterior."

"Shhhhh. Don't let anyone hear you say that." He grinned. "It'll ruin my image."

Serenely enlightening me about himself, Gabriel told me he was the oldest in an Irish Catholic family of five children, and the only member living in Texas. He was born and raised in Burlington, Vermont due to paternal ancestors skipping Ellis Island, smuggling whiskey into America, and investing in the small state. He had a privileged adolescence, but life changed drastically during his teens after his parents divorced. Interested in architecture, Gabriel took a carpentry job as summer employment to help with finances, enjoyed it immensely, and voilà, it became his profession. His voice became quieter as he told about hastily jumping into marriage with his high school sweetheart, which generated hostility by her affluent parents.

Within two years he and Astrid welcomed two daughters, but things weren't "happily ever after." Astrid despised his profession and insisted he pursue a more respectable career. She hated his wood smell, repeatedly told him it was indicative of a common laborer, and demanded he change from his sawdust covered clothing before arriving in their subdivision. She also insisted he tell neighbors he was an architect. Although he changed into clean clothing at a service station nightly, he refused to lie about his profession. Animosity abounded in their home.

Gabriel's revelation was interrupted by the unusually loud a cappella rendition of *Mention My Name In Topeka* by Murray, the silver haired, cheap old fart whose fat rump covered the center barstool from shortly after opening until late-thirty each night. "Hope he doesn't fall down." Gabriel watched Murray's swaying serenade at the bar.

I looked up and saw Beau motioning me to the phone. "It's Wesley," he mouthed.

We did a brief routine of me shaking my head NO and Beau shaking his head YES, before I finally walked over to the bar. "God, Beau," I moaned. "Why won't this man leave me alone? Tell him I just quit. Or died. Tell him anything. I'm scared to death of that horrible man and his threats."

Beau cupped his hand tightly over the mouthpiece. "Get on the phone this minute!" he insisted. The only time I'd seen such anger on Beau's face was the night he fired sexy black-haired dancer Gypsy for soliciting prostitution. "You tell him to come on over and kill you right now, because you'd rather be dead than be with him!" Beau stared into my eyes.

Murray tried to cop a feel. The old lech had likely fondled more ass than a proctologist, but in my outrage for Wesley, I slapped Murray's hand and pointed my finger at his forehead, daring him to touch me. Keeping my eyes focused on Murray's bulbous nose and red rimmed eyes, I blurted Beau's message into the phone, handed it back to him and hurried back to the table.

Gabriel stood up and pulled out my chair. "Hey Blondie, I agree with Al, your hair looks really nice."

"*Ohhhhh Mention my Name in Topeka. . .*" Murray started loudly singing again.

Gabriel took a Marlboro from the pack. "It's getting long and shiny."

"What?" I glanced around the room.

"Your hair looks beautiful. And you're a million miles away." He inhaled smoke smoothly into his lungs. "Anything you wanna talk about?"

I gave him a brief rundown on the Wesley situation. Gabriel listened intently, shook his head crossly a couple of times, and then took my hand, concern covering his face. "I'll call to check on you the next few days. So, if you need anything, just let me know. Okay?"

"Oh pleeeeease." My voice quivered. "I'm fine."

"Yeah. . . You sure?"

"I'm certain," I answered. "You certainly convey a lot of meanings with the word yeah."

"Yeaaah?" Gabriel drawled caringly. "Kinda like you do with please?"

"Kinda."

He and Al stayed later than usual and Gabriel squeezed my hand before heading to the exit where he looked back, caught my eye, and offered a goodwill nod. Even though Katie-Laura and I stayed extremely busy the remainder of the night, I constantly thought about our kiss. "I saw that mouth-to-mouth between you and Gabe," Kat said on the drive home. "Looked like you two were in some sort of trance." I didn't know about him, but I certainly was, and it was different than my myriad of self induced trances. When I got in bed around three-thirty, the kiss and its magical feeling played over and over in my head.

The following night, I found myself constantly watching the club's door, hoping my guys would make one of their infrequent Saturday night short visits, which Al had even dragged his wife along on a few times. Around nine o'clock as I rushed around taking orders, I glanced toward the entrance, and there stood Gabriel, smoking, observing. I delivered the drinks on my tray before walking toward him, but almost tripped in transit. "Where's your partner?" I tried to regain balance as I looked behind him for Al.

"I'm flying solo tonight," Gabriel said softly.

"Oh," I responded, almost wetting my sequined panties. The partners *always* came in the club together. I led him to a table, noticing he was looking somewhat ill-at-ease in his crisp dress shirt and slacks.

Unaware of Gabriel's "arrogant asshole" reputation, a new dancer with protruding front teeth plunked her fanny in the chair at his table, and instantly leaned in to ask for a cocktail.

Distractedly and without hesitation, Gabriel dryly said, "I'd rather give you money to see an orthodontist."

His brutal honesty often left those around him speechless, but not this time.

"Keep your money and buy yourself some manners!" She flipped him the bird as she walked away.

"I see you never got around to taking that Dale Carnegie course either," I teased.

"Even if I had, I wouldn't waste diplomacy trying to influence the likes of her. And tell Beau he needs to make sure this one's been wormed and has all her shots."

We gabbed about personal habits of dancers flitting around before shifting topics to current events like sit-ins, teach-ins, love-ins, John and Yoko's wedding, and the Supremes breakup. Our banter bounced from the dim witted *Hee Haw*, to the sharp witted *Dick Cavett Show*, as we grabbed every possible moment to chat. He laughed aloud several times and when he softly snorted mid-laugh, I asked if he needed Primatene Mist. He seemed relaxed and happy, unlike his usual gruff self. I savored this tiny peek into his psyche.

Staying Saturday-night-busy with no time to sit, I felt Gabriel's eyes follow me from customer to customer, so I made countless stops to check his beer situation. After three beers, he said, "I need to stop with Budweiser and start with the real thing." Coca-Cola had recently revived their old slogan and I don't know how often he reiterated, "the real thing," but Coca-Cola would have been mighty pleased. The parlaying of impolite personal remarks to each other vanished, and the guy I once considered a human affront to women hadn't once said, "I'd do just about anything for a piece of ass."

Suddenly, the Jewel Box didn't seem such a dreadful place.

6

Gabriel began coming in almost daily before prime time, sometimes with Al but often without. He drank Coke while we chatted like long lost friends, and he left before the crowd arrived.

"Gabe's dour look is changing into semi-pleasant these days," said Kat, who wasn't one to beat around the bush. "And it's because of you. The man never walked through these doors without Al before."

"Really," I casually responded.

"Yes, really. Even Beau's noticed the change in Gabe."

"Are there more candles in back?" I inspected the one in my hand a bit too thoroughly in my attempt to be blasé. "Several need replacing." For the first time ever, I couldn't tell Katie-Laura how I felt. I wasn't sure myself. Gabriel's presence made me lose my train of thought. Made me stumble. Made my pulse rise. Made me more fuzzy headed than usual. And after our unexpected mouth-to-mouth kiss, the fuzziness moved south to totally inappropriate places. But he was married. And don't think my mother left out any quotes on adultery. Those ranked right up there with "Thou shalt not kill."

Didn't take long before Al heard about his partner's frequent visits to the club without him, and one night after several drinks, Mr. Infatuation-turned-church-deacon took me aside. "You know Gabriel may be miserably married, but he does have two young daughters."

I stared into his road-map red eyes as he preached. *Blah, blah, blah.* Lacquered, bouffant hair was all Al needed to look as hypocritical as those TV evangelists. Al's wife apparently approved his stopping by the Jewel

Box on a regular basis, but it's doubtful she'd approve if she got wind of the recurring rise in his jeans, courtesy of certain dancers.

"Gabriel is a real decent guy," Al appeared to be winding down his mini-gospel hour. "So please just cool things with my partner."

"You're blowing things way out of proportion, Al. Gabriel and I are in a club packed with people—which I understand he frequented long before I began my illustrious career here." I took a deep breath. "Lighten up. It's not like I'm one of Homer's Sirens luring him into this joint, but I'll cool things."

I turned back to my two Jewel Box buddies, listening at the bar. "It'll likely take a blizzard to cool things between you two." Katie-Laura winked and raised her eyebrow.

"Indeed," Beau chimed in. "It's been years since I've seen a connection like theirs."

"You mean the way Blondie stutters and stumbles when Gabe's in the club?"

"That, and how Gabe no longer looks at Cherie, but looks *into* her."

"Something's brewing between 'em." Kat cocked her eyebrow.

"You guys need medication for your delusions." I blushed.

৩

Shortly after Reverend Al's "Sermon in sin city," he fell in love again. This time the object of his affection was a sultry nursing student, moon-lighting as a dancer. Teddy Bear's flawless honey color skin, lion-colored locks, and angelic yet strikingly seductive blue gray eyes qualified her as belle of the ball. Al said she made Raquel Welch look like leftover gravy. Always dancing to Creedence Clearwater Revival songs, Teddy Bear seemed brighter than the other girls, and managed to escape sarcastic pseudonym typically bestowed by Al and Gabriel.

"Hey Cherie," Al piped up one night as I served their drinks. "Gabe and I wanna take you and Teddy Bear to lunch this week."

"Someone accidentally shoot a hole through your skull with the nail gun today?" I glanced at Al, then Gabriel. Butterflies did acrobatics in my tummy at the thought of seeing him outside this noisy club, but I was sure Beau's rulebook didn't permit rendezvous with customers. "Beau's not about to allow that."

"You my friend, are naïve." Gabriel grinned.

"You think this is common practice?"

"I don't know, Blondie, you'll have to ask Beau. Al's assumption surprises me too, but this ain't exactly a church we're sittin' in."

Beau laughed when I told him what Gabriel said. "You tell Gabe we'll be having a revival next week if he's interested. But go ahead and have lunch with them—they're harmless. Just don't make it a habit. If men want company, they'll have to come to the Jewel Box."

Laura thought it a bad idea, but two days later Teddy Bear and I met the guys in front of the Jewel Box for our lunch date. I'd been dreaming about what to order at one of Sonny Looks great restaurants when we pulled into the parking lot of Gulfgate Mall. Houston's first mall, once glitzy and now beginning to show signs of decline like many other southeast side businesses, didn't thrill me. Nor did the Picadilly Cafeteria where Al pretty much salivated over Teddy Bear the entire meal. Still, he and Gabriel behaved like real gentlemen, and during conversation that ranged from the sublime to the ridiculous, Gabriel used clichés and made analogies mixing historical characters with current events. My prior pain-in-the-ass guy had impeccable table manners. Until we stood to leave. Gabriel punched his finger into all untouched rolls. "You're strange." I wrinkled my nose into a sneer, all the while feeling charmed by his weirdness.

A week later at Gabriel's suggestion, the same foursome wound up at a matinee showing of *Butch Cassidy and the Sundance Kid*. Gabriel's dark moustache wasn't as long and wild as Redford's and his blond hair wasn't as tousled, but other facial characteristics made me feel like I was sandwiched between two versions of the delicious Sundance Kid.

Beau demanded punctuality from waitresses, so I rushed the others from theater to the club where the four of us sat around talking until I was forced to work for a living. After waiting on a few customers, I hurried back to the table just as a new dancer, Sugar Box, was dragging a chair between Teddy Bear and Al. Almost as pretty as Teddy Bear, this loud mouthed, thigh slapping, long legged dancer with ebony eyes and blazing black hair didn't use seductive behavior to make her money. When it came time for her to dance, she darted from the table and chose *Sittin' on the*

Dock of the Bay for her dance routine. Sugar Box blackened two teeth and turned her gimme cap backwards, before sitting on the little stage with slouched shoulders and a fishing pole in hand, acting out her rendition of Mr. Redding's words. She dramatically peered into the crowd while Otis sang of watching the ships roll in, and slowly bobbed her head until he began whistling, at which time she loudly but pathetically whistled along.

Taking outstretched dollars and drink offers from men as she made her way back to our table, Sugar Box sat unladylike, spreading one leg on the back of Al's chair and the other on a vacant chair. "Lovely." I frowned.

"Gotta air my crotch," Sugar Box said, then told a joke so vulgar it even brought a blush to Gabriel's tan face. Al bought her a drink. She poured it down her throat. "Buy two more so you don't have to keep dragging out your wallet." Al complied and Teddy Bear daintily sipped her Kool-Aid cocktail, trying not to show her irritation. On Sugar Box's fifth cocktail, she began telling Al about her ex-husband who had the largest love bugle she'd ever been blessed to blow. That's when Teddy Bear stormed away from the table. Ten minutes later, Sugar Box took off to make money elsewhere, and Al went gloomy on us. "For Christ's sakes, man." Gabriel punched his shoulder. "That one's probably seen more penises than a first year urology resident."

Crude Sugar Box was incorrigible, but smart enough to sell more cocktails every night than most dancers combined. Lord only knows how much she made in dancing tips, and in a few weeks she was gone with the wind.

Teddy Bear never went to another lunch or movie, but her participation spawned a practice that soon became Al's calling card. Gabriel and I were elected chaperones each time Mr. Looking For Love In All The Wrong Places fell in heat, so we saw countless movies and often shared lunch, with Gabriel keeping his impeccable manners thing going—along with his finger into untouched rolls routine. I never got over the sensation derived from our mouth-to-mouth kiss, but had a new kinship with him. We definitely shared an attraction to the inappropriate and a sense of reckless impulse.

Even though her tenure longer than most, when Teddy Bear departed, Al turned Father Flanagan and befriended a dancer who was a major contrast to the sexy nursing student. With a pathetic, downcast face and glum expressions that ran the gamut from mourning to despair, Rosemary could have made a living doubling as a bloodhound in Disney movies. Gabriel nicknamed this repugnant goddess of grime, "Rosemary Rotten-crotch." Her stringy dishwater blonde hair always looked dirty, her acne covered face qualified as a *before* photo for Clearasil ads, and poor Rosemary radiated gag-inducing body odor.

"She's uglier than a twenty dollar mule and smells like she slops pigs before coming to work," Gabriel said, swigging his Budweiser at the bar.

"I doubt any farmer would hire her to slop hogs, but every evening around midnight there's plenty of men in this joint willing to spend money on her." Beau stacked bar napkins.

"Yeah, like Al." I grabbed some stir straws. "After too many drinks, he gets real chummy. That's why Gabriel leaves the table and comes up here."

"That old bastard better not suggest an outing with this verminous creature. This one's an infectious disease just waiting to happen. I swear I saw a fly land on her the other night and instantly drop dead." Gabriel polished off his beer.

I pursed my lips in a little moue of distaste, something I learned from Mother. "Al just feels sorry for her, that's why he slips her ten bucks to dance to Stevie Wonder's music."

"Hell, I love Stevie Wonder, but I'll give her fifty—make that a hundred—not to dance at all!" He nodded at Beau for a refill.

"Behave." I pinched Gabriel's arm. "Al's being humane instead of horny, for a change."

"I'm glad Al gives her money." Beau slid Gabe his beer. "Otherwise I'd have to pad her drink sales. She's the only dancer not breaking a hundred every night."

"Cause she can't get near anyone without causing them to puke," Gabriel said.

"Baby, can you and Laura give her some deodorant and toothpaste?" Beau pulled a twenty from the register and handed it to me. "Maybe school her on hygiene?"

"We can try, but installing a shower might work better."

Other than dancing to the trio of songs by Stevie for Al's payoff, Rosemary repeatedly danced to *Love Grows Where My Rosemary Goes*. Without fail, when the Edison Lighthouse song began to flow from the jukebox, Gabriel turned his back to the stage or headed to the men's room, saying he had to go puke his guts out.

Like the constant stream of dancers, Rosemary soon disappeared and was replaced by "Annie Oakley," who had aptly named herself, much to Gabriel's chagrin. Moseying around with a lightweight rope she utilized to lasso customers, Annie desperately tried to look the part, pulling her long, reddish brown hair into braids and wearing western garb, complete with cheap boots and spurs. Her western hat was black felt with a cord that pulled around her face and locked with a wooden bead under her chin. Hardly the style worn by true cowgirls, but she was damn proud of it, and constantly shifted the bead to lift the hat and tip her head at men as they walked through the club. Annie had knock-knees and Howdy-Doodie gap teeth that caused her to whistle when she spoke, but the feature men often commented on was her eyes. Even though she wore thick Coke bottle type glasses to correct her vision, she constantly squinted to see her surroundings. Every time she went on stage, men moved their chairs back in fear of being injured during her attempts to display her roping abilities. Laura and I had to clean up many a broken glass behind Annie before she ended her Jewel Box stint. We didn't miss her one bit.

෴

Gabriel and Al celebrated my twenty-third birthday at the club with me, and Al got so drunk you'd have thought it was his special day. Gabriel practically carried him out, then came back inside and walked up behind me at the waitress station. "Wanna go see *M*A*S*H*?" he asked, so near me I felt his breath in my hair.

"Does Al have a new love for the Seventies?" I stepped back.

"Not yet. You just like movies so much, I figured maybe I could pick you up on Sunday and we could venture out alone. If you don't have plans."

"I usually groom my beard that day." I looked over at Beau's ear bending our direction. "But if you don't mind unruly facial hair, I'll go." No Al with his flavor of the week. Just us. Sounded like fun.

After our first solo Sunday and Gabriel meeting my sister's family, it soon turned into a regular event. Gabriel drove to West Houston, picked up

Nikki and me at Ellen's, took us for lunch or ice cream, and then dropped Nikki back while we went to a movie. During those months he got to know my sister and her husband—who thought he was a fairly swell guy for a philanderer. Yes. They questioned our relationship, asking how his wife felt about it. I repeated Gabriel's explanation: Astrid demanded time alone and didn't give a rat's ass about his whereabouts. His marital status didn't seem germane to our friendship.

❦

Al's next love was a short and sassy dancer named Betty, whose ear hugging, fluffed up bob of brightly tinted red hair noticeably contrasted her black, inch long, false eyelashes. For several nights she completely ignored the partners because of their attire, but when she noticed Al was a big spender she was all over him like stink on you-know-what. The partners nicknamed her "Red," and of course Al fell head over heels for her, saying she exuded sexiness. Gabriel said, "Al wouldn't know sexy if it stung him on the scrotum and left a calling card in his crack."

"Gotta admit her turned up nose and pouty lips are fetching." I accentuated her positives.

"But only Bozo can pull off that god-awful red hair color." Gabriel shook his head.

"I can't believe Al fell for her haughty demeanor."

"Hell, how can he stand her abrasive voice? It cuts straight through my shoulder blades every time she laughs."

Betty (now dubbed, Red) walked around the club in a tube top, skin tight mini skirt, and six inch stilettos, holding her purse as though she had the Hope Diamond inside. She constantly flashed her fake smile while holding her head high and slightly tilted to one side like she expected the paparazzi to snap her photo at any time. Pretty snooty attitude for someone working in a topless club. But maybe that's what rang Al's bell. Old love stricken Al spent a small fortune on her, but she still refused to go out with him, even with Gabriel and me as chaperones.

After weeks of Al practically getting on his knees and begging for a date, Red agreed to let him move her into her new apartment. "Al has butt blemishes older than this girl, but he's trying to get a piece of ass and now

57

I'm roped into helping him move her goddamned furniture," Gabriel complained. "The old bastards' hornier than a broke-dick dog."

"Where do you get these weird aphorisms?"

"Shakespeare," he answered.

"You my friend, are strange."

"Me? Take a gander at my partner who'd give his left nut to make that conceited bitch happy. We should've never started the lunch and movie bullshit."

"At least that creepy caterpillar finally crawled off his upper lip. Your moustache is fetching, but his was. . ." I stuck my finger in my mouth to replicate regurgitation.

On Saturday the guys came to the club after the move, Gabriel looking thoroughly put out, and Al smiling like we were giving away free beer and growth hormones.

"What's with Al, did Red let him kiss her elbow or something?"

"No." Gabriel frowned. "The crazy fucker talked her into having breakfast with him tomorrow morning, so he can get more sexually frustrated. Naturally we have to go along." He looked at me, a broad beam shining from his eyes. "But that's okay, since I'll get to see you earlier than usual. Just don't make me look at her disgusting face so early in the day."

"You can look at me." I winked. "But I might dye my hair bright red for tomorrow."

"Don't make me puke! Speaking of hair, aren't you doing something different to yours lately?"

"Letting it grow back to its natural champagne blonde with only highlights from the sun."

"Yeaaah?" He pulled a smoke from his shirt pocket. "I kinda liked that platinum color."

"Oh pleeease! That snow white shade is fine for dark clubs and Hollywood, but in the real world it tends to draw a lot of attention. Cat calls from choir boys and that sort of thing."

"Ye watchers and ye holy ones, Bright seraphs, cer-u-bim," he sang.

I rarely got to bed before three-thirty in the morning after washing my smoke permeated skin and hair until the water ran clear, and I usually slept late due to exhaustion and my nightly dose of Phenapen (no longer needed for pain, just sleep). Still, I was looking forward to an eleven a.m. breakfast. Up before nine, I primped longer than usual, wanting to look my best, and when Gabriel arrived at Charles and Ellen's I was reading *One Fish, Two Fish* to Nikki. Being around him out of the Jewel Box was a nice treat and I appreciated how he overlooked where we had met, treating me as though we were introduced at a church social. Okay, maybe more like a truck pull, but he treated me special and it seemed we'd known each other since we were in diapers. I knew we wouldn't be dining at the Ritz, but had dressed appropriately for a public setting, wearing a tasteful lime green sundress (suitable for church social or truck pull).

"I like your dress," Gabriel said with a glance that validated his sincerity.

"Thank you, my friend. And I like your shirt and slacks, but you need to look for some sawdust cologne. You're just not the same without your signature scent."

"Yeaaah?" he drawled almost shyly, opening the passenger door of his brand spanking new white Ford Ranger pickup truck.

"Wow, I'm surprised you left the dealership without customized long horns on your hood."

"They're on back order." He grinned. "I'm in line behind six thousand other Texans."

I rolled my eyes in a show of distaste.

"Meanwhile I've gotta find the perfect ten gallon hat and armadillo belt buckle," he said while backing out of the driveway.

We headed across town to some little out of the way restaurant to meet Mr. Mid Life Crisis and Little Miss Shit Don't Stink.

Al was either wearing lifts or had optimistically stacked condoms an inch high in his boots. And Red must have been half asleep when she got dressed. The fashion craze was bare midriffs, but the *haute couture* would have found her rendition of the Paris attire mind blowing to say the least. All her tube tops must have been dirty because she arrived in a crop top that barely covered her boobs and short shorts that failed to cover her bum. She completed her ensemble with four inch clogs. Gabriel nudged my waist and facetiously mumbled something about her shorts begging for mercy. Red overheard his comment, took it as compliment, then flashed him one of her fake smiles. "Damn! Take a look at her face," he whispered in my ear, "if you can stand it."

I wish he hadn't done that. It was like passing the scene of an auto accident and seeing mangled bodies. It's hard to keep from looking, but even a quick glance can leave you with a nasty memory you'll not soon forget. One of Red's eyelashes had come unglued and was dangling with every flutter of her lash as she flicked cigarette ashes everywhere but in the ashtray. Al was too busy getting his ego stroked to notice. But her dangling lash and flicking ashes were diddly, compared to her eating habits. Besides putting out cigarettes in a pat of butter, Red smacked her food and slurped coffee while she talked and laughed at Al's cornball jokes. I dodged flying spittle. "I've seen better table manners on Animal Kingdom," Gabriel said. Al busied himself manhandling Red with his eyes. Slurping, smacking, and letting go her abrasive laugh, Red intermittently regaled Al with far-fetched tales about her fabulous life. When she started in with some crap about Charlie Manson's sex appeal, Gabriel pushed his plate aside and crowded into me.

"Puullease!" I whispered to him, "This chick is a bonafide weirdo."

His lips went against my ear. "She was definitely left in the birth canal too long. And if her eyelash falls into that plate, I'll guaran-damn-tee you, we're leaving."

He had barely completed his sentence when Red dropped egg yolk all over her crop top and failed to notice yolk dribbling down her chin while she blabbed. We're talking gauche table manners, folks. Familiar with Gabriel's brutal honesty and total dislike for Red, I prepared for a Woody Allen restaurant scene when he rose from the table. He surprised me. "I told Blondie about the apartments you moved to, and promised to take her over to see them today. She's looking for her own place, ya know."

I stood beside him. Red was clinging to Al's left arm and tossing him sugar coated compliments he was lapping up like ice cream after a tonsillectomy. She gave him a real sense of pride, you could tell. The odd couple barely noticed our departure.

"I was gettin' ready to puke," Gabriel grumbled, opening the truck door for me. "I'd rather chew on rat guts or get kicked in the groin before tolerating the company of that avaricious shrew again."

60

"Puke. Rat guts. Groin." I repeated a few of his words that would've once grossed me out. "I've always longed to meet a poetic James Joycean kind of guy."

"Hey Blondie, does it feel to you like we met on Noah's ark?"

"Yeah . . . it does." I reflected. "And thanks for getting us away from those two animals."

"Pleasure's all mine. Did I mention this apartment complex has furnished models, so you won't have to buy furniture? It'd be closer to work for you, and easier than drivin' out to the west side every weekend for me."

"You're fun to know." I leaned against the passenger door with the comfy casualness of a school girl. "But in a strange kind of way."

"Yeaaah? Well so are you." His blue eyes sparkled.

"That was the caption by my yearbook photo." I rolled down the window.

"Fun to know in a strange kind of way?"

"That would've been better than just 'Fun to know.' Of course, my mother was unhappy it wasn't 'Virtuous to know'—ya know."

"Watch out Blondie, you're pickin' up my pitiful grammar."

I had discussed getting my own place for some time, but a lingering fear that psychopath Wesley might find me again gave me qualms about moving anywhere alone. Hidden behind trees and only blocks from Interstate 45 South, the St. Patrick apartments looked pristine and homey, which made me instantly like them. But when Gabriel asked if I wanted to stop at the office and see a furnished model, I declined. He gave me an understanding nod. "Well, at least you know what the place looks like when you feel more comfortable about moving out on your own."

"Thanks for bringing me by. Maybe I'll stop and look at one of the models sometime soon." I fidgeted with my bangle bracelets.

"You don't sound very convincing, Blondie."

"Maybe I'll enroll in acting classes, Dagwood."

My sister and her husband had been exceptionally hospitable, and Nikki thought Jimmy was her brother, but we had lived with them for six months. It was time for us to be our own family. Before going to work on Friday, I drove my brand new, blue Ford Mustang to the St. Patrick apartments with security deposit in hand. They were as cozy on the inside as they looked from the outside.

"You made any decisions about moving to the south side?" Gabriel asked, after taking Nikki and me for ice cream on Sunday.

"You're starting to sound like a lobbyist who suspects I have political power over the rising cost of barley and hops."

"Am not," he responded. "I'm just tired of puttin' so many miles on my truck."

"Yeah, right." I reapplied lip gloss. "Well, Ellen and Charles can't be guardians forever, and I can't imagine having a better neighbor than Red."

"Blondie, don't tell me you moved next door to that disgusting wench."

"Opposite side of the complex."

"Thank God!" He helped Nikki out of the truck and watched her skip back inside to play with Cousin Jimmy. "Just let me know when you're ready to move. I know a mover who does a good job and it'll only cost you a couple of Budweisers." He winked, and then crouched down to pat a neighbor's Welsh terrier who wandered onto the driveway.

"Look at you. You never fooled me with that arrogant façade—I always knew you were human."

"Yeaaah? Always?"

"Well, initially I thought you were a human affront to society, but I'm incredibly intuitive. It's a gift God gave me in place of math comprehension."

"See ya crazy girl," he said before reaching over to give me a quick kiss.

Yikes. Our lips slipped again. This second mouth-to-mouth was quicker than our first, but triggered identical feelings in me. I shivered. And had a strange sense that Mother's moral radar was somehow tracking the inappropriate feelings flying through my body.

7

Some 80,000 peaceful demonstrators had gathered in Washington to protest the Cambodian incursion, and in Houston colossal clouds floated across brilliant blue skies making May ninth a lovely Saturday. Great day for a move. I intuitively knew Wesley would never bother me again. Everything just felt right—like on prom night when your lacquered beehive hairdo is impervious to humidity, gale force winds, and the ever-present idiot spewing champagne from a bottle.

Gabriel arrived at my sister's house in an unusually cheerful mood for someone who worked all morning. My brother-in-law helped pack his truck with boxes of household items I'd bought to replace what Wesley stole, and the two chatted like military comrades who'd spent fox hole time together.

"Can't I stay a little longer with Jimmy?" Nikki pleaded as they loaded my last box.

"Aren't you excited to come see our new place?"

"Just one more night, Mommy. Please?"

"Okay. My lovey-dovey." I kissed her goodbye. "Your uncle Charles is keeping my Mustang to buff out its new bumper dent, so you can stay until Kat brings me back tomorrow."

"How'd that happen?" Gabriel glanced at it before walking toward his truck.

"My reckless soon-to-be neighbor, Delilah. She backed into us outside our complex office when I stopped to sign final paperwork."

"Glad no one got hurt." Gabriel waved at everyone heading back inside, and opened his truck door for me.

"Thank you."

"Oh I'd do just about anything for a piece of ass, Blondie."

"Stop it. The day's too pretty for your silly vulgarities. Even the clouds look like giant scoops of whipped cream."

"Cumulus clouds," he enlightened. "Usually mean fair weather, but sometimes they form thunderheads when it gets really hot. Some even carry rain."

"Thank you Mr. Wizard."

"Anytime." He cranked the engine, turned up the radio to *Aquarius/Let the Sunshine In,* and loudly accompanied the 5th Dimension.

"Sing along, Blondie."

"Tiny Tim sings better than me."

"C'mon," he insisted when Smokey Robinson started singing *The Tracks of My Tears.*

Didn't take much urging before I chimed in. Thankfully the windows were rolled up as we harmonized in pathetic white folk voice along with Motown greats all the way across town. With a background of great music, we discussed everything from Pan Am's first commercial journey by a Boeing 747, to white lipstick and black lights until we reached the St. Patrick Apartments. Gabriel lugged box after box inside, hesitating only to harass me about my habit of walking on my tiptoes while I unpacked and placed my new things.

"Ay Chihuahua," he shrieked, and dropped a box when he walked into the bedroom.

"Silencio José!" I plugged in my radio. "I like my nicely furnished apartment. It's an eclectic mix of furniture, but at least my living and dining rooms are decorated in traditional style."

"Nothing wrong with Spanish décor in a bedroom." He frowned.

"Well it wouldn't be so horrendous if I hadn't had a moment of Andy Warhol warpism, and bought the red bedspread to accent the Spanish theme."

"Whose huge matador wall hanging is that?"

"Told you, I was having an Andy Warhol moment."

"You planning on entertaining Don Juan's ancestors?"

"I'm planning on grabbing a quick shower while you grab that last box, please. I'm a grimeball."

"Impossible. Says the worker bee to the queen." He sailed by, his sawdust scent lingering in the air.

I took a speed shower and threw on my button down sundress before walking into the living room where Gabriel was singing *You've Made Me So Very Happy* along with Blood, Sweat, and Tears. "Group named themselves after hearing Winston Churchill use the term in one of his speeches."

The guy was a real receptacle of musical trivia. "You're certainly in a great mood."

"You noticed?"

"Gabriel if you were wearing a mood ring its illumination would blind us."

He didn't respond and a weird quietness filled the room. The move had come to an end, and the time for Gabriel to leave had commenced.

"Well, Blondie, that's the last box. Unless you left something at your sister's." He held out his right hand and briskly rubbed his thumb across the tips of his fingers.

"Circulation problem?"

"Just a strange habit." He casually pulled a Marlboro from the pack and fired it up. "Didn't we leave a box behind? Forget something at the store? New element charts. Fishing tackle. Pickled pig feet. Kerosene, mariachis, world atlas, abacus. Anything? Surely there's something else we need to do."

Mr. Calm, Cool, and Collected was babbling!

"Guess I can call to see if Charles finished working on my car so you could take me back. Otherwise I have to impose on Katie-Laura tomorrow. She's covering my shift tonight."

"Uh."

"That's profound commentary."

Not responding with his usual flippant retort, he shuffled momentarily at the front door when radio music got interrupted by a report about Walter Reuther dying in a plane crash. Gabriel made some comment about the UAW, and then awkwardly cleared his throat. I sat on the arm of my rented sofa and nervously scraped off nail varnish just as *My Cherie Amour* came across the air waves. I briefly lost my balance, but didn't topple onto the floor. Singing along with Stevie, Gabriel walked over, stood squarely in front of me, looked into my eyes as he removed the Marlboro from his lips, and then put his hand behind his back. I shifted uncomfortably. A stream of smoke drifted up over his shoulders as he leaned forward and placed a long kiss on my lips. His lips were so soft, so warm, and so moist on mine, I melted. "Don't kiss me that way unless you mean it." I giggled nervously, trying to calm down. Trying to harness the feelings flying through my body. Trying to make the room stop spinning. And trying to return the atmosphere to a wholesome one. MARRIED MAN! I screamed internally.

Gabriel placed his Marlboro in an ashtray I had purchased just for him, and in a cautious voice said, "I do mean it." His hand rose to my face and he repositioned his lips on mine.

My body trembled as goose bumps began breaking onto my inner thighs from the feel of his hand gliding across my cheek. Feeling his damp hand, I knew he was as apprehensive as me when he began kissing each of my fingers in turn. An involuntary chill swept through my body as he effortlessly swooped me into his arms, and gently kissed my lips, my nose, and my eyelids, while carrying me into my bedroom.

Everything seemed in slow motion as Gabriel placed me onto that hideous red bedspread. Feeling a blend of guilt, passion, and intoxication, I absorbed his scent like a human sponge, wanting to seize as much of his aura as possible. Through our clothing, I felt his body pulsating as he slowly moved back and forth across me, his rough and calloused hands gliding ever so gently as he unbuttoned my dress, touching, sampling, and tenderly caressing newly exposed skin. And just when he had ignited a panoply of unknown desires in me, he stopped abruptly, jumped up, and stood beside the bed. I sighed a mixed-emotion sigh, thankful he was strong enough to leave before we did anything wrong.

Gabriel pulled his T-shirt over his head, dropped it on the floor, and looked down at me. "I'm going to savor every inch of your body," he said almost inaudibly. Then he slipped out of his jeans and white briefs, revealing an incredibly muscular physique. This was my third sexual partner, yet the first man whose body I allowed my eyes to slowly gaze up and down, memorizing every inch. Gabriel's V-shaped torso reflected his years of physical work, his arms and legs were sleek and sinewy, his chest almost hairless, and his belly taut. "As soon as I take a shower!" he said.

My body was still shaking when he climbed back onto the bed. His hand trembled so much when he touched my cheek, I joked about him having one of those illnesses that affect voluntary motor functions. I touched his hard edged muscles as he smothered me with kisses and wrapped his arms around me, melting into my body. With Aretha crooning *Natural Woman* in the background, I surprised myself by how greedily I accepted him, pulling him closer inside as quiet echoes of "Cherie" rolled from his lips. A certain sense of destiny spiraled through my mind as I drifted into Aristophanes mythical speech from Plato's *Symposium*. I had found my missing link.

"Your heart's beating like crazy. . . Or is that mine?" He gently stroked my hair. "This feels like an illusion. An out-of-control, wonderful fantasy, spilling over into reality. I want it to be and I don't want it to be," he whispered, his voice trembling, his eyes searching mine.

He couldn't shut up and I couldn't speak. I could barely breathe. This man had perfectly connected all the wires to my home entertainment unit. I had been untouched until now. And what do I do during my first orgasm? I burst into giggles. They began softly, and grew louder until I was giggling uncontrollably. What had he done to my central nervous system? Gabriel's eyes questioned my reaction as I broke into tears, then he wrapped his arms around me. "Ooooh girl, what have you done to me?"

"Whoooa," I said in shaky voice. "What have you done to me? Here I am, the mother of a three-year-old, feeling like I finally lost my virginity. And where did those giggles come from? How embarrassing."

"Yeah, for a split-second I thought you were letting me know I'm hysterically funny in the sack."

"Well, funny ain't exactly the word for it."

"Look out Blondie, you're startin' to talk like me."

We lay silently together for a few minutes, sharing soft kisses. "I need a smoke." He climbed out of bed and walked into the living room. Tactfully leaving the scene, I presumed. But he returned and set his ashtray on the ever-so-gaudy Spanish nightstand before climbing back into bed. Lying together, we expressed views about Nixon, Vietnam, flower power, and even Earth Day. But when he attempted to talk economics, I cringed. "That's a guy thing, like politics. So pleeease keep those discussions between men friends. Do you read mythology, specifically Plato's *Symposium* in which Aristophanes explains the origin of love?"

"Now that legendary 'Split-apart' crap truly is a girl thing—like tampons and douches."

Exhausted and totally satiated as he lightly stroked my arm, I fell into a sound sleep. Hours later he started kissing the back of my neck, which I presumed were departure kisses. Once again I presumed wrong. Round two went even longer, and he caressed my worn-out body as we drifted to sleep for a couple of hours.

Round three. *Really?* No mistaking that nudge. But just as every pore of my body began blending with every pore of his, Gabriel mumbled, "God, this isn't right. . . No, I can't. . . Please God, don't allow this!"

Took the snap out of my garters. I swallowed back tears, realizing this Catholic man was regretting his actions. Then he softly whispered, "Cherie, I love you! It isn't right and I shouldn't, but God help me I do."

I couldn't respond as he pulled me into his arms and began softly snoring. I slept an hour.

Awakened by the softness of his lips on the back of my neck, I realized the night hadn't been some bizarre, incredible dream, and then the tightness of his arms around me confirmed it. A dream? Even my overactive imagination couldn't have conjured a dream of this magnitude. Besides, my thighs and lower body were weak as I rolled over to face him.

"This is right," he said softly.

"I know Gabriel," I assured him. Then tried to shove those sneaky old guilt feelings my mother had so skillfully planted, to the back of my head.

At sunrise Gabriel slid from bed, showered, and kissed me goodbye. I didn't know where he was going, but knew he'd be back.

∽

"Wanna do lunch before taking me for my car?" I asked Kat when she arrived.

Her normal grin went ear to ear as she walked inside my apartment. "I knew it! I knew it!" she trumpeted. "I saw the looks between you two and watched Gabe's attitude change almost overnight. He actually seemed compassionate. Well, I guess with you he was more like passionate."

"Is it that obvious?"

"You've got the look, cutie."

"Well, unless I was having convulsions last night, I finally know what the big O is all about. Plus I learned simultaneous orgasms don't just happen, they're brought on by thoughtful men who hold back until you're ready for glorious uncontrollable body spasms that leave you tingling for hours. So to speak." I shivered.

"I'm just happy you finally had an orgasm!"

"You're happy? Before Gabriel, I never knew what the word meant."

"So. . ." Kat fluttered her eyelashes. "Gabe the asshole was great in bed?"

"Oh pleeeease! Even if I never see him again, he's being listed in my will. Let's get going and I'll tell you all about it on the way."

After a quick lunch filled with every juicy detail, we arrived for Nikki, but she pleaded to spend a few more days with Cousin Jimmy. I usually felt rejected when Nikki chose to stay apart from me, but today I handled it well, kissing her about a zillion times before leaving.

Around six in the evening I heard a knock and knew it was Gabriel before opening the door. Dressed in different clothing than he wore earlier, he hugged me tightly. I inhaled his woodsy scent. "Never open a door unless you know who's knocking." He held some gizmo in his palm. "Hell, ya never know when a deranged carpenter might be lurking about."

"You work on Sundays?"

"Not often. But today I just had to get out of the house."

"Oh." My voice sputtered. The reality of him having a house, a wife, and children, suddenly resurfaced, making me uneasy.

"Where's your mini-mouthpiece?"

"Nikki decided to stay a few more days with her favorite cousin."

"Well, c'mon." Gabriel pulled me into the entry foyer with him, closed my apartment door and busily installed a peep hole. "That'll make things a little safer for you two." He held out one hand and briskly rubbed his thumb across the tips of his four fingers as though trying to get circulation going. Then his face turned solemn. "Cherie, we have to talk. I can't get you out of my mind. I've never felt this way about anyone and I'm not sure how to handle what's going on here. When I went home this morning, Astrid didn't say a word and acted like I was merely leaving for a short vacation when I put a few clothes together." Sadness flooded his eyes. "I just kissed my daughters goodbye, and walked out the door."

My heart hurt for his little girls and a deeper sense of guilt unfolded. Involvement of children made our actions more injurious than reckless adultery. Shame overshadowed the wonderful emotions I previously felt.

"I brought enough clothes to stay a few days and contemplate my future," he said shyly still standing out in the foyer. "If you don't mind having a grouch underfoot for a few days."

Mind? I was ecstatic. Yet at the same time feeling guilt. *Homewrecker!* Gabriel stood staring at me for an answer. "Just don't interrupt me when I'm watching *The Mod Squad.*" I pulled him inside.

The evening began on a somber note, but turned passionate as we repeatedly made love and fell asleep in each other arms. I knew I was in love with him. It was a visceral sense that I did not question. Even knowing how great the odds were of getting my heart broken, fear nor guilt could keep me from embracing this experience. Here was a man who listened with undivided attention when I spoke, even about trivial stuff, yet when he spoke, I often lost thought mid-sentence, due to memorizing everything from his head to his toes.

The following morning, I cooked breakfast while Gabriel showered for work. He thanked me for the meal, helped clear the table, and insisted we do dishes together. As he washed, I dried while swooning and thinking I should pinch myself to make sure this wasn't some great fantasy I'd somehow brought to life.

The Jewel Box had become more tolerable after Beau deemed Kat and me as waitresses only, but returning was difficult. I asked Kat if she could handle work without me a few more days and she eagerly accepted, wanting the extra bucks. When Gabriel knocked on my door shortly before six, I met him with kisses.

"You expecting company?" He glanced at lit candles on my romantically set dining table.

"My distinguished guest just arrived." I kissed him. "I think I'll enjoy some sawdust sorbet before my caviar."

"I'm distinguished?" He pulled me closer.

"Well, you've got a special kind of *je ne sais quoi.*"

"You takin' French lessons, girl?

"No, I just heard it somewhere and like the poetic way it sounds."

"Poetic? You're really into that muse-mush crap, aren't ya?"

"I enjoy some poetry, but mostly I dig anything French. And despite your vile mouth, you make me feel as romantic as an evening in Paris."

"Oh girl, you don't know what you do to me. Ummm," he moaned. "Well, I better not get sappy this early in the evening." He gave me a mini-lip massage before jumping into the shower.

With a towel tied around his chiseled waist, Gabriel walked into the kitchen. "Wanna swing by tomorrow morning and see the carpentry job I'm doing?"

"Twist my arm," I tried being cool when indeed I was drooling inside like he'd just declared undying love for me and unveiled plans to purchase adjoining burial plots for us atop some picturesque mountain in Montana. How could any woman not be in love with this man? He was kind, considerate, fearless, gentle, intelligent, organized, and Lordy, Lordy was he ever an incredible lover. The kind of lover who tosses your soul onto new horizons, across the black void, into the sparkling universe, and causes you to speak languages you never studied. I would've traded my sponge curlers, bell bottom jeans, driver's license, library card, voter registration, and every Beatles album I owned for more time with him.

Days later, I drove to a nearby subdivision where my guy was working. Gabriel escorted me through the enormous house that looked crudely unfinished, and I sauntered around complaining about wanting to see a more exciting version. "This is bland and boring."

"Behave or I'll send you home."

"At least there's air conditioning there."

"You my friend, are spoiled." He gently guided me to another room. "But, I know what you mean about the heat. I was having a sinkin' spell before you walked in."

"Ooooh pleeeease! What a beautiful stairway."

"That's what we in the business call a hand crafted spiral staircase. You like it?"

"My inarticulate tongue is groping for words to express its splendor."

"Groping tongue?" He raised eyebrows Groucho fashion and leaned against me. "You're giving me chills talkin' that way, Blondie."

Since I was picking up Nikki early the next day, I decided to stay and watch him work. Moving around the house, Gabriel explained plans for several rooms while schooling me on circular saws, molding, swag, dowels, cornice rafters, louvers, joists, and studs. My slow walking, crude talking, chain smoking, arrogant acting carpenter was creative at heart. And busy.

"See you at home later." He used my elbow to politely guide me to the door.

"Just one sec." I bent down and picked up a tiny wedge of wood from the front foyer. "I'll use this as a doorstop when I move into my house near the ocean and keep windows open to let breezes fly through."

"You're such a dreamer, Blondie."

"Everyone needs to dream a little. Otherwise, not much happens in life."

I reflected on that little wedge of wood while stretching across the bar to bask in the moonlight beginning to trickle through the shop's showcase window. Memories of that long ago summer in 1970 seemed forever etched in my mind. Even dubious times.

Fetching Nikki from Ellen's always entailed an explosion of tears over parting from Cousin Jimmy. Even though my daughter begrudgingly climbed into my car to go to our new apartment, it didn't take more than five minutes until she was in love with me again, chattering as I drove across town. Her Q&A seemed endless, but that's the great thing about three year olds—they ask easy questions. Like, "Can we go to the park today?" or "Do lions like monkeys?" They almost never ask, "Are you working in a top-less club?" or "Are you having an affair with a married man?" Between her frenzy of questions, I managed to ease the news that on nights I worked she would be staying with a sitter who lived in our complex. Instead of being concerned, she looked at me with her big blue eyes and poised her pouty red lips, eager to interject her two cents as I told her about Delilah. Her petite heart shaped face and champagne blonde tresses were the only features of mine visible at her young age, but boy could she talk.

"Mommy where is Gabriel? I miss him, can we see him today?"

"He's at work, lovey. But I'll bet he stops by tonight."

"I'm sure he's missing me, Mommy."

"Absolutely," I agreed. Nikki assumed everyone missed her something fierce if she was away, even for brief times. If only I had a smidgen of her self-confidence.

"Maybe he could take me for ice cream again."

"Maybe. But remember it's impolite to ask favors."

"Okay, Mommy." She nuzzled against my arm.

Prior to my picking up Nikki, Gabriel suggested we alter our living arrangement to one more proper for her. I was learning a great deal about the person he pretended not to be.

Nikki and I were watching TV anchorman, Dave Ward talk with Ed Brandon about another humid Houston day when we heard Gabriel's light tap on the door. I dashed to open it, but the miniature affection moocher got to him first. "I'm jealous." I joked as he hugged Nikki. He then embraced me, which created an urge to say, "Na na na na na nah," but being the adult, I refrained. My insecurity shatters the theory that breast fed babies grow up confident.

Gabriel followed me into the kitchen. "Gimme your hand." He placed a penny in my palm.

"Are we going to a penny arcade later?"

"Al said you were going to get my last cent, so I thought I'd give it to you now." He winked before strolling into the living room.

"Such wisdom from a man who's still waiting for *Encyclopedia Britannica* to come out in paperback. When he grows up he might learn all women don't behave like his dream girls," I said with sexy sarcasm, not about to let my irritation at Al infringe on our home life. I wrapped the penny in foil, took it to the bedroom, and put it in my lingerie drawer by the wedge of wood.

During dinner our usual conversation changed to include that of a three-year-old as Gabriel talked about Sesame Street, telling Nikki people thought he was "Oscar the Grouch." She childishly disagreed and laughed at other silly stories he invented, before regaling him with stories of her daily adventures. After dinner Gabriel and I began our nightly dishwashing routine with assistance from Nikki, but when he kissed the back of my neck, she frowned.

"Maybe I should get a hotel room for the night," Gabriel whispered.

"Whatever you think is best." I was disappointed about being without him, but didn't need additional guilt regarding doing the right thing.

Gabriel unfolded the paper as Nikki crawled onto his lap. He attempted to read while she warbled in his ear. Unable to read, he switched to the evening news. When *Flip Wilson* came on the two laughed ridiculously. Okay. I was a little jealous about her invading my place on his lap.

"Time for your bath and then I'll tuck you into bed," I motioned to Nikki.

"Mommy, can Gabriel read my bedtime story tonight? Please?"

Seriously? "Uh. Okay, lovey."

He read two of her favorite books, and then she begged him to tell a story. So much for mommy-daughter loyalty.

"Okay, kid," Gabriel started. "There was a mama bear, a papa bear and a baby bear by a previous marriage."

I walked to the doorway. "It's time for the Grimms' renegade brother to get going."

We kissed goodbye and he squeezed me. "Hey, wouldya unlock your patio door and get her to sleep?" he whispered in my ear. "I can't sleep without you."

"Wood eye!" I bounced up on tiptoes.

"Let's just be discreet about it, Harelip."

Ever so quietly, Gabriel slipped in through the patio door, showered, and crawled in bed beside me. We spoke softly for a few minutes before attempting hushed lovemaking. Thank God Nikki was a sound sleeper. The following morning Gabriel awakened early, kissed me goodbye, and left via the patio door. Our morning routine of his reading and relaying the news to me while I cooked breakfast had become special to me. But I had to buck up and understand this was the respectable way to handle our disrespectable relationship.

"Mommy, someone's knocking on our door." Nikki sleepily walked through the hall, rubbing her eyes. I looked through my viewer, and there stood Gabriel with the *Houston Post* morning edition in hand. The three of us sat down and enjoyed a leisurely breakfast while Nikki and I dominated the conversation. Both helped with dishes. When Gabriel kissed us goodbye before leaving, Nikki snagged an extra kiss, then shot me a "Na na na na na nah," look.

"Bye, love." I shoved him out. "I've got to scratch several gifts off someone's birthday list."

Nikki gave me the evil eye. Gabriel honked his horn twice, so I walked outside. "That's my 'I love you' signal," he shouted as he drove away, blowing kisses until he was out of sight.

Nikki and I had a fun filled day, playing games and discussing everything from scientific developments in space to spray cheese. She was too young for discussing or understanding Gabriel's affinity for prolonged foreplay or his exceptional talent in the oral gratification arena, so we stuck with less mystifying subjects. When Gabriel came home, once again Nikki beat me in the hug race, and settled on his lap to tell him about her day while I cooked. "I'll be taking Nikki to the sitter tomorrow, before I return to work."

"So soon?" Gabriel asked.

"Yes. This has been fun, but I can't live on love alone. And without income Nikki might wind up running around half naked and hungry."

He scowled and went mute. No doubt the "running around half naked" fragment of my sentence irritated him. Wordlessly, we stuck to our usual routine, and as we did dishes in companionable silence, he crowded close. "Let me pay rent and buy groceries for a while. You can take a few weeks off can't you?"

"I can pay rent and buy groceries if I work," I said defiantly. Then remembering Al's comment, my tongue went caustic. "Besides, I wouldn't want to take your last cent."

"Fine, Cherie! Be stubborn," he said, in a sarcastic tone that couldn't compete with mine.

"You don't know stubborn, my friend!" I threw my dishtowel on the counter, spun around so fast it looked like a half pirouette, and walked into the bathroom to draw Nikki's bath. She was notoriously oblivious to unpleasant changes in my mood, and could persist in discussing recent dialogue between Kermit and Big Bird long after one's interest in the subject had vaporized and turned to thoughts of frying frog legs and yanking yellow feathers. Other than our initial clash at the Jewel Box, this was my first brusque exchange with Gabriel, and tonight it had a polarizing effect. Instead of feeling furious, I had overreacted, then felt vulnerable and upset, yet determined to take care of myself. Even if my job entailed running around half naked.

Gabriel and I remained polite but quiet for the remainder of the evening while Nikki cheerfully fed her dead goldfish. I didn't have the heart to tell her it had blown its last bubble. Gabriel tucked her into bed and I read her favorite bedtime stories until she fell asleep. When I walked in the living room, we apologized in unison and held hands as we watched *The Dick Cavett Show*. "I just want you to know you don't have to do anything you don't want to do."

"Well, if it makes you feel any better, I've cut my hours and won't be working twelve hour shifts any more. Gives me more time with Nikki and time to change professions."

"You call this a profession?"

"Unfortunately it is for many women. For now, it's what I'm doing. Strangely enough, I'm becoming independent in a male dominated society by catering to men, and I'm learning things at this club that Psychology 101 doesn't teach. Please try to understand."

"I'll try." He snuggled against me.

The following morning after our routine of wake-up kisses, patio exit, front door arrival, hello kisses, news time, breakfast, dishes, and goodbye kisses, Gabriel left for work and I pried Nikki from Sesame Street to go across the courtyard and spend a few minutes with new sitter, Delilah. Other than remembering the day Delilah banged her Camaro into my Mustang's bumper, Nikki knew nothing of this girl to whom I was about to entrust her care. Fortunately my daughter easily adapted to new situations.

"Hey kid, have a chocolate donut," Delilah offered, cigarette dangling from one hand. She obviously used perfume to combat tobacco smells. Loads of perfume. "And some Pepsi."

"No thank you," Nikki declined both, likely because of our big breakfast.

I wasn't keen on Nikki eating junk food, but the environment seemed safe. Not sophisticated, just safe. "Lemme get my baton for you." Delilah bolted into her bedroom.

I prayed she wouldn't repeat a tale she told me about being a former baton twirling tease, known for sending horny boys home with blue balls. "Maybe you can show her later," I said. "I'll bring her back around five."

"Okay. But look quick, Nikki." Delilah balanced her baton on her nose while belching.

Delilah was rough around the edges, but Nikki seemed fascinated by her. Juvenile behavior in adults is quite the kid magnet.

"You nervous about going back to work?" Gabriel asked on his third call of the day.

"I'm totally fine," I assured him, feeling jittery as all get out.

"Hey, I'm knocking off early today. Why don't I drive you to work?"

"Oh sweetie, that would be great. But I need to leave by five-thirty."

"Yeaaah. You think I don't know that, Blondie? I pay more attention to things you say than you realize. See ya in a bit."

He had obviously detected my anxiety and I was glad. Walking in the club would be easier with him by my side, but I didn't want him staying until three a.m., and then getting up for work three hours later. As we headed to the Jewel Box, I became a bundle of nerves, chatting nonstop and moving as close to him as possible. When we arrived, I sat glued to the seat, not wanting to leave his side. "Thanks for coming with me."

"I'd do just about anything for a piece of ass."

"Then get medication to curb your filthy comments."

"Be nice if you want me to come inside with you."

"Mmmm." I licked his ear. "You'll come inside for a minute or so?"

"Twist my arm," he said before jumping out to open my door.

∽

Five days away from the club brought just as many new dancers. No surprise. Topless dancers were a transient bunch. Gabriel headed to the men's room as Laura rushed over to give me a big hug. Beau squeezed me and whispered in my ear, "Didn't I tell you some men who come in these places are nice?"

I grinned at my spiritual guide through sin city. "Yeah, but I thought you were lying."

"I never lie." Beau winked. "And I think Gabe's a good man."

"Your support means a lot," I said as he went back behind the bar. "Of course now I can't shake that damn Lord Byron quote you shared with me weeks ago."

"Baby!" Beau grabbed my hand. "If you're referring to Byron's *What men call gallantry, and gods adultery, is much more common when the climate is sultry. . .* please believe me that your relationship with Gabe is considerably different. He never entertained women in this 'sultry' joint before; you two got to know each other over many months, and the profound love you feel is as evident as the remorse I see on both your faces. Sometimes these things simply happen. It was obvious Gabe wasn't happily married, and I don't believe you ever intended to fall in love—so just enjoy your time together."

Beau was a good judge of character and his approval was paramount, but in my heart I realized that even without his endorsement, I was hanging onto this carpenter. While Beau busily tended bar and Gabriel stood alongside, in walked Reverend Al. I made an irritated face, despite appreciating the company he offered my guy. I breathed easier with Gabriel in the club, so I grabbed Al's hand and dropped a penny into it. "Apology accepted for your asinine last cent comment." Al turned beet red, and then grinned like a jackass.

Soon the three of us were sitting around just like old times, and before you could say "Got any quarters for the jukebox?" a redhead carrying a big confederate flag and wearing an iridescent red, white, and blue ensemble complete with elbow length, star-studded arm cones, came by our table to introduce herself. Perched on a pair of red skyscraper sandals, "Dixie" stood beside Al, looking as if she was in a galaxy, far, far away. Al ogled "Tiger," the dancer on stage who had a full back tattoo of a Bengal, and didn't invite Miss Patriotic to join us. Gabriel glanced at the huge flag draped over her shoulder, and lightly jabbed Al. "You'd have to throw that flag over her face and fuck for Old Glory." Got him a sharp jab in the ribs from me.

Moments later when Gabriel and I were discussing France's success with the first nuclear powered pacemaker, Dixie interjected in a high pitched voice, "That's a fact and not a fiction." Without acknowledging her presence, Gabriel leaned closer to me and lit a Marlboro. Al danced in his chair to *Who's Making Love To Your Old Lady?* while clapping for Tiger, like he was Jim Fowler and we were on *Wild Kingdom*. Gabriel mentioned chief justice Earl Warren's retirement about the time Dixie swung by our table, and once again she trilled, "That's a fact and not a fiction," before dashing away, flag flying wildly.

"Her dumb look must be a ploy for money," I whispered to Gabriel. "She seems fairly hip on current events."

"You're wrong, Blondie. She was up at the bar when I was talking to Beau, then she sat at the table to our left for awhile. Consequently I've had to listen to her falderol, and she says 'That's a fact and not a fiction' in response to everything."

"*Falderol?*"

"Gibberish, prattle, mere nonsense." He snubbed his cigarette. "Trust me, she doesn't have enough sense to drink through a curly straw."

"Maybe she's just faking dumbness."

"Yeaaah? I'll bet she can sing the entire Flintstone's theme, but can't sing one line of the National Anthem."

"Oh pleeease."

"You're so gullible, Blondie. But that's one of the things I like about you. 'Course, I still haven't figured out why you like me so much."

"You've got just the right amount of velocity for me," I joked.

"That's a fact and not a fiction," Dixie interrupted, stopping once again.

Okay. Maybe Gabriel was on target about her. I decided to check if she was as brainless as he thought. "I like your costume. Does it have any special meaning?"

"Well, I'm proud to be an American. I was born and raised just a few miles from here. I love Houston."

"It's a rapidly growing city. Do you think Welch is doing a good job?"

"Who?"

"Louie Welch," I added his first name for clarification.

"Don't have a clue." Dixie looked up at the ceiling like a magic 8 ball might appear.

"Mayor Louie Welch," I said incredulously. "He's serving his fifth term."

"Well, you learn something new every day!" She sailed away.

"You're right." I leaned against Gabriel. "The girl is breathtakingly dumb."

When Gabriel and Al left around ten that night, I got queasy. The Jewel Box wasn't as revolting as before Gabriel entered my life, but I counted the minutes until he picked me up at two-thirty.

"How'd it go, Blondie?"

"Oh, it was tolerable. But I really missed you." I smothered his face with kisses.

"Yeaaah? You missed me?"

"Yes! Yes!" I serenaded. He could have asked for my first born son and received the same response. "But I don't want you wasting time hanging around here. Besides, your absence will make me work harder to get the hell out of this so-called profession. Tonight was almost as tough as my first night."

"I hate your being there. Remember you don't have to do this."

"Remember, I *do* have to do this. You don't need another dependent and independence feels good to me," I said firmly. "It won't be for much longer, so please don't make it more difficult than it already is."

"Whatever you say, Ms. Steinem."

Astrid filed a divorce petition, establishing Gabriel's visitation privileges with his girls as Sundays only—in their house. Gabriel occasionally watched Nikki in the evenings, but mostly spent time with me at the Jewel Box, where I dropped Saturdays, my best money making night.

Gabriel filled my days and nights with wonderful memories, and for the first time ever, I didn't indulge in dreams. Incredibly diverse and well read, he unknowingly educated me, and I recalled almost every word he spoke. I could have been blindfolded and identified him in a crowded room just by feeling his hands: those wonderful hands that carefully crafted wood, casually combed hair from his forehead, thoughtfully rubbed the side of his face near his mouth when he was in deep thought, and gently caressed every inch of my body. Our lovemaking was an extension of caring and conversations that ran the gamut as we got to know each other, and I lay in bed at night listening to the softness of his snoring, memorizing the outline of his face and wondering why this gentle, kind man found it necessary to masquerade as a crude, arrogant jerk. We went to movies, had romantic dinners and lived like a normal family. If you call a family that includes one member who is married to someone else, one child who is bonding rapidly with said member, and one member who works in a topless bar "normal." Other than my job, my life was filled with happiness. Our quiet, relaxing weekends were altered only by Gabriel's visitation time with his daughters.

Soon, I changed my work schedule to four nights a week for more family home evenings with Nikki and Gabriel.

After Red quit the Jewel Box to work at the larger downtown *Red Baron* club, I rarely saw her around the complex, but Gabriel ran into her constantly which irritated him no end. One day he came through the door whistling happily. "You'd think as much money as Al spent on that wench, she could afford something other than tube tops and shorts to wear every day."

"No foul words for Red? You're in a great mood," I said.

"Yeah, goddamnit, I had a splitting headache this morning and took some of your Midol by mistake. Hell, everyone at work ribbed me about being so damned pleasant!"

"I don't have Midol in my medicine cabinet. You must've grabbed my hit of acid."

"Blondie, I'm just kidding." He kissed me. "My good moods are all your fault and it's pissin' me off. Hell, I've been a grouch all my life."

"Oh sweetie, you're a grouch about like I'm Simone de Beauvoir."

"Who?"

"Pleeease, Gabriel. Your little subliterate act ain't flying. You pretend to know nothing of Franz Kafka or George Eliot, but when I say I know nothing about politics or finance, that's a fact and not a fiction."

"You sayin' you can't define MLR, GDP or demagogue?"

"Precisely. And I don't appreciate that language in the presence of my daughter."

"Fiduciary!" he goaded with a grin.

"Now I need something for my splitting headache."

"You don't really have acid in your medicine cabinet. Do you?"

"Yeah, but it's not for me, it's to enhance Nikki's childhood memories. I sprinkle it in her Cocoa Puffs since I'm not able to take her on exciting trips at this time."

Thus began an evening of stories about his childhood with four siblings, an attractive and persuasive mother, and an erudite, college professor father whose vicious temper led to countless job losses and constant upheaval. After all family members suffered physical and mental torment inflicted by their father; his mother divorced him and moved to Boston near her parents. Gabriel began working during his early teens while attending high school, and being oldest, took an active role as caretaker.

He pulled me closely to him in bed and solemnly told me about his estranged wife's personality. "Everything in the house has a proper place and under no circumstances are the girls allowed to play anywhere other than their playroom."

My house was clean and orderly, but Nikki ruled our domain, eating and playing anywhere her heart desired.

"Astrid's been taking uppers every morning and downers every evening for years, never noticing my comings or goings."

"That's so sad." I thought about his girls. The time to stop swallowing Phenaphen had commenced. My pain was long gone, so I vowed to dispense with the darling green and black capsules that once helped me make it through the night. But what Gabriel said next, almost made me regret my anti-drug resolution.

"Now she's threatened to file additional divorce papers naming you. I can't have that, so I'm going to lease an apartment and tell Astrid we split up. No need to involve you in this legal mess."

I didn't jump for joy over what seemed a reasonable solution.

Gabriel constantly reminded me his leased yet basically vacant apartment was less than a mile and only one minute away. He kept clothing and toiletries at my place where he stayed nightly and weekends (discreetly, for Nikki's sake).

"Blondie, this is getting more and more difficult," he said one Sunday night after returning from visiting his daughters. "Lauren, my oldest, keeps asking me when I'm coming back home, and Skylar clings to me and cries until I leave." His body shook as he hugged me. "I feel like the world's biggest jerk." Guilt was inescapable, and beginning that instant an ominous dark cloud hung overhead.

Within weeks, Gabriel began living within himself, periodically withdrawing for two or three days at a time. My attempts to intrude into his world only made him more distant and for longer durations.

9

At the end of May, Gabriel's younger brother flew from Massachusetts for summer work with Gabriel and Al's flourishing construction business. Almost a carbon copy of Gabriel in size and build, Sean O'Quinn had the same chiseled facial features, but with wheat-infused, light brown hair and translucent amber eyes, he reminded me of the late James Dean. He had a special aura that seemed to brighten anyone in his presence. Sean slept at Gabriel's apartment, but spent spare time at my place. He entertained Nikki by playing games, giving her piggy back rides until his knees were almost raw, and reading every book she hauled into the living room.

Gabriel worked solo on Saturdays (his Zen time), so Sean always arrived at my place with a bundle of 45rpm records, and played hits like *Imagine* by John Lennon, *Mercy, Mercy Me* by Marvin Gaye, and other songs by artists who made social commentary sound pretty damn sexy. In the following weeks Sean and I shared countless private moments, engaging in philosophical discussions deeper than Gabriel cared to venture, with Sean seemingly oblivious to everything around us while absorbing only the rapport we were developing. "I'm more liberal than Gabe," Sean broached the subject of politics.

"Isn't everyone?" His brother was as Republican as Eisenhower's infamous field jacket.

Sean let go a soft laugh. He possessed the same gentle qualities that made me fall in love with Gabriel, but didn't spout crude comments. Sean idolized JFK and Martin Luther King, and was always contemplating and discussing ideas to help resolve our country's civil unrest. Their brother Ben (older than Sean but younger than Gabriel) was in Vietnam, and unlike Gabriel, Sean often voiced his concern for everyone fighting that war. While other teenagers were into pop festivals, the drug culture, free love, and musical artists like Black Sabbath and Jimi Hendrix, Sean's main concern was ending the war, and healing within our own country.

"I worry about my young brother Conner. He misbehaves, and I'm not sure Hope can control him. My young sister is lovely and delicate. The opposite of our mom, Gloria."

"Really?"

"Gloria's lousy with finances, but so charismatic she manages to get most anything she wants."

"How 'bout your dad?"

"Hardly knew him." Sean picked up *The Last Picture Show.* "You like McMurtry?"

"I do. Beau loaned me that copy, but you can read it. Check out my Book-Of-The-Month selection." I handed him Maya Angelou's *I Know Why the Caged Bird Sings.* "It's amazing."

Nikki watched cartoons as Sean scanned the pages, and I listened to soft background music. "I thought the South was predominately racist," he said.

"Supposedly. But my mother sure wasn't. She taught us we're all God's children, told us to embrace similarities, appreciate cultural differences, and respect all races."

"Your mom sounds pretty rare."

"Oh yeah, a real archeologist's find. Granted, Mother was caring and kind, but we never connected like she did with my sister. I've recently gained new respect for her, but I'm cautious since her righteous viewpoint holds little regard for those who fall from grace."

"Well, she nurtured you into a special being." he said with sincerity.

"Unfortunately I've done things that would crush her if she ever found out."

"I understand." He lightly touched my hand. "I really do."

"Thank you, Sean. I just love the way we can talk about everything."

"Well, my brothers would break my balls if they knew half the stuff I discussed with you."

I tapped my ear and pointed to Nikki, reminding him she was listening.

86

"Ooops, sorry," Sean apologized. "But speaking of my brothers, Gabe sure is head over heels in love with you."

"He admitted that to another male?"

"No way. I can just tell. When we're at work, his face lights up when he talks about you. And I think he's envious of our time together."

"Only because he can't be here every minute. Gabriel tries to disguise his emotions, but I'm wise to his facade. When we watch *The Dick Cavett Show* he listens to guests like Gore Vidal and Bill Buckley, but should a guest get too philosophical or be too artistically inclined, he pretends he's reading. Five minutes later he says stuff like, 'People who believe in symbolist poetry shouldn't be allowed to vote,' then hugs me and says, 'You don't wanna vote do you, Blondie?'"

"My older brothers have a tendency to protect their vulnerabilities with a tough exterior. Especially Gabe, who took the brunt of our father's abuse."

"That explains some things. I don't know if Gabriel told you how we met, but it was in a place he went only because he was caretaking Al."

"He still does. Every day on the job. It's like he needs to protect anyone incapable of doing it themselves."

"The night we became true friends, Gabriel offered to protect me from a threatening maniac I once dated. We came together under most unusual circumstances."

"Synchronicity." Sean's amber eyes seemed to gaze into my soul.

"Don't let your brothers hear you talk that way. Gabriel calls my talk about meaningful coincidence or influence of the heavens, mumbo-jumbo. But I think astrology is significant in our lives."

"So does Gloria." He reached over and playfully pulled Nikki's hair braids.

"Why do you guys call her Gloria instead of Mom or Mother?"

"I'm not sure who started it, but we all do. Except Hope. Gabriel and Ben claim Gloria doesn't want to be called 'Mom' by her older sons because then she can't lie about her age. Whatever the reason, she prefers we call her Gloria."

"Can we go to the playground?" Nikki asked.

"Jump on my shoulders," Sean obliged.

"Have fun!" I waved to the duo, envisioning a thirty minute nap for *moi*.

ᗏ

On July 1st, New York state made abortion a matter between a woman and her doctor, which generated mixed feelings nationwide, and conversation over dinner at my place. Nikki excused herself, likely to sneak into my perfume. More of Delilah's influence showing up on our turf. Sean and I began discussing birth control pills and beliefs of the Catholic Church when Gabriel interjected, "Hell, I think the pill is great. Its primary side effect is promiscuity, and I'm all for that." He raised his eyebrows Groucho style.

"There's nothing worse than a fallen Catholic, except perhaps a fallen Lutheran." I flashed Sean a smile.

Gabriel crisscrossed his knife and fork on his plate, and said with a precise pinch of gravitas, "I'm not a fallen Catholic. I have strong morals and I'm still religious." He leaned back in his chair. "Just not to the point of human sacrifice—like some people."

"You having a serious conversation in the presence of another male is about as likely as my mother talking sex with me." I tossed a dinner roll on his plate. "Here, amuse yourself."

"So, what's the deal with you and your parents?" Sean rested his arm on the table.

"Now there's some serious conversation." Gabriel grinned.

I challenged his grin with a wicked arched eyebrow, and then turned to younger brother. "My 'atypical job' and the stigma attached to living with Gabriel caused me to distance myself from my parents. Ya know, *Don't tell my mother I'm living in sin,*" I began.

"*Don't let the old folks know,*" Sean chimed in.

"*Don't tell my twin I had breakfast on gin,*" we finished in unison. "*He'd never survive the blow!*"

"A.P. Herbert," Sean informed.

"Ah, that's the author." I was impressed by Sean's literary knowledge, but mostly by him revealing his sensitive side to his brother. "Anyway, I'm living a necessary lie, if such a thing exists. But Gabriel's compassion somewhat helps alleviate my guilt."

Seeming embarrassed about me calling him compassionate in his brother's presence, Gabriel shifted. "Let me know when you two conclude your poetry spouting session, and I'll offer praise with a heartfelt burp."

"Very funny," I scoffed. "Better bring that humor to bed tonight so you can entertain yourself in lieu of romance."

"At least I add spice to y'all's conversations." Gabriel sauntered into the living room.

"Puuleeese, Jacy Nicole!" I fanned my face as Nikki returned smelling like a mix of my Guerlain perfumes. She sat on Gabriel's lap to watch TV. Sean and I jumped into a discussion about women's rights, followed by the civil rights movement and senseless deaths at Kent State. Sharing his concern about America's declining morality, Sean talked about how virtues were instilled way back around 8000 BC when hunters/gatherers first organized grain growing communities to embed family and civic values.

"Family values and civic virtues, my ass!" Gabriel interrupted from the living room. "I'll guaran-damn-tee you, the only reason they grew grain was to brew barrels of beer."

"Watch your mouth, please," I said.

"Sorry. Better let Sean entertain Nikki now." Gabriel walked over and hugged me, his body scented with French perfume. "We can do dishes and discuss biology and anatomy."

Gabriel had yet to spend the night with his summer guest, but I let him know how impressed I was by his younger brother.

"He used the term 'balls' today, but compared to you he's ready for sainthood."

"Boy, he fooled you." Gabriel dried a glass. "Foul words will soon be runnin' nonstop from his mouth, cause he's as vulgar minded as me. Hell, he's only working to pay for hookers when he gets back to Boston."

Detecting a twinge of jealousy, I goaded. "That boy would never have to pay. He oozes charisma."

"Hey, what about me?"

"Vulgarity is not charismatic, my friend."

⁘

As Nikki spread way too much butter on her pancakes, she pouted her lips, looked across the table, and woefully whined, "Mommy, why does Sean have to go faraway on a plane? I'm gonna miss him."

89

"*Going to* miss him," I corrected. "And so am I, but he's been here for months and needs to get back to school."

"Can't he go to school here?"

"I guess he could, but don't you think his family misses him, and wants him home?"

"But I want him to stay, Mommy."

"Well he can't." I kissed her tiny nose and forehead, sharing her sentiment. "So stop pouting and put your energy into drawing a picture for him to take home."

"Okay Mommy." She took a sip of milk from her glass. "And I'm gonna . . . I mean 'going to' draw lots of pictures for him to hang on walls at his house."

"Let's limit your art work to one picture for his suitcase. Okay?" I retied her hair ribbon.

"Only one? He'll miss me so much I've got to draw a zillion pictures to send him."

"Please don't plunge into one of those Crayola frenzies like you did when you were young."

"Mommy, I'm still young!" She swung her bouncy ponytail. "And you're silly."

"So are you. Now, let's freshen up before Gabriel and Sean get here. No one likes grubby bye bye kisses."

"Pancake syrup kisses are not grubby," she said while washing her face.

⟳

There are certain people who cross your path and from the instant you meet, you know that even if you never see them again, a distinguishable mark will remain forever. Sean was a peaceful soul whose heart was filled with so much unconditional love, positive belief and good intent, he was contagious. The summer of '70 had passed much too quickly. Sean, Nikki, and I shed lots of tears while Gabriel rolled his eyes. "Stop the damn lachrymose goodbyes."

We cried harder. "You are the most melodramatic threesome in Houston. Now get your ass in the truck, Sean, 'cause I'm not waiting around the airport with you if we miss this flight." Gabriel tossed Sean's luggage into the truck. I swear his eyes were misty.

Nikki missed Sean's piggy back rides and story book readings, and I missed his cheerful attitude and our long talks. She drew pictures and I wrote letters. We also kept in touch via Ma Bell, and during one of our frequent calls, Sean put their mom Gloria on the phone insisting she and I get to know each other. Gloria was pleasant. I was stuttering nervous. What do you say to a mother when you're sleeping with her married son?

By October our calls subsided. Sean was busy with school and I had returned to my hectic schedule trying to stash away money so I could eventually quit. My inner conflict about working at the Jewel Box grew daily and it was obvious Gabriel detested my being there. He rarely stopped by, and when he did the conversation always turned to me "getting the hell out of that den of iniquity." His divorce had catapulted to a grueling, bitter stage, and he was paying an exorbitant amount of child support and maintenance. Instead of quality time between him and his girls, visitation degenerated into arguments when Astrid threatened to move near her parents in Phoenix. The constant turmoil and thoughts of having his daughters taken so far away to live near maternal grandparents who despised him, sickened Gabriel. My heavier work load and his crazy divorce proceedings led to less time together.

In a matter of weeks my world went upside down. Delilah had apparently sent her accountant/musician husband off to work with soup-in-a-baggie for lunch one time too many (she said he left her bowls at work), because they were divorcing. And her desire to work a nine-to-five job with the possibility of meeting men far outweighed her desire to babysit. Then Mother called. "Kent's living in Houston again and wants to see Nikki."

"Pleeease! The guy who thought parenting ended at conception and never paid a lick of child support, suddenly wants to see his daughter?" Things were chaotic enough in my life without a visit from Father Fantastic. "Tell him you can't reach me."

Tension took a toll on me and after a week of jittery nerves, teary outbursts, and gaining ten pounds almost overnight, during a regular doctor visit came the discovery that Miss Tilted Uterus was pregnant. No nausea or vomiting, and in less than six weeks I gained more weight than during my first four months with Nikki. Either the doctor who theorized my pregnancy chances as one in a million was a total quack, or Gabriel and I had hit that magic number. Thrilled about having his child, but aware of his mammoth support and maintenance payments, I delayed the news.

෧౨

"Hello," Nikki said to the young girl who walked into our complex laundromat.

"Hi there, precious," the girl answered in mellifluous voice.

"You're pretty." Nikki looked up at her. "What's your name?"

"Rachel." She smiled. With rings on several fingers, a flower in the braid of her long, chocolate colored hair, and a gauzy, flowing dress that fell only inches above her leather anklet, Rachel looked like she might have celebrated her eighteenth birthday at Woodstock.

"Do you live here?" Nikki prodded.

"We just moved in. I'm a newlywed."

Nikki kept asking questions, while I glanced at Rachel's "I do ironing" note she tacked on the bulletin board inches from my sitter request. She needed extra money. "Do you ever babysit?"

"No, but I adore tending my nieces and nephews."

"Do you think there's any way you could watch Nikki until I find a permanent sitter? Nurseries close at six p.m. and I work nights."

"I'd love to!" Rachel's face lit up. "We're waiting awhile before having our own."

Within days, Nikki was in love with her new sitter. Having a maternal warmth Delilah lacked, Rachel took Nikki to the playground and read to her every day (a big contrast to Nikki's former entertainment, which consisted of Delilah attempting to fart Sam and Dave's hit song *Soul Man*). And Rachel made sure Nikki ate home cooked meals. Delilah's cooking consisted of Chef Boyardee and other dishes requiring only a can opener. Nikki didn't seem to miss chocolate donuts and Pepsi for breakfast. Rachel also worked on ironing out a few negative traits Nikki picked up from Delilah—like sneaking perfume without permission.

I was cooking smothered pork chops when Sean called, and didn't realize we'd talked for thirty minutes about his return to Texas until dinner became a bit beyond well done. When Gabriel got home to blackened pork chops,

I handed him the phone. Sean dropped hints about returning and working full-time after graduation, but Gabriel skirted the issue. After five minutes of Nikki and me quietly circling him and begging him to bring Sean back to Texas, Gabriel whispered to me, "I don't want Sean in the middle of this messy divorce, so he'll have to wait until things settle down."

"Whispering is impolite," Nikki promptly informed.

The probability of things settling down seemed slim. One week after discovering I was pregnant, Gabriel learned Astrid had filed a continuance to delay their divorce. It might be ages before things got finalized. Every night I dreamed of having a blond haired, blue eyed baby boy, but couldn't find the right time to break the news to Gabriel.

Mother called again. "Kent's angling to establish visitation rights and child support payments so he can see Nikki."

I didn't know how to respond. The man had picked one helluva time for getting paternal instincts. Thankfully Gabriel walked in, giving me reason to end the call. "Gotta go, Mother. Please stall Kent a while longer."

My lover barely kissed me before pitching a stack of bills on the table. "Astrid's expenditures for the month." He grabbed a beer from the fridge.

"Wow." I sifted through receipts. Along with countless cosmetics, she had charged expensive shoes, purses, bras, girdles, panties and slips, by the gross. "Hell, if I were in her Ferragamo shoes, I'd probably do the same thing if my husband lost his mind over some fast talking, tiptoe walking, South Texas, topless club waitress/dancer."

Instead of responding, Gabriel put a lip lock on the longneck. He was pissed.

"Maybe all the lingerie means she's dating and your divorce will actually get finalized." I kissed his neck.

"I hope so." His mood brightened. "I'll even throw in a bonus check if he'll take her off my hands in thirty days or less." A smile lit his eyes.

Maybe it had been too long since we'd shared a lighthearted moment, but for some ungodly reason, this was the split second I chose to interrupt the love of my life mid-sentence. "I'm pregnant."

His smile swiftly departed as his expression turned thunderstruck. "You sure?"

"Positive. I've seen a doctor and I'm seven weeks."

"Christ," he sharply interjected, a grimace falling across his face. He shook his head as though it might make me recant my statement. Almost inaudibly he asked, "What do *you* want to do about this?"

"What do *I* want to do about this?" I snapped. "Why don't *I* get back to you after *I* make a decision?" I rushed into the bedroom and slammed the door.

He followed me and leaned against the door jamb, looking straight into my eyes. "I'm so sorry. I'm in a precarious situation already, and don't want you named in this rancorous divorce."

"I realize we're in a big mess." Tears rolled down my face, soaking my hair. "I'm sorry things happened this way. I'm sorry you met me and turned your life upside down."

"Oh Cherie, I wish I'd met you years ago." He walked over and gently brushed tears from my face with the back of his hand. "I wish I weren't paying thousands in support, and I wish Astrid wasn't threatening to take my daughters to Phoenix."

"Well, on top of everything else Kent has moved back to Houston and wants to see Nikki. What if he tries to take her from me?"

"He can't do that. You're a good mother."

"Good mother? I'm working in a topless club, for Heaven sakes! And not only am I pregnant out of wedlock, I'm living with a man engulfed in hostile divorce proceedings."

"Let's go to sleep and maybe tomorrow we'll think more clearly." He rubbed my tummy.

I don't know when we fell asleep, but for the first time since May ninth, we did not make love. Funny how pregnancy, finances, and the threat of having your children taken away, dwindles sexual desires.

The following morning, I woke up to throw up. Other than my butt bulging out of my sexy bikini undies in unsexy fashion, it was my first sign of pregnancy. That night, Gabriel came home and displayed a side of himself I'd never seen. Totally inebriated, he waltzed into the apartment loudly singing lyrics to *My Cherie Amour* before walking over and snupping out my scented candle with his hand, spattering wax everywhere. "Why do you make this place smell so sickeningly sweet?" he asked as prelude to an argument. I responded by noisily raking his dinner into the trash. My moodiness and his drunkenness created tension, but we didn't argue. Keeping fragile temperaments and comments to ourselves, we went to bed and once again fell asleep without making love.

❧

I was the one who made the decision and located the abortion doctor. When I told Gabriel about my appointment, his only question was "How much money do you need?" His only question! Then when the day rolled around, he benignly asked if he could take me. "It's not like escorting me to mass, Choir Boy," I snapped. His face went wounded child, but he transferred five hundred problem solving dollars from his hand to mine.

Too humiliated to tell my best friends, I kept the ugly secret from Kat, Beau, and even Rachel, who agreed to watch Nikki overnight and the following day. For some reason, I burdened Delilah with my guilt. Ever so accommodating, she took the day off work to oversee my dirty deed, and dropped me near the Gulf Building in downtown Houston. Chain smoking Winstons, Delilah got a tad preachy. "I'm worried about you having this illegal procedure without someone familiar nearby. Let me tag along."

"No thanks." I gave her a smile.

"I like Gabriel, but he's a damn jerk for not being here. A school chum went through the Big A, and then went bonkers. Still don't know where she wound up. So if you wanna back out, I'll help however I can. Either way, I'm always here if you need to talk." My eyes filled with tears as I bounced out of her Camaro before she could shift into PARK. I vanished before she saw which direction I flew.

I was fuzzy headed when Delilah picked me up on the corner four hours later, and pushed away her customary offer of Pepsi before tearfully wailing about aborting Gabriel's child. She listened and attempted to console, burping between comments.

When I got home, I felt irritated with Gabriel for what I considered obsequious behavior—him acting like the innocent partner in an unspeakable crime.

Days after my abortion, the vacuuming sound heard through my grogginess that afternoon became a relentless noise in my head. I suffered such self-reproach I constantly invented scenarios in my mind, taking me back to that room and somehow allowing me to save the tiny shred of life they sucked from me. And although I loved him dearly, I could barely stifle my bitterness toward Gabriel for never once attempting to stop me from that horrid procedure.

Gabriel's divorce was taking an emotional toll on him, and I couldn't count the number of times I found him looking in his wallet at photos of his girls.

Beau intuitively sensed problems between Gabriel and me. "There's a Shakespeare quote about lust bringing glorious pleasure that's often followed by agonizing torment," Beau attempted to soothe me one night as we were closing shop.

"It seems Gabriel and I are teetering into the bard's agonizing torment segment."

"I know. That's why I've hired a part time waitress. You and Gabe can use time together. Go see *The Last Picture Show* or take a little road trip."

"Thank you, Beau," I leaned across the bar to kiss his cheek. "Gabriel mentioned wanting to travel around Texas."

"Then don't come back here for several days, baby. I want to see that smile back on your face. Now go!"

Ellen kept Nikki while Gabriel and I travelled west to Palo Duro Canyon. Our noon arrival offered a spectacular view of primal red-orange ridges surrounded by mother-nature inspired lighting. No wonder Georgia O'Keefe loved it. Gabriel wanted to see the canyon the way cowboys once did, so our second day was a guided horseback tour. I would've been a pitiful pioneer chick. When we got back inside Houston city limits Gabriel bummed me out by driving past his former Braeswood neighborhood and pointing out the house where Astrid still lived. "Why?" I foolishly asked while frowning. The upscale area was impressive and the elegant house was enormous, but all I could think about were the two innocent young girls inside. Then it hit me. That's all he was thinking about.

On Christmas Day, Kent and his straight-laced wife came and took Nikki to their home for celebrating. Gabriel and I went to the Tower Theater's encore presentation of *Doctor Zhivago*—a tear jerking melodrama too similar to our situation—and Gabriel never let go of my hand throughout the movie. I was his Lara and he was my Yurii. Fortunately we lived in a warmer climate than Russia, but unfortunately a wife and children were involved.

Soon, an ominous cloud began lingering overhead as I tried to suppress guilt over Gabriel's divorce and my abortion.

Calls from Sean helped me stay sane, somewhat suffusing the awful vacuuming sound inside my head. Our verbal and written conversations were always filled with excitement over his anticipated return to Texas. I answered his letters immediately, but could never fill as many pages as he had penned to me. We were sharing so much of ourselves, there were times I felt a kinship with him even stronger than mine with Gabriel. I relished his letters and waited with bated breath for his weekly calls. He usually called on Sundays, so when Nikki and Gabriel were both visiting family, I got the entire hour to myself.

"Hey big sister," Sean enthusiastically boomed into the phone. "I've got a surprise for you and it's pretty special."

"Yea! I love surprises."

"Guess what I found at the book store yesterday?"

"Books?" I teased.

"A special one. But you've gotta guess the author."

"McMurtry or Updike," I said. We shared mutual admiration for both authors.

"Updike! *Rabbit Redux*," he boasted. "It just came out and it's amazing. I can't describe it well enough to try, so I'm dropping it in the mail tomorrow. Believe it or not, it's better than *Rabbit Run*."

"For real?" I looked into my fridge. "How so?"

"Ways I can't define, but it's full of social situations that struck a chord with me. I read it fast, but you'll likely savor it. Just keep it aside and I'll read it again when I get back to Texas."

"It's that good, eh? Must have lots of sex."

"It's got its fair share, but it's mostly about changes in attitudes about Vietnam, minorities, and other things important to family structure. I'm not good at critiquing, but just know you'll love its eloquent rhythm. You're one of the most unprejudiced people I've ever met, so it'll touch your heart."

"Sean, I'm lucky to know you." I took a deep breath, absorbing my affection for him. "How the heck did I find a guy with similar taste in novels?"

"My brother," he responded with a chuckle. "Speaking of Gabe, I'd better chat with Nikki for a few minutes then talk to him. I don't want him thinking I'm pressuring him to put me on his payroll again, but I do want to say hello."

"He doesn't think that, he's just overwhelmed by his divorce predicament. He's over visiting the girls now and Nikki is visiting her dad. My first Sunday alone in eons."

"How nice for you. So, whatcha been doing with all that free time?"

"I'm almost embarrassed to admit I was curled up on the sofa reading *Cosmopolitan* when you rang. Now I'm grabbing a Tab to curb my appetite since Gabriel promised to take Nikki and me out for dinner tonight."

"Well, have fun. I guess I'd better get off this long distance call. Tell Gabe I said hello and tell him to give Nikki two piggyback rides for me tonight."

"Oh, she's going to love you for that." I took a sip of cola.

"Okay. I'll call next week to discuss *Rabbit*. Stay safe until we talk again. I love you, big sister."

"Nikki and I can hardly wait till you're back in Texas, so *you* take care! I love you too little brother." I hung up.

"I was afraid of that," Gabriel said dryly. I hadn't heard the key jingle and almost dropped my drink on the floor when I saw him standing inside the door. "Now my kid brother is in love with you."

"He's not in love with me, he just loves me." I walked up to him. "And I love him!"

"Yeah, I know." He frowned.

"There's a big difference in the two." I kissed him. "I love you and I'm *in* love with you."

"I second that emotion." He sat on the sofa and pulled me onto his lap. "Just be careful. Sean's young and impressionable, and we've got the same blood running through our veins."

"Well, please do everything in your power to get him back here soon. Otherwise Nikki and I are making a trip to Boston."

"Chill your heels, Blondie. You Southern girls could never survive the cold. I'll get him back quick as I can, so try to live without him a few more months."

"Okay." I pouted, put my Tab on the end table, and pressed my lips against his.

Kent lived in Houston, yet sporadically saw Nikki after the holidays and began sending support checks; things settled down between Gabriel and Astrid with their divorce only weeks from being finalized; Sean and I planned his move back to Texas, and I took a typing course to increase job prospects. Topless go-go girl wouldn't exactly enhance my resume. Always talking in song lyrics, Gabriel said true love travels on a gravel road, but things were finally on a smooth course. It had been eight months since that night in May and I was madly in love with the man who had surpassed the number of wonderful things any man might do just for a piece of ass.

10

After an unusual evening of restless tossing and turning, Gabriel and I had finally fallen asleep when my phone rang. Sleepily reaching over to answer, I barely recall his brother Ben asking to speak with him, but vividly remember Gabriel's side of the conversation. His first comment: "Oh God!" His second: "How's Gloria holding up?" Third: "Guess it's a blessing it was instant." After that, Gabriel's responses were somber grunts until he ended by saying, "I'll be there soon." He placed my phone back in its cradle, laid flat on his back, and wordlessly stared at the ceiling. My heart pinging in my chest, I reached over and touched his shoulder knowing something horrible had happened. In a glacial, matter-of-fact tone, Gabriel said, "Sean's dead."

"No!" I shrieked, bolting upright in bed. "No, God, no!" I kept screaming. "It can't be." I jumped out of bed and knelt on the floor, loudly praying for someone to wake me from this horrible dream. My stomach felt like it was being violently kicked while a female in our bedroom moaned, "Not Sean, not my Sean," over and over. Then I realized the eerie cry was coming from me. Too weak to stand, I prayed for strength to climb back under my sheets until the nightmare ended.

Through faint lava lamp lighting, I saw Gabriel laboriously swallow while keeping his eyes firmly focused on the ceiling. "He just ate a telephone pole," he responded in the same horribly cold timbre.

"No God, please no!" I yelled at the top of my lungs as my hands flew to my head and yanked my hair in frantic motion. *Lies. Lies. Lies!* Without realizing where my hands went until they started stinging, I found myself hitting Gabriel. "Say it isn't true. Say it isn't true."

He continued staring at the ceiling in total silence. I cried hysterically. Shushing me, he reached over to hold me. "Don't shush me, I have to know what happened to Sean!"

Gabriel remained silent. Tears cascaded down my face as my sobs grew louder. Minutes ticked by. "God punished me by taking Sean's life in exchange for the life I aborted," I screamed.

Gabriel pulled me closer in a tight grip, never saying a word. I couldn't stop calling Sean's name and asking forgiveness. Nikki slept soundly as always in her room, while Gabriel and I stayed wide awake. He internalized, I ululated. His tacit pain juxtaposing my vocal sorrow.

The next day as Gabriel prepared to leave for Massachusetts, he explained Sean had been at a party and taken a ride home with two friends, one who was stumbling drunk. As his friend raced down the highway Sean pleaded for him to stop and let him drive. According to the boy who survived, Sean's concern was for his friends to get home safely. Before he could convince the driver to swap places, they crashed into a telephone pole, killing Sean instantly. The driver died hours later.

Devastated by losing someone I dearly loved, my grief intensified when I realized I would not attend Sean's funeral. Nothing was said. I simply understood. How do you bring the dishonorable, other woman to a sacred family event?

After Gabriel left I kept tears inside and held Nikki against me as I clutched the copy of *Rabbit Redux* Sean mailed weeks earlier. For Nikki's sake, I blamed my pain on a tummy ache as I functioned in a lifeless fog waiting for Gabriel to return. When Nikki played or slept, I reread Updike's words that meant so much to Sean—and sobbed uncontrollably.

∽

"I'll be over after I put away some of Sean's belongings I brought from Boston." Gabriel called from his apartment. An hour later he tapped lightly at the door instead of using his key. I felt uneasy. I opened the door slowly and looked at his red rimmed eyes welled with tears. He pulled me to him, hugging me tightly as he kissed my forehead. We stood by the doorway in an unwaveringly embrace, holding each other in total silence. He knew and I knew. Still, I felt faint when I heard the anticipated words. "You know I have to do the right thing and go back home to my wife and children, don't you?" His voice was so tender and so tinged with sadness, I trembled, choking back tears. I would not break down and seem weak. Gabriel's guilt over abandoning his young daughters had grown before my eyes, and it was obvious Sean's death deepened his remorse.

After slowly gathering his few belongings, Gabriel placed his key on my dining table just as *Yester-Me, Yester-You, Yesterday*, by Stevie Wonder came on the radio. The floodgates opened. Hitting the radio OFF button as tears trickled down my cheeks, I tried to brush them away, not wanting him to see me this way. Tears rolled down his face, but he just ignored them while trying to hold and comfort me. I had never known a man who would openly cry before, and it made him even more special. I ached for him, but pulled away. "Please leave! I understand why you have to do this—so just go. Right this minute. The longer you stay, the more I'll hurt."

He reached out and took my hand up to his mouth, his blue eyes filled with pain as he allowed his tears to drop onto my skin. "Cherie, I'm so sorry. I've hurt enough people already and God knows I don't want you to hurt."

Once again I pulled away. This time he rushed out the door. When I heard his engine start, his horn honk twice to send me his "I love you," signal, I broke down and sobbed. A gut wrenching, lung-heaving sobbing that left me limp.

I hated work, but went in knowing Beau would soothe my pain. "Here, baby." He gave me McMurtry's novel *Movin On*. "You don't cry at the drop of a pin, but there are similarities between you and restless, sharp tongued Patsy Carpenter."

"Yeah?"

"Her fascinating charisma keeps her adrift in affairs of the heart. She's gutsy despite frequently bawling over minor issues."

"Thanks for everything." I kissed Beau's cheek before leaving.

I never stopped crying long enough to read the thick book.

Kent's calls about taking Nikki for visits never came to fruition, so Ellen insisted she stay with them instead of watching me come unglued. After

Nikki left, I felt worse without her to hold. I suppressed my sobbing and phoned Gloria. Incredibly consoling, she seemed to understand my pain. "Not only have you lost Sean, you've also lost Gabriel." Gloria attempted to comfort. "Come to Boston. Bring Nikki if you'd like, just get away."

"I'm not sure that's the best thing for me to do."

"Cherie, get on a plane, come and stay with us as long as you'd like," Gloria said with sincerity. "Distance from Gabriel might help."

Hearing his name caused my suppressed sobs to surface with a vengeance.

"Cherie, Sean would want you and me to be together. And being with someone who was so special to him would help me."

"Thank you." Tears garbled my words. "I'll let you know."

Gloria had lost a son, yet showed incredible compassion for my feelings of loss. Hoping distance would help, I decided to visit Massachusetts. Ellen said Jimmy missed his surrogate sister and agreed to keep Nikki. Beau was predictably sympathetic, assuring me the club would get along without me and welcome me back. He insisted on paying my airfare as his way of expressing condolence to the family, but I rejected four hundred dollars he tried to shove in my fist for spending money.

Bawling as I boarded the plane, vanity had taken a leave of absence as black clumps of mascara rolled off my cheeks and onto my blouse. I didn't care what anyone thought. I just hoped being with the mother of my favorite men would make my pain disappear. Looking like I'd been in the back of a turnip truck for three months instead of an airplane for three hours, I arrived in Boston an emotional wreck sporting red, puffy eyes.

"My darling, Cherie," Gloria greeted me in the airport. Absolutely stunning, she could have passed for Liz Taylor had her eyes been violet. Gloria's hair was almost black with a plum cast and her deep olive skin and ebony eyes were a surprising contrast to fair haired Gabriel and Sean. Gabriel swore her affair with their blond postman had produced him and Hope. Gloria hugged me tightly. "Sean said nothing but wonderful things about you."

"That's true," said Hope who was just as Sean described. At fifteen, she was the epitome of beauty and gentleness with the classic looks of Princess Grace; long flaxen blonde hair, ivory skin, and a delicate smile that revealed perfect teeth.

Younger son Conner politely shook my hand. "Call me Conn. It sounds more like Sean." An abbreviated name seemed his only resemblance to siblings. Conn had his mom's olive skin, dark hair and eyes, but the boy didn't know how to shut up or sit down. Gloria scolded him several times when he got carried away entertaining me with arm farts on the drive home.

"Ben's gone back to the Air Force, so dinner will be quiet," Gloria watched as Hope put food on the table. Everyone had impeccable table manners, and Conner cleared the table to help Hope wash dishes. Easy to see where Gabriel picked up his considerate kitchen traits. Lord knows who influenced his foul mouth, but hearing "I'd do just about anything for a piece of ass" would have been music to my ears right then. "C'mon," Gloria insisted. "Let's sit on the sofa."

The four of us talked for hours about Sean's kindness and loving ways. When Gloria reached over and held me in her arms, saying she loved me because Sean loved me, we both began crying. My waterworks continued long after my head hit the pillow for a few minutes of sleep.

৩৩

"Thankfully Hope took on 'mothering' duties the minute I started working outside the home," Gloria said the following morning as Hope fussed over Conn. The two did breakfast dishes while Gloria and I stayed in her bedroom talking about everything—including sex. She thoughtfully tried to cheer me up, but I grieved for Sean and felt heartsick without Gabriel.

Later in the evening Gabriel called Gloria. She allowed me to overhear her side of the conversation. "I know, son," she comforted him. "Yes, I'll take good care of Cherie." She hung up. "Gabriel is worried sick about you. I've never heard him so depressed." A sympathetic look crossed her face. "He kept telling me how much he loves you, but he's trying to do right by Lauren and Skylar."

Again, I cried myself to sleep.

Two days later Gabriel called again. Gloria spoke briefly with him. "Here, darling." She handed me the phone, kissed my trembling cheek, and walked into another room.

103

"How are you, Cherie?" Gabriel asked.

"Fine." I tried to hold back tears.

"Well, I haven't slept or eaten in days. And I might just go mad without you."

We both started crying and in a loud, tear filled voice, Gabriel said, "I can't function without you, Cherie. I'm taking a five o'clock flight to Boston, so I'll see you in a few hours. I love you more than you could possibly know."

"I love you too, Gabriel."

"Yeaaah," he whispered. "Now I know how Zhivago felt without his Lara. Promise me you won't go runnin' off to Russia before I get there, Blondie."

"I promise. Besides I don't own a fur coat, and the only Russian word I know is *ostranenie.*"

"Must mean something naughty, if you memorized it."

"It means defamiliarization of art or 'making strange' of common perceptions."

"Blondie, why the hell does your knowing that not surprise me? Just hang tight till I get there . . . promise?"

"I'm not good at hanging tight, but Gloria just walked in with some rope and duct tape."

"Love you, crazy girl. See ya soon."

Gabriel arrived late. "I missed hearing you say pleeease, and watching you walk around on your tiptoes." He hugged me tightly.

I couldn't speak as my tears fell onto his shoulder. We barely touched each other while chatting with his family, but the only thought crossing my mind as words casually flowed from him, was how I wanted to leave lip prints on parts of his body currently covered by clothing. Gloria must have read my mind. She suggested Gabriel and I retire to her bedroom.

෬৩

"We gunned the engine and peeled away from Sean's gravesite," Gabriel told me as we walked out to his rental car the following morning.

"Sean would've wanted it that way," Hope agreed before elaborating on Sean's sense of humor. "He wasn't just about global harmony and unconditional love," she said.

Warm hugs and kisses were exchanged, leaving everyone teary-eyed as we backed down the drive. "Wish we could move to Texas," Gloria said.

"That would be wonderful," I answered.

Gabriel interrupted by loudly gunning the engine. Conn and Hope waved goodbye.

"Your family has an odd sense of graveyard humor." I snuggled against Gabriel. "But I'm sure Sean would've appreciated the peeling away from his grave site."

"Yeah, he'd have also liked a less traditional grave marker. Maybe one with a naked woman on one side and a prophylactic on the other."

"I think you're describing the headstone you'd want on your gravesite."

"Hell no, Blondie. I don't want a funeral or any of the formalities that go with it. Just drop my happy ass in a vat of Budweiser."

"You're strange, my friend."

"Yeaaah?" He tightened his arm around me. "But now you know it's genetic and not acquired."

"Try again. And if it is indeed genetic, when can I expect to see some of their fabulous familial traits surface in you?"

"You better hope never. When it comes to traits, Gloria is one of the most conniving women you'll ever meet, so you don't want her behavior up in me."

"Conniving! Why would you even joke about something like that?"

"I'm not joking, Blondie," he said staunchly. "Unfortunately she had to resort to scheming and lying to handle life with our dad, and regrettably the cunning nature remained."

His comment stunned me, but I was too tired to discuss it as we rushed to catch our flight.

Back in Texas, Astrid reactivated divorce proceedings, I remained in my apartment, and Gabriel pretended to live in his. One Sunday after Gabriel pumped petro at a local gas station, he walked over and leaned inside my window. "Don't look now, but Astrid's sitting in the full service lane." Without moving my head, I cut my eyes to the side and glanced at the woman with primly cut driftwood colored hair, surrounding a pale face that was tilted ever-so-properly upward (as though she'd have to look up the definition of fellatio if someone accidentally uttered the term in her presence).

"I guess the girls are with a sitter—she looks dressed for an evening on the town," Gabriel said as he returned to the driver's seat. "Hey, you okay?"

"She's pretty." I took an acute breath. "And she definitely looks like the silver-finger-bowl-at-every-meal type. Very prim and proper."

"That's dreadfully prim, proper, pompous, and rigid."

"Which is what my mother wanted of me."

"You're just prim and proper enough."

"Oh, pleeeease," I interrupted.

"And you're beautiful, loving, impetuous, charming, and most importantly..." He threw his arm around my shoulder. "I love you!"

"Thanks for being so sweet. Guess you could tell seeing her made me a bit nervous. I can't help but feel like a home-wrecker."

He shook his head. "There's no such thing as home-wreckers; only wreckable homes. Hey Blondie, May ninth is just around the corner."

What a guy. He remembered our one year anniversary.

The following week Astrid took the girls to Phoenix for a visit with her parents, and Gabriel took me along while he fetched a few items from the house. The place was like a museum. Beautifully decorated, yet antiseptic and uninviting. Until we reached the cheery playroom he had created for his girls. It was filled with toys and books, but its most noticeable feature was delicate woodwork, painted pastel pink and white in carousel decor. When he told me about reading the newspaper in this playroom so he could be near his girls, I felt sad for them. It was the only room with any warmth and now their daddy was gone. Just as guilt crept in making me uncomfortable, Gabriel led me out.

Gabriel was a patient, loving, prince of a man, but within months, I was back to changing moods with underwear. Abortion guilt. Blame for Sean's death. The wicked vixen who split Gabriel and his daughters— whom Astrid was soon moving to Phoenix near her parents.

And I despised my job. Saying the harrowing lifestyle had taken away a part of her, Kat quit the club only days before Beau became ill and was hospitalized with chest pains. Although I talked with him daily by phone and visited when possible, Beau's absence and Kat's departure made me feel even more miserable every time I walked into the place. In addition, Beau's uptight wife Celeste stopped daily at the Jewel Box to oversee financial aspects, and it was obvious she didn't appreciate being around any of the girls. Especially me. I'd worn a red sundress to work the first day she showed up "in charge" and wasn't about to wear lingerie in her presence, much less jump on stage. Thus began my transition of waitressing in street clothes. Beau once mentioned his wife seemed jealous when he told her about taking me under his wing and he got a good laugh out of it. Being almost thirty years my senior, Beau appreciated the compliment. A savvy business woman whose striking beauty was accentuated by designer fashions one might find in a Neiman's catalogue, Celeste always donned oversized sunglasses when she walked into the club, even on rainy days. She really needed to loosen her sphincter. It was obvious she didn't want to be seen slinking out of her black Jaguar and slithering into the Jewel Box. Beau said when he explained the potential money involved in said undertaking, Celeste initially balked, but gave in with stipulations. It would be a short-time enterprise and first-class. Ha ha. Despite Beau's integrity and attempts to dignify said business, I'll always consider the term "classy strip joint" the ultimate oxymoron.

Beau recuperated and returned to the Jewel Box. I followed Kat's footsteps and quit. But unlike her, I kept my alias. Gabriel knew my given name was Jill, but Cherie was the one he screamed in ecstasy. That pseudonym was here to stay. I began looking for business opportunities to invest my savings, yet loved not working, which gave me more time with Gabriel and Nikki.

I still relished conversations with Beau and swung by the Jewel Box one afternoon after a job interview. "Keep it quiet, so dancers won't bail before due time, but the Jewel Box is being demolished soon to make way for the new South Freeway."

"Oh, Beau." I felt a wave of sadness. "What'll you do?"

"I'm already building a neighborhood bar on the proper side of the Medical Center."

"Don't go getting too high and mighty on me."

Beau laughed like I'd said something really funny.

∽

It was a couple of months before Nikki and I stopped by to check Beau's club progress. Some unusual music played on a portable cassette player near the door as we walked inside. Beau, dressed in coveralls, was busily working. Even Sean Connery couldn't make farmer garb so appealing.

"You're a man of many talents, Beau."

"Hey, baby!" He turned and met us with a warm smile. "I didn't hear you two walk in."

"My mom can sneak up on a ghost." Nikki rushed to Beau.

"Keeps you on your pretty little toes, huh?" He reached down and gave her a hug.

"Yes, sir." Nikki said, before skipping over to his tape player.

Beau hugged me. His broad shoulders always made me feel so secure. "I love a man who's not afraid of hard work or getting his hands dirty, but please wash up for lunch."

"How thoughtful, baby." He washed his hands and grabbed a deck of playing cards.

"Who's singing this pretty song?" Nikki asked, leaning closer to the music.

"The Little Sparrow, Edith Piaf," Beau answered. "Singing *Non, je ne regrette rien* which means, No, I regret nothing."

"I like it," she said. "A lot."

"Precocious for her five years." Beau nodded toward Nikki. "Ms. Piaf is a famous French singer who led a tragic life that we'll discuss when you're older. Here, take this cassette and I'll buy another."

"You don't have to do that, Professor Higgins," I said, despite wanting to hear more of her mesmerizing voice.

"Take it." He placed the tape in my hand. "I insist. Now c'mon, Nikki." Beau motioned her to a booth with a window view.

We ate deli food I fetched in transit, and Beau taught Nikki a new card game and a few magic tricks. "Teach her your 'Jack of Clubs' ruse."

"Now, baby, you know that's more than sleight-of-hand and took me years to master while working Vegas."

108

"Right." I grinned. "Even though it's only been closed a few weeks, do you miss the Jewel Box, Beau?"

"Well, it was an exciting adventure that made a ton of money, but also created tremendous tension with Celeste. One being club gals, the other, her elitist pals. We live on the outskirts of River Oaks, so my sweet wife of privileged youth felt anxious her socialite friends might learn about the go-go joint." Beau was careful not to use the term "strip" in Nikki's presence.

"I understand that fear, but not her jealousy of you and club chicks." Flattery was Beau's only flirtatious act, and despite countless girls trying to bed him, he tactfully turned them down and went home to Celeste and their son Gilles.

"Human nature. Celeste is a beautiful woman who loves to look great and get compliments from men, but by God, she didn't want me looking at any women."

"You shouldn't use God's name in vain," Nikki chastised.

"I'm sorry, precious one." Beau squatted to her level. "Do you forgive me?"

"Of course!" She allowed him to lift her high for a farewell hug and kiss on the cheek.

"God's name in vain...whose input is that?" he whispered to me after she grabbed our basket to take to the car.

"My sister or mother, I'm guessing. I don't hang out with many chaplains."

"Well, please come back and see me again. *The Grapevine* should be open for business in a month or so."

"The Grapevine?" I asked, honored he named it from my song choice of long ago.

"I thought it a good name for a little neighborhood wine bar."

"Oh yeah." Silly me. Who the hell remembered my spastic dancing to that song?

"This arched doorway you walked through will be covered in grapevines, and the brick entry will remain, but a new door is being built from French oak to replicate a wine barrel, and it'll have a wide leather strap as its handle. Hopefully the front will be a cozy invitation."

"And once inside you'll be playing Edith Piaf as background music?"

109

"French, Italian, and American music. Can't show prejudice, but nothing sets a better mood for drinking than Italian crooners. Being on the opposite side of the Medical Center from the Jewel Box, I doubt this place will be a gold mine like that go-go club, but getting it up and running is satisfying in itself."

"I'm glad you're enjoying life, Beau."

"You too, baby. By the way, I've got another McMurtry book for you to read."

"Can't wait!" I kissed his cheek. "And thanks for your continued efforts to cultivate my mind."

"No effort involved. I enjoy sharing things I like and I'm glad you get such a kick out of some of my obsessions. Hell, life is twice as exciting when you share the fun."

"Yeah." I reflected back to the Jewel Box, getting mixed emotions.

Beau seemed to interpret my thoughts. "Baby, life is a unique and wonderful journey, so relish all memories—not just the good ones."

Beau was more than my spiritual guide through sin city. He had touched my soul with his warmth and wisdom, and left an indelible mark on me that would never vanish. My plan was to never be too far from the sound of his bass voice and heartwarming laughter. Laughter I was sure could bring about world peace.

11

"My Camaro's in the shop and I need a ride to the east side." Delilah jumped into my car before it came to a complete stop in front of my apartment.

There was no shoving her out. "Jeez, I just failed an interview and need some alone time."

"Please, Sha-reee. I gotta get somewhere pronto."

I backed out, left our complex, pulled onto the freeway, and headed east while she babbled between spitting out directions. "Take that exit!" She pointed ahead. "We're gonna get stoned together."

"Sweet offer." I gave her a disapproving scowl. "But I'll pass."

"C'mon, smoke some pot and get in the groove. When we get to this dude's we can get an all time high. I hear it's really happenin' at his pad." She slouched in her seat.

"Well, it'll be happenin' without me. My daughter needs a cognizant mom when she gets home from Rachel's."

"Oh yeah, little Nikki . . ." she said as though she had already forgotten my child.

As we passed a dilapidated yellow frame house with a porch full of junkyard debris and a trashed out lawn overgrown by weeds, Delilah bolted upright. "Back up, I think that's the place."

I looked at the rusty washer-dryer combo sitting next to a shabby sofa on the porch, then at a beat up VW bus with flats all around, then at Delilah like she had water on the brain. "For crying out loud." I made a U-turn. "It's Tobacco Road, Texas style."

Delilah ignored my comment as a young hippie girl walked onto the porch, sporting a mop of hair that appeared immune to grooming. The young girl in teensy tank top and blue jean shorts, dropped a bowl of food on the porch, yelled toward two mangy dogs lying under a tree, and then waved at me and Delilah before turning to go back inside. Her shorts had the rear end cut out, leaving only the seam going up the crack of her ass—showing off dual tattoos. Left cheek read "Eat," right cheek, "Me." That keister will be the highlight of some mortician's day when she passes to the great beyond.

Delilah invited me to cruise inside with her while she picked up a dime bag. I declined her invite and raised my radio volume to sing along with recently departed Texan, Janis Joplin. Suddenly a male voice was crooning *Me and Bobby McGee*, and filling my Mustang with his rank breath.

"Tragic death," said the bearded ox, covered head-to-toe in tarantula tattoos. As his sweaty body inched further inside my open car window, I slid out the passenger door and into the dude's happenin' pad. The time to catch and release Delilah had commenced.

The sun seeped feebly through tiny portions of long windows, opaque from years of accumulated dust and grime, and partially draped with towels and sheets that had seen better days. Tossed throughout the house were leprous mattresses occupied by two or more grimy individuals and over-stuffed bean bags serving as beds. With beads clicking and swaying behind me and *Spirit in The Sky* blaring around me, I stepped over beer cans and dirty laundry as I wandered room to room searching for Delilah. Sitting on a sofa that held slightly more appeal than the filthy floor, she was opening a bag of grass when she saw me.

"C'mon. Sit." Delilah casually motioned me over.

I sandwiched myself between her and a kid who looked much like Sean.

"Groovy," he said. His soothing voice reminded me of Sean, and I allowed myself to lean against the sofa and temporarily drift into memories. "Want a hit?"

"No thanks." I gazed at the plaster peeling walls with their shrines to Jimi Hendrix as he passed the joint to Delilah who took a long drag before passing it to others.

"There you are, purty gurl!" The tattooed, bearded guy reappeared and squeezed in beside me and the kid, adding more grime to the sofa.

112

"It's time to pick up Nikki from Rachel's." I thumped Delilah while rising from the sofa.

"Peace," said the young man.

"Bummer." Delilah stood beside me, flashing the peace sign to her newfound friends.

"Indeed. Thanks for my introduction to Houston's drug scene." I grabbed her arm to keep her from stumbling over a naked couple and miscellaneous other clutter as I navigated our way out the front door.

ᕞ

Meanwhile, Gabriel and I seemed to be on different wave lengths in general, with him wanting to talk when I didn't, and vice versa. No surprise when he started spending excess time with Hank, an outgoing wilderness-type business associate near his age. Who could blame him? Wallowing in guilt, self pity, and sleep deprivation due to post-abortion nightmares, I wasn't exactly a weekend at the Brazoria County Fair.

Poor Nikki, coping with a moody mom and absentee father. Kent promised to pick her up for visits, but usually called with excuses why he couldn't come. Doubtful any "#1 Dad" cups were in his foreseeable future. My anger rose each time she lugged her packed, tiny suitcase back into her room, gloomy with disappointment. I'm not the violent type, but seeing her so sad made me want to kick his teeth up through his nose.

"Well, Blondie," Gabriel said in solemn tone when I answered my phone. "Al called to say he just drove past the Jewel Box and saw bulldozers plowing it down."

"I might cry." I went flush with melancholy. Despite a few unpleasant memories, that place brought me to Beau—a compassionate father figure when I desperately needed one—and to the love of my life.

"Tears won't help. City planners are making way for the new South Expressway come hell or high water."

"Well, I hate progress and hearing that really makes me sick to my stomach. That noisy, little club was where we shared special memories. Like secretly carving C/G inside that shelf of Beau's mahogany bar the night he was too busy counting money to notice our monkeyshines."

"Blondie you're too sentimental. It was ironic we met in such a place, but still it was just bricks and mortar. We got lots of time for making memories."

Demise of the Jewel Box triggered a surge of sadness. "I miss Sean. He died too young to keep making memories."

"Don't," Gabriel sternly warned.

"But I feel guilty." I broke into tears.

"Cherie, God didn't take Sean's life because you had an abortion, so drop your guilt and stop being so goddamned morose." Suddenly he was shouting. "Sean's dead! It's not your fault, and we can't bring him back. I'm sick to death of your poetic soul wrenching and your deranged attachment to the past!"

"Deranged attachment!" I screamed back. "Screw you, Gabriel."

Click.

His slamming the phone left me listening to static and acknowledging the distance growing between us. I cursed him for not stopping me from having the abortion—an event I constantly relived in my head, but never spoke about.

ᐴ

Kent exited Nikki's life as abruptly as he re-entered it, leaving a pitiful support check he sent sporadically as our only remnant of him. Wise for her age, Nikki intuitively stopped packing suitcases and waiting around for her "No show" father. Spending more time with Ellen's family was my antidote to Kent's absenteeism.

Nikki was spending another weekend with Cousin Jimmy when I fell into abysmal depression. Unable to shake the guilt associated with my abortion, Sean's death, or causing two precious girls to be without their father, I proceeded to get considerably drunk. I couldn't walk a straight line, but the cashier at *U-Tote-Em* sold me two bottles of *Nytol*, which I knocked back with orange juice on my way home. Apparently Gabriel called and failed to rouse rational commentary from me, until I said something about joining Sean in Valhalla. He called paramedics who came and broke through my door.

In the ambulance they pounded my chest and asked questions. I didn't answer. I didn't want to be rescued. I wanted to end my pain and confusion. I called Sean's name, and saw visions of him as I drifted in and out of consciousness. Through the darkness a shadow seemed to swirl into a funnel of wispy smoke, and I reached for Sean's hand. "I'm sorry" I kept saying as I struggled to grab onto him, but as my breathing weakened, he slowly faded away.

They pumped my stomach at the hospital, and later fed me breakfast through a tube. Several days and several psychiatric consultations later, I was released to Ellen's care. I looked at Nikki as she sweetly rubbed her tiny hand across my cheek. How could I have been so incredibly weak and stupid? Leaving a dependent child without a parent is a selfish crime, not a heroic self-sacrifice. Mythical Valhalla would have accepted Sean, a hero who died while trying to save others, but I would have been rejected and sent straight to Hell.

Justifiably angry, Gabriel called daily and spoke only with my sister about my condition. It took days before I could dial a phone, and I spoke in fragmented sentences for weeks, constantly groping for words. As I slowly recovered, Gabriel slowly dismissed his anger at my actions and returned to my side. Though I knew I would never attempt such a foolish act again, Ellen kept a close watch over me. Like a hawk. She was always there for Nikki and me, but never made me feel worse than I already felt, by asking "How could you?" or "Why?"

Months passed without communications from Kat, so when she called and left her number with Ellen, I couldn't wait to hear her sassy voice. Oh, my! Kat found the Lord. She married a minister, moved to some small southeast town near Galveston, and was hanging out with other born-again Christians, quoting scriptures and doing whatever else holy rollers do. I'm sure she didn't mean to come across as overly pious, but after my adultery and abortion, talking to those of the holy cloth ranked right up there with Tabasco enemas. After numerous strained conversations with Kat trying to save my soul (possibly her atonement for helping tarnish it), and me ending the calls abruptly, we eventually lost touch.

In typical terse fashion, Gabriel dismissed my moments of grief over lost lives by kissing me instead of allowing me to articulate my heartache. I appreciated the passion, but wished for a little compassion from him every now and then.

And although she hadn't been the best babysitter for Nikki, Delilah's warped personality somewhat kept me from wallowing in guilt. She'd quit smoking pot and started stalking me for recreation. Of course, Delilah and I had *that* bond. I don't know where I was when Neil Armstrong walked on the moon, or who was with me the day Kennedy was shot, but I'll never forget the person who chaperoned my abortion.

Every time I took Nikki to the pool for swim lessons, Delilah appeared.

"Under water, lovey," I instructed my daughter to duck her head and ears. Delilah's topics were a bit risqué for youngsters.

"I'm sick of these son-of-a-bitch losers in my life," Delilah complained.

I said nothing. No need to invite more tales about the wayward men she socially entertained.

"Course I thought I'd hit the jackpot with my Greek God fireman. Cherie you should've seen his 'down under' arsenal!"

"Hey lovey, can you show Mommy how long you can hold your breath down under?" I encouraged Nikki.

"Yep, he helped me drain three quarts of Boone's Farm strawberry wine, and then made hot, burning love to me in his Corvette while I wore his official firefighter's helmet."

I figured Nikki couldn't interpret the meaning of "healthy throbbing hose," but other adjectives Delilah used to describe his fiery unit caused me to cringe.

"Fantastic," I said to Nikki as she resurfaced. Delilah assumed I was commenting on her affairs, and opened her mouth to continue. "Can Mommy time you?" I asked my girl, who quickly ducked down holding her nose.

Delilah swigged her Pepsi and burped. "But I haven't heard a damn word from that bastard."

What a surprise, I thought as Nikki's head popped up to knock water from her ears. I assured her she had set a new time record for holding her breath underwater, and then tactfully changed subjects by asking Delilah about her new job. Details about Methodist Hospital's pharmacy department were anything but boring and spiked my interest.

"They're hiring and I know you can pass their prerequisite tests," she announced as I towel dried Nikki's long hair. "And you're welcome to all the *Valium* you can sneak out every day."

"What are valley ums, Mommy?"

"Grown up vitamins and nothing we need." I rubbed after-sun lotion across her shoulders. I no longer ate pain meds, but desperately needed a job—especially one that didn't involve serving cocktails and trying to avoid getting hit in the eye by twirling tassels.

An extraordinary role model, Rachel continued caring for Nikki after I was hired for Methodist's three to eleven shift. The time was perfect for apprentices, late hours suited me to a T, and the challenging job beat the hell out of dressing scantily and slinging beer. I missed Beau something fierce, but Gabriel showered me with so much love my life seemed fairly complete.

Gabriel's brother Ben was still traveling the world courtesy of the US Air Force. Astrid relocated Gabriel's daughters to Arizona, and shortly thereafter, Gloria and her two youngest children moved to Texas. Gabriel said her move would save him Western Union fees. "Gloria can borrow direct instead of me wiring cash every month." According to him, despite earning adequate income as a travel agent, she bought foolish luxuries first and paid bills if any money remained in her account.

Gloria moved near Gabriel, and I absolutely loved visiting her. Somewhat cluttered, and comfortably furnished with overstuffed sofas, soft lighting, bountiful plants, an aroma of potpourri always filling the air, Gloria's home felt like one had walked right into a Norman Rockwell painting. Gloria met visitors with a cheery hello, a wide smile, a tight hug, and welcoming conversation that made one feel special. Weekends were often filled with noises of friends and family, but a quiet corner could always be found when the hustle bustle became overwhelming. A blithe spirit who talked about things my mother would have never considered proper, Gloria and I shared a special relationship. This hip, middle aged woman placed her copy of *Cosmopolitan* with Burt Reynolds posing in nothing more than a smile, on her coffee table. Gloria and Hope pampered Nikki constantly, often babysitting while I spent romantic evenings with Gabriel or worked late, or covered Delilah's shifts. Her absenteeism was becoming problematic.

Delilah fell for a bass player and spent way too much time in clubs waiting for last call or hanging out wherever musicians hang at three in the morning to have jam sessions and fry their brains. Flip had a wild look in his eyes, and was the first guy I'd met who could go from attentive to withdrawn, happy to depressed, angry to ecstatic, calm to hysterical, all in the same hour. Delilah's temperament made it difficult to tell if she was popping pills with him, but when I became assistant purchasing agent, I noticed the pharmacy was going through Quaaludes like they were blue light specials at Kmart.

In December, Gabriel's middle brother, Ben, came home on leave from the Air Force. Several inches taller and more muscular than Gabriel, Ben walked with a mammoth air of confidence, spewed more curse words than Lenny Bruce, constantly voiced wicked thoughts, and always wound up the center of attention. Gloria made him curb his language in Nikki's presence, so he got good at spelling obscenities faster than most people could say them. He was crude Christmas entertainment.

Houston's holiday weather was warm and humid as usual, but Gloria's house was like the winter wonderland one reads about or sees on television specials. A festively decorated blue spruce tree centered the living room windows and overflowed with a quaint mix of old and new ornaments, some hand crafted, some store bought. The myriad of colorful twinkling lights flickered through swirling angel's hair, conjuring visions of an enchanting childhood where sugarplum fairies happily danced. A pleasant change from Yule seasons of my youth in which a disheveled yet spirited Santa (with amazing resemblance to our dad) bulldozed gifts while stumbling around Mother, arguing his sobriety. At Gloria's, Christmas music filtered through laughter, chatter, and Ben's endless innuendo and spelled-out obscenities, as everyone exchanged gifts. Gabriel made sure Nikki had a gajillion presents to unwrap. He gave me fabulous gold jewelry, but my favorite gift was a music box that played *Raindrops Keep Falling on my Head*, from our first movie, *Butch Cassidy and the Sundance Kid.* It was a post-card perfect Christmas, just like those the *Saturday Evening Post* always promised.

Our family of three joined other siblings to bring in another year over a huge breakfast at Gloria's. She always made sure grace was said before the boys took over, and albeit she attempted to keep an air of decorum during all meals, she never succeeded. "Happy New Year!" we said in unison, clinking coffee cups and other juice glasses in the air. Nikki excused herself for a bathroom break, which Ben took as invitation to mouth off. "Gloria," he boomed, getting everyone's attention. "You should know that yesterday I saw your youngest son out front jerking off behind that big oak tree."

Gloria blushed. Conn defensively screamed, "I was not!"

"Hell, it's okay and you don't need to deny it," Ben interjected dryly. "I do it myself from time to time, but you don't need to be embarrassing the family by pulling on your dick in the front yard."

Gabriel shook his head slowly, a mischievous grin surfacing.

"I wasn't jerking off!" Conn slammed his fist on the table.

"Ben, be quiet," Gloria said.

"Boy, don't you know you can masturbate yourself into a coma?" Ben scolded.

"You cannot . . . and I wasn't jerking off," Conn protested.

"Look, I saw you doing it." Ben casually leaned back in his chair. "And I'm gonna tell you right now, I know a guy who got cancer from constantly yanking on his dick."

"Ben!" Gloria sternly interrupted as Nikki walked back into the room to take her place at the table. "Please stop so we can enjoy breakfast."

"Okay, I'll stop." He cocked his head to the side, slowly looking around the table. "But I wanna warn everyone before they spoon up any of that white gravy, to think about what might be in it. And don't even think about passing it my way!" He put his hand up in Stop signal fashion. "I mean it, I don't trust the boy. He's a M-A-S-T-U-R-B-A-T-I-N-G machine."

Following Ben's lead, Gabriel looked at the gravy with disgust, and pushed the bowl away from our end of the table. Hope became furious. "This isn't funny and there's a five-year-old child present!"

"I'll be six in June." Nikki blotted her milk moustache with a napkin.

"Mother," Hope continued, "I'm sick of hearing this kind of talk every time my brothers get together."

"Your guilty conscience bothering you, Hope?" Ben shot Gabriel a smug look.

Hope took offense at anyone teasing Conner, but trying to control her brothers was futile. Ben and Gabriel had moved onto other lightly veiled, vulgar conversation. Gloria and I weren't doing well at holding back grins. When Gloria broke into laughter, Hope angrily jumped from the table, carried away her and Nikki's plates, and then stormed back for Nikki. They finished their meals in her bedroom.

Before the end of the year I switched to Methodist's day shift, making my time with Nikki along the same hours as most families. Besides, leaving work at four thirty in the afternoon left only limited time for dealing with Delilah's antics.

Most evenings after Nikki fell asleep my spare time was spent with Gabriel, holding hands while discussing everything from Cronkite's coverage of Nixon and Watergate, to flight characteristics of the Frisbee. The emergence of some great soft rock and pop artists like Fleetwood Mac, Steely Dan, Chicago, The Eagles, and especially Texas blues band ZZ Top, filled our place with music. We were still grooving to our favorite Sixties tunes, but an underlying current made me sense our little love song was hitting some low notes. I couldn't shake my adultery/abortion guilt or analyze Gabriel's strange, three day silent moods and remote attitude. I hated when he went into detach mode.

ᦔᦗ

Houston's unemployment rate soared in '73, creating a shortage of homebuilding that negatively affected Gabriel's booming business. While he pondered his future, I threw myself into my job while shooting for a normal life. So to speak. Attempting to bond with my own family, I made personal pilgrimages to Mother's.

"Spray starch in a can doesn't work nearly as well as the boiling method." Lynn straightened her single strand of pearls.

"Really," I replied to my persnickety mother. I hadn't starched one article of clothing since leaving home.

"I pride myself on getting George's cuffs and collars crisp as can be."

I curled my lips to keep a grin from surfacing. Dad may have left our home in shipshape starched white shirts, but often returned looking like he'd jumped overboard.

"Oh, I just got a recipe for lemon-almond cake. It takes a couple hours to make, but it's delicious. Let me write it out for you."

"Face it, Mother. I'm your home economics failure."

"You are not," she said with sincere conviction.

I watched as she jotted instructions. Two hours? Flouring almonds? Gently folding eggs? I would never attempt such a recipe. I quietly stared at Mother's beautifully buffed hardwood floors as she painstakingly wrote ingredients. Further attempts at conversation proved untenable, and my inability to connect with my loving mother discomforted me.

Back in Houston, I scheduled an appointment with my mental hygienist, but didn't tell Gabriel who had the same aversion to psychiatrists as he did IRS audits. A few sessions of my shrink nodding when I questioned my need to bolt from uncomfortable situations, motivated me to sign my final check. No sense in wasting good money when a compassionate and highly competent counselor was just a stone's throw away.

"Good to hear your voice, baby!" Beau greeted into the phone. "When are you stopping by *The Grapevine* again?"

"Soon. I need to return *All My Friends Are Going to Be Strangers*. It was a quick read and I liked it."

"Short or long, I love reading McMurtry's memorable Texas characters."

"Well, you're my most memorable character. Maybe he'll write about you someday."

"Baby, you really need to get out more often!" Beau chuckled.

"Indeed I do. What day are you free next week?"

"Come by *The Grapevine* anytime. I'd love to see you and can tell by your voice you need to talk. This place isn't thriving, so we'll have plenty time to sit and visit."

"Thank you, Beau." I felt instant relief by his offer.

~~

"Good news is I sold my part of the business and dissolved my part-nership with Al," Gabriel said via Ma Bell. "Bad news is I'll be building houses outside Houston to survive."

"What area around Houston isn't affected by this recession?"

"None. I should've said outside Texas. First offer I got was from the East Coast."

"Say it isn't so," I whined into the phone.

"Fraid so, Blondie."

Gabriel began working out of state, yet made time to visit Lauren and Skylar in Phoenix as often as possible. They lived near Astrid's parents, which he feared meant getting his daughter's young minds pumped full of toxin toward him.

With Gabriel travelling so often, I moved into an apartment closer to the rapidly expanding Texas Medical Center, and put Nikki into a school with after care. Gabriel and I went from speaking daily to sporadic phone calls, and rare moments together. I truly believed we would always be together, but couldn't deny the obvious. We were drifting apart.

12

Nikki liked her new school, but missed Rachel whose temporary babysitting job lasted three years. Despite Rachel's serene guidance, as Nikki grew I witnessed familiar characteristics from my family tree springing to life. Short on years, but long on attitude, Nikki was daring, defiant, and a nonstop talker who loudly voiced her opinions. Neither of us would have been welcomed at Quaker gatherings. I worked extra hours just to keep her in private school and ballet lessons (hopeful prerequisites for keeping her out of sequined pasties and white go-go boots later in life), and she showed appreciation by whining about my absence. My childhood dreams of a luxurious life in the big city seemed an elusive fairy tale.

Gabriel occasionally called from whatever state he was working. Maybe time apart would help us forget negatives that soured our relationship. Somewhere along the way, I began blaming him for my abortion and even Sean's death. And I was fairly certain he blamed me for Astrid taking his girls away.

Gloria's calls became as rare as Gabriel's, which didn't surprise me much. I learned firsthand how Gloria meddled in her children's affairs when she trashed a letter Ben wrote to Mei, a girl he met in China, instead of mailing it. When Hope dated a boy Gloria disliked, said suitor soon vanished. But, we all have faults, eh? Mother drummed said sentiment into our heads by quoting Shakespeare: *Condemn the fault and not the actor of it* while reminding us to *love the sinner, not the sin.*

And I rarely spoke with Beau while he coped with marital and business problems. "You should go out with that hospital administrator, baby."

"Did I mention he looks like Burt Reynolds and acts like the obnoxiously sarcastic Don Rickles?"

"Rickles is kinda funny, and women adore Burt."

"Some women. Did I mention Phil is well known for his inexcusable pedantry?"

"No." Beau chuckled. "But Gabe's not calling, so go enjoy life."

Phil Parnell flirted with me for weeks before I eventually accepted his invite to a hospital function. I needed a change of pace, even if he wasn't vaguely appealing to me. I endured the date, but when he walked me to my door and kissed me goodnight I turned my head to miss a mouth-to-mouth. Phil didn't push the issue.

No calls from Gabriel, so before you could say "forget that carpenter" I was dating a suit wearing, briefcase carrying Aggie. And by dating, I mean watching television. I urged him to try water sports. He urged me to watch football. Our only common interest was ice cream.

"That no good Marvin Zindler!" Phil stood in front of the TV, his face reddening.

"I think it's hilarious." I looked at ABC's evening coverage of our local white-haired Channel 13 reporter getting national air play for his efforts to close LaGrange's Chicken Ranch.

"He needs to stick with dirty restaurant reports and leave this Texas shrine alone."

"Sounds like you have a sentimental attachment, Phil."

"Bullshit." He turned away from the tube. "I'm just mad at this idiot."

"My gosh, man, don't come unglued. Grab some Kleenex and let those tears flow."

"Ha ha." He sat rigidly beside me. "The Chicken Ranch is a legend in this state."

"Yeah. A house of ill repute frequented by UT Longhorns and you Texas Aggies."

"Reportedly," he shot back with the precise amount of venom to kill our conversation.

As obscenities were being bleeped on TV, we looked over just as the tenacious news reporter got a fist in the face from La Grange's Sheriff Jim. Wowza. Finally some fun news.

In late summer of '73, Marvin Zindler succeeded in closing the infamous whorehouse, so every time ZZ Top's hit song, *La Grange* played, I turned the radio full blast to irritate Phil. He busied himself distributing "I'm a Friend of Sheriff Jim" bumper stickers as "a joke." Yeah, right. He was a frugal Aggie, the Chicken Ranch's eight dollar Monday night special was gone. You be the judge.

Phil was a narcissist with a penchant for arguing, but oddly enough he rarely debated my comments about being hopelessly in love with Gabriel. And even odder, when Hope and Gloria told me Gabriel was dating some bank secretary, I surrendered to Phil's libidinous mating call. But only to a point. Kissing on the lips was just too personal. I always turned my head so all kisses went off sides. No intimacy, just one-two-three we're done. Minor arguments ensued, but Gabriel's lips were the only ones I wanted pressed against mine.

Delilah married the fry-brain bass player, gave birth to a darling baby girl, got knocked up a second time (her words), and absolutely despised Phil. When I told her about Gabriel's fling, she drove to his apartment one evening, interrupted their dinner, checked out the secretary, took a pungent poop in his toilet, didn't bother flushing, and left. Now that's what friends are for.

Nikki stuck like glue to Cousin Jimmy and I got marginally closer to my sister and her hubby. Ellen and I even discussed our differing relationships with Mother. She felt our priggish mother was simply sheltering us from our often inebriated dad. Logical conclusion, but my easy-going, high-spirited dad remained my favorite parent.

I spoke to Gabriel occasionally. Pleasant, but strained talks. He was still surviving the recession by working far from Houston, and I was still trying to get over him.

By October, Phil was dropping matrimony hints. The man was faster than a rabbit in more ways than just sex. "I think it's time we discuss marriage." He scratched his bushy, dark moustache.

"It's a social union or binding contract between people in love."

"I know the general definition." Phil raked fingers through his course hair, continuing his irritating addiction to personal grooming. "And it's time for us to make this legal."

"Legal?" I reached over in primate gesture, pretending to pick a flea from his neck. "Like I keep telling you, I'm in love with someone else."

"Well, my love for you can overcome anything. And marrying me is a sure-fire way to stop your foolish sentimentality for Gabriel."

I almost laughed out loud. Even if his plan included attaching a slow drip methaqualone IV to my wedding ring finger, marriage to him could *never* make me forget my true love. Phil was brilliantly book smart, but stupendously street stupid.

༄

"Hey Blondie, got any Cokes at your place?"

"How about Tab?" I asked casually, my heart beating wildly.

"I need the real thing. Handed to me by the most beautiful woman alive."

"Phony flattery might sway floozies at truck stops, but I'm not letting you come over."

"It's not phony flattery. And I really need to see you."

"And I really need to say *au revoir*."

"Yeaaah? Well you can speak French in person, I'm coming over."

"You can't do that! I'm involved with someone."

"So am I, but I'd love to see you again. For old times' sake."

"Old times' sake my ass, Gabriel."

"See ya in a few."

Nikki got hustled through her bath and put to bed in record time.

I opened the door and Gabriel stood back, slowly shaking his head. "Maybe my standards are low, but I like what I see."

"No kidding you have low standards, but I'm living nicely without your insolent mouth," I flat-out lied. I wanted his mouth and all other marvelous body parts he possessed.

"My insolent mouth," he drawled. "You should talk."

"Rumor has it I talk too much." I touched the hairy growth on his cheek. "What are you doing hiding your sweet face with a beard?"

"Grew it for winter. . . but talk about sweet faces." He grabbed the front of my blouse, bringing us nose to nose.

"Whoa." I got a whiff of barley and hops. "You've been drinking. How 'bout some coffee?"

"Coke is fine." He moved over to my sofa and lit a smoke. "I only had two Budweisers."

Goosebumps raced up and down my legs as I walked to the fridge to retrieve a Coke I'd kept just for him. Pathetic, I know. Exhaustion laced his voice as he told me about his travels, happenings with his family, and other innocuous subjects. Somehow I got the nerve to ask about the woman in his life. He awkwardly offered vague details about Victoria. Just hearing him say her name made me feel like thumb tacks were trickling down my left ventricle. I interrupted in wobbly voice, volunteering details about Phil as though Gabriel wanted to know. Somewhere mid-sentence, he reached over to shut me up with a kiss. That was all she wrote. For about three hours. I'd forgotten how fabulous five star love making felt. But after his usual smoke and a few kisses, he rolled out of bed and put on his faded jeans.

"You cannot possibly be leaving." I was taken aback.

"I'd love to stay the night." He pulled his Polo shirt over his head while leaving my bedroom. "But I have to leave early tomorrow morning for West Texas."

He had always stayed overnight with me. "I don't believe this!" My face flushed with anger. "All gracious Southern ladies know that if a man doesn't spend the night cuddling and caressing you after he's fucked you, he's not a true gentleman."

"Ah, such language from a Southern lady."

"I'm hardly a debutante school graduate, and picked up most of my language from a particular blond asshole carpenter."

"Either way, your mother would be real proud." He slid a Marlboro into his mouth.

"Oh, I think a few snapshots from 1969 would be enough to fill my mother with pride."

Giving me an "enough said" look, Gabriel slowly moved toward my front door. My wrath diminished and I turned sentimental. "God, I miss your sawdust scent."

"Yeaaah? I'm sure you're accustomed to men wearing expensive suits and exotic after shave."

"Oh, pleeease!" I straightened his shirt collar. "You still don't know me like I know you."

"That's probably a fact and not a fiction. You know me better than anyone does, but you're still an elusive butterfly."

I wanted to pull him tightly against me and never let him leave my side. I *did* know him. But I wouldn't let him see my weak side. "You should marry that girl." I brushed his blond hair from his forehead with my fingertips. "Since she's willing to deal with your arrogant attitude and your traipsing about the country."

"Well, you should marry that guy. Grab onto anyone willing to put up with you walking around on tiptoes and living in dreamland." He quickly kissed my forehead.

"So." I stepped back. "This really was our 'one last time' for old times' sake."

"What do you think, Blondie?"

"That's between me and my shrink."

He distorted his face, like "shrink" a worse term than any of his four letter words. Then he broke into song. "*Yester-me. . .*"

"*Yester-you*," I said in whiney voice.

"*Yesterday*," he concluded, inching closer.

"Still using lyrics to say what you can't." I took a significant breath.

He pulled me tightly to him. His lips were warm and his kiss was slow, as though he were memorizing it for the long trip ahead. Then he walked out my door seemingly moving in slow motion, walking backwards down the stairs, and blowing kisses until he was out of sight. Honking his horn twice, he knew and I knew. No matter how much time or space came between us, it wouldn't alter our feelings for each other. The time for us wasn't now and it seemed marriage to righteous others might wipe out all guilt, absolve all former sins.

∽

"You win some, you lose some." Beau called to say *The Grapevine* was failing.

"I'm sorry to hear it."

"Don't worry, baby. I'll open another club once things improve on the home-front."

"Yikes. What's wrong?"

"No real problem. Celeste just needs me," he said with a laugh. "She can't keep a maid, and I'm a decent floor sweep and expert dishwasher with time on my hands."

"As long as you're doing okay, I'm happy. Now, I've gotta dash. This new guy is determined we go see the movie, *The Way We Were.*"

"I know you're not crazy about Phil, but going out'll keep your mind off Gabriel."

"The movie's premise sounds as enticing as a bone marrow transplant, but Mr. Burt Reynolds lookalike bribed me with the promise of Milk Duds."

"Then savor those chocolates. And come see me at *The Grapevine* soon, baby."

Phil glanced at his reflection in the theatre window as he escorted me inside, where he bought me a huge box of Milk Duds, then foolishly selected back row seats as though romance was in his near future. My only emotions were tears due to Redford's resemblance to Gabriel and the movie's depressing ending.

"You gotta get over that carpenter guy." Phil attempted to comfort me (or maybe cop a lubricious feel) as we left the theatre. "So it's about time we get married."

He went into overdrive for what seemed hours, trying to convince me marriage to him would eradicate memories of Gabriel. Oh, how I wanted to believe him, but this was like telling me blow jobs were the solution to global hunger. A revelation that could make major changes in the world as we know it—if only it were plausible.

"No sense in dragging things out. I'm ready to make you my wife, immediately."

I felt lightheaded. And not in a giddy way. "Immediately?"

"Three, maybe four months. No longer. I've got you and don't intend to lose you."

He didn't have me, but was damn sure wearing me down as he yammered on. I'm not sure if it was my emotional instability, my need to get Gabriel out of my bloodstream, filibustering by Phil that would have made our state legislatures envious, or the bulge in his wallet, but at that chaotic moment, I agreed to marry him. "Okay, fine."

Phil hugged me. "This calls for a drink!"

I clinched my jaw tightly to keep from recanting my eloquent, "Okay, fine." acceptance speech. Being drug free doesn't always assure prudent decision making. Here I was sober as hell and agreeing to marry a man who found mathematical equations erotic.

∞

For weeks *The Grapevine* phone rang without answer, so eventually I drove by to see Beau. The workmen inside said they were remodeling for Mr. Tabor and knew nothing of a man named Beau Duvalé. I cussed myself for procrastinating. He was under Celeste's thumb now.

Feeling more lost every day without Beau to talk to, in a few weeks during a discombobulated state of mind I frantically coordinated arrangements to marry Phil at his family's Piney Point hacienda. Another nonmensa moment. My quickly planned event yielded four hundred guests who showed up to celebrate and witness me getting beyond swirling drunk. Luckily intoxication got me a two day pass on consummating our vows.

Within weeks I learned from Gloria that Gabriel had married during the same week. My heart plunged when I heard that news. Didn't matter that I had wed; my reason for rushing down the aisle was to get over him, get over us, get on with living. I equated marriage to Phil with financial security, while he equated it to having sex on a regular basis. Phil had his definition of regular and I had mine. Viewing Pioneer II's pictures of Jupiter with its large moon Callisto was twice as stimulating, and a gajillion times more memorable than coitus non-gratis with Phil. Once again sex was nothing more than perfunctory, servile motion. Phil was the fourth man with whom I had swapped body fluids, yet the first who seemed to enjoy arguing during the act.

"What's on the menu for breakfast," Phil asked when he walked into the kitchen where I was watching my blender whirl.

"Check with McDonald's." I slapped my home blended cucumber mask onto my face. Two weeks of marriage and Phil had the opposite effect of Gabriel, who never asked, yet kindled some Julia Child instinct that had me happily cracking eggs and browning bacon.

"You don't cook and you hate sex," he shouted.

"Hey, you were the one making fairy tale predictions, not me."

I never volunteered sex, and when Phil insisted, I closed my eyes and tried to imagine he was Gabriel. Even pretending left me grinding enamel off my back molars. Sexual treats were exclusive for you-know-who, so when the topic of oral sex infiltrated our bedroom, I informed Phil there were folks on the seedy side of Westheimer who would happily accommodate.

⁓

"Well, another bass player bit the dust," Delilah informed via phone.

"What happened to Flip?" I grabbed yogurt from my fridge.

"His shock therapy didn't go as planned, so I'm divorcing him."

"Oh, that's sad news for your children."

"Not as sad as living with a man who's pooping his pants more often than our toddler."

I threw my half eaten yogurt into the trash.

"So," Delilah paused for a drag on her cigarette. "I might drop by later with the kids."

"Sure," I said hesitantly. "But let me check with Phil to make sure we don't have plans."

Delilah never called, but showed up with kids only minutes later, ate a week's worth of groceries, and spent an hour irritating the hell out of Phil. "I took a toxic dump in Burt's bathroom and didn't flush," she told me on her way out. Occasionally I appreciated her antics.

The only inkling of marital bliss with Phil came when he pulled strings to assure my best friend a job with his cousin's IT company near Methodist.

131

Said best friend just happened to be Gabriel's sister. Hope and I spent lunch hours dining, shopping and talking about everything but Gabriel. "I'm not going to mention my brother unless you ask," she assured.

"Thank you. That's truly considerate."

"But. . ." she took a sip of tea. "I think you'd like Gabe's new wife, Victoria."

About as much as I'd like the new "daylight savings time" America just put into effect. Not good at faking emotions, I gave Hope a cynical half-smile.

13

Wheel of Fortune made its television premier in January, Saigon surrendered on April 30th—unofficially marking an end to the Vietnam War, and on July 4th, I attended Willie Nelson's annual picnic with 90,000 others in Liberty Hill, Texas. Phil didn't appreciate Willie and stayed home. After I eighty-sixed ice cream from my diet for bikini season, we had zilch in common.

The summer of '75 sizzled while my marriage to Phil fizzled. "Please take me to Marfreless," he pleaded, refusing to drop the subject.

"When Jupiter aligns with Mars," I rejected his pleas for finding the clandestine bar. An unmarked make-out place in Houston's River Oaks area, Marfreless has a reputation for boundless hedonism supposedly taking place in the upstairs area. Phil was not the person I wanted to walk through the blue door with, much less sit around in pitch black darkness and smooch on the couches. His insistence dulled my occasional good moods.

"Fine," I dressed up one Saturday night after a day of his non-stop begging.

My plan to hopefully shut his pie hole once and for all, found us driving around mid-town Houston for hours. Finally I led him to an infamous joint I'd read about in a local rag, with an ambiance poles apart from Marfreless.

"You sure this is it?" Dick head asked.

"Reasonably sure," I lied while leading him into the biker bar.

The door greeter was a one-arm, good looking blonde girl.

"Oh, my god," Phil whispered and nodded toward her disfigurement.

"Hey, Clockarm!" Patrons entering behind us sweetly saluted the pretty greeter. I had read about her fan following and her affection for her Clockarm nickname.

I stepped aside not wanting to be seated, while watching others convivially salute and hug the pretty blonde.

"It's not very dark in here," Phil moaned as though darkness would make me frisky.

"Guess this is the wrong place. But I'm too tired to look elsewhere." I turned and said farewell to Clockarm. Phil stormed out the door. The man had absolutely no sense of humor.

∞

Months passed without hearing from Beau, intensifying my miserable life. Gabriel called occasionally, just to say hello. Even knowing when he was out of town, I still did double takes every time I saw a white Ford Ranger or a blond guy in blue jeans. Nikki was seeing more of Hope and Gloria as they busily planned Hope's August wedding to a handsome stock broker, but when my soon-to-be flower girl returned with news of seeing Gabriel, I changed subjects faster than my mother always had when I tried to talk sex. Hope chose St. Anne's Catholic Church, but confided that Gloria selected everything else including flowers, cake design, and even the wedding gown. Sweet tempered Hope didn't seem nearly as upset as me about Gloria usurping her sacred bridal territory. A bright girl being so easily swayed by her mother annoyed me, but by August I jumped back on Hope's happy bandwagon. Obviously Gabriel would be at his sister's wedding.

Nikki and I arrived at the church early, so she could get dressed with other members of Hope's bridal party.

"Oh, Cherie," Gloria called out. "This is Gabe's wife, Victoria."

I managed a polite greeting of "Hello."

"It's so nice to finally meet you!" Gabriel's new wife greeted me with a big beauty contestant smile. "I've heard wonderful things about you!" Smile. Smile. Smile.

She kept rambling in a voice so sugary sweet, I almost puked. Tall, slender, and impeccably dressed right down to her brightly polished dagger-red fingernails, Victoria looked like she was born to model designer fashions: walking confidently while radiating a condescending air. Her shiny chestnut brown hair fell loosely around her shoulders and surrounded a gorgeous porcelain complexion from which honey colored eyes looked out on the world like guardians of a great treasure. Doubtful she'd be shopping at those new Walmarts opening up all over Texas. "Gabriel's getting here a little late," she flashed another huge smile, showing off her perfect teeth. "He's coming back home from Phoenix." Her eyes actually sparkled. *Really! How lucky can one girl be?*

Gabriel's not being there didn't seem to faze her. During pre-ceremony activities as everyone busily prepared for the event, you could hear Victoria's laughter bouncing off ceilings and walls. Vivacious was the only word to describe her. I wanted to shave her head bald.

Seated three pews in front of Phil and me, Victoria kept glancing at the church entrance for late arriving Gabriel. The ceremony was approaching vow exchanges when the church door opened. I took a quick glimpse, and turned just as Gabriel walked up the aisle. In a flash his eyes met mine. My heart pounded wildly. Phil nudged me and asked if this was Gabriel. I indicated yes with a nod. Had he noticed our eye contact or simply recognized him from my descriptions? Gabriel and I linked eyes again after Hope and Troy made their way back down the aisle. This time Phil definitely noticed. Ask me if I cared. Gabriel looked delicious.

During the reception, with glasses clinking toasts to the bride and groom, Gabriel and I unexpectedly ended up alone in the hallway. Walking in opposite directions, as we passed each other Gabriel moved so near me I could feel his breath. I inhaled his unforgettable scent (sans sawdust), drawing in deeply to savor the moment. Fearing our bodies might touch, I moved slightly to one side, almost tripped, and nervously glanced back toward other guests.

"You look beautiful," he whispered as his thumb flew auto-pilot against my cheek.

Took my breath away.

Then Hope appeared out of nowhere, grabbed my hand, and led me away. What she said is still a mystery. All I remember was seeing her mouth move and hearing words echo around me as I looked back at Gabriel, who was leaning against the wall.

Thirty minutes later, we wound up sitting directly across from each other in a room crowded with others. Gabriel stared at me. I attempted to get my pulse under control, as he wordlessly mouthed, "Let's talk," and tilted his face toward the hall. Spontaneously nodding in agreement, I slowly stood.

"Ouch," I yelped in response to a jab against my waist.

"You two are asking for trouble," said groom Troy.

"And if you and Gabe think you're going unnoticed, you're dead wrong," Hope added. "So, please behave. Phil might be oblivious to your body language, but Victoria won't be."

My butt went back into a chair.

Gabriel and I attempted to inconspicuously flirt throughout the evening, but every time he came near me, he was whisked away by Victoria or some other annoying individual. Nikki wrapped herself around him on occasion and each time I warned her not to wrinkle his suit, I envied her position. And every time I walked into the same room with him, I clumsily tripped. "Champagne," I assured. "Yeaaah?" He grinned, knowing damn well it wasn't the bubbly.

Phil made a lame excuse to leave early, and before the engine warmed he leaped into commentary about Gabriel. "He doesn't look anything like Redford," he barked, sardonically.

"Are you saying he's not handsome?"

"He's okay, but he's certainly not God's gift to women like you say." Phil adjusted the rearview mirror to gaze at himself.

"I never said any such thing."

"Well that's how it comes across when you talk about him."

Took every ounce of will power I had to keep from bringing statistics, measurements, and League Standings into this argument. Instead, I held my tongue, trying to enjoy the ride home by recalling some of Gabriel's impressive stats.

"And those clothes he was sporting didn't appear to have designer labels," Phil continued.

"He's secure with himself. Unlike you, he doesn't need Calvin Klein for validation."

Phil groomed his God-awful beard in the mirror for the hundredth time, before leaping into dissertation about why the Catholic Church was no longer relevant in the twentieth century. Pleeease! I tried tuning him out, but he switched subjects and began loudly announcing my miscellaneous shortcomings. After he used the words narcissistic and oedipal together in a sentence one time too many, I interrupted him by saying I was hyper-oxygenating and would vomit all over the car seats if he didn't shut up. I jacked up the radio volume as Nikki and I sang along with Carl Douglas to *Kung Fu Fighting*. Oh-oh-oh-oh.

That brief encounter with Gabriel at the wedding got replayed in my head a million times. I was rewinding my mental video when the phone rang on Christmas Eve, smack in the middle of Phil's family gift exchange. I grabbed a phone in the foyer.

"Thank goodness you answered," Gabriel said. "I didn't wanna have to hang up on Burt."

I was speechless.

"You know I love you, Cherie. And I know you love me. Christ, we'll always be in love, but I guess there's nothing we can do about it."

I looked into the living room at those observing me with puzzled expressions, and cleverly responded, "Oh."

Having deciphered each other's verbal utterances for years, Gabriel interpreted my open syllable as total agreement and continued professing undying love. Okay. He'd had a few glasses of holiday spirit. But his words were fact and not fiction. "Thanks for wishing us a merry Christmas, Gloria," I lied to deceive onlookers. "I love you too."

Returning to the festivities, I faked enthusiasm as Phil handed me my annual gift. A bottle of Joy parfum and the usual "I put no thought whatsoever into this," Sak's Fifth Avenue, thousand dollar gift certificate. I pulled on my happy mask, trying to hide thoughts of how special the holidays would have been with my carpenter. Like him, I got drunk and melancholy.

∽

"Victoria got a secretarial job at an accounting firm near Methodist, so she's joining us today," Hope casually mentioned during lunch.

I felt nauseated. Breaking bread with the woman who had *my* man seemed unpalatable, but I tried to out smile her when she walked in.

"It's absolutely thrilling to see you again," Victoria greeted, like I was someone famous.

"You too," was all I could manage. My mouth was going to hurt like hell from fake smiling.

Surprisingly enough, Victoria's boisterous personality made me comfortable. Until she started talking about life with Gabriel. Everyone in the restaurant probably heard the thunderous beating of my tell-tale heart.

Hope began frequently having lunch with her hubby while Victoria and I lunched or shopped together. I missed Hope, but Gabriel's wife number two and I soon became friends. Okay. Maybe *friends* is an exaggeration, since I constantly fantasized about slipping her some magic potion to make her uglier than Eleanor Roosevelt, and she openly envied my marriage to money. Sure, to naïve small town girls like Victoria and me, Phil was considered wealthy, but I learned right away that the rich subdivide into the haves and the have mores, and Phil barely slid under the haves line. Victoria often complained of boredom, saying Gabriel's work kept him out of town. I never complained when Phil worked late to pursue advancement. Time without him was glorious.

"Got another promotion," Victoria announced during our weekly lunch.

"Good for you!"

"My raise should be on next month's paycheck." She lightly brushed a linen napkin across her red lips. "You've been so great about buying lunch and giving me money to send Gabe's girls. I really appreciate it and just want you to know that soon, I'll pick up all our lunch tabs."

"Not to worry." I plunked Phil's credit card on the table.

Her constant bragging about big promotions and raises, followed by borrowing money from me happened so often, I almost suggested she pursue a career as a professional fund raiser. Victoria knew my feelings of guilt about Gabriel's daughters and didn't seem the least bit uncomfortable each time she asked to borrow three or four hundred dollars to send them in Phoenix. That cash came from my savings and I doubted Victoria would repay me. Giving money for Lauren and Skylar seemed the least I could do for them.

It must have been my masochistic side that allowed me to continue my Chinese Water Torture lunches with Victoria. Despite her talk of raises, she hadn't yet paid for one meal. She slowly dripped verbal acid into the soft spot of my brain, which swiftly penetrated my heart, as she discussed life with Gabriel. Her words always left a powerful sting and my voice usually wavered as I stammered some asinine response while cringing. Still, I customarily picked up the check as though it had been the most fabulous event of my day. Maybe I just needed to hear every tiny detail about Gabriel, even those including her.

"Guess what?" Victoria asked excitedly at our weekly lunch.

"You got another promotion," I said, biting into a mushroom and trying to avoid the beams of happiness shooting from her eyes.

"Something better," she said, pushing her plate aside. "I'm pregnant!"

Only women who are hopelessly in love with someone else's husband can understand the sick feeling that overcame me. I almost choked on my salad. "Congratulations," I said with the most sincerity I could muster.

"Isn't it the greatest?" She asked, and then looked my way. "Oh, my gosh. Your mouth is bleeding!"

I tasted blood. Must've bitten my lip fighting back tears. "It is the greatest!" I blotted my mouth and signaled our waiter

"Are you alright, Cherie? You look pale."

"I'm fine, but woke up with a nasty headache this morning. Maybe I'll try to see my doctor. But congratulations again!" I picked up our tab and rushed to the cashier.

Doctor, indeed. I had been "without therapist" for awhile, so my search for a new one would soon commence. I had to get rid of all feelings for Gabriel—even if it meant hiring an exorcist.

14

I couldn't locate my beloved Beau, yet couldn't lose the ubiquitous Delilah. Although she quit Methodist and moved northwest near Cypress to work as a waitress in some country western honky-tonk, she found time for me.

"I had to wear falsies to pass my job interview," Delilah said after an unannounced visit that included a drag along with her kids and new boyfriend.

"Whatever makes your heart happy." I closed the door behind them, checking out her new look. She'd gone instant hillbilly with heavily teased hair, magenta rouge and lipstick, and donned a gaudy cowgirl outfit with gaudy cowgirl boots. "I see you're still sporting sizable cups there, Calamity Jane."

"You betcha!" She latched onto her latest lover, a rugged character wearing tattered jeans and a battered wide-rim western style hat. A contrast to her usual musician type. "This is Scooter."

Delilah's three-year-old flew past us and onto my sofa where she tested the resilience of my cushions.

I took a risk and shook Scooter's hand, without wearing latex gloves.

About the time toddler Buzz started whining because his sister Bitzy wouldn't let him join her bounce-a-thon, cowboy wannabe Scooter started reiterating, "Don't let the bedbugs bite" and "Don't take any plug nickels" like Houston was overrun with bedbugs and street corner hustlers trying to pass off plug nickels.

"Sex with this buckin' bronco is wilder than a rodeo and makes me freaking moan 'til the cows come home!" Delilah wrapped her arms around him and boasted. Her distasteful depiction aroused an inappropriate kiss from Scooter.

It was a sad thing for children to see. His tongue went deep. Thankfully before the duo punctured each other's lungs, Bitzy crashed into my coffee table and began screaming. Buzz harmonized with an earsplitting demand for Beanie Weenies. I was fresh out of that delicacy. Delilah finally disengaged from Scooter's tongue and attempted to control her children by whacking their rear ends. Thought I'd never get rid of them.

༆

A brilliant, multi-dimensional pharmacist joined the Methodist staff, and fortunately Patrice found me interesting enough to befriend. Almost everyone seemed magnetized by this gregarious, book smart, street savvy, ebony haired, smoky eyed lady whose infectious laugh even evoked smiles from pharmacy curmudgeon, Ed. Studying for a degree in corporate law, Patrice had varied interests, but I was intrigued by her comprehension of metaphysics. She urged me to continue my education, and inspired my enrollment in an evening paralegal class.

Other than spending more time with Patrice and less time with Hope and Gloria, my life revolved around Nikki, whose life revolved around friends and Cousin Jimmy. At age ten Little Miss Priss was mature for her age, an honor student who excelled in Literature, and much more logical than me at her age. When I decided to enlighten her about the facts of life, she listened intently and then asked, "Exactly what attire is appropriate for such an event?" before announcing she was going horseback riding with friends.

I almost fell off my chair when I saw the name Beauregard Phillipe Duvalé in Methodist's pharmacy care charts. Not a common name. I phoned the room. "Oh, my long-lost beloved," I gushed. "What are you doing in the hospital?"

"Baby, is that you?" Beau asked.

"Yes. I can't believe you're only steps away from me. What's wrong?"

"Been having some shortness of breath and chest pains. Nothing major. And can probably be cured with a hug from you."

"I'll be up in five minutes."

"Baby," Beau opened his arms for an embrace when he saw me at the doorway.

"Of all the hospitals, in all the towns, in all the world, you walk into mine," I doctored a famous *Casa Blanca* line. "Thank goodness!"

We talked a mile a minute, catching up on old news. Beau had divorced his first wife Celeste and remarried a second younger woman—who had recently divorced him. He'd lost his highly profitable *Night Owls* club to second wife Lola, and opened a giant sports bar in Sugar Land, a small city southwest of Houston.

"This new club has built-in aquariums, dart throwing areas, ping pong and pool tables, small dance floor, band area, and fifteen TV sets for sporting events. It's my first sports club, so I named it *Beau's Place.* Maybe having my name attached will keep future wives from getting it."

I fluffed his pillow, trying to make him comfy. Then he brought up the subject of Gabriel. "I always thought y'all were one couple destined to be together."

My heart sank. "Let's change subjects. "Have ya had any bedbug bites lately?"

Beau looked at me like I needed medication. When he told me about selling the beautiful mahogany bar from the Jewel Box to a local restaurant owner, I felt somewhat melancholy, but when he started talking about some of the girls and incidents from the club, I got panicky. Far too many times I'd awakened in a cold sweat after nightmares of being on that little round stage, and it took days to retrieve my self-confidence.

"Remember that black haired girl I fired on the spot, when I found out she was turning tricks in the parking lot?"

"Gypsy," I quietly answered.

"Yeah, that was her. Anyway, she snookered some sap into buying her a small garden shop right down the street from *Beau's Place.* I saw her when I was buying plants to decorate the club and diffuse the smoke smell."

"Oh," I responded, worried this might turn into a lengthy tale.

"She cussed like the devil while telling me about using her sexual prowess to entice the dim-wit into forking over even more money for gardening lessons. Hell, her brain was stuck in neutral, so she had to connive men with her body."

Please be quiet! I wanted to say, but kept my mouth closed.

"Place looked nice for a while, but about the time I finished renovating the club, there were more brown plants out front than green ones. So much for those horticulture classes. I passed by last week and her little shop was belly-up."

"Reminds me of a Dorothy Parker quote." I lightly stroked his arm.

Beau nodded. *"You can lead a whore to culture, but you can't make her think."*

"One of America's greatest writers." I attempted to stick with conservative topics.

Beau considered happenings from the Jewel Box just more of life's entertaining adventures, but the last thing I needed was hospital employees overhearing details about my past. Besides being a secret I wanted concealed forever, if Phil learned that tidbit of trivia, he would divorce me quicker than you could say sequined pasties and white go-go boots.

"Always liked Mrs. Parker, but I'm still a McMurtry fan. His latest book, *Terms of Endearment* is a doozey. I've set it aside for you and know you'll love it. The primary setting is Houston, even though McMurtry failed to mention any of my clubs—especially the Jewel Box."

"What kind of writer is he, not to mention you and your honky-tonks?"

"A smart one, baby."

Seeing Beau's distinctive black cowboy boots beside his bed, I remembered times Gabriel and I went to breakfast with him after hours. His boots made a powerful sound when he walked, and once the tab came, Beau pulled hundred dollar bills from them. "Great boots, Beau."

"Paul Wheeler custom-made these ten years ago and they're still so comfortable I could sleep in 'em. His son Dave wants me to try their flashier designs, but I'll leave bright colors for the younger set. Gotta love that cowboy boots are the modern man's high heels." Beau chuckled.

I reached over and kissed his cheek. "See you later, but I'm sending my friend to lessen your boredom. I think you'll like her."

"Oh, baby, you're not trying to fix me up, are you?"

"Never. I just adore both of you and think you should meet. Now, swear you won't mention my go-go days to Patrice."

"I won't. But you've got to embrace your past one of these days."

144

"One of these days, I just might."

"Might what?" Patrice entered his room.

"Complete the stack of work on my desk," I said before introducing Patrice and Beau.

Patrice returned to the pharmacy in high spirit. "I'm awed by Beau's *bonhomie,* and his sincerity. He kissed my hand in gentlemanly French fashion. Not many white men his age would touch a black woman—much less kiss their hand."

"Beau's a special soul."

"Before I left, he asked me to watch after you."

"That's my spiritual guide." I smiled. "But I worry he needs someone watching after him."

"He'll be fine. I intuit he's surrounded by people he guided in the past."

"Well, I'll always be there for him." My eyes misted.

Beau stopped by the pharmacy after his release, and albeit dressed in simple slacks, white shirt and tasteful suspenders, co-workers commented on his debonair appearance and movie star swagger. Young and old women swooned. He handed me a business card for recently opened *Beau's Place* and made me promise to bring Nikki by. "I'm counting on seeing you two soon, baby." Beau's voice boomed as he headed toward the elevator. There wasn't another man on earth who could call me "Baby" and produce a smile so heartfelt it could light my face for hours. When I walked around the corner to my stack of paperwork, a *Jack of Clubs* card lay across it. Damn, Beau was good!

Sales of Elvis Presley records soared past the two million mark within days of his death, and it was rumored the king's funeral cost forty seven thousand big ones. But life with Phil rolled along, while our marital rhythm continued like a bad song playing on the radio. One of those tunes you think you'll never get out of your head until you die. We slept in the same bed; however I mastered the fine art of faking sleep comas. Out of bed we continually engaged in an ongoing battle of caustic carnage, fighting about everything and nothing. I couldn't stand the sight of him—much less his touch, and after painting our bedroom every therapeutic color available, I claimed his snoring stole my sleep, and then moved into the guest room. His requests for conjugal visits were denied. Even marriages with tremendous love have problems, so the demise of our loveless one was no surprise.

∽

Putzing about in my flower bed, I barely heard the phone ringing over Nikki's blaring stereo. Off with my gardening gloves as I walked inside to answer while my ten-year-old sang *Rock And Roll All Nite* at the top of her lungs along with Kiss. My preppy kid loved hard-rock.

"Hey, Blondie. I had a boy!" Gabriel proudly announced.

I couldn't force even one syllable from my lips.

"Did you hear? I had a son."

"Congratulations," I cheerfully managed, while demonic creatures did cartwheels in my belly.

"I just wanted you to know. He's healthy and looks just like me. Why don't you bring Nikki out to the house so y'all can see him?"

"I'd love to. And as soon as Gloria or Victoria invites us, we'll stop by. Congratulations on your new son."

Gabriel was elated. I was ambiguous. I was happy he had a son, but thought about the son I once dreamed of having with him.

From that call forward, I kept busy with Nikki and evening classes, which wasn't easy since Phil and I were constantly performing medleys from *Who's Afraid of Virginia Woolf*. The primrose path Phil led me down and I feebly followed, was overrun with thorns and stinkweed, so in January we began divorce proceedings. Mother called long distance insisting I should be more giving, more tolerant, more subservient to men, yada, yada, yada. She ended by rattling a quote about a sharp tongue being the only tool that grows keener with constant use. Thank God it was her dime.

Fortunately, Beau and Patrice were always available to help me maintain a modicum of sanity while I went through a chaotic divorce with Phil, who would argue with his pet rock. I took no money from our joint savings, no home equity, no furniture or art purchased together, and even returned my wedding ring, but apparently Phil wanted a few vials of my blood as keepsakes.

"You and Nikki are spending a few weeks at my townhome until you find your own place," Patrice insisted.

"Are you sure you can handle a pre-pubescent kid under foot that long?"

"I adore Nikki, and think she adores me. She confides in me on occasion."

"Uh oh. We're beginning to butt heads, so no telling what comes out of her mouth."

"I'll never repeat, but you're lucky, Cherie. Now pack your bags and get over here."

"But you're studying for bar exams."

"And neophyte Nikki can be my quiz master. I thrive on pressure and adrenalin."

She didn't have to ask twice. I removed Phil's name from my personal savings account, took mine and Nikki's clothing and personal items, jumped into my El Dorado, and left Phil with a beam of happiness surrounding me.

Living with Patrice proved two people who instantly connected on a spiritual level, hardly knew each other. Nikki and I arrived on a Saturday morning, which meant an introduction to *Soul Train* and mandatory dance lessons. I attempted moves that worked muscles previously unknown to me. Almost threw out my back. In thirty days we discussed background differences, racism of every nationality, and social obligation. We laughed and cried, realizing it would take more than our personal friendship to change world attitudes.

"I'm going to miss you both," Patrice said, but hugged Nikki tighter than she did me as we left to move into our own home.

Unfortunately I saw Phil's mug every day at the hospital. After working at Methodist for five years, the time to look for a new job had commenced.

15

In April, my dad called to wish me a belated thirty-something birthday. He could never remember my exact age. The happy lilt in his voice made me smile, even though his jokes about my aging were brief. He rolled into "world expert" mode, offering solutions for the recent oil spill polluting the Gulf of Mexico and Atlantic oceans, before predicting serious problems for the US as a result of Iran voting to become an Islamic Republic. On the local front, he insisted I follow the career of US House of Representatives member, Ron Paul, the former Lake Jackson OB/GYN doctor. I tried to talk about me, but his listening abilities were hampered by something in his bloodstream. Dad was an avid fan of most music by native Texans, but when he turned his radio window-shattering loud for Meat Loaf's *Two Out of Three Ain't Bad* it was obvious Dad was hanging with Jack Daniels while Mother was out stocking up on home goods. *Bat Out of Hell*, indeed. Lucky for me, Patrice rang the doorbell, offering my excuse to end Dad's call.

An only child whose parents were long deceased, Patrice asked me to attend her distant cousin's funeral, wanting my companionship and saying I would appreciate the experience.

"I'd better clue you in, before we head out." Patrice looked inside my fridge. "Black funerals are like huge family reunions." She curled into my overstuffed chair with a huge box of leftover Valentine chocolates she found. "Relatives from every state in the union will show up ready to party like its New Year's Eve."

"Party?"

"You know, grilling, eating, drinking, dancing, and singing before and after services."

"White people do similar things, Patrice."

"I've attended several white funerals, and never once seen a coffin mourner." Patrice munched on her second dark Bordeaux. I loved how she embraced her body, eating sweets whenever she pleased, not just on special occasion—and especially not out of stress, like me.

"Death is painful for the living." I reached over, snagged a raspberry truffle, and popped it into my mouth. "All nationalities mourn, Patrice. Some just do so quieter than others." Guilt crept in, filling my head with god-awful visions of truffle induced ass dimples.

"Showing grief for the deceased is Old World—and I can assure you my kin hired professional mourners to attend and do their thing. But upbeat, spiritual music somewhat counteracts the whooping, hollering, passing out, and flinging of bodies over and occasionally into the coffin."

"Sounds like fun!" I grabbed my purse.

"Just don't feel obligated to buy if anyone claiming to be my dearest relative tries to hawk their latest album. Well-heeled blondes are perceived as easy marks by con artists."

Patrice displayed reverent grief during the service, but I found myself in awe of people unabashedly showing sorrow for the passing of a loved one. And I partied with everyone else.

On the drive home, my kindred spirit and I chatted about my fear of transitioning from Methodist to the Ray and McCreight law firm.

"Why not try a female psychologist for a change?"

Wow. Apparently I wasn't the feminist I thought, since this idea never crossed my mind. Lady Freudina, here comes your next head case.

◦◦

I actually liked my new therapist. She promptly advised me against intimate relationships with men, especially attorneys. She didn't deem me emotionally ready to play with big boys, and said lawyers she knew rarely played in honorable fashion. I liked her, but I wasn't a Stepford Wives patient. Before you could say strobe lights and disco fever, I was doing the hustle with Randall, a friend of an attorney. Close, but no counsel.

Investment banker Randall was a tall yet chunky, fair haired Texan who lived up to his introductory line, "What I don't have in looks I make up for in personality." He owned a couple of deep dimples that grooved his cheeks, but I was a bit leery of charismatic men after watching news accounts of Reverend Jim Jones persuading nine hundred cult members to join him in Guyana for poison punch. Still, after Phil's incessant insults Randall's compliments had me spellbound.

Randall wore Stetson hats similar to those worn by the cast of *Dallas,* and never went anywhere without his boot-size cellular phone. He introduced me to Eggs Benedict, Oysters Rockefeller, Cartier jewelry, Judith Leiber handbags, Bob Mackie clothing, and sad but true, New York discos. I learned to shake my groove thing a bit better than I had on that tiny Jewel Box stage, but Tina Turner's shimmy queen title wasn't in jeopardy. Randall always arrived for dates with gifts ranging from Fauchon chocolates to Rolex watches. Occasionally he included Nikki in our evenings of elegant dining and lavish shopping sprees, insisting she should become accustomed to the finer things in life. I didn't want him spoiling her, but I was busy getting accustomed to those things myself.

"You're all grown up." I shook Gilles hand. He was tending bar for his dad at Beau's Place on weekends. Beau claimed "pre-college experience," but old wise one was utilizing his strapping, handsome son to bring in female fans.

"Nice to see you," Gilles said, obviously not remembering me from his youth.

"You too." I had to catch my breath. What a gorgeous man he'd grown into.

"Be sure to bring Nikki tomorrow." Beau handed me directions to his new digs.

"She wouldn't miss it. She's a sappy Vinny Barbarino, John Travolta fan.

"Well, I hope she's lucky enough to see and talk to him."

"I'll let you guys get back to work." I leaned across the bar, gave Beau a peck on the cheek, and waved at Gilles who was busy entertaining a troop of young ladies.

We visited Beau at 2016 Main, a swanky high-rise in downtown Houston, hoping to see stars while they shot scenes for *Urban Cowboy*. Nikki never spotted Travolta, but we got a glimpse of Texan Jerry Hall, who was playing one of the Sexy Sisters. Even without celebrity interaction visiting Beau was delightful. And bittersweet. Distance and conflicting schedules would take a chunk out of our time together.

Patrice accepted an in-house counsel position with a law firm in Manhattan—without consulting *moi*. In her desire to see the world, she only applied to large firms offering travel. I dreaded her May departure. My summer of '79 would definitely lack close female friendships. Unlike some chicks who won't leave home without an entourage of girlfriends, I never easily bonded with those of the feminine persuasion. Go figure.

∽

On my tenth date with Randall as I nibbled pâté de foie Strasbourg truffle at La Colombe d'Or, he mentioned his upcoming trip to the Orient (where he traveled often), before reaching across the table, taking my hand, looking into my eyes, and murmuring through perfectly capped teeth, "You look like a Bottecilli Angel. Not only are you gorgeous, you're something I think could be my everything, so no place but in the middle of that is where I want to be."

A well rehearsed line if I ever heard one, but I gave him an A for timing and delivery.

"I'll miss you while I'm in Japan." He slowly stirred ice in his whiskey on the rocks. "*Ay ishete imasu.*"

"Pardon?"

"That's Japanese for I love you," he whispered across the table.

I was surprised he hadn't murmured the Japanese translation of *Love to Love You Baby* since Donna Summer's song was ritual background music he played to enhance lovemaking. I didn't know Japanese for "You're interesting and wealthy, but you're not Gabriel," so I flirtatiously shook my long hair and said we should get home before Nikki violated the building code by cramming too many friends inside our place.

Time spent with Randall meant less time with Beau or even Hope, who was in marriage counseling after several squabbles with Troy. Conn claimed the newlywed problems were mother-in-law influenced—something Hope wouldn't dare admit. Instead, Troy's happy ass would get dragged to therapy until he learned to live with in-law issues. Comply or say bye-bye. Gabriel once claimed Gloria was as conniving as she was charming, and I was beginning to believe his statement might be indeed a fact and not a fiction.

Gloria insisted Nikki and I go with her for a visit to see Gabriel and Victoria's young son at their new home. We arrived just as Gabriel drove up. "Look at that new blue van." Gloria cocked her penciled black eyebrow. "His and Ben's construction business is booming." Gabriel smiled and grabbed Nikki's hand, rushing her inside to show off Luke. I walked behind, sucking up sawdust fumes. Gabriel seemed enthralled with fatherhood. Victoria seemed disenchanted and irritated. Lost sleep and added pounds will do that. Much to Gloria's dismay, I respectfully cut our visit short. And all the way home my mind stayed cluttered with his scent, blue eyes, blond hair, mannerisms, *mere existence*. It was time to step up therapy sessions or consider a lobotomy.

Other than Nikki's melodramatic, smart mouth pre-teen behavior exasperating the heck out of me, things were running relatively smooth in my life. New relationship, new therapist, new job. So why wasn't I happy? Maybe it was Gloria's relentless calls, insisting Gabriel was unhappy in his marriage. I regaled her about life with Randall being grand, until she told me to stop my charade because she knew I was still in love with her son. Two days later, said son called. "Hey girl, I saw Chevy Chase impersonating you on *Saturday Night Live.*"

"I think he was impersonating former President Ford."

"Yeaaah? Well, it sure looked like he was mimicking you."

"Believe it or not, I don't stumble or trip around anyone but you, Wiseass."

"Hey, if you're gonna talk crassly, I'll hang up."

"Oh, pleeease! I thought vulgarity was an aphrodisiac to you. I guess you've become virtuous with old age."

"What do you think?"

My therapist's words to let go of him and our past history, and Gloria's words that he and I belonged together were clashing in my brain. "Actually I think I shouldn't be talking to you. Take care of yourself, Gabriel." I forced myself to hang up the phone, thinking how pleased my therapist would be. Of course, she had also suggested I stay the hell away from his family.

∽

With Hope and Troy in therapy, I rarely saw her, and saw Gloria only when fetching her youngest. She and Hope had been so generous to tend Nikki, I wanted to reciprocate in the child care arena. Conner O'Quinn had turned drugstore cowboy and taken to wearing pointy toed, roach killer boots, western shirt complete with pearl snaps, tight jeans, and a belt buckle the size of Texas. He irritated preppy Nikki something fierce.

"Gonna take care of me again this summer?" Conn asked.

For several years I had watched him while Gloria and Hope traveled to Tahiti for ten days, courtesy of Gloria's job. She worked for a travel agency and always won the annual competition, thus whisked Hope off to their favorite hideaway.

"I think I've told you 'yes' a hundred times, Conn." Even when Gloria wasn't traveling, Conn called often, asking me to chauffer him somewhere or other.

"Darlin' I'm just making sure. I don't get to see you often enough."

"Ha," Nikki said as we drove away from the theatre where we'd watched *Caddyshack*. About twice a month we took Conn to the movies or hauled his butt around Houston, giving Gloria a break.

"Darlin' can you please buy me a Coca-Cola? Please?" Conn begged me to stop.

"You guzzled two at the movies," Nikki reminded him.

"I'm gonna die of thirst!" His voice turned adamant.

I pulled into a convenience store to appease him, all the while knowing Gloria wouldn't be thrilled about me getting him jacked up on sugar so late.

Conn stayed inside longer than necessary—likely trying to peek inside a *Playboy*—and had barely returned to my car when his older brother suddenly appeared.

Gabriel hugged Nikki, my central nervous system went berserk, and Conn pitched a hissy fit when Gabriel asked him to sit in the back seat while he talked with me. Conn's hissy soon turned into a full throttle tantrum that made Delilah's kids look docile. Twelve-year-old Nikki temporarily placated the sixteen-year-old prattle mouth while Gabriel and I chatted.

Gabriel told me about forming O'Quinn Brother's Construction with Ben (retired from the Air Force), how business was booming, and how he was busy doing the woodwork he loved. He had several crews on multiple sites, but still worked his hands in wood alongside his employees every day.

"Whooooa!" Conn yelled. "Let's get this show on the road."

Nikki's bored-but-dealing-with-it attitude went instant irritation when Conn began bellowing like a wounded bulldog. "Time to take the Rhinestone Cowboy back to Gloria's ranch house," Nikki raised her voice louder than his.

I nodded in agreement and turned the ignition key. "You better give up your front seat before teeth start flying from the rear," I warned Gabriel.

Just as he leaned into me to say something, Conn opened the car door, practically yanked him out, and bolted back to shotgun position.

"Thank you," Nikki said while waving goodbye to Gabriel.

∽

Chats with Patrice were rare as she traveled with work, and I missed her. From time to time I called Mother, but her homemaking tips and tedious quotes bored me something fierce. And my therapist was getting on my nerves with an undercurrent of advice to avoid the O'Quinn clan, so I dropped out of therapy and once again opted to use Beau as my sounding board. We spoke by phone and occasionally shared lunch, which seemed more beneficial than pricey therapy.

Determined to distance myself from Gabriel's family, I kept busy going places, doing things, and attending lifted pinky soirees with Randall when he wasn't in Japan. Functions where you cheerfully greet haughty people, hug, kiss air, then lie about how marvelous everyone looks while discussing preferences in skiing St. Moritz or Kitzbühel. At Halloween, Randall bought us Batman and Catwoman costumes, and requisitioned a black helicopter to drop us at three different parties. Impressed the hell out of me. Still, it took me a while to get used to his lifestyle and I never got comfortable with it.

Randall took me to Dallas to meet his family. I'm sure my mouth flew open as we drove through gates and around the winding drive, where Rolls-Royces were being buffed by men in uniforms. Ditto as we walked through ornate double doors, opened by a doorman named Albert. I attempted to shift into blasé, sophisticated mode when I looked up at Lalique chandeliers that seemed to propagate as we walked through the hallways. Then I met his mom and aunt. Both were proper and gracious, but as I spoke with them, all sense of sophistication promptly vanished, and just as I was feeling terribly out of place, a servant arrived offering tea. I lifted my pinky and delicately raised an almond crumpet from the silver tray, not daring to breech etiquette by dropping one tiny crumb. Randall's mother sat upright with hands folded across her lap, and a Greta Garbo smile stretched across her lips. I could almost read the thought bubbles over her head. Her ancestors? Breeding? Social status? Finishing schools? Not for my son!

Unlike his family, Randall was totally unpretentious and down to earth, with the only exception being his preference for Dom Perignón's 1939 and 1947 vintages. Highly adaptable, he could comfortably mingle with elite jet setters or those traveling via lesser means, and he enjoyed everything from Willie Nelson's *Crazy* to Bach's fourth *Brandenburg Concerto*. We did simple things like spending weekends aboard his yacht or watching old movies. But mostly, we attended polo matches (yep, they play polo in Texas, y'all), plays, operas, museum openings, or were whisked away by limo or jet to extravagant parties. For one of mediocre upbringing, opulence was an aphrodisiac—and we all know faking orgasms is a female prerogative indoctrinated way back in Biblical times.

"I'm taking you to St. Barts," Randall flashed tickets under my nose.

"Yes!" I hugged him tightly.

"And here's my credit card to buy lots of sexy bikinis, high heels, and whatever else you want."

"Can't I just buy moo-moos when we get there?" I teased. "You're the best!"

When I told Nikki about our trip, she whined. Then her whining advanced into dribbling fake tears for several days. To combat her childish

156

behavior, I brought home one of McDonald's newly introduced "Happy Meals" and put it on the table. "Get jolly, lovey."

"I can't believe you're going on a great vacation without me!" She sobbed real tears into the decorative little box.

I ignored her and she reciprocated by refusing to speak to either of us. I found her silence refreshing. Randall couldn't handle it, and the day of our trip, he gave her five hundred dollars, concert tickets for her and Jim, and countless rock 'n roll albums. This soon became a pattern, with Nikki making out like a bandit, me opposing his actions, and him dismissing my protests. When he wanted extra time with me, he simply handed Nikki money. I became so entwined in grandiose privilege I only glanced at every other white Ford Ranger or blue Chevy van. Still looked at every blond guy in faded blue jeans though.

As much as he loved Texas, Randall's decision to move permanently to Park City, Utah, surprised me. While making a land deal in early 1980, he found his own *Rocky Mountain High* in a fabulous villa nestled just beneath the peaks of Utah's Wasatch Mountain Range. Randall began flying me back and forth on weekends, while proposing marriage. My capricious nature allowed me to be elusive without him asking for reasons. Maybe it was my distinct distaste for cold weather. My need to be near a warm body of water. My insecurities. My inability to feel comfortable around the extremely wealthy. Okay. Fine. I didn't love Rich Boy. And I longed for my blond carpenter.

๛

Hope and Troy called a family meeting to announce they had smoothed out marital troubles even though they'd recently learned Hope couldn't conceive. Troy wanted several kids, so devastated Hope said counseling would continue.

Speaking of counseling, Delilah had gone from country to rock, and stopped by after midnight decked out in a skin tight, silver Spandex jumpsuit, drunk on wine and drowsy from downers. "You gotta meet my new Elvis impersonator boyfriend. He's got a tattoo of Graceland on his penis."

"And my boobs get perkier with age. Delilah, you shouldn't be driving while plastered."

"Ugh," her voice choked as she rushed into my bathroom, stuck her head in the toilet and threw up all kinds of crap through her nose. Door wide open—for my viewing pleasure.

"Please spend the night," I urged.

"No way." She turned and sat to take a whiz that went on forever. I prayed she wouldn't fall face first onto my tile floor.

As she struggled to get back into the snug outfit, I begged her not to get behind the wheel while thoughts of Sean filled my head. She wasn't fit to drive. I felt helpless as she bolted past me to the front door.

"Long live the King!" Delilah yelled loud enough to wake sleeping neighbors. "I'm off to get me a hunk-a, hunk-a, burnin' love."

Praying for her safety, I made a mental note to talk with her about alcohol abuse when she sobered up.

⟳

In the fall of '80 I flew to Park City for a weekend with Randall, and stepped into the tiny private airport, where I was greeted by a glowing Randall, countless bouquets of flowers, a musical quartet, local television crew, and several scripted banners. The banners and Randall were covered with the proposal, "Cherie will you marry me?" Talk about mixed emotion city. It was a daring gesture and typically Randall, but being offered the freedom and happiness that supposedly comes with millions, I had never felt so trapped or mysteriously miserable. Surrounded by onlookers and a television camera, Randall whipped out a six carat diamond ring and popped the big question. Unable to answer, I placed a flimsy kiss on his cheek, and when a female reporter pushed a microphone to my mouth, I barely mustered, "Randall and I will talk about this privately." TV chick looked like she was in the middle of her first televised *faux pas*, but Randall beamed broadly as he pulled me tighter. "That's my girl, always upstaging me."

When we reached Randall's mountain home, I refused to let him carry me over the threshold, and told him I needed time to think. Didn't exactly make for a fun filled weekend, and as usual, I fell back on my Biblical prerogative. By the time I arrived home Sunday night, I was questioning my judgment. This really nice, really wealthy man wanted me. And I wanted my really nice, really wonderful, Gabriel.

Time with Beau went from scarce to quick calls to voice message tag, and finally nada. I was busy, his business was booming and he was spending any free time in Vegas after admitting two failed marriages and a few romantic fiascos made him miss the bright lights and forget-it-all environment. The less I saw him or spoke with him, the more I missed him. And boy did I need his sage advice.

Meanwhile, Randall proposed weekly, and most people encouraged me to marry him. Nikki being his number one proponent. She extolled his kind and generous nature with such accolades you'd have thought he was running for office—but that's what happens when you give a teenager lavish gifts and cash. Or was it possible Nikki felt I should move beyond Gabriel, and Randall was her favorite candidate?

"Randall's aura is too dark," Patrice warned from her trip to France. "And I'm worried about his inability to give you cosmic orgasms."

"I agree with your orgasm sentiment."

"Not to mention he's somewhat chauvinistic for insisting you end your association with Delilah."

"Randall can't stand her," I admitted. Delilah easily annoyed many people.

"That doesn't give him the right to indict someone based on egregious behavior."

"C'mon, Patrice. You're the one who said conversations with Delilah were so low-brow you could barely stay awake."

"Yes, I did. But I've never once suggested you dissolve that friendship."

"True," I admitted. Delilah seemed intent on remaining my friend—so persistent in fact, after too much wine she often joked about revealing my illegal abortion to my new circle of friends. "Be careful in your adventurous travels, my gutsy, spirited friend."

"Be careful in your amorous trials, my whimsical friend. Love you!" She ended the call.

16

Friday nights meant free drinks at the Cadillac Bar courtesy of our boss Arne, but I ducked out early and headed home for some "me" time. With Randall in Park City, I suspected he was the caller ringing my phone off the hook while I attempted to unlock the door.

"Hey Blondie," Gabriel cheerfully greeted. "How was Utah?"

"How'd you know I'd been to the mountains?" My heart fluttered.

"Heard it through the grapevine."

"Oh yeah? Was that grapevine Gloria or Hope? How are you Carpenter Boy?"

"Better, now that I'm talking to you."

He talked about the work he was doing in a house in Kemah, just off Galveston Bay, and sounded absolutely great. Okay. He could've been discussing hemorrhoid remedies and still sounded marvelous. The calm voice with the slow drawl was describing wainscot paneling when my stomach turned to knots. I was dying to see him, but he was still married to Victoria. A heartbreaking state of affairs, if you asked me.

"I'd really like to see you," he said softly. "I'd even let you buy me a Coke."

"How about a Tab?" I waited for his usual response.

"Gotta have the real thing, Blondie. That's why I called you."

"I shouldn't do this." I thumped the phone against my forehead.

"Yeaaah? And I shouldn't ask. But I did and I hope you will. For old times' sake."

"Oh pleeease! I remember the last time you said that."

161

"It won't be like that. We're just good friends."

"Well, that's what friends are for—delivering Coca-Cola to their pals. Just give me directions, and I'll try to swing by tomorrow."

"Try?"

"Yes, try. Something tells me your directions may lead me to the River Styx."

"Yeah." He chuckled. "Just pay the old ferryman and he'll make room for you on a safe rowboat high above the fiery water."

"I hope you get bit in the ass by a three headed dog for lying to me all these years about not knowing Greek Mythology."

"Hey, be nice to me. We'll both probably wind up in Hades one of these days, and you just might need my protection."

"Uh huh," I said. "Keep your nail gun in its holster and tell me how to find this house if you want me driving south."

Jittery as all get out, I scribbled directions and hoped I wouldn't get too lost.

On Saturday I took an Opium bubble bath and dusted in Opium powder, before trying on every casual piece of clothing in my closet. Opting for jeans, cashmere sweater, and Cole Haan loafers, I arrived at the job site in Kemah, but sat in my car a few minutes before timidly walking inside. Gabriel rushed over, greeting me with his confident smile, and looking like a million undervalued dollars. The sight of him caused me to stumble. Dammit! He placed his hand gently against my elbow attempting to steady me. "Still impersonating Gerald Ford?"

"No, Wiseass. I'm channeling for Charlie Chaplin."

"That's Mr. Wiseass, if you don't mind."

"Still trying to dignify your epithet, I see."

"Trying is about as far as I get." He leaned forward and lightly kissed my cheek.

I nervously stepped back. Engulfed by the smell of sawdust flowing from his body, I had forgotten what wondrous emotions his nearness could evoke.

"I was having a sinkin' spell, before I saw you, but I'm wide awake now. Christ, you smell great! Whatcha wearing?"

162

"Opium," I answered. *My forever fragrance beginning now.* He'd never complimented my perfume scent before.

As he stood smiling at me, seemingly oblivious to other workers who were busily working throughout the house, his eyes reflected a luminescence that said "I've missed you." And after years of numbness, I felt sensitivity again. We hadn't been intimately alone since that October night in '73, before each of us married. I shook my head. *Stop remembering.*

"How are Victoria and Luke? And how's small town living?"

He wrinkled his nose. "I love my son and I like living in a small town. Otherwise, I just exist. My house has great potential, but I'm not motivated to renovate it." He held his right hand out and briskly rubbed his thumb across the tips of his four fingers. "So, what've you been up to Blondie?"

"Working at the law firm, running around the country with Randall, trying to keep Nikki in tow, yada, yada, yada."

"You gonna marry Ole Moneybags?"

"I don't know, Gabriel. It just doesn't feel right. Money can't buy love, you know."

"Yeaaah, I know that. I just thought it was prerequisite for you."

"Prerequisite?" I tossed my hair over my shoulder. "Why would you say such a thing?"

"You can't stand there in those overpriced clothes and deny liking money."

"Pleeease, Mr. Sears Roebuck Wash-N-Wear! I only buy expensive clothes and shoes when they're on sale. Most of my paycheck goes direct to savings."

"Can you teach Victoria? Hell, she goes through money faster than congressmen."

"And you my friend, embellish like one."

"I'm serious. She's perceives herself a 'social climber' and spends tons of money sucking up to prominent Pearlanders. At least those she can schmooze with her ingratiating bullshit."

"Prominent Pearlanders. Isn't that an oxymoron? Or does that refer to the ones without chicken coops in their front yards?"

"Blondie, that's a fact and not a fiction. The small town now has million dollar homes in it." He sounded slightly offended.

"Yikes, I didn't mean to trespass on your farmland. I'll change subjects. How's business?"

"Ben and I are doing exceptional." He blew a stream of smoke out the side of his mouth. "He's great to work with and has really settled down."

"You mean he's learned to control his vulgar mouth?"

"Christ, no! But he keeps it shut for the most part. I still do all negotiating with builders and homeowners, and he oversees operations, keeping crews in line. Ben's somewhat of a control freak."

"No kidding. I noticed his need to be in command when he came home from the Air Force. Guess that's indicative of being a military officer."

"Absolutely. Ben's the only sibling who boldly demands control. Maybe some is inherent since Gloria likes to dominate. She's just more subtle at swaying people."

He was so sure of himself. So strong. So gentle. So calming. With just the wind for background music, we stood and talked for over an hour, until I realized I had to get away from him. Being near him felt too good. Would I ever stop feeling lightheaded by his presence? Would I ever stop feeling he was the perfect man for me? Would a lobotomy eradicate his memory from my mind or just remove vital facts necessary for me to function in life?

"I'd better leave." I took a long, boundless breath, wanting to inhale as much of him as possible as we walked toward the front of the house. Stepping out into the cold wind, I blurted, "I love the smell of you and this silly sawdust."

He flipped his cigarette butt into the air, pulled his sawdust covered T-shirt over his head, and handed it to me. "Here! You like my goddamn smell so much, take this shirt. Now is there anything else you want?"

You bet your ass there was. I wanted him to do delicious things to me for the rest of my life and then some. "I'd better take the fifth on that question." I wasn't about to say anything that might encourage the break-up of his second marriage. "It could lead me back to therapy."

"Save your money." He grinned. "Freud himself couldn't penetrate your psyche."

"That's a fact and not a fiction," I said, but wanted to scream, "I'll love you till I die," cling to his body and never let go. Instead, I turned to leave, clutching his sawdust covered T-shirt.

"See ya, Blondie," he called out as I hurried down the sidewalk and he strolled to his van and pulled on a fleece jacket. Then he honked twice, jumped out of his van, blew me kisses and waved while walking backwards toward the house. I got into my car and sped away.

T-shirt never got washed, and turned into my sleep aid on restless nights.

༄

Beau phoned to explain he had been MIA due to remarrying his second wife, Lola. No surprise. He'd shown me photos of his five-foot-nine, stunning brunette wife who was blessed with sultry teal colored eyes. Model-esque Lola was four years older than me and about forty times hotter. Beau admitted he got terribly lonely after a nasty upper respiratory bout, so he worked hard to rekindle their romance. It started with a diamond necklace, and he admitted that sentimental token soon turned into requests for more trinkets of love to keep her happy. *Whatever Lola Wants!* Thankfully his sports bar was going gangbusters and raking in the dough. Beau admitted he wasn't truly happy with wife number two, but his fear of being alone motivated him to rejuvenate the love they once shared. He had always imparted so much wisdom to me; I was surprised by his actions. And somewhat shocked when he said Lola was a bit jealous of our friendship. "Forgive me if I don't call as often," he'd said. I understood. Beau wanted this marriage to work, and although I treasured our conversations, I respected his quest for a happy life. Our friendship in limbo meant therapy for me. I couldn't handle a sassy teenager, pine over lost love, and navigate a relationship that wasn't fair to Ole Moneybags without help.

Speaking of Randall, he flew to Texas for the Christmas holidays, but left Christmas morning for Park City, fairly upset I wasn't joining him. I'd given him Christmas Eve and my warm natured ass wasn't going to the mountains. Besides, Gloria had invited Nikki and me to stop by Christmas Day to visit with Hope, Troy and Conn with his betrothed, Kim. Barely eighteen and ready to marry? I accepted her invite after Gloria assured me Gabriel, Luke, and Victoria wouldn't be at her home. While Conn spouted irrelevant commentary about Gabriel and Victoria, I tried to minimize my facial twitching. Gloria must've noticed my anxiety. She grabbed my hand, led me to her bedroom, told me Gabriel was miserable with Victoria, and ended by saying, "It's obvious that other people in your lives are just filling a void until you two can be together." Maybe I should have felt sad that Gabriel wasn't happy, but Gloria's message made my eyes sparkle more than the lights on her Christmas tree.

I didn't sleep much that night and when a ringing phone woke me around seven in the morning, I was still groggy.

"Let's do lunch," Gloria trilled into the phone. "My treat. Noon today at Brennan's?"

My sleep deprivation made me recall my sweet friend, Katie, and how much she adored Brennan's. Kat often dined there, especially after a great money making week at the club. I also recalled Brennan's delicious food and ambiance didn't come cheap. "See you there, Gloria."

Looking stylish as always with her perfectly coiffed hair, Gloria hugged and complimented me, even though I'd hurriedly applied makeup and my dress wasn't nearly as dazzling as her expensive pant-suit. She made more than average income as a travel agent, but her eye-catching presentation lent Gloria the appearance of a woman of high social status.

Gloria was uncharacteristically quiet during lunch, offering pleas-antries to the waiters and such, while letting me talk about Nikki. But when the main entrée plates were removed, she took over the conversation. "Cherie, I shouldn't tell you this, but Gabe's marriage is crumbling. It's just awful."

"I'm sorry to hear that." Not a total lie. I felt bad for Luke.

"Well, it's inevitable." She stuck her fork into her chocolate dessert. "It's not a matter of if, it's a matter of when. And I think it'll be very soon."

"Oh," was all I could say as I forked strawberries from my fruit cup.

"I don't mean to seem pushy, but I think you should move to Clear Lake City when your lease expires. Be there for Gabe when his marriage falls apart."

Gloria knew I relished the idea of living on a lake. "I've always dreamed of being near the water and watching boats go by, but daydreaming never has paid my bills."

"NASA and high-tech businesses are thriving. Employment won't be a problem."

"I'll think about it." I was enchanted by Clear Lake's sunset views and small town feel.

"Just do it!" Gloria said. "There's a delightful future in store for you with Gabe, so make yourself available as soon as possible." Cupid in her plum pantsuit was being pushy.

But saying things I wanted to hear. Gloria insisted on covering the tab, and her attitude was so upbeat I figured she'd recently sold a mega travel package.

⁊

"These men go wild when it comes to being romantic." Patrice called from Venice, Italy after a whirlwind international business trip ended in a brief vacation.

"So I've heard. Licking the face to show appreciation, etcetera."

"Not exactly, but overly affection men irritate me as much as guys who want to tie me up and spank me."

"There's a happy medium somewhere," I said. "Nothing personal against black stiletto boots, leather corsets, spiked collars and cracking whips—when appropriately applied, but I'll take face licking over sado-masochism any day."

"You've always appreciated nice guys who were a tad aloof, Cherie. Which brings me to ask. . .have you heard anything about your old flame, lately?"

"Funny you should ask. I had lunch with Gloria recently. She says my old flame is miserably married and soon to be divorced."

"Just be cautious when dealing with that woman. They're announcing my train departure, so I've got to dash. We'll talk more later. *Arrivederci,* for now."

I had always trusted Patrice's judgment and appreciated her intuition, but the harsh timber of her voice when she said "that woman" took me aback. Maybe she was overly tired. Jet-lagged, train drained, or suffering skin irritation from those Italian face lickers.

17

Cupid Gloria called so often I thought she was trying to get a telephone solicitor license. Lightly veiled with trivia, she regurgitated details about Gabriel's disintegrating marriage and the wonderful life awaiting us once we reunited. Used car salesmen had nothing on Gloria.

Shortly after Gloria numbed my ear one night, her son called. "If I worked my hands in wood, would you still love me?" Gabriel sang into the phone.

"I doubt your wife would appreciate you singing those lyrics to me."

"Soon to be ex-wife. We talked about the one thing we both agree on and that's divorce. Hell, I almost creamed my jeans when she said she'd be out of here in a few weeks."

"Okay trash mouth," I blurted, my heart pounding with mixed emotions, "But please tell me this wasn't because of my visit to Kemah and the T-shirt episode."

"Heavens, no. Victoria never even noticed my coming home bare-chested. It was just bound to happen. When two people would rather swallow fish hooks and yank out vital organs instead of spending time together, it's best to end things. Besides, she's dating some banker already."

"Sorry to hear that, Gabriel." Again, not a total lie.

"Well I'm glad. Now he can pay for her outrageous spending."

"Just keep things cordial for Luke's sake."

"That's what I've been trying to do. And I'll keep doing whatever it takes to make sure my son isn't hurt." He paused. "Hey, I heard it through the grapevine you might move near Pearland in a few weeks. Let me know if you need a mover. I know a guy who does a good job and it'll only cost you a couple of Budweisers."

"Didn't I fall for that line about ten years ago?"

"Can't blame a poor ole carpenter for trying."

I hung up, my heart dancing in my throat.

I gave notice to my landlord. Notice to Randall would follow—once I summoned enough courage. Removing the six carat diamond ring was a start. He wasn't returning to Texas for two weeks. I had time to prepare. My natural instinct was to return the ring via courier, vanish without forwarding info, and let it go at that. Randall was smart enough to figure out the details. But during my last visit to my therapist (last, being my decision— not hers) we had discussed conquering my "exit: stage left" tendency by confronting uncomfortable situations head-on. I vowed to try as I told her goodbye. But I am a natural born runner.

My engagement ring indentation was still visible when Gloria called. "Cherie, I have dreadful news. Victoria's going to live with Gabe longer than expected, possibly post divorce. It's difficult to explain."

Yet Gloria gets designated as spokesperson? Where the hell was Gabriel?

"Victoria has to upgrade her credit rating enough to buy a house."

"What happened to her so-called banker fiancé?"

"He's knee high in divorce proceedings. Cherie, Gabe's decision is because of Luke."

"Well, wish them well, Gloria." I hung up.

After a week of not hearing from Gabriel, my vacillating about ending things with Randall came to a screeching halt. My battered self esteem needed buffing, not more dents. With no therapist on my payroll, I agreed to move to freezing Utah and make wedding plans. I resigned from the law firm, but did not tell Gloria. Having witnessed her knack for convincing people to see things her way, I avoided the talented debater.

Nikki had mixed feelings. She loved Texas and didn't want to leave friends she acquired over thirteen years, but Randall's lavishing of gifts likely swayed her vote to head west.

⚬

The packing crew was wrapping our belongings when Nikki grabbed the phone, and then handed it to me. "Cherie, please hang tight," said mouthpiece Gloria. "Gabriel's working on a plan for you two to be together."

I wasn't buying her rhetoric this time. "Do *not* drain that tank," I wailed at the packer, who apparently couldn't read. "It stays with our neighbor."

"I'm getting a cat when we get to Utah," Nikki told him. "My first ever 'hands on' pet."

"What on earth is going on over there?"

"We're moving to Utah so Randall can add another notch to my wedding ring finger. Beats the hell out of hanging around Texas while Victoria and Gabriel play house."

"Cherie, don't be foolish."

"Gloria, these guys are trying to empty Nikki's aquarium despite the 'Do Not Pack' sign hanging on it. I really can't chat."

"Oh, Cherie," she coaxed. "Please believe what I'm saying and don't do this. You love Gabriel and you know he loves you. His daughters were in town the past week, so he needs more time to sort this out."

Damn mover kept dipping fishy water. Realizing he couldn't speak English, I tried hand gestures. "Gloria, you're right that I love Gabriel, but I don't appreciate his not calling to offer a personal explanation. Besides, I don't want to be the home wrecker of his second marriage."

"Don't do this, Cherie. Gabriel's trying to arrange things so you can be together."

"Nikki, please get him away from that fish tank!" I yelled. "Sorry, Gloria, I can't handle this emotional tug. Distance will be best for me. Gabriel's doing what's best for him so please allow me the same privilege. I can't be in this state without going mad thinking of them together."

"But it's for Luke," Gloria protested.

"That doesn't make it any easier. And like I said, if Gabriel isn't man enough to tell me his reasons, he's not the man I once knew."

"Cherie, he's crumbling inside and just trying to keep things together."

"Wish him the best. Now, I must go. Love you Gloria."

"We love you too Cherie." She was crying. I felt sad, but knew I couldn't handle the torment of Gabriel being with Victoria for any reason.

Nikki employed sophomoric sign language to successfully stop the packer from draining her aquarium. It was promised to our neighbor since fish couldn't endure the trip and Nikki had found the breed of cat she wanted. I was a dog person, but having never allowed furry pets in our home, I accepted Nikki's choice.

I was supervising movers when the phone rang again. I heard Nikki explaining to Gabriel that we were packing for Utah and she'd be getting a room twice the size of any she'd ever had. With their special closeness, sharing her excitement was only normal. "It's Gabriel, Mom." She handed me the phone, totally oblivious to the emotional turmoil he and I were experiencing.

"You're alive!" I snapped. "Guess I can put my black veil back in the wardrobe box."

"Cherie, please don't do this. I'm sorry I haven't called, but I tend to clam up and try to internally correct things before discussing with anyone."

"So, I'm just 'anyone' now?"

"No!" His voice was loud, but quavering. "You're the woman I love. I just have to make things right for Luke. It's not going as smoothly as I'd hoped. And now I'm in a state of shock that you'd so easily run away."

"Let's not talk about shock, okay? Forgive me Gabriel, but I have to go oversee packers before they put Nikki in a box." I didn't wait for his response. Click.

After the packers left, I sat on the sofa holding back tears while Nikki talked endlessly about decorating her new room. The phone rang just as she switched subjects onto possible cat names.

"Gabriel just left my house and he's an emotional wreck." Gloria sniffled. "Cherie, you must realize his being with her for even one day more is because of Luke."

"I understand Gloria, truly I do. But I have emotions too."

"Would it help to know that Victoria has a boyfriend?"

"That's what Gabriel said, but I don't know anything for certain these days."

"Please don't run off to Utah. We'll work out these details as a family."

"This house has already been leased."

"Cherie, we're a strong family who'll get through this. Everything's going to work out for you two."

"Really?" I desperately wanted to believe her, but another part of me was screaming to get the hell away. Besides, Nikki was excited about a big bedroom, and I had disappointed her too many times in her young life.

"Yes, really. I'm not sure how it'll be handled, but believe Gabriel when he said he wasn't about to let you run off."

I looked around at all the boxes. Poor Nikki. Uprooted again.

"And I know you and Gabriel will soon be married," she insisted.

"Oh, Gloria." I sighed. "Will you please ask Gabriel to call me? I hung up on him earlier but think I can speak calmly to him now."

"Of course I will, you needn't ask. We all love you, Cherie. And we love Nikki, too."

Gabriel never called. After waiting two hours I called Gloria to see if she had relayed my message.

"It's very late and Gabe's confused. You being packed and ready to rush to Utah, then unwilling to listen to him was a hurtful blow, Cherie."

"Well, the hurt is mutual. Doesn't he know my hearing from *you* about him living with Victoria was what generated this move?"

"I think he does. He's feeling vulnerable and wants to do the right thing for Luke. But I know he'll call soon. Please don't leave. Just stay near your phone."

In spite of Gloria's encouraging words, I felt apprehensive and confused as I sat by the phone waiting for Gabriel's call. I fell asleep on the sofa.

The following day after basically sitting on my phone, I was startled when it rang at ten in the evening. My anxiety broke the minute I heard his voice, and I started crying.

"Calm down, everything will be okay," he assured. "Don't you know that together we can face any problems?"

"I'm sorry, Gabriel. I tend to run from problems, rather than face them."

"I know you do," he said in a low serious tone. "And I clam up. But here's the plan. Victoria is moving into an apartment, and I'm paying her rent for six months."

"What happened to her banking lover?"

"His divorce got ugly, so he's staying low key. Just forget them and get ready to move to Pearland with me. We can work out minor details, Cherie. I promise. And you know I don't make promises lightly."

"I know you don't. And I know you clam up, but I'll try to teach you the art of candid conversation with the woman who loves you. Oh yeah, we need to get Nikki a cat."

"A cat?" he moaned. "Oh man, I'm a dog person."

"So am I, but no argument. Randall promised Nikki a cat and her heart will be broken if she doesn't get one. A bigger room will have to come later down the road."

"Don't say 'down the road' Blondie. No more running away from me."

"I love you Gabriel, and I'm sorry for acting irrational."

"Just cancel those cross country movers and I'll handle the rest. Love you, Blondie!"

Gabriel was my tranquility base. I hung up and immediately called Randall with an honest explanation. He reacted like a true gentleman, never asking me to return the ring. Maybe he knew I would. After all, I broke our engagement. Besides, I was careless when it came to sporting that huge rock and felt fortunate none of my friends got injured during my storytelling gesticulations.

I left my job at Ray and McKreight and wound up moving to Pearland instead of Clear Lake. Not as close to water, but close to the one I loved. Gloria brought food for a "moving in party" while the brothers arranged furniture and provided crude entertainment. After everyone left, Nikki tumbled into bed exhausted. Gabriel held my hand as we walked through the house turning off lights, and when we got to the foyer, what began as an embrace ended as passionate lovemaking against the wall. Finally found a fabulous use for foyers.

"Sorry I was such a reticent asshole," he apologized softly against the side of my neck.

"I understand." I pushed closer to him. "I'm sorry I was ready to haul ass."

He squeezed said ass. "I never want to be without you in my life."

"I second that emotion. I'm the luckiest woman alive."

❧

In the following year, Delilah turned over a new leaf after meeting and marrying a genuinely caring guy who treated her like she'd had proper upbringing, and treated her kids like they sprang from his loins. She purchased a custom T-shirt shop and snagged contracts with athletic departments of several schools, but also used the business to display her uncensored thoughts across her chest.

Youngest O'Quinn member, Conner, married a nice (and naïve) girl named Kim, who overlooked his screwball behavior. Most importantly, Nikki loved our life with Gabriel. Although I never regretted leaving Kent, I felt guilty for working during Nikki's formative years, thus substituted material things for time and love, adequately molding a spoiled brat. Ironing out the wrinkles in her melodramatic personality wasn't going to be an easy task.

Right off the bat, Gabriel bought Nikki a Himalayan kitten and barely cringed at the price tag. He pretended not to like Mistletoe, but trained her to fetch like a dog as she grew. Gabriel threw a stick that she retrieved no matter how far she had to run or how many bushes she had to maneuver. He whistled. She came. And every morning Mistletoe walked alongside Gabriel's leg as he strolled down the driveway for his daily newspaper.

Gabriel was still succinct, using few words to get to the point, and I was still incessant, using thousands of words, but never quite getting to any point. Our morning routine was similar to that of the Seventies, with me walking him to the back door, kissing goodbye, and waving to each other as he honked twice to say "I love you." Around five each day, I cooked dinner while listening for his van, and then met him at the back door. Occasionally when Nikki locked her door to write in her journal, we utilized the laundry room to make quick love on top of our washer/dryer. If you've never shagged on a Maytag, you don't know what you're missing. Love those spin cycles.

My Julia Child's bon appétit thingy was hit and miss, (oh, the boiled pork chops incident), but Gabriel raved about every meal I cooked, even hot dogs. We ate out a lot. We saw movies. Visited museums. Attended music festivals. And spent hours star gazing. Sometimes when I went into overdrive thanking him for being super nice about things, he'd fall back on his idiosyncratic one-liner: "I'd do just about anything for a piece of ass, Blondie."

⁓

Their excuse was "Houston summers are too humid," but I was sure Lauren and Skylar stopped coming for summer visits because their dad was with me again. Still, Gabriel and I spent many weekends at the family lake house—and by family, I mean a house Gloria found on Clear Lake, made a minimum down payment with money she borrowed from Ben and Gabriel, purchased under her and Hope's names, and then needed Gabriel as co-signer since her credit was sub-par. Gloria never made a single payment, thus called it the family lake house, saying technically it belonged to all her children. Gabriel bought a boat and skis (mostly for me), so everyone swam, fished, read quietly, watched TV, or played indoor games. Then came the beauty makeover. On the fourth of July, Hope helped fifty-five-year-old Gloria "go blonde" to hide her proliferating gray hairs.

"I don't like it one damn bit," Conn said after Gloria left the room.

"Yeah, it looks like a gaggle of geese flew over and shat on her head," Ben added.

"I really liked her dark hair," I quietly told Gabriel. "It accentuated her olive skin."

"Persuade her to dye it back," Troy told Hope.

"Better keep those opinions to yourselves," Gabriel said to everyone. "Otherwise you'll be seeing some real ugliness surface from this newly tinted blonde."

An exhausting day in the sun was followed by an evening of watching holiday fireworks on the water. When the last Roman candle fell from the sky we rushed inside to rotate turns in the shower, before racing for prime sleeping quarters. Once the brood finally settled into beds, Hope and I started chatting from nearby rooms.

"Hey, stop the goddamned girl talk and say goodnight," Ben called out.

"Goodnight Troy, goodnight Cherie," Hope complied.

"Goodnight Hope, goodnight Gloria," I shouted from our room.

Gabriel yelled, "Goodnight Luke, goodnight Nikki," prompting a series of goodnights throughout the house.

When Kim's signoff finally reached Ben, he shouted, "Goodnight Kim, goodnight Conn Boy—don't be milking your mongoose in the moonlight." We were the Waltons, gone awry.

The Eighties had brought a more mature, kinder, sensitive Gabriel than the one I knew in the Seventies, and watching his father-son relationship with Luke added a new chapter to my Omnipotent Gabriel book. He had fought long and hard for joint custody of Luke, who visited often. Good to the bone, Gabriel was charitable to persons of lesser means, always cared for stray animals, and his reticence was no longer mistaken for coldness. He loved sitting outdoors in the peacefulness of nature and made a point of watching sunsets and sunrises, claiming they could persuade an atheist to believe in God. In the late evenings he often called Nikki and me outside insisting we view the constellations as he taught her the quiet wonders of our universe. I listened as he and Nikki exchanged ideas and information, thrilled she was seeing him in *almost* the same light as me.

The lighting for us was soft and reflective, but powerful. Taking care of business around the house, we couldn't pass each other without a quick touch or auto-pilot kiss. I was intense and fast moving, garrulous and insecure, he was patient and slow moving, soft spoken and self-assured. And my creature of habit still raked his hair from his forehead with his fingers; still kept Marlboros in his shirt pocket and always used matches; still rubbed his thumb across the tips of his four fingers as though he were dusting away grains of sands; and still sported a short moustache that drove me up an erotic wall. I loved his idiosyncrasies and every one of my personalities were totally, helplessly in love with every one of his.

18

Gabriel savored solitude, and after serving time as a waitress, I wasn't exactly "hostess with the mostess," but every weekend we wound up with a houseful of family. "How did our house become party central?" I asked, hearing the first visitors arrive. We lived miles from everyone.

"You can thank Gloria." Gabriel grunted.

"I'm starving," Troy shouted as he and Hope walked inside. I gestured to the kitchen.

Despite directing folks to food and booze by pointing our fingers instead of offering to serve, social Saturdays were fun. Thanks mostly to Ben O'Quinn. He could still spell obscenities faster than most could speak them, and although sometimes annoying, his antics had us spraying drinks out our noses. Ben had married a soft-spoken Beijing beauty he met while in the military, and when he finally brought her to Texas, we were surprised. Mei was unlike Ben in almost every aspect, but the two connected in a special way.

"We are here," Mei said sweetly, carefully enunciating each word. She was delightful. "Bennie's helping Gloria bring in some food I make for everyone."

Mei had a positive effect on Ben who she endearingly called "Bennie." Adding "ie" to a man's name instantly lowers his macho level a notch.

Gloria walked in with Ben who was lugging a basket of goodies. Conn and Kim followed. Gloria stopped to chat, but the younger crowd made a beeline to our kitchen.

"Jur hair look berry pretty tonight," Mei said to Hope.

"Thank you!" Hope smiled before entering the powder room.

Gloria made a quick frown at Mei's broken English, and then blew air kisses at her daughter-in-law as she went into the kitchen to help Bennie set up her Chinese cuisine. Gloria squeezed into a tiny spot at the end of our sofa where Gabriel lay sprawled across two cushions.

"She's sweet, but it breaks my heart that Ben married outside his race," Gloria whispered to him. It wasn't the first time she'd expressed anti-Mei sentiment.

"You fucking bigot," Gabriel bolted upright, and passed Hope on his way to our bar.

"Sorry about his mouth," I said quietly to Gloria. "But you know Sean would have embraced Mei without bias." Hope flipped through a magazine. She adored Mei, but turned a deaf ear on her mother's snide remarks.

ᢒᢙ

Kent remained financially and emotionally absent, so before school started in fall Gloria finagled the legal changing of Nikki's last name to O'Quinn. "She'll fit in better," Gloria claimed. "Being part of a cohesive family."

"Yeah, before long we'll all have the same last name." Gabriel winked at us girls. Usually it's the bride who decides her wedding date, but Gabriel was adamant about ours falling on May ninth—the date we consummated our relationship in 1970.

"Shake a tail feather, lovey," I called out for the umpteenth time on Nikki's first day of school. No response or sighting. I'd gotten an earful of exasperation about the new school when I woke her, but with minutes ticking away, I needed some cooperation. "You can't possibly still be getting dressed," I raised my voice a few octaves. I knew she wasn't applying makeup or fussing with her hair since her idol Hope was into the natural look. "C'mon, Nikki!" This time I screamed loud enough to break windows or at least some cheap wine glasses. "Get out to the street!"

"I can't believe I have to ride a stupid school bus!" An unhappy Nikki entered the living room.

"Suck it up buttercup." I stood my ground. She'd never been on a school bus before, but our life was changing and we'd discussed the transportation situation, ad-nauseam. "The bus arrives any minute and you'd better be on it."

She mouthed something before slamming our front door, almost unhinging it.

Hours later Nikki blasted through the front door, "I despise Pearland and all the hicks at that school."

My heart sank. "It can't be that bad, Nikki."

"These are the most boring, backwoods people in the world!"

Where had I heard that before? "Things will get better. You'll soon have all kinds of new friends and I'll bet most of them won't be comparing designer labels."

"Uh." She rolled her eyes. "Only because they've never heard of Calvin."

I wanted to smack the smirk off her face. "Don't be a little snot, Nikki. Before Randall, you weren't wearing such high-falutin' clothes and carrying handbags that cost more than my car payment. Adjust your attitude."

"Change my attitude? You want me eating possum for lunch with everyone else?"

"That's enough!" My face felt flush with anger. Gabriel was so prideful of this little town, I didn't want his feelings hurt. "Now promise you'll make an extra effort for Gabriel."

"I'll try." She grabbed her books and headed to her room. "For him."

I took a deep breath, counted to ten, and prayed to all the gods around us.

Gloria continued making big bucks as a high-powered travel agent, and before you could say nepotism, she got me hired as part-time assistant to company owner, Eduardo D'Alessio. Our boss did most of his own paperwork, making my job a breeze. Gloria barely tolerated him, and often made negative remarks about his sexual preference. The guy was so gorgeous he likely had a string of women praying nightly he would switch teams. I instantly clicked with this sensible yet sometimes silly, educated but not snooty, bighearted guy. Eduardo was a discreet homosexual, but even if he had flaunted his lifestyle à la Liberace, it wouldn't have bothered me. "Live and let live," Mother always said. Eduardo dubbed me Farrah, so I tagged him "Roarke"—the character portrayed by Mexican-American

Ricardo Montalbán on TV's *Fantasy Island*. Albeit much younger than the mysterious Mr. Roarke, Eduardo kept his age top secret, tried to teach life lessons to employees, believed in fantasy vacations, and was super suave even without wearing a white suit. His office décor was eclectic, with unusual furniture and rare art. Eduardo also had countless non-autographed posters of Lupe Velez, a Mexican film actress who began her career as a dancer and later worked in US vaudeville. Being innately dramatic, Eduardo believed his mother's notion that his upper crust family was related to Lupe.

Eduardo enlightened me on many amazing aspects of indigenous Mexican culture in Texas, since two things he enjoyed as much as theater were Texas history and Halloween.

"Farrah, did I mention Halloween's my favorite holiday?"

"Tattoo mentioned it," I straightened Eduardo's personally auto-graphed poster of Dolores del Rio that seemed off-kilter between original Frida Kahlo and Diego Rivera paintings. "That's the day you kick-off your kick-ass annual contest."

"That's right, missy. Whoever sells the most tour packages by the end of November wins the grand prize of a trip for two anywhere on the globe, all expenses paid for seven days. Competition is open to all employees, not just travel agents, so pony up and sell some trips."

Gloria had won the competition five years running, and always took Hope to Tahiti during August, Houston's hottest month. The woman could sell Brylcreem to bald men.

I rarely spoke to Beau while he and Lola struggled through issues dur-ing their second-go-round, so when he called I was elated. A father figure who *actually* listened. And listen he did as I told him everything from concerns over Nikki's disdain for small town living to comfort with my new job. When I mentioned Eduardo's competition, Beau seemed unusu-ally interested.

"Baby, I'm going to a party for June Wilkinson this evening, and should see my old buddy Bill Ruel. I might call you with some good news next week."

"Actress June Wilkinson? Who married Houston Oiler Dan Pastorini?"

"Yep, but they're divorced now, baby. I've known June for decades."

"Your list of acquaintances amazes me. A Playboy bunny!"

"Well before Hef discovered her, she was the youngest topless dancer on record."

"Is that how you knew her?"

"Lord, no. She was only fifteen and lived in London. I met her in 1961 when she was doing a West Coast stage production with Milton Berle. I think it was *Norman, Is That You?*"

"Milton Berle. Jeez, Beau."

"I met Milton in Las Vegas during the late forties, when he was packing showrooms at Caesars Palace, The Desert Inn, and other casino hotels."

"How about Elvis. Did you ever meet him?"

"Oh, we're still best pals. He's alive—just not feeling so well," Beau joked. "But remind me to tell you an interesting story about the King and I some day. Lola just drove up, so I'll call you soon. Bye for now."

The following day, Beau called with unexpected news. His friend Bill Ruel was planning a surprise party for his wife's fortieth birthday and wanted to book one hundred and ten guests into a hotel in Barbados on New Year's Eve. Beau asked Bill to book through me.

Employees could not divulge sales (Eduardo kept bookings secret), so excitement ran high during November as everybody including the janitor pushed trips to friends and relatives. Everyone assumed Gloria would win the international travel, but we all sought second place of a four day weekend at Houston's luxurious Warwick Hotel. Not to mention third place of five hundred dollars. Clever Eduardo was making more in sales than he was paying in prizes, but it was spirited competition. On December 1st, Eduardo summoned employees into the board room for his theatrical production—red carpet leading to a small stage where a table covered in gold satin held three "Eddie" statuettes. First place was a replica of Eduardo in pilot uniform with cocktail in hand. Second place model had Eduardo dressed as a bellhop, holding a hotel key. And the third place Eduardo statuette was decked out in pimp attire, flashing a fistful of cash.

"First of all, I want to thank my hard working employees for making this our best competition ever." Eduardo stood center stage in his expensive emcee suit. "Even those who aren't called for prizes today will find some extra jingle in your Christmas stocking this year."

Everyone clapped and awaited Eduardo's "Texas History" trivia. He took employees back in time to the mid-Sixties when River Oaks socialite Candace Mossler was charged along with her nephew Melvin Powers of murdering her millionaire husband, Jacques Mossler. Candy's love affair with her young nephew was common knowledge, and the two were so brazen with their lust, everyone was sure they would fry. Until infamous attorney Percy Foreman joined their team. A bouncy, platinum blonde, former model, Candy charmed reporters with her southern accent and on camera charm. When asked about allegedly murdering her husband and having an incestuous affair with Mel, she held the microphone and boldly stated, "Well, nobody's perfect." After her acquittal, Candy kissed every juror.

"I know you all dig tales of Texas oil money and greedy cheating spouses that lead to murder without convictions," Eduardo continued, "but I suspect you'd rather learn the winners of our contest. Interestingly enough, this year's three largest producers could easily impersonate some famous Texans." He took his sweet time looking around the room at each employee, making us wonder who the hell we resembled. Some people fidgeted in their chairs, a few women crossed their arms as if to say "enough already" and two men lit smokes.

"So with this said," Eduardo finally continued. "Will the freshly tinted blonde who now resembles Hot Wells native Texan, Mary Kay Ash, and could sell Bibles to an atheist, please come forward?" He nodded toward Gloria who was already halfway to the stage.

"Next up is the man who looks so much like native Houstonian Kenny Rogers—it's been rumored he sells trips by promising women he'll sing *Lady* to them all night." Daryl Moss rushed forward to stand beside Gloria.

"And last but not least, can our other Texas celebrity lookalike, the lovely Ms. Farrah Fawcett please join us?" Eduardo stretched out his hand. I walked forward, tickled pink, but thinking I should update my layered haircut.

A collective gasp filled the room. Thanks to Beau's assistance, I had outsold some hard-hitting agents. Still, Gloria and Daryl had hustled big time the past thirty days, so I figured my take would be the five hundred bucks. Employees applauded through forced smiles since their chances of winning were gone. I stood beside Gloria, who squeezed my hand while we waited for Eduardo to announce the big winner.

"And I've got a twenty dollar bill for the first one who can name Farrah's birthplace." He winked at remaining employees.

"Corpus Christi," was shouted in unison by at least five guys.

"Can't believe so many of you knew that one." Eduardo shook his head, and slowly passed twenties through the crowd. "But then most of you probably still own a sticky copy of her famous 'red swimsuit' poster."

Gross Neal from accounting let loose a long whistle. Gloria shifted impatiently, and squeezed my hand tighter than ever. Eduardo was attempting to amplify suspense, even though everyone knew Gloria would win the top prize yet again. I was mentally spending my cash on Luke and Nikki's Christmas.

"Drum roll, please." Eduardo thumped his microphone several times. "Our third place winner with sales of one hundred and seven travel packages goes to. . ." Long pause. Longer pause. And, finally—"Goes to our bearded gambler, Mr. Daryl Moss."

Daryl's look of defeat was obvious as he ungraciously accepted the glittery pimp statuette with its fistful of fake money. He had bragged about beating Gloria this time, so he grumbled a measly "congratulations" her direction and rudely left the stage. Then it hit me. Daryl's loss meant I had won the mini-vacation at the Warwick's Black Label Suite!

"And now. . ." Eduardo winked at me and Gloria. "Since we're down to two lovely ladies and only one can win the international trip, let's fast forward to our second place winner." No fast forward. Eduardo milked his moment in the spotlight—left eyebrow arched high while he pensively scratched his chin and strutted between Gloria and me. He looked dashing with his sable hair slicked back.

Both Gloria and I smiled happily as we held hands on the stage. We were visualizing our vacations as Eduardo continued to draw out his presentation.

"Houston's Warwick Hotel," Eduardo elaborated, "has hosted celebrities such as Princess Grace of Monaco, the Duke and Duchess of Windsor, Imelda Marcos, the Shah of Iran, and Bob Hope. In 1979 when Phil Donahue asked the entertainer to name the most beautiful view in the world, Hope named the Warwick. Bob had stayed in a suite facing south, and noted that guests staying in the Black Label Suite could enjoy a splendid view from their balcony bathtub."

"You're going to love it," Gloria whispered in my ear. I was giddy.

"Okay, then." Eduardo began thumping the mike like Ringo Starr on acid. "The winner of a four day stay at Houston's grandest hotel for selling one hundred and eleven packages is Gloria O'Quinn!"

Gloria dropped my hand. I stepped forward to accept the tiny bellhop statuette and was reaching for it when Eduardo stopped me. "Farrah's in shock. Should I slap her?" he joked. "Cherie, this award belongs to Gloria."

I looked at Gloria. Her cheek muscles tightened and her eyes narrowed as she smiled. I stood stunned.

"Congratulations, my darling Cherie," Gloria said as she snatched the statuette. My feelings were mixed. Having never won anything in my life, I was elated to win Eduardo's "Tripping the Light Fantastic" contest, but felt awful for Gloria whose smile seemed frozen on her face.

"And for selling one hundred and fourteen packages." Eduardo handed me the tiny replica of himself as airline pilot with cocktail in hand. "Our first prize goes to Cherie Parnell." I remained stunned. Even though I hadn't paid attention when Eduardo was announcing the number of packages sold, I knew Beau's friend had only booked one hundred and ten. There must have been a mistake. I revealed my thoughts to Gloria, which turned her gloomy expression to a happy one. We needed to confer with Eduardo once the room emptied. When the last person finally trickled out, we cornered our boss. Together we learned that Beau had called the agency days earlier when I was at a doctor's appointment. He spoke directly to Eduardo and booked an additional four packages for a trip to Las Vegas with Lola and her parents. Beau had sworn Eduardo to secrecy, wanting to surprise me. Poor Gloria. Her glimmer of hope was now completely gone and her face fell sad again.

❧

"Thanks to you I won the grand prize by three packages!" I called Beau from work.

"Good for you, baby," he congratulated, but his voice echoed despair.

"What's wrong, Beau?"

"I'm not going to bend your ear with my problems."

"Then I'll never yap about mine to you. Talk to me, please."

Silence filled the airwaves and when he finally spoke, his voice was shaky. "My marriage is falling apart and this time I can't seem to pull any tricks from my sleeve to make Lola happy."

"I'm so sorry. You know I'd be there in a New York minute for you if I could. But Lola wouldn't appreciate my presence, so here comes a giant phone hug."

"Thanks, baby. I needed that." He sounded a little more upbeat before ending the call, but still couldn't hide his pain.

Mixed emotions swirled in my head, dulling the thrill of my win. I felt bad Gloria was miserable, but it saddened my heart to know Beau was dealing with the excruciating misery inflicted by lost love.

19

"Gloria never dreamed you'd outsell her," Gabriel said when I got home. "Otherwise, she'd have baked something other than laxative brownies during the contest. She wanted all competitors busy on the throne instead of the phone. Luckily you only eat sugar-free crap."

"She did not do that," I chastised.

"Tip of the iceberg, Blondie. She even buys laxative gum."

I'd seen Gloria passing out gum, and Daryl missed a couple of days due to stomach problems. Surely Gabriel was joking.

"Gloria's a sore loser. Don't take any food or drinks she offers the next few months."

"Stop it," I responded reprovingly.

Gabriel couldn't hide his excitement about our seven day trip to France, while Nikki's excitement sprang from her and Mistletoe spending time with eighteen-year-old Cousin Jim, home for college break. My decision to visit Paris two weeks before Christmas was such short notice, finding a hotel became a head banger until Eduardo offered a marvelous bed and breakfast on the Right Bank in the Marais district. It's great to be connected.

The quaint B&B was cozy yet romantic, and Paris was all I dreamed it would be. On our first day: Eiffel Tower for photo ops. Our first evening: dining at La Closerie des Lilas where I closed my eyes and visualized Hemingway (the young, handsome, square-jawed, rosy cheek version) sitting nearby, writing diligently. Okay. I'd consumed lots of French wine.

189

Gabriel indulged all my adventures from walking along the river Seine in an area where Anaïs Nin reportedly lived on a houseboat, and even strolling Pére Lachaise Cemetery, burial site of famous folks like Edith Piaf, Oscar Wilde, Frédéric Chopin, Marcel Proust, Gertrude Stein, and its number one attraction, Jim Morrison. No objections to visiting Parisian cabaret, Le Crazy Horse Saloon for an hour of tasteful burlesque, or taking cooking classes, traveling the cobblestone streets of Rue Cler, viewing Monet paintings at the Musée Marmottan, or shopping at all the quirky, funky shops near our B&B. We returned each evening to share a gourmet French meal with other guests, before flying up to our room to drink wine and engage in multi-orgasmic sex, complete with giggles. As a courtesy to other guests, Gabriel's loud screams got ramped down to quivering moans of "Oooh...baby, baby."

Vive la France!

We returned to Houston exhausted, but ready for a nice family Christmas. Little did we know what had happened while we were enjoying France. Gloria believed the contest was a conspiracy between Eduardo and me, and confronted him. In an apparent flash of rage, Gloria called Eduardo a tamale eating faggot. He fired her on the spot. A week before Christmas.

Eduardo and I shared a great business relationship, so when I returned to work I immediately apologized for Gloria's inappropriate remarks. He politely refused my apologies. "Absolutely unnecessary, Cherie. Those words didn't spring from your mouth, and it's always been clear that you're nothing like your future mother-in-law. I rarely say anything negative about others, but believe Gloria ranks up there with Cruella de Vil. Watch your back. I suspect Gloria's bigoted behavior is only one of her malicious traits."

I understood Eduardo being pissed, but those were mighty strong words. Still, my first day back at work ran smoothly and by Friday it was obvious Eduardo held no ill feelings toward me. Other employees treated me with respect instead of jealousy over my win. I left work feeling all was right in my world.

Gabriel and I were snuggling in bed when the phone rang. He answered, and then held the phone away from his ear to avoid hearing loss. Hope was shouting at him, but her hostility was aimed directly at yours truly.

Eventually Gabriel managed to interrupt her rant. "Goddammit Hope! Gloria lost and Cherie won, fair and square. No cheating involved."

I leaned against my pillow offering explanations about Beau's generosity, and Gabriel acted as moderator for a few minutes, before handing me the phone. Hope was yelling that she didn't want to speak to me when I put the receiver to my ear.

"I'm on the line, Hope. Let's settle this."

"You caused my mother to lose the best job she's ever had," she said in menacing voice. "You're a brown-nosing sneak and should be ashamed, Cherie."

All I could do was gulp. Hope's words stung.

"My mother is too old to be looking for another job. If she gets sick over this, I'll never forgive you," she screamed. "You'll pay for this mess you got my mother into."

"So I'm to blame for Gloria's racist outburst?" I asked, infuriated by her remarks. "How did I suddenly become the villain?"

Apparently Hope didn't hear my question. "Remember, Cherie, blood is thicker than water. Gabe may be defending you now, but he'll side with family before this is over." She took a short breath, and I almost got a word in. "I've never hated anyone like I hate you, and I don't blame Gabe's girls for wanting to avoid you." Slam.

I couldn't believe she hung up on me. I couldn't believe my once dear friend hated me. I couldn't believe my stomach felt like it might come up through my nose. Hope's words about Gabriel's daughters avoiding me were swimming in my head, doing side strokes with Gabriel's comment about Gloria being a sore loser.

Gloria didn't seem one bit resentful, and invited us to her annual Christmas Eve family gathering as though nothing had happened. We arrived early and got busy drinking Gloria's special eggnog. She was quiet. "Where's Hope and Troy?" Conn kept asking.

"They're running late because of commitments with Troy's family."

I doubted that. In my years of knowing them, this was the only Christmas Eve that Hope hadn't been the first one through Gloria's door. "I feel like the Grinch that sprayed graffiti on the family's Rockwell print," I whispered to Gabriel while watching the hands on Gloria's grandfather clock make more rounds.

At ten o'clock, our family left for Pearland to get Luke and Nikki asleep before old St. Nick fell down our chimney. Hope and Troy pulled up the minute we drove away.

Gabriel reassured his brothers Eduardo's competition was not rigged while Hope tried to convince them I'd double-crossed Gloria. Kim and Mei called in support of me, saying Hope had gotten spoiled to their summer vacations in Tahiti. I was miserable. Gloria was depressed. Gabriel was stuck in the middle. Although he had initially shrugged it off, each day he seemed to be withdrawing, and I began feeling guilty-as-charged by Hope.

Meanwhile back at the ranch, Nikki was in a snit about school. She informed me Lee High was only thirty miles from Pearland, while I rejected her pleas citing the drive as reason enough. She was persistent. I caved. How could I blame her for not wanting to attend Hooterville High? I'd done the same thing decades earlier.

I never found the nerve to tell Gabriel about Nikki's school change. "It'll be our ugly little secret," I told Nikki. Lying through the teeth seemed better than wounding his Pearland pride.

"I'm sorry for causing such a mess, Mom." Nikki hugged me.

"Well, I don't want you unhappy in school and I certainly don't want more problems for Gabriel."

Along with my partner in crime, we made the round trip from Pearland to Houston daily praying he would never find out. My first dishonesty with Gabriel brought overwhelming guilt, but I couldn't fess up. Things were bad enough with Hope and Gloria angry at me and unhappy with Gabriel for defending me.

❧

"Baby, I don't know much about your life, but worry about the controlling nature of Gabe's mother." Beau said during a brief chat.

"Life is good. I just want to resolve this family issue."

"I know *you* do, but be careful about what you sacrifice. Take care of number one."

"I am. So much so I've actually been dishonest with Gabe."

"That's not good, baby. Were you dishonest to protect him or to protect yourself?"

"Me, I'm sorry to admit. Nikki didn't like her school, so instead of hurting his pride and giving him more to worry about other than his upset family, I failed to tell him."

"Then tell him first chance you get. Lies, no matter how small, can wreck havoc on trust factors."

"I'll try. Just gotta find the right time."

"I can tell you from experience, the longer you put it off, the more damaging the aftermath." Beau sighed deeply. I've got to run now, baby. I'm wrestling my own issues over here."

I didn't prod. Beau was ringing in the New Year with divorce and asset settlement.

Gloria soon landed a new job, but unfortunately it paid much less than her annual forty thousand plus bonus earnings from Eduardo. Still, she made efforts to mend things between us. Hope remained distant. Restaurant gathering were noticeably void of her and Troy, with Gloria offering excuses. I missed Hope and couldn't understand her animosity. One Sunday morning as Gabriel and I sat in the kitchen, I whined about Hope's coldness toward me. He acted like it was no big deal.

"She'll come around, just give her time." He sipped his coffee. "Remember we have the same blood running through our veins and you know how stubborn I can be. All my siblings can put up a wall and shut out the world if necessary. Christ, our childhood dictated it."

"Don't remind me how well you can put up a wall."

"Well, Hope can do the same thing."

"Heaven help me." I shivered.

"Just relax and smell the roses, Blondie. She'll come around. Hey, wouldn't a rose bush be nice in the garden outside this window? We could look at it while we drink coffee and talk."

He was getting better at segueing than me. But I couldn't be upset with him for pretending the family problem was no big deal—after all, I was pretending Nikki was attending Pearland High.

Soon the split between Gloria and Hope was overshadowed by a bigger problem. Nikki's sudden goofy behavior suggested the leaf drawings on her notebooks were something other than a personal tribute to Canada. There's not much worse in life than discovering your child is on drugs, except being a parent whose method for handling problems entails running from them. I couldn't abandon Nikki, so every day became a three-act drama. I screamed at her, Gabriel calmed her. I threatened, he compromised. I pleaded, he set rules. She and I cried, he comforted. Father Intervention, at Sybil's rehab. After weeks of bizarre behavior and countless talks with Cousin Jim, Nikki finally fessed up. We assured her we would do whatever necessary to help, but if Gabriel hadn't been the most patient man on earth, she might have ended up on the streets. My mothering skills ranged somewhere between June Cleaver and Joan Crawford.

Beau hadn't called for months and dialing his number got me an annoying "no longer in service" message. I wanted his advice, but had too many issues going on to hunt him down.

༄

"Mommy, please come get me." Nikki called from school, sounding like my sweet little girl for a change. "I can't go to the water fountain without being offered drugs."

Nearing hysterics, I rushed to Lee, withdrew Nikki, and drove around Pearland wondering what to do about another fine mess I'd gotten myself into. Gabriel despised lies. The following day I embarrassingly regurgitated the ugly truth.

"Cherie, there are two things I detest. One is conniving and the other is lying. I understand why you felt you had to lie, but it doesn't alter the fact that you lied to *me*."

"I'm sorry," was all I could choke out. I didn't blame him for distrusting me, but the dejected look in his eyes crushed me.

He stared at me for what seemed an eternity before he spoke. "Put her back in Pearland High."

"I'd rather go to Lee and get high." Nikki threw a fit.

I threw a bigger fit.

"Then we'll enroll her in parochial school," Gabriel interrupted my ranting.

"You're the best!" Nikki hugged Gabriel.

He popped the top off his Budweiser longneck.

I popped the top off a canister of Pillsbury chocolate frosting.

Our family of three checked out Mt. Carmel together. Sister Mary Francis warned us narcotics were inescapable, but assured us the school kept a close watch on students and the arduous academic schedule left little time for getting into trouble. I hoped that Nun wasn't lying. We registered Nikki to begin classes and Gabriel crossed his fingers in the air before writing her tuition check. I prayed to God that He would somehow undo my upbringing and remake my daughter into the perfect teenager. It hurt my heart to think my years of selfish neglect could have easily caused me to lose Nikki to drugs.

20

Nikki began her tour de Mt. Carmel, and I continued working part-time for Eduardo, which enabled me to deliver and collect her from school daily. Gabriel and I theorized less idle time would translate to less time for illegal deeds. Working for the travel agency seemed a bit like pouring salt on Gloria's wound, but I adored Eduardo and the flexibility he offered. Tending my child took priority over a paralegal career. Thankfully, Nikki loved her new school and her friendship with Gabriel flourished, with both constantly joking about her being his illegitimate child. In the looks department, she'd gotten Kent's long eyelashes and my heart shaped face, but her pale blue eyes and red, full lips were Gabriel O'Quinn personified. At an early age she developed his odd mannerism of mid-laugh snorting, but apologized after doing so. "It's not very feminine and only happens when I'm really tickled," she claimed. Possibly via osmosis, Nikki had acquired Gabriel's less-than-subtle dry wit. After repeatedly asking us to keep a lid on things in our bedroom at night, she nicknamed me the giggler, him the screamer. One morning she entered the kitchen half asleep, but mouthy. "Could you guys lower the noise after nine o'clock? I'm just a teenager, ya know."

"We'll turn the TV down from now on." I sipped some java.

"Oooh. . .baby, baby," she moaned, flipping her hair over one shoulder before joining us at the table. "It's not the TV keeping me awake. Try things that go bump in the night."

"See, Blondie." Gabriel blushed as he jumped up for more coffee. "I told ya we should've given her away when she was three years old and adorable."

"I'm still adorable," Nikki piped. "And old enough to log parental abuse."

"Watch out, sweetie. She's serious with those diary threats. I haven't read it lately, but suspect an entry about wire hangers is forthcoming."

Aspiring journalist Nikki jotted anything she felt noteworthy, filling her room with composition books, diaries, letters, and notes written on any handy paper. She was evolving into a fairly happy teenager and I was thrilled. Having experienced the agony of Nikki's drug use, it upset me that my irresponsible behavior once drove her to escapism via mind-altering chemicals.

There was no denying we were walking a wobbly bridge over troubled waters. I spent more quality time with Nikki in my dedication to be a better mother. Whatever it took to keep my child from raising the national recidivism rate for teen drug users.

During the week Gabriel helped Nikki with her math, history, theology and even literature homework. I wanted to bop his head while they discussed everyone from J.D. Salinger to Gertrude Stein. Fourteen-year-old Nikki was absorbing the happiness that filled our home, and like myself, gathered Gabriel's pearls of innervision as though they were precious gems. I smiled each time he discussed authors with her whom he once pretended to know nothing about, but didn't smile about her replacing proper English with Texas drawl or other colloquialisms he spouted. In fact, I complained loudly. They told me I needed medication for my delusions.

Gabriel made everything seem easy, but the absence of Gloria and Hope hung over me like a dark cloud. Nikki talked about how Hope had always treated her like a grown up instead of like a child. Gloria had become a mainstay to me from the minute we met after Sean's death. She couldn't be all bad. After all, her genes produced some wonderful children, especially my crude talking, humorous, sexy man, delightfully bundled in blue jeans and T-shirt.

February found us staying up late to watch a new show hosted by David Letterman. Cavett was no longer on the tube. Dave reminded me of Gabriel—smart, calm, and a little wacky despite his often eloquent vernacular. Gabriel appreciated the way Letterman defied the system by wearing

198

white gym socks and tennis shoes. Our bedtime that consisted of talking, laughing, and semi-quiet lovemaking, suddenly included Dave. Some *ménage à trois*! We lost sleep Monday through Friday, but even with sleep deprivation, Gabriel woke up happy. My transition from night to morning person hadn't exactly been a glowing success.

"Just one more month," he announced early one morning. No need for crowing roosters or alarm clocks in our home.

"Really?" I said distractedly, trying to hide my excitement about our May ninth nuptials.

"And we're keeping it a low-key, private ceremony with just us and Nikki."

"Gabriel, we can't exclude your family." Even though Hope had wrapped her pretty self in bitterness ribbons, I sensed Gloria was attempting to mend things.

"Ah, who cares about that crazy family?" He rubbed my arm.

"You do and you know it. Stop trying to act like a hard ass. I've known you too long."

"Hey, I am a hard ass, goddammit."

"A hard ass who misses the family closeness. I don't want to make things worse and hurt Gloria's feelings by marrying without her attending."

"She'll get over it." He pulled me against him. "Now forget about them and focus on me."

It truly seemed like my first and only, but since this was the third marriage for each of us, we decided on an unconventional wedding at a justice of the peace in neighboring Friendswood. No frills, flowers, music, or guests. I slipped into an ivory lace sundress with ivory pumps, before attempting to expedite my daughter's dressing efforts.

"You're yanking me bald," Nikki complained when I tried to brush tangles from her long hair that was inching closer to her butt crack than our agreed upon length.

Gabriel walked into the living room wearing dress shirt, slacks, tennis shoes and white Letterman gym socks. "Well girls, I've never been married in tennis shoes, so maybe this marriage will work." He reached over and kissed me.

Nikki utilized our smooch to slip away and do her own brushing.

"How could you be doubtful of us?" I reached up and scratched his sexy moustache.

"Cause I'm part of *us*, and I'm far from perfect."

"So am I, but together we're Plato's perfect fit."

"Damn weird philosophers," he said with a grin. "Leave 'em at home and let's go."

"Look. The sun's shining," Nikki said as she slid in the car. "Do meteorologists ever get it right?"

"My positive vibes for good weather trumped their prediction of rain." I fastened my seat belt.

"I do. I do," Gabriel said several times as Nikki and I chatted along the drive to Friendswood.

"Why are you reiterating *I do?*" I finally asked.

"Cause I don't want to screw up in the presence of clergy and say I'd do just about anything for a piece of ass."

"Seriously, Gabriel. How bout as a wedding gift you retire that stupid line?"

"What? It bugs you?" The corners of his mouth edged upward.

"Kill it, bury it, and never resurrect it!"

"Whatever you say, Ms. Steinem."

Radio saved his bum. As we pulled into the JP's driveway, *Chapel of Love* came across the airwaves. "Someone's taking care of the musical arrangements after all," Nikki said. When we walked inside, the JP handed me a bouquet of yellow roses before beginning the ceremony. I looked at Nikki, who was smiling precociously as though all the little unplanned pieces had magically fallen in place. Gabriel stood beside me and darted his eyes down the top of my sundress while Nikki lifted her eyebrows Groucho-style— another of his habits she acquired. After the epithalamium when we were pronounced husband and wife, Gabriel and I locked lips.

"Save something for the honeymoon." Nikki bolted out the door.

We returned to our car after the quick ceremony, and the first song on the radio was Paul Stokey's *Wedding Song*. "Which one of you called the radio station?" I asked.

"You think I'm that resourceful or sentimental?" Gabriel winked at Nikki.

"I swear we didn't." Nikki lifted her hand, testimonial style. "It must've been a higher power."

"Yeaaah, maybe Jimmy Swaggart," Gabriel joked. He wasn't a fan of TV evangelists.

"It was kismet." I leaned against him. "I'm on Cloud Nine."

"What else is new, Blondie?" the two chimed in unison.

I never thought it possible to love Gabriel more, but life after marriage was glorious. He verified everything I always dreamed love could be, and with passion and compassion perfectly blended, every day was Valentine's, every night the Fourth of July. When I did stupid things (which I did often), he acted like he did dumber things all the time. I could have blown a hole through the roof, and he would have calmly said "Great, I was thinking about putting a sky light up there anyway." He listened to every word I spoke—even trivial ones—with such quiet concentration it flattered me and made my imperfect feelings vanish. I gave him rubdowns when his legs ached. I loved doing his laundry and folded his socks and underwear as though they were the shroud of Turin. When he did yard work, and I brought iced tea or Budweiser for his riding lawnmower trek, he cupped his hand over his mouth and blew me kisses until I disappeared inside. We were that annoying couple at red lights too busy with each other to notice light changes, causing people to lay on their horns. For us, love was simple. I didn't try to analyze our happiness, we just were. He colorized my black and white world and I knew beyond a shadow of a doubt, I was his life as fully as he was mine.

But oh, his idiosyncrasies. The man who had never belched in my presence, read cookbooks and moaned while reciting recipes like he was reading a Braille version of *Playboy*. He often shoved a pair of my panties in his back pocket, claiming he wiped the sweat from his brow with them during the day. "Beats a raggedy ass ole bandanna and makes me think you're right there with me."

"Do it once, you're a philosopher. Do it twice you're a pervert."

"Blondie, where do you get these expressions?"

"Yeah I know." I handed him my car keys. "You've never heard of Voltaire."

Gabriel was teaching Nikki to drive.

"She drove into the gate and knocked the side mirror off your car, so we're moving onto Body Shop 101. She drives wilder than you. Put two Budweisers on ice for me."

I watched out the window as he instructed Nikki on checking air pressure in tires and all fluid levels. They walked inside laughing, with Gabriel affectionately calling her "Boy."

"Thanks, Old Man," she warmheartedly said while he slugged back a beer. "You're the most patient guy on Earth. Good thing you're teaching me to drive 'cause Mom and I would've ripped out each other's hair by now."

Gabriel slid behind her and pretended to yank hair from her head.

Many weekends were spent with Ben and Mei boating on Clear Lake, and afterwards we often stopped by Gloria's for a quick visit since her house was along the way. I desperately wanted things to return to the way they were, and soon Gloria began dropping by our home. Brief visits only, but I felt hopeful. Hope made no efforts, even though I called repeatedly trying to reopen communication lines. Mending family fences became my goal.

Shortly after Gabriel returned from visiting Lauren and Skylar in Phoenix, Astrid called, saying she had had quarreled with her parents and they froze her trust fund. The chick who had never worked a lick in her life couldn't find a job. Gabriel agreed to send money. "Little Miss Finishing School said she was so desperate she almost lowered herself by working as a waitress."

"Oh, the horror." I flung my hand across my mouth, and then smiled as visions of me waitressing half naked to support myself and Nikki flashed before my eyes. Ironically that inglorious job allowed me to meet my glorious dream man. From a young age, I dreamed I would be swept away by an Adonis wearing a three piece suit and mesmerizing me with iambic pentameter, and here I was, head-over-heels in love with this rugged blond who wore faded jeans and charmed the pants off me with eloquent prose like, "Git in the truck, Blondie."

෬ඁ

"How are you and that cute husband doing?" Patrice asked in one of her rare calls.

"Words can't explain the emotions that evolve from knowing the love I feel for this man is one hundred percent mutual."

"You're lucky, indeed. Especially with this scary malady sweeping the globe. AIDS has certainly put a damper on my recreational sex. I'm taking the abstinence route until scientists unravel this mysterious disease."

"I feel for all the singles out there dating. And thank God for this wonderful man. He works more than I'd like, but other than wanting more time with him, nothing is lacking in my life."

"That's a significant statement. Other than time, nothing is lacking?"

"Really. We consider ourselves the luckiest couple alive. Just yesterday Delilah said Gabriel and I have a 'fairy tale' love because in real life people subject themselves to each other's bodily functions. Then she belched. Or farted. It was hard to tell over tell over the phone line."

"She's still crazy and crude, I see. I'm just happy your life is nearing perfection."

"Well, as close to perfect as I've ever imagined. We attend a small neighborhood church that's awakened our anesthetized spiritual sides and somewhat soothed my lingering guilt. Gabriel still has regrets about being apart from Lauren and Skylar."

"Not seeing his girls blossom into young ladies must be tough. Of course you'll be supportive since you still regret Nikki's abandonment by her dad."

"True. I cheerfully send Gabriel off on trips to visit his girls in Arizona, happy for their connection and hoping one day they might accept me."

"How could they not?"

"They're teenage girls, Patrice. I'm the woman they believe broke up their childhood home. Do the emotional math."

"Tough equation, but don't give up hope."

"I haven't. It's just that Gabriel and Victoria made marginal progress during their marriage, but since we tied the knot all small steps forward seem to have turned into giant leaps backward."

"Sounds like you have a ton of work ahead of you. Speaking of which, I've got to finish a project I've been ignoring. Otherwise I could be looking for a new job soon."

"You would never have to look. Jobs always find you. Bye, Patrice. Love you!"

21

After weeks of trying to reach Beau by phone, I took time to drive to his sports bar. Vacant! The "For Sale" sign listed a realty company contact, but I couldn't squeeze Beau's personal info from them. Probably for the best. If Beau and Lola were resolving marital problems the last thing they needed was my intrusion.

On the home front, Nikki and Gabriel grew so close, at times I felt excluded, especially when it came to their obsession with cooking magazines and Leon Hale's *Houston Post* column about travels through Texas. Meanwhile I helped Gabriel co-parent mischievous, five-year-old, Luke. Boys sure are different than girls. One Saturday night as I took my bath, Luke came into the bathroom. "Have you seen my dad." His eyes went auto-pilot male to my breasts.

"He's not under these bubbles." I lowered myself while checking the proximity of my towel. "So grab your Etch-A-Sketch and draw his likeness to keep you company until he shows up. Now scoot!"

Seconds later Luke reappeared, eyes firmly locked on my boobs. "Can't find him."

"Your dad's not here," I shooed him off again.

He looked back intently while closing the door. I intuitively added more scented soap bubbles. On his third return, I narrowly escaped spine injury when I banged into the bottom of our shallow tub. "Gabriel, please pry Luke away and put a leash on him so I can enjoy my bath."

Gabriel materialized, sporting a wide grin. "You just don't understand the intricacies of the male mind."

"Obviously." I blew soapy suds from my chin.

"Seeing you naked could cause premature puberty in any boy, especially one with my blood." He herded Luke away, raising his eyebrows Grouch-style. "Wood eye."

Gloria began stopping by on weekends to see Luke, and soon Gabriel and I were attending family functions at her home or the lake house. Hope seemed detached, despite my attempts to chat. Gloria assured me she would help bridge the gap between us, but the situation was taking on a *River Kwai* look to me.

And when Gabriel's grandmother came from Boston in January for a family reunion, explosives were detonated. The minute we arrived at the gathering, Hope and Gloria acted as though hugging me was comparable to licking a microscopic slide with an AIDS virus on it. I retreated to a back bedroom. I had not imagined their rudeness. Conn's wife Kim followed, and in a soft voice informed, "Before you got here, Hope told Nonna that you're a condescending snob."

I shrugged.

Kim continued. "Then Gloria said they were surprised Nikki was at the reunion instead of out making indentations in the back seat of some boy's car."

I jumped up. Insult me and I'll work toward peaceful resolution. Insult my daughter—game over. Respect for Gabriel kept me from making a scene. I returned to the gathering and sat quietly beside Nikki.

When we got home, I told Gabriel about Hope and Gloria's venomous comments. He exploded. After phoning Hope and filling her ear with expletives, he called Gloria for a modified chastising.

Hope withdrew once again. Gloria acted like a cordial martyr. Gabriel shunned both, making me feel awful. When his mother called inviting us to events, Gabriel rejected without consulting me. No doubt I was blamed for his declines. Then when sharp pains invaded my forehead inducing mega migraines, Gabriel joked that Gloria had fashioned a voodoo doll in my likeness.

Gabriel's jokes soon subsided and despite his denial, I sensed him missing his relationship with Gloria and Hope. "Stop and visit Gloria on your way home from work." I insisted. He did. And my insecurities escalated. Personal time with Gabriel shrank while he habitually visited the woman who disdained me. The ominous cloud we fell under during the Seventies once again reared its ugly head.

Lauren and Skylar phoned occasionally, but never said much to me when I answered.

"They still consider me a homewrecker," I told Gabriel.

"Stop feeling guilty about the past and stop making unjust presumptions." He got furious.

Maybe I was a delusional moron. My once loving husband seemed less attentive due to work, and evenings spent talking after dinner changed considerably. He calculated job bids aloud. I straddled his lap and purred, "Ummm." He kissed me and said, "Five more minutes." I pressed against him and licked his cheek. He kissed me and said "Four minutes." I wiggled closer, he continued the countdown. We had a script.

What began as communication difficulties, soon became talking less to avoid misunderstandings. Aware of our slow drifting apart, we agreed to professional counseling. One small step toward solving our problems—one giant leap for Mr. I Hate Therapists. I even agreed to Gabriel's contingency clause: if no major breakthrough happened in three visits, bye-bye therapy. First visit was a non-productive history gathering hour. Second visit entailed me doing most of the talking and question answering, while Gabriel nodded or grunted when asked for input. Third visit; dreadful! After Gabriel told our counselor he loved me and wanted to do whatever necessary to fix us, I broached the subject of Gloria and Hope. Gabriel wordlessly shook his head as though the family feud a figment of my imagination. He stood, wrote a check, and walked out. I followed. And that was that.

Gabriel suddenly became jealous, questioning my lunch habits and who I chatted with during the day. Regardless of my answers, he cocked his eyebrow suspiciously and asked, "Yeaaah? You sure 'bout that?" In all my years of knowing him, he'd never exposed a jealous bone. Maybe insecurity caused it to surface, but I didn't like it. One evening I walked outside and found him searching my car. My tight-lipped husband instantly volunteered info. "I'm clearing your car to vacuum it."

"You can stop looking for condoms—I keep those at the office." My tummy violently alerted me things were going haywire just like they had in the Seventies.

"This is crazy!" He grabbed the vacuum and took it into the garage.

"Let's please talk." I followed him.

"About what?" he asked without looking up, Marlboro dangling from the side of his mouth, Bogart-style.

"Why we can't talk, for starters."

He inhaled intensely, and finally moved his hand to remove the cigarette. "You're the big talker, the one who always got me to talk. Now you seem to have a problem doing that."

"Which is what I'm trying to do now Gabriel," I said cautiously. "But you seem to have a problem listening."

He looked at me, threw a tool across the garage, and shouted, "Unsalvageable!"

"So, you're throwing in the towel?" I yelled back.

"I was talking about the goddamned tool, not us."

"Right. You and your stupid tools."

"Look, I know you're embarrassed about how I make my living. I think you want me to be some successful executive, so you can have a life filled with fancy clothes, glitzy parties, and expensive champagne."

"How can you say that? You're talking to a woman who once worked in a topless club, remember? Gabriel, you own a successful business and love your work. I'd wear rags, eat sardine sandwiches every day, and drink sewer water if we were happy like we used to be. I think you're the one with insecurities."

"Don't start with your goddammed pop psychology."

I stormed out of the garage in tears. Instead of following me, he turned up the radio to listen to some damn AM talk show.

Gabriel and I began losing sleep and our sex life changed. Drastically. Cliffs Notes foreplay, five minute sex (give or take a minute), and within weeks, we seemed like strangers occupying the same house. If I tried to talk, he clammed up. If he tried to talk, I jumped in my car and drove to the lake. I couldn't understand what was happening, and Gabriel rejected my pleas for continuing therapy.

Suddenly the kitchen—our favorite room for talking—became a room filled with confusion and question, where we walked around for hours in interrogatory circles. One night, he stopped me and held me at arm's length. "Cherie I don't know what the hell's happening here, but our inability to talk is tearing me apart. . . Why the fuck can't we communicate?"

"Because you won't talk about the real issue."

"What real issue?"

"I think you resent me for separating you from Gloria and Hope. And your daughters."

"Bullshit, Cherie! That's your goddamned excuse." He threw his hand angrily into the air. A moment later, he looked into my eyes and gently rubbed my arm. "I'm scared to death I'm losing you and I'm trying to protect myself from the inevitable."

"The inevitable?" I leaned against his hand enjoying the feel of his touch. "Gabriel, I love you with all my heart, but I'm coming apart. Why won't you go back to therapy? Make some kind of effort."

His hand fell from my shoulder. "You know I don't believe in that goddamned quackery! I'm guessing you want more than I can offer, and you're just looking for reasons to leave. So go ahead, Cherie, blame it all on me."

"I'm not blaming anyone. But maybe if you weren't working so much." I hesitated, searching for the right words. "Maybe your business is growing too fast for you to handle."

His face became animate with anger and hurt. "I may not be able to make a marriage work, but I can damn sure run my business," he roared.

A cold silence filled the room as he emptied his ashtray and went to bed.

♾

I desperately needed Beau. Discussing my marital problems with other friends seemed moot. Sensible Patrice suddenly seemed irrational when she began dating a married man; Delilah was bored with her nice guy husband; former sitter Rachel worried her husband was doing drugs; and even our neighborhood preacher was having an affair with the church secretary. People

busy with their own secrets and deceptions, while their marriages kept rolling along as usual. Gabriel and I truly loved each other. He wasn't having
an affair. And I damn sure wasn't. Our energy was spent trying to stop our
disintegrating union.

Nights were incredibly bad. Unable to comfort each other, we rarely
slept, and Gabriel often left our bed to lie on the living room sofa, thinking
his tossing and turning bothered me. One night I got out of bed to sit at
the kitchen table, hoping an answer would transcend from our once favorite
place. In the quietness I heard a match strike across its box, and saw a flame
across the table.

"What's happening to us?" Gabriel asked gently. "Where the hell are
the two people who could share their innermost feelings about everything?"

"We're right here, and we've got to talk." I pulled my chair close to
him.

"Oh, Cherie." He shook his head hopelessly. "How can we fix this
mess?"

I wanted to hold my hands against his cheeks and feel the touch of his
moustache while kissing his lips, but instead I gently touched his knee,
knowing my next comment would upset him. "Give therapy another try?"

He just sat there pretending not to hear. Or he thought I was Kreskin.
I waited for what seemed ten minutes, before getting furious. He asked
how to resolve things, and then went mute like it was all on my shoulders.
I jumped up, shoved my chair under the table and stormed away.

By the end of February our home had become a house. Our conversation had turned to interrogation. Our happiness had turned to sadness. Our
euphoria had turned to depression. Interwoven with all the confusion was
some strange life-force that kept us clinging to each other.

Then came two days of silence by Gabriel. I reacted by driving to the
lake as usual, but this time stayed for hours, staring at the water for a solution to the unknown. I got home late, walked down the hall toward our
bedroom, and overheard Gabriel talking on the phone. "I'll drop off five
hundred tomorrow and another five next week. That should tide you over."

Gloria was having another financial crisis. I walked into the room, and
Gabriel looked at me as though I'd caught him making an appointment
with a hooker. "I'll talk to you tomorrow." He abruptly ended the call.

"He speaks!" I snapped, my voice shaking from fear and anger. "For a while I thought I was living with Helen Keller. Sorry to interrupt your *personal* call. I can leave again."

"Do whatever you want, Cherie."

"Like you?"

"What do you mean?"

"That you secretly support your mother, despite saying her reckless spending irritates you."

"I'm embarrassed and angry that I can't say no, and fork over cash every time she comes crying to me."

"Gabriel I don't care if you fund her irresponsible behavior. What bothers me is how you've stopped sharing information with me."

"Enough said," he barked. "This is my personal issue."

"Then perhaps you should be *sleeping* with your personal issue."

Dead air filled the space between us. Gabriel had always internalized instead of talking, but nothing infuriated me more than his silence. I rushed into our guest bedroom to spend the night, wishing I had been composed enough to keep inflammatory remarks in tow. I'd said enough already. Or hadn't said nearly enough. I was tired of being upset and frustrated about our inability to dig out of the quagmire that was zapping our emotional strength as it pulled us under.

The following morning Gabriel politely refused to acknowledge my existence. Sure, I used the words "sleeping" instead of "having sex," but he interpreted my hateful message.

Daily, we withdrew more and more. I rarely cooked, and if we did dishes together it was in total silence. One evening as Nikki and I sat watching television, he walked in with one of Gloria's Corningware dishes, placed it in the fridge, and then cut through the living room ignoring both me and Nikki. Instead of responding to her cheery greeting of "Hi, Old Man" he just nodded. I looked at her puzzled and hurt expression and felt upset over our collapse affecting my daughter who dearly loved him. Then thoughts of his daughters having been affected for years because of our actions filled my head. At that very minute, I confronted the only solution to our ultimate insoluble dilemma.

After an evening of ear splitting silence, Gabriel showered then sat in the living room reading the *Houston Post* and smoking. The calm face my eyes always loved to linger on looked as handsome as ever, even with his damp hair combed straight back. I leaned against the wall separating the dining and breakfast rooms, then looked at his profile in a bewildered, soft-focus, sort of way. As he slowly inhaled his Marlboro, I lovingly etched that memory in my mind and wondered how the hell everything got to this awful point. He sensed my presence, looked over, and curtly asked, "You need something?" Without answering, I walked through the living room, into our guest room, closed the door, threw myself across the bed, and cried myself to sleep.

When Gabriel left for work the next morning, I felt fairly certain he knew I wouldn't be there when he returned. As soon as his van left our driveway, I phoned in sick, called Mother to say Nikki and I needed to stay with her for a few days, and then called movers. Nikki was on school break, so when she woke up, I told her we were leaving. "I don't understand, Mom. You and Gabriel love each other." She began crying.

"We always will, but love doesn't conquer all. Even if it were possible, the O'Quinn familial bond should never be broken or bent like it is now. I won't make Gabriel choose between me and his blood line."

Together we cried and packed our belongings along with the moving company I hired who guaranteed to have our house packed and in their truck by four o'clock. We alternated giving information to those rushing about our house, each of us answering questions when the other was crying too hard to speak.

22

We arrived at Mother's house with me brushing away tears while Nikki comforted. "Are you okay?" Mother asked, standing in her sensible pumps, starched apron over her floral dress, and white dishtowel across her shoulder.

I nodded yes. Instead of prying, Mother hummed and rattled pots and pans in her immaculate kitchen. She was such a contrast to Gloria. Quietly passive yet always forgiving and supportive of her two children and husband without choking us with her apron strings. Dad stayed in the den playing a tune on his harmonica he'd likely heard in some smoky honky tonk. Mother and Nikki were pushing food at me when Gabriel called.

"What the hell are you doing? Please come home."

I ached for him, but couldn't go back. "I'm allowing you to be with Gloria and Hope again, and most importantly, Lauren and Skylar."

"Bullshit, Cherie! Are you out of your fucking mind?"

He was still cursing as I hung up the phone.

The following morning I woke up in a pool of sweat and a state of panic over a horrible nightmare. Then I looked across the room at Mother's armoire, realized it wasn't a nightmare and rushed out of bed to throw up. I threw up until I doubled over with dry heaves, fell onto the bathroom floor, and howled into a towel. Getting through the day was agonizing, but I exercised false bravado to calm Nikki. My lovey almost stroked the fur off Mistletoe.

When I phoned Eduardo, he reminded me he was leaving for a two week vacation, and insisted I take as much time off as needed. Others could catch his phone and paperwork would wait. Major relief.

213

Gabriel called every night for two weeks. The hurt in my heart contrasted anger at him. Maybe our breakup was inevitable, even without Gloria's interference. Beau once said happiness taken at the expense of others often turns to sadness. Ours had, tenfold. But I believed Gabriel should be with family, and refused to return home. I sobbed nightly and rarely slept. Then Gabriel's calls stopped.

Not hearing his voice was torture. I prayed for strength, certain I was doing the right thing for him. After a few days, I phoned my former home desperate to learn Gabriel was okay.

"Yeah," he gruffly answered the phone.

"Gabriel." I gulped, nervously. "I just wanted to check on you."

"I'm great, Cherie." His voice was cold.

"You don't sound great." I attempted to soothe. "Emotionally."

"Emotionally? I'm void of emotions. Something you stirred in me that I never knew existed, then goddamn yanked away."

"Gabriel you know I had to leave." My heart pulsated insanely. "And you also know I love you."

"All I know is that I loved you more than I knew was possible," he said angrily. "Christ, you were my life. Just because we couldn't work things out overnight, you rushed away."

"Gabriel, I left for the well-being of your relationship with your family."

"Don't try to glorify your leaving on philosophical grounds. You ripped my heart out, then kept slashing it with constant rejection."

"I'm sorry," I cried. "When I stopped hearing your voice, I knew I was wrong. As long as we talked, I guess I still felt connected."

"You mean as long as I called and begged you to come back, you felt good. Well, I felt like hell. Goddammit, Cherie, you hurt me and it'll goddamn never happen again."

"I didn't mean to hurt you. We just need time apart."

"You've got all the time you want." His hostile tone cut straight through me. "I've built a wall that no one can tear down." Click.

I threw up.

I called Eduardo and told him I could no longer work for him. He sympathized and advised. "You don't have to work for me, but get back to the city where you can take care of yourself and Nikki."

After far too little sleep and far too much upchucking, I managed to stumble into survival mode. Back in Houston, I went full-time paralegal with a huge firm, leased a townhouse, and enrolled Nikki at Memorial High to finish her senior year. Despite staying super busy, my active life failed to keep me from feeling like a part of me had died

Gabriel and Nikki's relationship continued, with her visiting our former home, talking with him on the phone, and occasionally meeting for lunch. Through Nikki, I knew Gabriel was okay. My heart was broken, but I was determined to let go and let him reunite with his family.

∽

I spent my fortieth birthday at a bar getting swirling drunk and trying to forget. Under the influence of vodka, I swallowed a small tablet called XTC that a girl I hardly knew placed in my palm. "It's totally vogue and one hell of an aphrodisiac," she'd said. Within minutes I was feeling astatic instead of ecstatic, and began waxing rhapsodically about my undying love for Gabriel. If it had an aphrodisiac effect, I never felt it. Maybe ECT (Electroconvulsive Therapy) would have been a better alternative. Within weeks, I'd moved from Ecstasy to cocaine. Freud took cocaine, so what could it hurt? Along with cocaine came any sleeping meds I could get my hands on. It's hard to catch Z's when Bolivian oblivion ignites ones central nervous system into overdrive. But the white powder couldn't repress thoughts of Gabriel or keep me from reaching out in fitful sleep for the feel of his flesh.

"You okay, Sis?" Ellen awoke me by phone. She was becoming my alarm clock.

"Fine," I lied.

"I'm here if you need me. Anytime."

"Thanks, Ellen." I headed to my kitchen for coffee. "And please tell Mom I'm sorry."

"Why?"

"She called one day rattling off self-help quotes and I told her to mind her own damn business."

"Mother will be just fine. But Jim said Nikki moved out."

"Yes, my daughter diplomatically chastised my behavior before leaving. She was sweet about it and even kissed me goodbye, but snooty Mistletoe turned her butt in my face."

I could've sworn my sister whispered, "Smart feline" before she hung up.

Disturbed by Nikki's departure, I struggled to stop my sudden yet significant cocaine use. By August I hadn't stopped, but I had *somewhat* slowed my intake.

Patrice checked in occasionally, but her goal to become partner didn't leave time for personal visits. She felt remorse for having dated a married man, and asked my forgiveness for her ultimate betrayal to women. I asked her to forgive me the same, and understood her regrets. Patrice then regaled me about her exploits with a plethora of unusual *unmarried* men; from astrophysicists to Zen gurus. Talking to her inspired me to lift my lugubrious ass from my sofa view of Iran Contra news and seek the company of live men.

"How's the dating game going?" Patrice asked.

"Disastrous. First up to bat was a drop dead gorgeous guy ten years younger than me who worked in the same office building. He left notes filled with Springsteen song lyrics on my car."

"Wasn't 'I'm on Fire' was it?"

"You guessed it. And he underlined the 'sheets soaking wet' part. Anyway I met him at Steak and Ale for dinner and drooled over him. Until our food arrived. His table manners were worse than that red-headed dancer whose breakfast with Al was a memory I'd shoved so deep, I figured only hypnosis could retrieve it."

"Not many things are as appalling as atrocious eating habits."

"Amen. So, I slipped away and found a phone book, and when he asked for my home number, I gave him the number to the Houston Zoo."

"That's a shame, but not enough reason to leave the game."

"I didn't quit. Second suitor on the mound was an older, less attractive, wealthy president of a small company. We'd chatted in the building lobby several times and eventually agreed to meet at Cyclone Anaya's for drinks and dinner."

"Arriba, margaritas!"

"Hardly. The Porsche driving, platinum card holder, pulled out a 2 for the price of 1 coupon, calculated the waiter's tip to the penny, snuggled against me like he was expecting sex for the meal he hadn't bought, and asked if we should welcome morning at his place or mine."

"Unpardonable," Patrice said. "How'd you get away?"

"Told him my ex-husband just got paroled from prison and we'd be lucky to leave the restaurant without gunshot wounds. No more dating men from the office building."

I didn't tell Patrice, but snorting coke with my madcap group of friends seemed more sensible. I quickly reverted to hanging with druggies. Not street corner thugs, just your typical run of the mill businessmen who functioned under the influence.

∾

During what I can only refer to as a six month blur, I struggled through work and lied to family and friends, including Gabriel, who called with concerns about my drug use. I swore I wasn't partaking that often. Just a partial frying of the brains. Okay. I had a problem. Cocaine isn't cheap. I was taking money from one credit card to make payment on another and Citibank was after my ass like horny hyenas in mating season. With my half-functioning frontal lobe, I began searching for Beau who wasn't listed with local information. I needed him. But with or without my spiritual guide, the time for voluntary withdrawal had commenced.

Counseling would've been wise, but I opted for exercise and working longer hours to kick my habit. Being naturally hyper, I'd never really liked cocaine, but it was the drug of choice among my friends. I detached from the wild bunch and met new friends at the gym, which resulted in much more than healthy benefits. Especially with Brandon, a shy, world travel-ing, chemical engineer who was engaged to a charming Columbian girl. He never flirted like most gym guys and despite his being heavy into politics (big turn off), we connected while treadmill walking and watching national news. Brandon traveled frequently, but introduced me to his anti-drug friends who lightly bonded with me while he was away. His financial guru friend thoughtfully schooled me in salvaging my credit rating.

Thanks to Brandon, his fiancée Bianca, some of their friends, and my darling, Nikki, I celebrated six months of blow free living.

"I snagged an interview with Kevin Dorsey," Nikki bragged. She was either visiting more frequently or I hadn't realized she'd been with me throughout my purple haze. Cocaine blizzards tend to impair one's vision. Still working on her degree in journalism while working part-time as a secretary, Nikki seemed indefatigable. "Took two hours and two cassette tapes, but I got a ton of Dorsey's opinionated viewpoints."

"Fabulous! Your first interview."

"With my favorite hard-rock radio personality." She was giddy.

My sweet daughter was blooming into a responsible adult despite inconsistent upbringing by her irresponsible mom. "But you must be excited about buying the house in West Houston."

"I'm closing tomorrow, moving on Saturday."

"Congrats, Mom. That area's supposedly the soon-to-be epicenter of Houston."

"New businesses, more subdivisions, great restaurants and fabulous shopping. And naturally horrendous traffic."

"I'll help you get settled. After all you start the new job on Monday, right?"

"Yes, lovey. Wish me luck."

Working for a patent and trademark attorney. Yawn. A monotonous job with a sixty-year-old boss was boring, but his not knowing the difference between cocaine and cocoa powder proved a positive contrast from prior partying firms. Minor traces of my snow daze lingered in my medulla oblongata, and my finances were getting back on the plus side after the nose dive they took during my all-inclusive Peruvian powder excursion.

Brandon wasn't around much, but when he was, I felt fairly comfortable confiding in him. Not one hundred percent. He knew about my prior narcotic use, knew about my attempts to get over Gabriel, and knew I was trying to locate Beau. I bent his ears repeating stories about my dear friend—especially Beau's clever *Jack of Clubs* trick—yet never divulged my true "pasties and go-go" history. I told him I once waitressed in Beau's bar, and let it go at that.

∾

"Mom," Nikki said into the phone. "You need to get in touch with Gabriel." Her voice conveyed a sense of urgency.

"Not happening."

"It's not personal about you two," she assured. "Respectfully call him, please."

I was hesitant after not hearing his voice in months, but dialed him up at Nikki's urging.

Gabriel answered somberly, and said something about the weather before stammering several confusing statements about us.

"What's all the double talk, Gabriel? In one breath you say we can't live together, in the next you say you'll never love anyone like you loved me. I'm familiar with past and present tense, so let's conclude this conjugation discussion."

"What do you mean?"

"Get to the point. For once, I'm not the one talking in circles and stumbling over words."

"Well, I'd like to get on with my life," he stuttered. "If you'd let me."

Oh God, the dreaded words. He was moving forward. Without me! Wasn't this what I wanted? For us to get on with our lives—independent of each other? "Well, I'm lousy at interpreting hem hawing, but my guess is that you're hot for someone and need a divorce."

"Yeaaah?"

"Tell me about her," I said in someone else's composed voice while yanking my hair.

"Well, I guess you could say Fran's your complete opposite. She's a boisterous Cadillac saleswoman who thrives in crowds and loves to party."

"Enough said," I interrupted. No need to go bald headed over some loud mouth peddler. "I suppose a four year separation is long enough." My heart plummeted. "Let's divorce."

"Since you have paralegal background, I'd really appreciate your doing the paperwork. I'm tired of paying divorce attorneys."

"I'll bet you are. I'm not familiar with family law, but I'll try to put something together." I was chewing my lip worse than I did the first month I gave up blow.

After two phone conversations with Fran, I threw together divorce papers, and agreed to meet her and *my* husband. Fran was polite enough, but her abrasive voice annoyed me no end.

I fought resurfacing emotions as I met the happy couple in a supermarket parking lot midway between Houston and Pearland. Fran was sitting behind the wheel of her Cadillac, but opened her door and jumped out, taking full command as Gabriel sat quietly inside. Odd. Feeling Gabriel's presence as though he was standing beside me, I briefed Fran on various legal procedures, and then as calmly as possible told her I was going to say hello to him. As she slid back behind the wheel to relay my message, I thought if beauty schools gave grants based on the amount of hair spray used in a style, she'd be a recipient. Looking as nervous as I felt, Gabriel opened his door and stood outside her car, leaving the door ajar.

"Jeez, I'm not going to bite you." I tried to hide my uneasiness. He had shaved his moustache—a minor turn off for me. Minor. He lost it a couple of times during our marriage, but I always begged him to grow it back since his sexy 'stache sent shivers down my spine. "I just wanted to say hello and tell you to take care of yourself."

"Hello Cherie," he said sotto voce, looking into my eyes. He shook his head then looked away. "I'll send you a copy of the divorce decree."

"Toss it. Unless it's wrapped in money, I don't need it."

Congratulating myself for being flip and not breaking down, I held my chin high, walked back to my car, climbed inside, cranked the engine, and *almost* got out of the parking lot before tears cascaded down my face. My heart was racing, threatening to combust. I needed Beau!

My zillionth attempt to get beyond Gabriel found me shopping with Nikki, watching French films with Ellen (my sister and I embraced our common interests), and visiting my parents. I'm not sure what transpired, but Dad said "good riddance" to liquor, and actually retained his supersonic personality—unlike some reformed drinkers. On the flip side, Mother said "hello" to convivial behavior. She was delightful to be around once she unearthed her wry little sense of humor. A personality obviously stifled due to tip-toeing around an alcoholic who frequently dropped the F-bomb around children she dreamed were destined to become princesses.

Staying super busy proved more comforting than the turbulent world of emotions. Then something wonderful happened. Brandon was competing in a dart tournament at a neighborhood sports bar when he noticed people talking to an older, impeccably groomed gentleman whose stature and bass voice fit my numerous descriptions of Beau Duvalé. Brandon introduced himself. Talk about kismet—the man was Beau! He wrote his phone number on a brand new deck of cards for Brandon to give me.

გ

How easily Beau and I renewed our friendship. I drove to his apartment, surprised to see him living so modestly after the prestigious addresses he'd held in the past. He and Lola had divorced again, and she drained him financially. He said he simply wasn't up for a bitter fight and after all, it was only money. Beau had emphysema and was much thinner, but still looked great. The smile lines around his steel-grey eyes merely enhanced his looks.

"Cherie, you're such a delicate flower," Beau flattered, "still coming into bloom."

"And you're still as handsome as Clark Gable." I allowed tears to fill my eyes.

"An aging Clark." He winked. Then he coughed. I was worried about his health. Too many years had slipped by and I felt guilty about not being there for him.

"Brandon says you split from Gabe."

"Oh, that's too tender a spot in my heart to discuss right now, Beau."

"Then how is Nikki?" He changed subjects. "She was the cutest little thing and so smart."

"She's doing well. God only knows how she managed to rise above my negligent parenting. You know where I was hanging out during some of her childhood years."

"Indeed," he said with a chuckle. "My *immoral* establishment—as you put it. Still, those were some fun days at the Jewel Box, huh baby?"

"Maybe more fun for you, than me." I rolled my eyes. Beau had a way of imparting humor and dignity to topless entertainment.

"I got a kick out of customers like blue shirt Tony. He blew a ton of money on the dancers, but didn't own a car and didn't have cab fare to get home most nights."

"I noticed he wore the same blue stripe shirt, but never knew he was broke."

"Hell, when he couldn't catch a ride, he'd wait for me to close and I'd take him safely to his shabby efficiency apartment. Making sure he got inside gave me a glimpse of his furnishings. Raggedy recliner, TV table with a tiny set, and a flimsy army surplus cot."

"Oh my. I'm pretty sure he was the one who forked over money for Paulette's bedroom suite that she bragged cost a thousand dollars. Of course she could've found a way to finagle money from a monk. She was one of the most beautiful and seductive girls to grace the Jewel Box. Remember her?"

"Only because she was a he!" Beau coughed and shook his head slightly. "So many girls came and went through that club, I barely remember their faces, much less their names."

"Thank goodness you remembered me."

"Who could forget you? You were totally out of place. Scared to death, but determined as hell. Soft spoken, but quick to spout jokes or state your opinion. Hell, I still remember some entertaining exchanges between you and customers."

"Yeah." My thoughts flew back to that small, special club.

"Until you fell in love with Gabe, and curbed your caustic tongue."

Hearing his name again caused me to gasp for air. I eyed Beau's oxygen.

"I'm sorry to hear about your break-up. Is there any chance for reconciliation?"

"No. I recently handed him his requested divorce papers."

"Oh, baby." Empathy filled his voice.

"Well." I choked back tears. "It's a long, sad story that I can't discuss right now."

"I'm sorry. Gabe was a real nice guy and I always believed you two would live happily ever after."

"So did I." Tears started to flow. "I can't believe I'm still crying over this guy."

"Here, baby." Beau handed me Kleenex. "I won't say another word until you're ready to talk about it, but I'm guessing his controlling mother and her daughter that she weakened into being her accomplice, were at the center of your split."

"Yes, ole wise one. And when I'm up for discussing it, I promise to call."

"Brandon said you two are just good friends."

"We are. Not friends like you and me, but he helped me kick my cocaine habit."

"I can't visualize you doing nose candy. But I'm glad you had someone to help you through what could've turned into a trip to the morgue. You're a strong woman, but everyone needs help when life gets rocky. Damn. What were the odds of you meeting Brandon, then me going into that particular sports bar that particular night, and having him actually recognize me?"

"I don't know, Mr. Las Vegas. I'm just glad the odds were in my favor."

"Speaking of odds, I'm betting you never read McMurtry's *Lonesome Dove* while under the influence."

"You're right. I completely missed that book."

"Well, it's a damn good western, baby. I saved the book and also taped the mini-series." Beau scurried off to his bedroom book shelf. "You'll enjoy his usual string of strong women."

"Thanks. I'll read it and we can watch your taped mini-series when I finish."

"I'm counting on it." He kissed me goodbye.

Not sure how Beau did it, but when I jumped into my Bronco, a *Jack of Clubs* card sat propped along the back of my passenger seat.

Bianca was in the US awaiting marriage to Brandon, before the two relocated to Peru for his assignment, Nikki was busy with journalism classes, Cousin Jim graduated college, Ellen and Charles became millionaires from their numerous fabrication shops, and although I had little time to spare, free moments were spent with Beau who lived thirty minutes from me. Lola had robbed him of his retirement, so any time a salvageable piece of furniture was left out for garbage collectors, he snagged it, refinished it, and sold for profit. He taught me how to refurbish, and lo and behold, I was actually good at it. Our time together usually included a visit to

Leon's Lounge, Houston's oldest bar, according to Beau. And occasionally we drove to Galveston to find our fortunes along the Seawall via some metal contraption he found. Gas for the trip quadrupled the cost of anything we uncovered, but Beau loved the thrill of searching.

Beau and I spent an entire Saturday watching his VHS taping of *Lonesome Dove*, with Beau expounding on the courage of Angelica Huston's character, "Clara moved onto a better life, despite loving Gus."

"Yes, she did."

"So get over Gabriel and move on with your life, baby."

"You need medication for your delusions, Beau. Now, tell me more Vegas stories."

"One day I'll record all my adventures. . . after I'm finishing having them. You know I intend to die in Vegas, not Houston."

"Yes, my favorite raconteur, you've told me."

"So, baby." Beau mischievously winked. "Would you like to come into my bedroom and look at my etchings?"

"You still burn cool." I followed him.

Inside his bedroom closet sat an old treasure chest with worn red satin lining. It was filled with memorabilia, but easily recognizable as the once beautiful chest that sat inside the entry of the Jewel Box decades ago.

"Remember these two?" Beau handed me a faded photo of policeman Zane and Wendy, the walleyed dancer he wound up marrying. "Don't know why I still have this." He shook his head. "What a pair."

"Yeah, a super hairy, horny cop and a gal whose one eye went straight to men's private parts."

"Her cute face couldn't detract from her ocular affliction, so we agreed she'd only work long enough to earn airfare to Ohio. Two weeks later she hooked up with Zane, who kept her at home. A blessing for everyone since her involuntary roving eye made customers uncomfortable."

"Who'd think zooming in on the crotch would bother a guy?"

"Beats me, but men did complain about her gawking at their southern regions."

"Probably insecure guys whose units couldn't handle close scrutiny," I said.

Beau chuckled and began showing me photos of him and Benny Binion at the Horseshoe Pub, a register from the private club he owned in Dallas with signatures of Lyndon Baines Johnson, Joe E. Lewis, and other famous personalities. "I could tell you a story about my brief association with Jack Ruby, but I wouldn't want you to think badly of me."

"There's nothing you could say or do to ever make me think badly of you. The respect you've shown and taught me over the years can't be undone that easily."

Beau seemed humbled as he fell into a long coughing bout. When he settled down, I monopolized the conversation so he wouldn't work himself into a frenzy regaling me with tales.

"I never want to leave Houston, Beau. Texas is my heart, so mosquitoes, humidity, traffic, flash floods, two blazing hot summer months and one freezing cold winter month are tolerable when we get to look up at these beautiful skies."

"Yeah, I've lived here so many years now, Houston's grown on me too. Gotta admit I love how foliage stays green year round, and most days I'm able to wake up with birds singing around me. Hell, I even get a kick out of watching squirrels scamper around the leafy old oak trees while I drink my morning coffee out on the deck."

My cue to exit. "Okay, I better leave so you can rest and wake up with the birds tomorrow."

Beau escorted me out the door, and kept it ajar. "Remember, baby, I love Texas as much as you, but want to be sitting at a Black Jack table in the new Mirage Casino and bellow 'Hit me again!' before keeling over. I'd love to be hauled out through the front with people saying 'Looks like we've lost another high roller' while they keep placing bets."

"Texas traitor," I yelled while walking away.

"Cosmopolitan cowgirl." Beau's raspy voice echoed into Houston's humid night air.

23

After Nikki left with her cousin Jim and his new bride Roxanne for a Christmas skiing trip in Aspen, the only holiday spirit filling my house was excitement about Brandon and Bianca's wedding. I was looking forward to being with Beau for the evening when the phone rang. "I'm just not well enough, baby," Beau apologized.

"I'll be right over."

"No, you won't!" His bass, fatherly tone rang through. "You'll go to that wedding and have fun."

"Ha. People think I'm a social butterfly, but I'm petrified of crowds. I just put on a good facade and a buttload of deodorant."

"Then mingle with millionaires and let the egomaniacs do all the talking."

"Please feel better soon, Beau. You owe me dinner."

Ten minutes into my reception mingling efforts, I noticed a towering brunet with resonant voice, putting a humorous slant on everything from antiballistic missiles to Zionism for an awe-struck audience. Entertaining like he was being paid for it, he recited JFK's inauguration speech by heart, then Patton's address to the troops. Nothing subtle about this man. Just as my mind wandered onto Gabriel's soft spoken mannerisms and how his dry humor flew past most people, the boom hit my eardrum. Perched slightly above my left shoulder, Scott introduced himself. Thirty minutes later I knew the life story of this former fighter pilot and former tax attorney turned lobbyist. Heaven help me. Taxes and politics. Scott told about dove hunting trips in Beeville, fishing at Kennebunkport, and playing golf with Vice President George Bush, before rolling into accolades for Reaganomics. As he egotistically described his Washington D.C. apartment with its spectacular view of the Capitol and his digs at The Houstonian, I scanned the room for an escape hatch.

There was no slipping away from this guy. He was ubiquitous. And no matter how minor the happenstance, Scott bounced into magniloquence that would have impressed Bill Buckley—or he rolled into humorous impressions of everyone from Pee Wee Herman to Henry Kissinger. He was unquestionably brilliant (Brandon said a 160 IQ), and by the end of the evening, I was laughing along with everyone else. It was obvious Scott had tossed back more than his fair share of whiskey, but then I was the only semi-sober one of the bunch.

After two weeks of persuasive calls from Brandon and Bianca, I agreed to a date with Gabriel's polar opposite. Scott had an unbelievable Valentino thing going, arriving with roses, complimenting everything from my head to my toes, taking me to a romantic dinner at Tony's, and quoting Shakespeare when appropriate. During our meal, Scott introduced me to several folks who stopped by our table. I didn't recognize most names, but certainly recognized Houston's hilarious sportscaster, Craig Roberts who spent several minutes chatting with Scott. I couldn't tell if he actually knew Craig or had simply covered his tab.

"Come with me to Houston's upcoming Consular Ball," said intoxicated Scott at evening's end. "It's a white-tie and tails gala event. You get to meet members of the Bush clan, Texas Attorney General Jim Mattox, Houston's Mayor Kathy Whitmire, and other dignitaries.

"What do I wear?"

"I'll take care of that. Just say you'll go."

Scott insisted on paying for my formal dress even though I assured him a personal relationship was not in our future. My evening gown was handmade by a tailor in West U (a wealthy city within a city, where local television celebs, athletes and affluent folks reside). It wasn't Armani, but a spectacular one-of-a-kind emerald green number. We mingled with local and international socialites while Scott proceeded to drink his stocky self into oblivion. I snagged his car keys, drove his Mercedes to my house, and then sent him to my guest room to sleep it off.

"What's he doing sacked out here?" Nikki stopped by the following morning and couldn't help but hear Scott's snoring. "I thought you weren't romantically interested."

"There's no hanky-panky going on. Even friendship with him is iffy. He's too high society, drinks too much, and is a flaming male chauvinist."

"C'mon, Mom. The only thing worse than a male chauvinist is a woman who won't do what she's told," Nikki joked while popping a bagel into the toaster.

"You're too young to be quoting Jack Benny and George Burns."

"I'm an old soul, Mom. Someone had to take care of you. And by letting Scott crash here you might've opened your doors as a half-way house for drunks."

"Don't forecast such horror. I'd have to move again."

She sat at the table slapping cream cheese on browned bread. "I spoke with the Old Man last night and he sounds mighty unhappy."

My heart fluttered and for a split second I weakened. "I'm sorry to hear that." I took several deep breaths. "But Gabriel moved on without me and I'm trying to do the same."

"Yeaaah? I think you both got stubborn and stopped communicating when your feelings were hurt, but I still believe you're meant for each other."

"Nikki, please don't say that. Our split was over blood being thicker than water."

"That saying is passé." She nibbled on her bagel. "Throughout time, people have murdered their own children, siblings, and other blood relatives. Trust and love seem just as powerful as blood to me—maybe even more so."

"You're young and gullible."

"Well, Mom, you vanished without a word, leaving him to come home to an empty house. Then you refused to return. That was an agonizing blow to him."

"And I apologized. But he still hasn't apologized for not supporting me over Gloria. Allowing him to get back to life with Lauren and Skylar was the best thing I could have done. He has a relationship with them now, and hopefully they're as close as he and Luke."

"Sorry I brought it up. The Old Man asked about you, I know you still love him, and I'm steering clear of this chaotic love story from now on."

∽

Unfortunately Nikki's prediction about the half-way house was on target. Scott stopped by my place at all hours when he'd had too much alcohol. Romance wasn't an option, but he seemed hell bent on a platonic relationship. Fine. Until platonic commences to suck the life from me.

Days later, Scott sat on my sofa polishing off a twelve pack while flipping channels between Kopple and Carson, oblivious to my ringing phone.

"Hello, lovey," I said, assuming it was Nikki calling so late..

"Hello yourself," Gabriel responded in dismal voice.

The television was so loud I could barely hear him. My heart pounding wildly, I interrupted Scott's clicking routine and asked him to hang up the living room phone so I could talk in the bedroom.

"So, Hot Shot, I can't drive on the freeways without seeing your gargantuan billboards."

"Ben's damn idea. We sure as hell don't need more business."

"Okay then." I changed subjects. "So, how are Gloria, Hope, and the rest of your family?"

"Everyone's fine," he said despondently.

"Except you."

"Yeaaah? I never could fool you, Blondie. You always see right through me. I'm unhappy as hell, how are you?"

"I'm happy Gabriel," I lied. "I'm dating again." Okay. Another lie. An air of mendacity filled the room as I transformed Scott into my pretend boyfriend. "He's your complete opposite."

"I'm glad you're happy." Gabriel fired up a smoke. "Blondie why do you think we chose opposites instead of working things out?"

We both knew damn well why we couldn't work things out. I wanted to shout "Family Ties," but kept my comment in check. "Well, the opposite you chose has blonde hair, like me."

"Yeah, but hers is cheesy looking crap that she plasters down with a can of hair spray."

Oh, I had noticed her truly impressive hairstyle. "How'd you end up with Francine?"

"I was confused and determined to get you out of my mind, and Gloria was trying to fix me up with every woman over the age of sixteen. Christ, Fran's boldness actually attracted me, can you believe that?"

"Sure. Victoria was outgoing and I'm not exactly shy."

"Yeaaah, but you're subtly sarcastic—like me." He paused, taking a drag on his cigarette. "Anyway, I was drinking during that time and one of the architects arranged a date between us. I didn't know about her Halcion use until much later."

"Oh pleeease, Gabriel. How'd you miss that?"

"Like I said, I was drinking too much and didn't snap that her passing out and falling off bar stools was anything other than booze. Besides, she has a couple of kids younger than Luke."

"And in steps Gabriel the caretaker. Even so, her bold persona surprises me. You were always in charge."

"Yeah . . ." he said.

"I'm sorry you're so down in the dumps, Gabriel."

"Well, selling the house on Windmill Lane has a lot to do with it, I suppose."

A lump formed in my throat. I couldn't speak. That house held special memories.

"I got cash for it," he informed. "And sunk it into a big farm house near Friendswood."

Last thing I needed to hear was some "Green Acres is the place to be" mantra, since I was no longer Farmer Brown's wife. I ended the call.

Scott was asleep when I returned to the living room, but woke long enough to ask about the call, and half-listened to my explanation. "Cher, you're a good friend to listen to him," he grunted. "Could you turn off that light and toss a blanket over me?" I'd asked him a zillion times not to

231

call me Cher, but before I could complain, his eyelids slammed shut and snoring resumed.

Didn't take long for me to realize Scott spewed more fiction than fact. Yes, he knew influential folks, but hanging with them didn't happen often. If at all. Scott claimed he was pals with Ken Hoffman, a new columnist for *The Houston Post*, whom Nikki and Gabriel adored. And Scott never introduced me to his beloved Morgan Fairchild, because she insisted their affair be clandestine to maintain her sex-symbol image. Hey, I understood. Johnny Depp asked me not to flaunt our sizzling tryst since his hectic *21 Jump Street* schedule left little time for him to answer questions about our age difference.

Nikki began hanging out in West U with law student Tad. The duo mostly hung out at preppy dive, Kay's Lounge, but frequented Houston clubs like Volcano, Numbers, Therapy, and Club No Minor, to name a few. Some were wild places, but my sequined pasties background didn't exactly sustain objections I voiced.

೧⁓ల

Gabriel called occasionally and somehow our conversations inevitably rolled into comparing Fran and my phony lover's remarkable resemblances. Both were proficient in hyperbole and decent enough when sober, but after throwing back booze they suddenly possessed the morals of maggots, and blamed alcohol for their actions.

"Fran seemed domineering, but pleasant enough when I met you with divorce papers."

"That was one of her better days," he said dryly. "Hell, she fell off the wagon right after that night. And not only is she a drunken mess, she's gained about forty pounds since then."

"Really?" I gloated inwardly, envisioning her ass looking like a keg of cottage cheese. "Well, Scott's gained weight himself. Still, he's brilliant and amusing with a redeeming quality of dazzling everyone with phenomenal vocabulary. He loves being the center of attention and can turn a simple occurrence into a mini drama or hilarious sitcom." No need to mention my faux boyfriend's propensity to prevaricate. Or Scott's drunk ass crashing at my house every time he left a bar in my neighborhood that he'd been supporting since he stumbled into it one day.

"You're lucky." Gabriel drew in smoke. "Fran thinks she's dazzling and taking center stage, but her drunken behavior is hardly a crowd pleaser."

"We could cite a litany of wrongs committed by our counterparts, but maybe we should consider our own shortcomings." Like me starting to lie almost as skillfully as Scott.

"Hell, that'd take all night, Blondie."

"That's a fact and not a fiction," I agreed, thinking of my years of analysis. "Even though my dad and I have grown closer since he stopped drinking, Patrice says I see Scott as a father figure and think if I can fix him, it'll be like fixing my dad. Repairing my childhood. Rescue him to rescue me."

"Yeaaah. Don't think I'm not familiar with the old white knight syndrome. I'm a caretaker too, especially if children are involved."

The young faces of his daughters flooded my thoughts. He had mended their childhood to the best of his ability, considering the damage we had done, and I realized all the pain I felt from leaving him hadn't been in vain. But we needed to keep our distance so things could remain repaired. "We better say goodnight. I need to get some rest and I know you still get up at some ungodly hour."

"And you still stay up watching Letterman. Say goodnight, Blondie."

"Goodnight, Gabriel. Take care of yourself."

I continued my alternative lifestyle with Scott. We were two troubled souls, fighting very different emotional dragons with little possibility of ever slaying our monsters. Worn out by my unconventional bond with Scott, during a weak moment I foolishly agreed to have lunch with Gabriel when he called. Beau knew something was up the minute he heard my voice. I fessed up about my upcoming tête-à-tête.

"Reviving a love affair is like warming up cold biscuits," he staunchly warned. "They never taste as great as they did when they were fresh baked."

"Pleeease, Beau. That's a cute analogy, but Gabriel and I aren't country cuisine. And we're not trying to revive our love affair."

"Well baby, you sure could've fooled me."

"Oh," I mumbled. Beau knew me too well.

"Did you ever read *Texasville?*" He changed subjects.

"I'm almost finished. Thank you again. I just hope the movie version does it justice."

"If McMurtry does the screenplay it'll be super. Just no *Lonesome Dove.*"

"Let's watch it when it comes out on video." I knew Beau could never sit in a theatre without coughing others out of their seats. "Can I call you back, Beau? Someone's knocking on my door."

"I need to hook up to my oxygen anyway. I'll call you tomorrow, baby."

Scott walked in with a six pack, started in on some narrative about National Security Advisor Colin Powell, then grabbed the remote and plopped his rear in front of the TV. He was rambunctiously gorging himself on a giant bag of pretzels I'd intended to keep in the family at least two weeks, when my phone rang.

"Cherie," a loud voice shrieked icily. "This is Fran O'Quinn."

"Yes. . ." I responded nervously, attempting to catch my breath.

"What's going on between you and my husband?"

I sat down on my bedroom floor, hoping she might tell me. And focusing on Beau's advice to keep quiet when a conversation was one of questionable content.

"I know Gabriel's been calling you because I found this number on his desk. Now what the hell is going on between you two?"

"Nothing. He's called here, but only to ask about Nikki," I lied.

"You sure about that?" she asked, phrasing it both as a question and the answer she wanted to hear.

"Yes." I shifted uncomfortably. "Gabriel and I are just friends." I glanced into the living room at Scott who was too busy putting a lip lock on a bottle of Coors to notice my conversation. "Fran I have company, so I need to hang up now."

"Okay Cherie. Thanks for answering my questions."

Fran seemed relieved by my inaccurate account, but for me it seemed like déjà vu all over again. I had spent too much money on analysis to let this nonsexual involvement with Gabriel get out of control. Besides, I'd parked my deceiving bum right in the middle of my bedroom floor and lied—yet again. These fibs had to stop. Lunch with Gabriel would not happen.

Beau and I spent an afternoon at Leon's Lounge and after wine, I told him about Scott's frequent visits to my "Drunks Drop Inn" motel. About Fran's call and my dishonesty with her. About my inability to detach from Gabriel. He listened patiently.

"I always liked Gabe and wish you could be together, but I don't want you getting hurt."

"When it comes to Gabriel, I can't hurt anymore than I have. And I don't want anyone else getting hurt. It's just hard not to talk when he calls."

"Toughen up, baby. This bond you've got with him isn't healthy."

"But, it's like he truly was my mythological split-apart and we're still seeking to return to our original union, Beau. Maybe love taken at the expense of others is destined to end like a Greek tragedy. All I know is that my life seems to be a series of attempts to get over him."

"I'm concerned about the animosity of his sister and mother. In-law interference has caused many a marriage to fail, but in this case they just can't keep you two apart."

"I know. So do you have any advice other than cute analogies about cold biscuits?"

"Not really. Just that you're in the middle of an emotional downpour of unsalvageable love, so please look out for yourself."

"You somewhat instilled 'look out for number one' in me years ago with Wesley, thus I've always remained emotionally detached with other men. With Gabriel, it's like he produces a conditioned reflex that accelerates my pulse, heightens my anxiety and sends me into a frenzy. If he weren't Irish, I'd swear he was related to Pavlov."

"That dog feeding, bell ringing, Russian scientist?" Beau coughed.

"That's right."

"Baby," Beau took a shallow breath before signaling the bartender for our tab. "Thought I told you years ago that everything you do in life, every friend and every relationship you possess is your choice. There's a dark side to every soul, but whether you lead or follow, do good or evil, the choice is all yours."

"Yes, you were talking dialectics and Nietzsche."

"Yep." Once again, Beau attempted to drag some air into his lungs. "And in my opinion, you should stay away from Gabriel as long as he's in the thralls of wicked Gloria."

"You're right." I jumped off my barstool to save Beau from expending energy by helping me down. Always the gentleman, he gave me a little frown that I shrugged off with a sweet smile.

"Every human being has ethical and corrupt tendencies and the merging of those is what makes us into who we are," Beau completed his observation.

"I believe in dialectics, but wasn't Nietzsche the one who hated women, then died of syphilis or some other sexually transmitted disease?"

"Life has no plot, baby."

"Hey." I thumped his shoulder. "That's my line!"

New Year's Eve was spent quietly with Beau, although we were guests of his friends for a celebration aboard a colossal yacht docked in Corpus Christi. Beau loved to mingle, but when I noticed him tiring, I found an isolated upstairs corner with a great view for observing others. We chatted about determination and free will, the cosmos, and harmonious structure. "Aristotle called metaphysics 'the first philosophy' and divided it into three parts," Beau informed as I sipped champagne. Who knew Beau was hip to metaphysics? My brain absorbed only minor bits of his explanation, but I absorbed his presence like a sponge.

Nikki and her new love, Tad, went to his family's beach house to drink champagne and welcome 1989 with his relatives, singing *Auld Lang Syne* or whatever happy people sing. Tad was a third year law student, following the footsteps of his attorney father. My girl was maturing into a responsible young lady who grew more like Gabriel every year. Besides possessing his mid-laugh snort, she listened to AM radio, made a production of watching sunsets, and often read recipes to me—complete with orgasmic sounds.

The year officially kicked off with Texan George H. W. Bush becoming the 41st President of the US in January. And in March the *Exxon Valdez* spilled eleven million gallons of oil in Alaska. Spring came and went with Gabriel calling intermittently, whilst calls from Patrice doubled due to her excitement about moving to London with potential of becoming a senior partner. "My salary is substantial, but so is the cost of living, not to mention taxes for Queenie."

"Ah yes, the royal pain in the commoner's ass."

"Speaking of pains, are you still in that symbiotic relationship with Scott?"

"How's this symbiotic for me?"

"He offers male companionship without making physical or emotional demands."

"And what benefit does Scott derive?"

"You give him credibility with his associates. It's likely you're the only sane woman who's stuck around for any length of time."

"I appreciate you calling me sane, Patrice."

"Just be careful. This guy is like one of those unsightly warts you can't burn off."

಄

Nikki stayed wrapped up in Tad all summer, which worried me some since they looked at each other the same way Gabriel and I always had. They weren't overly affectionate to the point of causing nausea in others, but no one else existed in their world. Leave it to my child to fall in love with a slow walking, calm talking, star gazing, nature loving, guitar strumming Irishman who made her giggle uncontrollably.

By the end of summer, my affiliation with Scott was making me weary. Beau made gentle allusions about my relationship being unhealthy, saying Scott wouldn't be showing up so often unless he was infatuated. Wrong. Scott was smitten with one thing only—and it came in liquid form.

As Beau's health declined, I spent much of my free time with him listening to his plans to return to Vegas. I always whined about his inevitable departure.

"Gosh, baby, you don't sound well enough to be out visiting," Beau said when I arrived after a non-contagious bout with upper respiratory.

"I'm channeling Marilyn Monroe," I whispered.

"I oughta shoot you for driving over here. It's obvious you don't feel well."

"I'm fine, I just sound awful." My illness had left me winded and speaking in hushed tones. "My meds kicked in, but I'm still wondering what the heck knocked me in my chest and battered my lungs like this."

"It's couvades." Beau rested his hand on my arm.

"You're cranking your oxygen too high, Beau. That term only applies to men and pregnancy symptoms."

"Well, I still think you're feeling sympathy pains for me."

"I am, but doc thinks I picked up some weird parasite, and prescribed antibiotics. 'Course, I think my parasite is a subspecies named Scott. If he's not travelling he's popping up at my place like an inebriated Jack-in-the-Box."

"Baby, what kind of powers do you have over men?"

"Mutual sick minds, I guess."

"Seriously," Beau said softly. "You've got to stop allowing others to drain your energy and dampen your spirit. When you totally take care of number one, you'll blossom into a magnificent flower. It won't be easy with your kind heart, but it's vital for survival of your soul."

"I still have Emerson's *Twelve Essential Essays* that you gave me my second week at the Jewel Box. You highlighted the volumes on Self-Reliance."

"You mean I didn't highlight Intellect?"

"Ha ha, and no you did not," I said in breathless undertone. "So it's your fault I'm a ditz."

"You're no ditz," he said in a voice fainter than mine.

Time for me to leave and let him rest.

The following evening Gabriel called under the pretext of sharing a comment from Ken Hoffman's latest column. "Hoffman's hilarious on occasion, but scoring good drive-thru food doesn't exactly entice me like it does you and Nikki."

"Ken only does food reports on Thursday. The other days he covers all kinds of subjects."

"Okay, fine. I'll check him out more often."

"First check out this beautiful sunset," Gabriel said.

238

I looked outside with a peaceful heart, remembering the friendship we shared before we became lovers. A friend who still made me feel so comfortable.

"Oh, yeah. Conn's wife Kim had a baby girl so you might want to drop by to see them. No need to call, they're always home and the little puke would love to see you. He always asks about you when Gloria's not around."

"Ah, someone on Walton's Mountain still cares." I took another glimpse out my window to see the sun set, and noticed Scott sitting on my sidewalk like a one man Welcome Wagon Committee. "Gotta go, Gabriel." I ended our call.

Yes, I allowed Scott's drunken bum to come inside while swearing to Beau it would be my last time to enable an alcoholic. And I booted him out before midnight, so progress was being made. Beau's comment about me taking care of number one was ringing in my ear when I fell asleep. Maybe I'd eventually learn to keep my distance from people of dubious integrity and negative karma.

⟲

"You awake?" Delilah boomed into the phone, waking me.

"Of course," I said, opening one eye to look at my bedside clock. "I'm up watching Reverend Falwell save sinners. Jeez, Delilah, it's five in the morning."

"I had to tell you what I did to Eric for falling asleep on the couch again."

I cleared my throat and rubbed my eyes, hoping she'd keep it brief.

"While he was sawing logs, I used Super Glue to bond his dick to his hairy leg."

"Not again. That's as bad as you throwing firecrackers into his lap on New Year's Eve when he doesn't stay awake until midnight with you."

She snickered. "Yeah, not too many men like roasted weenies."

Delilah behaved sensibly in business dealings, but otherwise didn't attempt to curb her immature behavior.

"I hope your kids aren't awake when Eric rises to go pee this morning."

"My teenagers spend every Saturday night with their goofy friends."

239

"Speaking of such, Nikki recently informed me that on her fourth birthday you told her Pluto and Goofy were homosexual."

"No, I said they were queer." She took a drag on her cigarette. "Well, gotta go. Eric's taking me to early mass this morning as soon as he wakes up and shaves his leg."

"I'll pray for your family and all your neighbors in Cypress, Delilah."

With Patrice living in London, Beau was my primary strength builder. His health kept him fairly homebound, and being with him helped keep my mind off Gabriel. One evening after dinner, he insisted I sit on his sofa while he searched for something. His hunt went long as I patiently waited for him. "Sorry to keep you so late, but I recorded something and want you to have it."

"Better not be an episode of *Step By Step*," I warned. Beau once mentioned he watched the sitcom because Suzanne Somers reminded him of me. Wasn't the first time I'd been compared to a blonde airhead.

"No, it's a recording of me reading a quote that I came across recently. It's right on target with my sentiment about taking risks."

"Oh sweet Beau," I yelled out. "Always trying to guide me through life."

"Baby, I just want you to become more confident. More gutsy."

"Oh." I relaxed on his sofa. Beau knew my weaknesses.

"Here, I found it," he said in muffled tone as he sauntered back into the living room.

I insisted he sit beside me, and made idle comments while patting his hand to let him catch his breath. "Now play it every day until you regain that self-confidence and spirit for life you once had." His voice was weak, but his tone was firm. He punched PLAY and we listened to his recorded voice: "Cherie, I read this quote on 'Risk' in some nondescript publication and recorded it for you because I consider you a dear, dear friend." Several coughs escaped between Beau's personal explanation and the actual quote:

"To laugh is to risk appearing the fool.

To weep is to risk being called sentimental.

To reach out to another is to risk involvement.

To expose feelings is to risk showing your true self.

To place your ideas and your dreams before them is to risk being called naive.

To love is to risk not being loved in return.

To live is to risk dying.

To hope is to risk despair,

and to try is to risk failure.

But risks must be taken, because the greatest hazard in life is to risk nothing.

The person who risks nothing, does nothing, has nothing, is nothing and becomes nothing. He [or she] may avoid suffering and sorrow, but simply cannot learn and feel and change and grow and love and live.

Chained by their certitudes, they are slaves who forfeit their freedom.

Only the person who risks is truly free."

I understood why the risk sentiment hit home with Beau, and wanted it to saturate my skull. Maybe the time for me to take risks and become truly free had commenced.

24

A setting sun ended my Saturday gardening as I finished a light watering of my English roses and Autumn Amethyst azaleas. I stood enjoying a small sense of well-being when Scott flew down the block in his Mercedes, driving and honking like he was the fire marshal and my place was ablaze. He'd been riding the silver bullet again.

"We've got to celebrate the Fall of the Berlin Wall—I brought my own Coors," he shouted while opening his car door. "Hey, you'll never believe who I had dinner with tonight."

He had that right.

"Dan and Marilyn. She's much more attractive in person, and Dan isn't as dumb as everyone thinks."

"Scott, I'm really tired. You need to leave."

"I'll only stay five minutes. Please, Cher. Please, please. . ."

"Dammit!" I threw down the garden hose and removed my gloves.

"So, what you been up to all day?" He set his car alarm before stumbling up the walk.

"Sitting at Jungman Library, reading up on stalker laws in Texas."

"Got anything to eat? I'm starving."

"Were you too busy talking politics with the Qualyes at *Ho Jo's*, to eat?" I asked.

"Hey, why don't you wear your hair like Marilyn's?"

"Why don't you head home?"

"You'd look great in that pretty flip style she wears."

"Not as great as I'll look after eight hours sleep. Please go home, Scott. Your nights of crashing here are over. I apologize, but I need time alone."

He looked stunned. I didn't care. Heeding Beau's advice, I turned away, walked inside, locked my door and prayed Scott would arrive safely wherever he was going.

Lakeside Drive was becoming a busy street. After work on Monday as I drove down the block, I saw Gabriel leaning against his van in front of my house. I panicked, knowing he saw me see him. I pulled into the garage, then got out and walked over to him. Beau said there's a big difference between compassion and passion and once you've had both, friendship is impossible without wanting the passion. Still, I wanted to try. Beau was a marvelous mentor, but let me extrapolate backwards for those who may have forgotten: I am not Mensa material.

"Just wanted to watch this sunset with you," Gabriel said softly. "If you don't mind."

How could I deny him a sunset? I loved him. And knew he still loved me. Our being together meant disrupting his relationship with every biological woman in his life. It was that simple and that complex. I could settle for just friends.

"Anytime, amigo." I looked across at him. Damn. He was once again wearing his melt-in-my-mouth moustache.

"Thank you." He nodded with a smile, but as he looked away from me and toward the sunset his expression seemed one of perpetual grimness. The calmness he always exuded was gone, and after reaching for a smoke, his hand trembled when he lit it.

We watched the setting sun in silence, and when his pale blue eyes turned to rest on my face, I noticed a perceptible twitch in his cheek muscle. The sky was shifting into nightfall.

"I'd better get inside. Got lots to do before bedtime tonight." I rushed into my house, waving as I went. Beau would've been proud of me.

It took me a few days longer than usual to complete *Texasville*, maybe because I was dialing Beau about every third chapter or so to leave messages on his answering machine. It had been well over a week since we spoke and I was getting worried about him. I attempted to catch him live to discuss

McMurtry's novel, but wound up telling it to his machine again. My phone rang immediately after I hung up the receiver. "Please, please be Beau," I said aloud before answering and tapping my speaker key to better hear his weak voice.

"Hey Blondie, whatcha up to?" Gabriel's voice amplified into my world.

"Checking out rehab centers." I hit the speaker key back to its off position.

"Yeaaah? You are one crazy lady."

"Just two fittings shy of a custom straightjacket. What's up, Gabriel?"

"Same old shit," he responded in dismal tone.

"You're still so eloquent. Maybe you should team with Delilah for T-shirt slogans."

"Don't make me puke." He wasn't a fan of Delilah. "That women is almost as bad as the one I live with."

"Speaking of Fran." I almost choked on her name. "She may have your phone tapped, so you might want to get to the point."

"No point. Just needed to hear your sweet voice."

Despite him sounding horribly depressed, he could easily weaken me. I wanted to be his friend, but wasn't sure how healthy it was for me. Hanging up was my only option. "I think I'm having a grand mal seizure. Better dash."

"You don't have that affliction."

"Right. But I do have to end this call. *Au revoir.*" I hung up.

He might've been in a miserable marriage, but our Seventies adultery had caused pain for all involved, and his girls were now part of Gabriel's life as were Gloria and Hope. None of these women would ever accept me and we both knew this. But like in our therapy sessions, he wouldn't address it. And as long as I allowed communication, we were still rhythmically committing sin while concomitantly adding guilt.

I was magnetized by Gabriel and didn't know how to demagnetize. Desensitize. Beau was still MIA, Patrice almost impossible to reach, so I dialed Delilah.

"I'm worried about Beau. He hasn't returned my calls."

"He's probably in Vegas. Didn't he say he was going there?"

"Yes, but he usually tells me his whereabouts. It's been two months."

"Is his answering machine still working?"

"Yes." I opened my fridge and inspected expired foodstuff on semi-empty shelves.

"Then he's fine. Otherwise his phone would be disconnected."

"You're probably right," I said hopefully. "I'm just concerned, and could sure use his wisdom."

"More Gabriel problems?" she pried.

"Not problems. He's just so ingrained in my heart it's tough to keep him in the friend zone."

"Because you two love each other. If it weren't for his family's interference you'd still be together."

"Maybe, maybe not. Still, the family situation happened and the damage is irreparable."

"It's sadly complicated," she said pensively. "But I'll always think of y'all as a great couple."

"Like Jane Eyre and Edward, once he lost his crazy wife." I trash canned some grey-green carrots and matching tofu. "Unfortunately, we lean toward Zhivago and Lara."

"I was thinking more along the lines of The Captain and Tenille. Hey, hold on a sec. I can't talk without a cigarette."

I heard Eric's voice and thought what a salt-of-the-Earth good guy her husband was, and how Delilah had become more responsible over the years. Still slightly warped, though.

"Cherie, you need to stop wallowing in the past." She paused to take a drag. "Go on a date—it'll help."

"Dating doesn't help. Every time I try to detach, he calls. Gabriel feels the same as me."

"Well, he won't do anything about it!" Delilah all but yelled. "Gloria and Hope are happy he's not with you, and maybe he thinks being miserable with Fran is his penance for what he did to Astrid and his girls."

"You're probably right." I found some grapefruit juice and poured myself a glass.

"Just feel lucky you two shared something great once. Really Cherie, put a lid on your memories, toss 'em on a shelf, and start dating again."

"There's gotta be more to life than smiling at lousy jokes during dinner, dodging lips after that, and ending the date by saying I'm not interested so take your penis elsewhere."

"Stop using Gabriel as a gauge for men, and maybe you could fall in love again."

"In the immortal words of Dionne Warwick: *I'll never fall in love again*."

"Cherie, if things are meant to be you two will be cashing your social security checks together and sitting your butts in rocking chairs when you're eighty, but until then, have some fun and enjoy life. Gabriel obviously hasn't put his life on hold for you."

Heaven help me. Delilah was right.

෫෴

M.C. Hammer was belting *U Can't Touch This*, and I was longing for some favorite Motown music when the phone rang. It was Beau! The best music my ears could ever hear. He had been hospitalized for weeks with a bout of emphysema, and then recuperated at his first wife Celeste's home. She insisted he stay at her house so their son Gilles could check on him when she wasn't around. Beau was happy to be back in his unadorned apartment, but talked about plans to head to Vegas the minute he was well again. Nothing could nip the joy that came from hearing his voice, but his frail utterance worried me.

A week later Beau called to say he was feeling better and had found an old side table and a ladder lamp table he was sure I could refurbish. I was so excited about our Friday date, I spent the week cooking and freezing casseroles to take him. I'd listened to KLOL's traffic updates in transit, but still wound up getting a ticket in my rush to see Beau. I would've risk jail time to hear him say "Baby" while wrapping me in one of his hugs. An embrace that evoked tears from me.

His wonderful smile lit my heart, but Beau looked pitiful. Pale, bone thin, and struggling to catch his breath between words, still he noticed my tears and immediately attempted to soothe my concern. "I feel better than I look, baby." And he rolled into story telling mode, easing my worry as he took me along on his favorite sentimental journeys. I would've been there all night had his lungs cooperated. Before he secured his oxygen for the evening, I hugged him extra long, making him promise to call anytime he wanted my company and especially if he felt ill. "Baby, if I get really sick I'll put your unlisted phone number in my wallet. My memory isn't what it used to be. It irritates me no end that this seasoned Black Jack player can't recall numbers."

"There's bound to be a tattoo parlor somewhere around here. Let's ink it on your arm."

"I've had too many needles poked in my arms the past few months." He was too tired for tattoo jokes. "But I'll be okay and will try to let you know if I'm not."

"Try?" I asked, in way-too-whiny voice.

"Baby," Beau attempted to speak, but began coughing something fierce. We slipped oxygen on him for a few minutes and I monopolized the conversation until a healthier color suffused his face. "That dang Lanny Griffith didn't help my cause tonight," I said.

"Who?"

"Houston's Master for Traffic in Bondage. He wears black leather and cracks his whip to keep listeners informed about traffic jams, but failed to keep me from getting a speeding ticket."

"Let me pay for that," he offered.

"No way. I'll take it to court, cop won't show up, and I'll win."

"You sure?" He started coughing again.

"I'm positive. And you need to rest so please don't say another word."

His neighbor arrived to help me load the old furniture into my Bronco, so I waved and blew kisses to a coughing yet smiling Beau as he sat watching from his apartment window. I looked up while driving away, and saw Beau flash a single playing card. I couldn't read it, but knew his weak hand was holding a *Jack of Clubs*.

25

Beau wasn't up to many visits and our talks grew rare, so I busied myself elsewhere, determined to forget what's-his-name. The '91 calendar was rapidly rolling toward May ninth when I rolled into the Sculley situation at Griff's pub where I watched Rockets basketball. Despite my attraction to this Irish advertising man with blond hair, blue eyes, and year round tan, I resisted his date requests. He was Gabriel in a tailored suit—sans moustache.

His simple "Hi, I'm Aidan Sculley," introduction back in 1990 was drenched in sensuality and accentuated by the flashing of his pearly whites.

"Oh, I've heard of you. Prone to tantrums, part-time bounty hunter, collector of belly button lint, wannabe priest, single helix DNA, and you were once caught kissing a corpse."

"Pretty funny," he said, uncertainty belying his comment.

"Well, I used to be pretty funny. But that was a while back."

"What happened?" He brushed his hand across the breast pocket of his suit.

"Let's just say I fell from grace with a family that was more like my family than my genetic family, so my only family now is my aboriginal family." I gazed into the crowd.

"Sounds interesting." He shot me a dubious look.

"What a coincidence, I used to be that too. But my wise personality just fired a warning shot reminding me to get away from the opposite sex, so I'll say *au revoir*." I looked at sportscaster Craig Roberts on a big screen TV, and laughed at his punch line.

"Can I buy you a drink?" Adian offered.

"I don't drink much, so thanks and buh bye."

"*Adios*," he said, yet never budged. The guy was either hearing impaired or hellaciously persistent.

"Bueños nachos," I responded. He had definitely derailed my train of thought. Although I suspected he was addicted to Binaca, there was no denying my physical attraction to him. Aidan was a very sexy piece of business. He stood stoically in his usurped post, forcing me to move elsewhere. My mercurial mind already hatching plans to substitute him for you-know-who.

Every time I saw Aidan he would do something incredibly asinine, like loudly sing the theme song to *The Fresh Prince of Bel Air* or suddenly break into discourse on Descartes. He was peculiar. My kind of guy. His athletic body verified his statements about being a health food nut, exercising regularly (participating, not just watching sports), and his casual dress consisted of walking shorts and wild print shirt, indicative of the Woodstock era. I learned through others that Aidan owned a small ranch in California, but considered himself a multifaceted rancher. Capable of roping and branding cattle, Aidan left such chores to hired cowboys while he enjoyed the great outdoors. His varied background intrigued me.

"Wow. Check out the callipygian." Aidan nodded to a passing girl as we sat at Griff's watching a Rockets game.

"Callipygian?" I questioned.

"Oh, it's an esoteric and rather useless word that means big-assed. I was an English professor at UCLA, so I remember minutia like that."

No way! I thought to myself, even more intrigued. "Then you could tell me all about Dorothy Parker." I attempted to check authenticity. Remember, I'd been involved for two years with Mr. Would I Lie To You Baby?

"Too easy." He slid onto the barstool beside me. "The sarcastic American writer of short stories, poems, plays, reviews and magazine articles, who was rarely without booze, attempted suicide several times, wrote 'Men seldom make passes at girls who wear glasses,' walked around without her glasses because she liked things blurry, and left her estate to the NAACP."

"I'm impressed, Mr. Sculley." I raked my bangs over my forehead, attempting to awaken any finesse I previous possessed for communicating with attractive, interesting men.

"Good," he said, observing me. "I'd like to impress you. My friends from California call all the time asking me to settle disputes on literature, history, politics, song lyrics and old television shows. I'm a vast receptacle of trivia. Feel free to indulge."

"I'll keep that in mind." I flipped my hair in flirtatious fashion, realizing my libido had suddenly sprang back to life. "Why did you stop teaching?"

"Mo' money, mo' money. And I wanted a job that entailed traveling."

"So." I nervously twisted my locks into a side ponytail. "What state did you go to first?"

"State? I went to countries. Starting with the Running of the Bulls in Pamplona, Spain."

"Hemingway must have known he'd ignite macho instincts in every man alive when he wrote about that strange Spanish custom."

"*Si, señorita.*" Aidan shook his head in agreement.

"*Hable usted Espanol?*" I mustered some Spanish and swept my tresses back to norm.

"*Si. Y tengo películas para provarlo. Soy un photografo fabuloso,*" he fluently replied.

"*Despacio, por favor,*" I asked him to slow down. "I don't have a clue what you're saying. I retained only a few words from seventh grade Spanish, and some vulgar street slang."

"I said I've got photos to prove it." He raised his right hand as if taking an oath. "I'm quite the photographer."

"I'm sure you are," I said with skeptical inflection, watching the callipygian girl stroll past us again.

"So, would you like to go to a movie or dinner sometime?"

"Oh, Mr. Sculley. Something about your looks warns me to say 'No way José!!' with double exclamation marks." I rubbed my ankle with my foot.

"My looks? I couldn't look more clean cut. In fact I've been mistaken for one of Christ's disciples before."

"Yeaaah? Would that be Judas?" I scurried away as he offered the bartender thirty pieces of silver for a Budweiser. If he smoked, something told me the brand would have been Marlboro.

୭

Shortly after Aidan began to earnestly consider a position as National Ad Director for a travel magazine in California, I accepted a date with him.

"*Dulce señorita.*" He grabbed his heart when I agreed to dinner. "I guess you make all men ask for a year, before agreeing to go out."

"It's a celibacy issue. I hear self-inflicted abstinence slows the aging process."

"Actually, it's just the opposite." He winked.

He probably had a plethora of sexual tricks up his bi-lingual sleeves, but he was leaving for California in the near future and I couldn't possibly become attached. So I decided to indulge in that predominately male game. Utilization of current resources. When you can't be with the one you love, check out tangible bodies.

Aidan arrived at *mi casa*, blue eyes sparkling as he whipped out a dozen orange roses from behind his back, saying they represented the number of months he had asked me for a date. He also informed his orange color choice signified enthusiasm, desire and fascination.

I lika this cowboy, I said under my breath while placing the roses in a vase. We went to Birraporetti's on West Gray, and after pizza I suggested venturing down the way to Marfreless. Didn't take long for us to find the crooked tree, rusty fire escape, and unmarked blue door. We didn't see much naughtiness going on in the darkness, so we conjugated verbs while Aidan drank bourbon and I sipped a raspberry martini as chill music played around us. Finally we stopped talking and kissed a few times before leaving. Doubtful we'd become regulars, but at least we experienced the little speak easy so we could brag to friends. On the ride back to my place, Aidan cranked up his Dylan CD and we sang all the way home. His live for today attitude somewhat conflicted his passionate reflections of the Sixties and Seventies. We had a lot in common. Married and divorced twice, Aidan admitted knowing his way around when it came to countless failed relationships. We also shared the joy of windsurfing and waterskiing, watching Letterman nightly, *Northern Exposure* on Mondays, and *Seinfeld* on Thursdays. When we returned to my house, Aidan grabbed a bucket with chilled champagne from a cooler in the back of his Land Rover. He popped the cork, poured bubbly into our glasses, then rummaged through my cassette tapes and inserted "Smash Hits of the Sixties" into my stereo. That was all she wrote, cowgirls. I dimmed the lights to cocktail lounge level and enjoyed the spontaneous combustion. Somewhere near the grand finale I murmured Gabriel, but Aidan took it in stride and never missed a beat.

"*Mama mia*!" Aidan gasped for air as he pulled me closer. "The earth just rotated."

"So that's why you screamed 'In dagoddadavita, baby' during climax."

"Did I do that!?"

I looked up at the ceiling fan and counted blade rotations. Some lies have fun potential.

Aidan slowly rubbed my arm, pulled me tightly to him, kissed me gently, and said "That was great!" Then he hesitated like it was my turn to comment. It *was* great, but I didn't say a word. Maybe it was his resemblance to what's-his-name, or my new rules on accolades after sex. I hugged him and sighed tenderly, wasn't that enough? The last thing I needed was post-coital brooding in my bed. He pulled me even closer, and I clung to him like an exhausted swimmer who had reached a brightly colored life raft in a dismal sea. Sex with Aidan: better than Nytol.

The following morning we laughed while conjugating more verbs and other things under the sheets, before Aidan rushed into the kitchen to prepare a breakfast treat for me. Great sex and Rice Krispies too? While he was cracking eggs, I got a micro-guilt thing going. Had I jumped in bed too quickly? Been too easy? Acted like a slut? At least I'd been mature about one thing. Besides, I appreciate the levity condoms can add to an evening. Just about the time I'd regressed back to Lake Jackson's obsession with reputation, wondering if he'd blab about our night together to our mutual friends before I saw them, Aidan returned to the bedroom with turkey bacon, egg white omelets, wheat toast—dry, and fruit slices on the side.

"How about a movie on Friday night?" he asked while gathering plates to take to the kitchen. "Maybe *Thelma & Louise.*"

Dying to see that film, I followed him to the kitchen like a woman under the influence.

"And I'd love you to join me Sunday for Easter Brunch at the Backstreet Cafe. It'll be just me and twenty of my closest friends from Griff's."

"I'd love to. Now leave so I can harvest grapes or plow the lower forty—I'm suddenly bursting with energy."

Walking backwards on my sidewalk, Aidan yelled, "Call ya later!" and waved goodbye. I put dishes into the dishwasher thinking how unbelievably close he came to filling Gabriel's shoes.

◦◦◦

Nikki phoned, but swiftly interrupted my details about my evening with Mr. Great Sex by telling me about a splendid job offer she received with a local paper. They wanted her to begin before graduation. She was pumped. Investigative journalism was her goal and this was a good start. Nothing yet on engagement to Tad, a subject Nikki addressed with calm confidence. Having witnessed my multiple marriages and failed relationships, I knew Nikki wouldn't commit unless she was one hundred percent sure. After dating two years, they knew each other well and neither seemed in a rush to walk down the aisle.

I called Beau to relay Nikki's career news, and although he struggled to speak, he sounded tickled for her. We hadn't seen each other much since the night he gave me furniture to refinish, so I insisted Beau let me come over and prepare his favorite meal: filet mignon—bloody rare, baked asparagus, and garlic baked potato. I loaded my car with groceries and flipped the radio to KLOL for traffic guidance.

When I arrived, the old treasure chest from the Jewel Box was empty of Beau's memorabilia, and parked near his front door along with a small table in desperate need of restoration. "I understand the table, but what's up with this, Beau?"

"All yours." He took a shallow breath. "Thought you'd like the old chest."

"Oh, Beau, I can't take part of your history."

"It's also part of yours, baby. With a little TLC, you can make it look decent or just keep it in your garage for storing things. Maybe one day it'll evoke some good memories."

"I have good memories." I walked over to hug him. "Especially of you frequently saving my naïve bum. I will *forever* treasure this chest, Beau."

"Well, I'm giving away things I feel might bring happiness to others. Gilles is getting all my valuable memorabilia and this would mean nothing to him, but much to you. By the way, there's a couple decks of playing cards inside that contain only *Jack of Clubs* cards."

"You sneaky bastard!" I lightly punched his arm. "Thanks again, Beau. This is already calling up old memories; some characters who traversed that great divide will be etched in my mind forever. Dancers and customers."

"Remember that knucklehead who gave discount coupons to waitresses in lieu of a tip? Fifty cents off everything from Windex to diapers." Beau chuckled.

"Mostly I remember old Murray, the millionaire who sat at the bar singing *Mention My Name In Topeka,* complaining about the price of drinks, refusing to spend a dime on any girl, but always managing to touch more breasts than Hugh Hefner."

"I heard he died shortly after the Jewel Box closed."

"Well, I'll pray for Murray's soul, next time I slap an old fart who tries to cop a feel."

Beau coughed. "He got slapped often, but was back to his groping game before the sting left his cheek."

I loved assisting Beau in reliving his past. "Yeah, I remember Red almost flattened Murray one night when she went to the bar for smokes. That girl was one tough cookie. Did I mention I ran into her several months ago? She owns a chain of liquor stores in southeast Houston."

"Who was that again, baby?"

"Well, Red was a nickname Gabriel gave her because of her atrocious hair color, but she was the only girl I met who danced under her given name of Betty."

"I don't remember her." He adjusted his oxygen tank. "But glad to know some girls turned their earnings into thriving businesses."

"She was a short, snooty, redhead with weeping, catawampus false eyelashes."

"No, still can't place her." Beau paused as though trying to recall. "But now that you mention it, I remember finding some damn creepy spider-looking eyelash almost glued to my bar ever so often when I'd open up before the cleaning crew arrived."

"Had to be hers," I said. "She was sloppy with glue and lost either a right or left strip of lashes about once a week. Ugh. I still remember how pitiful she looked parading around with one eye laden in lashes while the other was barely visible. But let's forget her and get some food in you!"

"Amen, baby." Beau agreed as I began setting his table. "You're my angel in an apron."

"Now there's a slogan for luring women into cooking for their man."

"Do you cook for this new guy in your life?"

"Nah."

"Well he's still damn lucky to have you."

"Glad you're not biased, Beau. And I'm happy you're feeling better."

"I'm feeling so good I went out to Half-Priced Books last week. Let me get you these books I stumbled across and read in four days. I like this new author as much as McMurtry. He's young, but writes like he's done a lot of living. Name's Tim Sandlin. *Sex and Sunsets* is a page turner." He headed to his bedroom.

"Sounds like soft porn, Beau"

"You know me better than that. But Sandlin is a tad raunchy. Still a damn talented writer, though. Start with *Sex and Sunsets*, then read *Western Swing*." He handed me two paperbacks.

I left his place with Sandlin novels in my hands and tears in my eyes. The sentimental overtones of Beau giving me the special treasure chest touched my heart.

❧

After our Backstreet Cafe brunch, Aidan and I joined friends at Griff's where he walked around talking to his guy friends as I sat at a table talking to their wives and girlfriends. When he passed by and kissed my cheek after a game of darts, Roz and Susie started asking questions. Like any pub, Griff's was gossip city and Roz was mayor elect, so I lit their fuse by saying we had great sex that left Aidan standing in bed afterwards screaming "In dagoddadavita baby."

Aidan buzzed by again and kissed my neck, creating chills so delightful, I almost didn't compare him to Gabriel. Then he turned my chair around to face him. "Everyone kept asking about our night together and I was being honorable, denying anything happened, when Dave said something about 'In dagoddadavita.' That's a good one."

"Ooops!" I cupped my hand over my mouth.

"It's okay." He pulled my fingers from my lips.

"Well, it's not like everyone can't tell. I'm all aglow here and it's not from the sun. Sorry about my mouth."

"Don't apologize." He was beaming. "I like your mouth. And now I don't have to worry about blurting out the wrong thing to my buddies—who, by the way, are asking. I guess we're pretty obvious. See, I'm all aglow too."

"That's because you think you've got enough signatures on your petition to reinstate those sexy Spuds McKenzie commercials."

He gave me a quick kiss. "Gotta run and get more signatures. Need a drink?"

"You bet. Would you bring me a glass of wine?"

"Would I?" He closed one eye.

"Harelip!" I twisted my mouth.

"I can't believe you know that joke." He laughed. "But that's what I like about you, you know all the old jokes and Sixties songs."

Watching him walk to the bar, I tried to shake the vision of Gabriel sitting in the Jewel Box telling me that joke. If I could zap that carpenter out of my thoughts, I might wind up having a nice summer for a change.

From an early age, Nikki often visited Beau with me, and I witnessed their intense listening to each other while gaining personal insight from their age disparity. But helping Beau celebrate his seventy-third birthday in Galveston, I selfishly wanted to travel fifty miles alone with him. We drove near the area where the Jewel Box once stood and talked about the decline of Houston's southeast side after Intercontinental Airport opened on the north side. Previously booming businesses around Hobby Airport had closed or deteriorated. The once luxurious Carousel Motel that revolved in the sky had become a hump-and-run joint where people paid by the half hour. NASA no longer held the attraction it once had, making us both sad. Beau enlightened me on Galveston's history, before asking about my youth, and then moving to his. Beau's presence warmed me and made me feel like an incredibly valuable soul. I loved hearing about the good old days, way before the Jewel Box—his one and only endeavor in the topless field.

Beau chose a cozy cafe and bar with a tropical, upbeat, Jamaican atmosphere. As a coterie of diners politely nibbled their salads and shared languid conversation, I never felt the least bit embarrassed as Beau spouted spirited stories about the Jewel Box. A place that once seemed so awful, led me to two wonderful men. Naturally Jewel Box conversation always gave rise to Beau's sentiment about me and Gabriel, with Beau saying no matter how great our love, my being ostracized by all important women in his life would never make for a happy ending. Beau was still trying to force his wisdom through my thick skull.

"That side table you gave me renovated beautifully, Beau. Thanks for kindling my love for restoring old furniture." My eyes sailed to an antique shop across the street.

"Why don't you open a small shop, baby?"

"Takes lots of money, and doesn't offer health insurance."

"Well, make it an antique shop that serves tea and crumpets from ten until four during the week, and I'll bet you could bring in enough to pay insurance premiums."

"I'm not as bold as you about putting all my cash into business gambles."

"Haven't you listened to that tape on Risk I recorded for you?"

"Yessssssss. . . I'm still a coward though. And I have lots going on in my life."

"You'll always have lots going on." Beau stared into my eyes. "Don't leave this life with regrets, baby."

"I won't. I'm just trying to make up for lost time with Nikki."

"Don't worry about her childhood." He read my mind. "Nikki turned out exceptionally well and you should be proud. Damn proud!"

"She's been the highlight of my erratic life whilst I created problems in her I assumed only years of therapy might correct. In her younger years, I overheard her tell a friend, "Sometimes my mom and I get confused on the mother/daughter, authoritarian/apprentice role.""

Beau chuckled. "Nikki always was a cerebral kid."

"Yes. And an even smarter adult," I bragged.

Sitting there with Beau, I felt thankful Nikki and I had finally developed a healthy relationship. Only took twenty-four years. "Do you have any regrets, Beau?"

"Just wished I'd saved more money. Otherwise I'm content. After Celeste and I divorced, I spent a lot of money on several gold diggers. Especially Lola. You'd have thought I knew better, but there's no fool like an old fool. Still, Gilles grew into adulthood better than my highest expectation, and I'm so proud of him. Beau's eyes misted. "Celeste and I put him through medical school, but she allowed him to live underfoot for twelve years. You've seen him so you can imagine her grocery bill." Beau beamed.

"He's the spitting image of what you must've looked liked in your youth."

Beau nodded his head, proudly. "Know what I dream about almost every night, baby?"

"Opening a restaurant or nightclub," I answered with a smile, thinking how often he revealed those dreams to me.

"Yep." His eyes brightened. "Sometimes it's a gigantic dance club, sometimes it's a tiny neighborhood bar, and sometimes it's a normal size restaurant. Sometimes I build them from the ground up, and sometimes I just remodel an existing place. Some are successful and some are complete failures." He laughed.

Oh, I loved hearing his heartfelt bass laugh and seeing the lines around his eyes deepen. Then he coughed. I patted his back, and signaled the waiter for our check. Beau would never allow me to pay, and knowing his funds were limited, I always tucked a fifty dollar bill somewhere in his apartment when visiting. "You sure I can keep these?" I asked when he rejected my attempt to return the Tim Sandlin novels he'd loaned me.

"All yours. I'm glad you liked him so much."

"I loved him! Might even become one of his groupies."

"Here, baby." Beau insisted I take his metal detector, which he'd previously offered me. I gave him an extra hug instead of wasting time arguing. He wasn't up to seeking hidden treasure anymore.

Beau valued his privacy, but the minute I got home I called. "Why don't you come stay with me til you get healthier?"

"I'll be fine, so stop worrying. We'll spend more time together before I leave for Vegas. Hell, maybe I'll teach you to count cards and bring you along so we can make a small fortune. I say small because we'll have medical bills when they break our legs for cheating."

"Me on crutches? Beau, I'm a total klutz."

"But wouldn't the thrill of it be cool?"

"Hey, you know how Katie-Laura described you years ago?"

"How's that?" He managed to ask between coughs.

"She said 'Beau burns cool' which initially mystified me. But I totally agree."

"Sounds like her. She was a good girl. I hope you find her again and rekindle your special friendship."

"I'm trying. Ladies are tough to find since our last names change with marriage. Now, let me get off this phone so you can rest." I could hear him struggling for breath.

"I love you, baby."

In all my years of knowing Beau, he'd never once said those words. "I love you too! Now go rest your lungs and call me when you feel better. Goodnight, Beau."

26

Shortly after our trip to Galveston, I couldn't reach Beau by phone and his answering machine wasn't on. Eventually I drove by his apartment. My heart dropped when I found it vacant. Intuition told me he had not gone to Nevada, but still, I dialed numbers he gave me of places he might stay in Vegas. No Beau. I chastised myself for not insisting he come live with me. I spent an entire Saturday calling local hospitals before attempting to reach his ex-wife or their son. Unlisted. We had become too close for Beau to lose touch with me and I knew something was terribly wrong. Still, I refused to believe he went to the big poker game in the sky without saying goodbye, and kept waiting for him to call.

Aidan went overboard trying to keep my thoughts from Beau's disappearance, which also helped keep my mind off Gabriel. The native Californian considered his state the greatest in the union, so occasionally I had to outshine his Golden State bragging with Texas trivia.

"You know, Texans don't just eat squirrel for breakfast and armadillo for dinner every night. We have culture and a few famous folks."

"Oh yeah, Bonnie and Clyde, Tex Watson, and Lee Harvey Oswald?"

"Howard Hughes, Walter Cronkite, Carol Burnett."

"Weak on athletes, though," the smug sports aficionado interrupted.

"Only if you don't count World Heavyweight Boxing Champion George Foreman, Indy 500 race car winner, A.J. Foyt, golfers Babe Didrikson Zaharias, Lee Trevino, Ben Hogan and Tom Kite, baseball great Nolan Ryan. . ." I took a breath, hoping to recall others.

"Well, Texas *is* a big state." Aidan looked around the room.

"And birthplace of Tom Landry, illustrious coach of the Dallas Cowboys, not to mention coach and athletic director of Rice University, John William Heisman who just happened to get a trophy named after him. Ever hear of the Heisman Trophy, Aidan?"

"You're killing me. Can I buy you a shot? Maybe one of those 'mind erasers'?"

I was revved up. "Houston built the first sports stadium with a dome in 1965, and speaking of domes, Austin's capitol building dome stands seven feet higher than the nation's Capitol in Washington, D.C."

"Bring this girl a shot of anything." He motioned to a waitress.

"The King Ranch is bigger than the state of Rhode Island; the world's first rodeo was held in Pecos in 1883; Austin is considered the live music capital of the world; and Texas-born musicians are too numerous to mention. But let's start with Selena—the Queen of Tejano music, since she's from my home town of Lake Jackson. And your favorite, Woody Guthrie is a fellow Texan to Barry White, Buddy Holly, Lisa Loeb, Edgar Winter, The Eagles' Don Henley, Dwight Yoakum, George Jones, Janis Joplin, Kris Kristofferson, Meatloaf, Roger Miller, Steve Miller, Roy Orbison, my personal picks, Stevie Ray Vaughn and ZZ Top, but since the list is so long it might take all night, I'll end with my absolute favorite from Abbott, Texas, Willie Nelson. Someday I hope to spark seeds with that legendary redhead."

"Shut it." He lightly placed his finger across my lips.

"And did I mention the word "buttload" is an official Texas measurement?"

This time Aidan used a kiss to quiet me. Yum.

Friends began saying it was nice to see me happy again. For the first time in ages, I was actually smiling from the heart. Until that weekend at the Westheimer Art Festival. After meandering through the artsy shops, Aidan and I went inside a booth filled with handmade wooden items where the craftsman was busily carving wood into whales. The smell hit me like a double Patsy Cline CD. Confronting the pitiful reality that my erotic epiphanies would always arise at the scent of sawdust, I rushed out of the tiny building and leaned against a tree, leaving Aidan alone for a few minutes.

"There you are," Aidan joined me. "Whatcha doin?"

"Pondering the crisis in the Gulf."

"We'll you can do that at Griff's. I'll even let you win a game of darts."

"I'll win more than one game, without handicap from you."

"Whatever you say, Ms. Steinem."

I'd heard that line before. "I say it's time for a drink and you're buying." I swept his hair from his forehead, wishing I could've been one-tenth as independent, strong, and intelligent as Gloria Steinem. My false bravado and stubbornness had deceived Gabriel years ago, and now Aidan.

"When have you ever bought?" He pulled my hand into his, heading to his car.

"Just making it clear."

⁓

Nikki, my nephew Jim, and his wife Roxanne were the ones who brought the tragic news of my father's death. Dad had been killed in an auto accident, which unfortunately seemed befitting, since he drove like a bat out of hell and like myself, could eat or read as he sped around town. We never had a strong closeness, but bonded some in the years after he turned his life around, stopped drinking, and flourished into a wonderful soul. I stepped up visits with Mother and realized that despite decades of dealing with his drunkenness, she never once said a negative word about Dad. She was the epitome of a gracious Southern woman. A trait she had fortunately passed to one of her two daughters.

Dad's death caused me to believe Beau wasn't simply missing. Losing my dad brought immense sadness, but still, nothing comparable to the grief I felt when Sean died. For days after Dad's funeral I functioned on auto-pilot, which is likely why I answered my phone on first ring.

"You okay, Blondie?" Gabriel asked. "I'm sorry to hear about your dad and just wanted to see how you're doing."

"I'm okay," I answered, unable to hide my grief. "Thanks for asking."

"You'll never believe what I did last week." His voice switched to "Cheer her up" mode.

"Probably not."

"I drove by the St. Patrick apartments—well, they're named something else now. Christ, they're old and dilapidated and should be condemned."

My heart fluttered. "Do you remember where I lived? And did you go by and see if the peep-hole was still in the door?"

"Of course I remember *our* apartment; number one-twenty-six. And no, I didn't get out of my van. Christ, Blondie—you tryin' to get me shot?"

"It can't be that bad."

"Believe me, you wouldn't wanna go there unarmed."

"Oh, that makes me sad. Those apartments were so special to me."

"I know what you mean," he said softly, as though tripping back in time.

"Gabriel, I need to go now." My heart was about to pounce out of my chest. "Take care of yourself."

"You do the same, okay? Again, I'm sorry for your loss. Please call me if you need anything."

I hung up and took ten deliberate breaths, as if fresh air would eradicate my longing for him. He still loved me. Why else would he go out of his way to go by those apartments?

Only months after Dad's death, Ellen and her husband Charles uprooted and moved back to Lake Jackson, near our mother. It wasn't a sacrifice for Ellen, who enjoyed small town living and was a spitting image of our straight-laced mother. But at age seventy, Mother's fun side emerged and she began answering the phone in her immaculate home, "Joe's mule barn."

"I'm worried she's getting senile," Ellen said.

"No, we're just seeing the perky personality that Dad fell in love with. I think Mom toned down to raise us kids while Dad ramped up and started raising hell."

"Maybe," Ellen agreed with a smile. "Let's just hope Mom doesn't get wild like he did."

"Not to worry, with her chromosomes."

Dad's DNA got me banned from a few bars in my earlier years, whereas Mother's DNA yielded virtuous Ellen. Saints and sinners. Beau always said life would be boring without both.

Aidan's job offer was reaching the stage where he had to decline or accept, which would entail his move to California. He seemed hesitant about taking the job, especially considering his love for the state and his small ranch there. Maybe it was salary or benefits or a combination. I was ambivalent about his news, not really caring if he'd accept the job and move. Soon, I was feeling apathetic toward him. Maybe it was losing my dad, missing Beau, or exhaustive furniture refurbishing, but suddenly I didn't see Mr. Great Sex as a marvelous man. Okay. Aidan just wasn't the real thing.

I went back to screening *all* calls to avoid conversations with Gabriel. Beau's words about me being in an emotional downpour of unsalvageable love, echoed in my head and gave me strength to stay clear of Gabriel's heart wounding zone.

27

I spent months reconnecting with pals from my past, and searching for others (like my daughter's beloved sitter Rachel, amazing Patrice, and even my dear Katie) while spending time with Nikki when she wasn't with Tad. Nikki still communicated with Gabriel, but respectfully kept their conversations to herself. Until Gabriel told her Gloria was hospitalized with a serious heart condition. Nikki conveyed Gabriel's concern. I had to call him.

"Gabriel, I'm sorry to hear about Gloria."

"She's not doing so well," he said. "Thanks for calling."

"Gloria was special to me for many years. What's her prognosis?"

"Dilated cardiomyopathy. Naturally she's determined to beat it."

"I'm sure she will. I don't know much about heart disease, but know Gloria's a fighter."

"This particular condition weakens and enlarges the heart, keeping blood from pumping efficiently. If they don't get things under control, it'll affect her lungs, liver, and so forth."

"I am truly sorry, Gabriel."

"Blondie I really need to see you. Wouldya come by and bring me a Coke tomorrow?"

His request took me by surprise, so I stalled until he cleared his throat several times. "Wood eye?" I broke the silence. "Just give me directions and I'll try to take a long lunch."

"Try?"

"I promise to fly by for a few." I gave in. Beau wasn't around to clip my tail feathers.

"See ya, Blondie."

At lunchtime I drove to Gabriel's job site, and then sat in my car twisting the brass buttons on my military style suit, wising I'd worn something simpler to work. Apprehension finally triggered more adrenaline, giving me enough courage to walk inside. Gabriel was nowhere in sight, so I wandered through the gargantuan house until I saw him jotting notes into his planner. I nervously leaned against a door jamb while sawdust flew around me, and watched him write a few things until he finally noticed me. Dark circles surrounded his eyes, making him look slightly older, and his hair seemed slightly thinner. His grim expression went auto-smile when he saw me. He closed his book, walked toward me, placed a quick kiss on my cheek, and ushered me out of the room filled with workers. I almost tripped over my own four feet. "Sawdust intoxication," I explained.

"Watch out!" He grabbed my elbow as Ben sailed around the corner carrying a large piece of lumber. Ben raised his eyebrows to salute me, leaned the wood against a wall, then marched over and delighted me with a gentle hug. He wasn't as gruff as he pretended either. I hugged him and offered condolences for Gloria's ailing. "And how is lovely Mei?" I asked.

"She's running O'Quinn Brother's now. Does all our bookkeeping, accounting, purchasing, and any other tasks we despise. She loves it!"

"That's terrific. Never hurts to be family owned and operated. Like the Mafia."

"Yeah, if only we were making that kind of money," Ben said with timorous modesty.

"Now you sound like your brother. Hundred thousand a year is hardly abject poverty."

Before Ben could respond, Gabriel walked over and ran his forefinger across the hash marks on my suit sleeve. "Admiral Halsey's taking me for a Coke. I'll be back soon."

Something of his aura of serene self-confidence had visibly diminished and he seemed almost vulnerable.

"You can slip out of your apron faster than most men slip out of their wedding rings," I said as he tossed his carpenter's apron aside. His ring finger still conspicuously void of jewelry.

"C'mon, I need to get out of here." He placed his hand against my elbow.

His voice, his smell, his touch, and my anxiety caused me to stumble over a board on the foyer floor as we left. He grinned, shook his head slowly, and called me a klutz. Didn't he understand why I became the clumsiest woman on earth in his presence? Didn't he know it had to do with jewel boxes; music boxes; Budweiser, Kool-Aid cocktails; sawdust; pasties; "Got a dollar for the jukebox?"; "I'd do just about anything for a piece of ass"; Woodstock; The Berlin Wall; tiptoes; sinkin' spells; Vietnam; Desert Storm; sunrise; sunset; harelips; wood eyes; Dick Cavett; David Letterman; the real thing; that's a fact and not a fiction; yada, yada, yada. Jeez, was I too complex for him?

We stopped at a convenience store just as a fine mist of rain began turning the sky a shade darker. He handed me my diet Coke, and I followed his directions and drove to a spot near Memorial Park that was shaded by enormous trees. Once parked, I stole glimpses of his delicious profile as he sipped his Coca-Cola and talked about Gloria. The strength he once reflected was drained and that made me sad. He gently rubbed my right arm, and then reached over to me. I froze. *Don't be an idiot! Don't let him weaken you. Not now, not ever again.* My intention to soothe his concerns for Gloria had gone awry. I moved away from him and raised the radio volume just as *This Old Heart of Mine* by the Isley Brothers was ending.

"What station is that?"

"KLDE. They play oldies and lots of Motown."

"Yeaaah, I listen to talk radio mostly. Oh crap," he groaned as *Yester-Me, Yester-You, Yesterday* by Stevie Wonder came across the air waves. Moving swifter than usual, he reached over and turned the volume down, then looked at me. "Can't take that today." He shook his head.

"Sorry." I looked out the window.

"I need one of your hugs in the worst way," he whispered.

Thawing slightly, I leaned into him and acknowledged a coincidental inclination. Once again he had intensified the need. The ache. After we embraced he cleared his throat. I wanted to speak but he knew everything

I had to say. Everything I felt for him. He sat quietly, doing what I referred to as his quirky hand jive.

"Why do you always rub your thumb against those fingers? It's like you have imaginary sand on them that you're trying to brush away."

"I do that?" He turned toward me.

"For years and years."

"Like you and your walking on tiptoes?"

"I've almost broken that habit," I lied.

"Well, I'll make an effort to stop with the finger moves."

"Please don't. I love that weird mannerism."

"And I love watching you walk on your tiptoes. He turned and looked forward at the trees as the rain picked up its rate of speed.

I looked at his hand resting on his leg, then glanced upward at the pewter buttons on his jeans, took a quick breath, and looked forward. How many times had I touched those buttons or felt them pressed against me? God, why couldn't he have been one of those sloppy, inconsiderate, two minute men instead of one who found foreplay more pleasurable than Monday night football? Maybe then my memories would be less vivid.

"What ya thinkin' Blondie?"

"Oh, nothing." I tried to shake tantalizing thoughts.

"What have we done with our lives?" he asked, in contemplative tone.

I wasn't about to let him shift this into a somber *The Way We Were* mini-drama, knowing one wrong reaction could break down the defense mechanism I'd been working to fortify. "Obviously we've screwed up big time, Gabriel. We're too old to have been crack babies and knowing our mothers, we can rule out fetal-alcohol syndrome. The blame falls on us. But we're not the types to cry over foolish mistakes, are we?"

"Christ, we'd need Noah and his ark," he said dryly.

"Please know I'll be sending positive thoughts to Gloria. I'm still not big on praying. Not sure who listens."

"Thanks, Blondie."

Thunder suddenly boomed around us.

"Hope this doesn't grow into a tornado. Although I wouldn't mind drifting up into the sky today. Like Dorothy and Toto."

"This ain't Kansas, Blondie." He let go a tiny grin. "But if you pass through Topeka, mention my name to Murray."

"Beau told me old 'Mention My Name in Topeka' died shortly after the Jewel Box closed, but I'll always think of him when someone mentions Topeka."

"Yeaaaah, me too," he responded softly.

I went mute as my mind rolled onto Beau. Now was not the time to wallow in Jewel Box memories. Gabriel stopped talking as our old comfortable silence returned. Like the quietness that once lingered in our home when we were doing separate things, but feeling content in each other's presence. I had to shake that pleasant feeling. As rain fell against the windshield, Gabriel smiled. He loved having a front row seat for Mother Nature's theatrics. I stared forward and shared his view, then felt his gaze on me. Our physical closeness hindered my breathing.

"What ya thinkin' now, Blondie?"

"That I'd better get back to work."

"Yeaaaah. . ." His voice drifted off and he cracked his knuckles before staring absently down at his hand. Aretha Franklin began crooning *Natural Woman* in the background. "We need to get back before we get in trouble."

I stayed composed enough to reiterate my regrets about Gloria's illness, and then cranked my engine. On the drive back not one word was spoken as he softly rubbed the top of my hand, which I habitually rested on the center console. I stopped in front of the house where we continued our silence while looking at each other in a puzzling sort of way. He reached over and gently kissed my cheek before getting out of my car. I waved goodbye and he cupped his hand over his mouth, blowing several kisses as he walked backwards into the house, getting drenched. I was tempted to honk my horn twice, but something kept my hands firmly attached to the steering wheel. Most likely that "something" was my spiritual guide named Beau.

❦

Aidan accepted the job in California and was in Newport Beach less than a month when he invited me out. "I'd love to visit. Distance from Texas might do me good."

"Wow, that's the fastest response I've ever gotten from you. I'll overnight a ticket before you can change your mind."

271

"Not to worry." I pulled luggage from my closet. "I'm packing as we speak."

"Yea! I can't wait to see you, my Cherie amour!"

Two days later I took off to be with the man I hoped would be the man to make me forget the man I truly loved. Surprisingly enough, I had a delightful long weekend with Aidan.

After my weekend in California, I avoided Gabriel, and weeks later when Aidan flew to Houston on business, he spent Saturday night with me. For twenty four hours, I became someone I almost didn't recognize, playing mind games, behaving seductively wicked and praising this gorgeous man for all he was worth. I desperately tried to fall in love with Aidan, but it just didn't take. Well, not on my end. Unfortunately my excessive fawning made Aidan think I had fallen head over heels for him. Before he left on Monday, he dropped to his knees, apologized for not having a ring in his pocket, and asked me to marry him. Little Miss Dysfunctional had an amazing man proposing marriage. I wasn't ready to jump into a relationship, much less marriage. Aidan interpreted my speechlessness as a request for more time.

In between Aidan's occasional visits, I stayed busy refinishing old furniture and reading McMurtry and Sandlin novels from Beau. I lived frugally, hoping to turn Beau's idea of a small antique shop with daily tea into a reality. Nikki and I drove to Galveston one weekend to see *Greater Tuna* at the 1894 Opera House, and arriving early, decided to go to the Strand and loiter at Colonel Bubbies—a gigantic military surplus store where worldwide collectors come seeking treasures. As we strolled past the little cafe where Beau and I shared our last lunch, a man was placing a "For sale" in the window. I jotted the number and dialed it. I was appalled by their asking price, but spiritually believed I was destined to own it. After all, Texans had recently voted the lottery into our Lone Star state.

⌒♥

Gabriel called on our May ninth anniversary, but only to say Gloria was soon to be released as doctors had stopped her acute symptoms. Albeit attached to a monitor and taking vasodilators and other meds for chronic failure, the news was encouraging. I kept the call succinct, hung up, and then wrestled with the idea of visiting his mom in the hospital; not wanting to offend, but wanting to wish her good health. An hour later, I was in the Bronco heading downtown.

After thirty years of exponential growth, the Texas Medical Center seemed almost unrecognizable, and it took a while to get my bearings. I parked on North McGregor Street and began walking toward Memorial Hermann. Realizing how late it had become, I stopped and sat on the curb. Was visiting Gloria the right thing to do? Not because it was almost nine, but because I would never want to upset her. Wishing for Beau's opinion, I sat outside, allowing the evening breeze to blow my hair as I took in a decent view of nearby Hermann Park.

"What the hell are you doing?" Gabriel asked, as he knelt beside me.

"Wondering if our meeting falls under the heading of kismet or terrible timing," I accidently blurted personal thoughts. "Sorry. I'm just trying to decide if visiting your mother is the respectful thing to do."

"You are some kind of crazy, Blondie."

I wanted to chew through his moustache and suck the lips off his face. How's that for crazy? "Yeah," I answered. "I'd be wealthy if I could find a way to use my personality disorder to make a living. Instead of spending money on shrinks, I should've invested in stocks."

"Did you say cocks?"

"No, I said you're perverted." I smirked.

"Is that a fact and not a fiction?"

"That's a fact, my friend."

The damaging effects from years of smoking had caused few visible changes, but his coughs had become pulmonary bulldozers.

"Hey, Doc Holiday, you need to stop smoking. I'm not sure you'd look quite as appealing lying naked in an iron lung."

"You think?"

"Smoking widens the ozone hole." I made a moue.

"Well before you go runnin off to work for the EPA or Green Peace, I've quit smoking. It's only been three weeks, but I'm sticking with it. Seeing Gloria stuck in that hospital bed is better than any stop smoking program. You know I can't be confined."

"No more tobacco? Congratulations!" I cheered. "Now, should I go visit or not?"

"She's taken her pain med, and was dozing off when I left." He nodded. "Hey, look up."

I followed his eyes upward to the deep blue sky reflecting a myriad of twinkling stars as moonlight flickered through the billowy trees, hypnotically. Sounds of nature mingled with workers and visitors to create a melody around us. Gabriel shifted to sit beside me. I didn't ask Fran's whereabouts. We sat in total silence for about twenty minutes before I stood to head home. That was one damn hypnotic moon.

"Gloria's going to be okay." I touched his arm offering assurance. "Nikki and I read up on the disease and predict she'll be one of its survivors."

"You two have the same closeness as Gloria and Hope—just a healthier one."

"Healthier?"

"Yeah, their bond formed by Gloria manipulating Hope into being her willing slave."

"Gabriel, I wish you wouldn't talk in such mean spirit about people I once loved."

"Well, they hate your guts."

He could have hit me in the stomach with a baseball bat and caused less pain. I took several breaths, fighting back tears. "Thanks for your brutal honesty, Carpenter Boy."

"They're not the only ones. My daughters hate you too."

What the hell was he trying to do? I knew his feelings about honesty, but had he lost all sensitivity?

"But I don't." He put his arm around me. "And you know my brothers don't."

"Lauren and Skylar don't even know me." I pulled away, struggling to hold back tears.

Gabriel grabbed me tightly, possibly recognizing my distress. "They blame you for separating me and Astrid." He cautiously reached for my hand. "And I'm sure Gloria's hammered it into them that you sabotaged her job."

"That sickens me!" I allowed him to hold my hand, which was visibly shaking. "Since you're so hell bent on honesty, tell your girls why Gloria lost her job, and also that a happy marriage doesn't end simply because of another person. It takes two to tango and I'm not sure who took the first step, but we were both on the dance floor."

"Yeah, we were dancin' along pretty good there for awhile."

"Like Fred and Ginger." I pulled my hand from his as tears welled in my eyes.

"Hey, I'll even dance with you right now, if you want." He put his arms around me, and then gently kissed my forehead. Had he finally noticed my anguish? "Cherie, you're the only person I'll ever love and I know why we ended up together. That's all that counts."

"Omigod!" I pushed him away and grabbed my chest. "Glad we're near a hospital in case I need some Digitoxin. You said you love me!"

"Did I say that?"

"In your round about way, you did." I smiled through tears. "It's amazing you can easily tell me about women in your life hating me, but can't manage to say you still love me. Doesn't matter, Gabriel. We both know why we'll never be together again."

He reached over and kissed the top of my head. "Don't say that, Blondie. And please don't pull away from me. I just need to hold you for a minute."

As I turned my head, he turned his, and without notice, our lips met. It was an ever so gentle kiss, filled with the hot breath of irony like a kiss shared years ago. The only difference was that this kiss was under the stars with nature's gentle sounds as background music—and there were no flickering dance lights or people screaming to be heard over a loud juke box.

I allowed his arms to stay wrapped around me much longer than his requested minute, as tears rolled off my cheeks and onto the grass. I didn't care who saw us and apparently neither did he. It was as if we both knew this would be the last time we would ever hold each other.

28

Even though I kept pushing Aidan's marriage proposals into a "No thru traffic" zone, we continued dating long distance. Occasionally he got a bit pushy, asking why I seemed to be withdrawing, why I couldn't give him a definite answer, why I postponed weekend trips to California, and so on. How could I explain? One must understand oneself before exegesis is possible.

Aidan's business brought him to Houston fairly often, and being with him was fun, interesting, and I gotta admit, a beneficial dose of sexual healing. Always whistling or humming, Aidan occasionally sang *Fifty Ways to Leave Your Lover* as though the lyrics might make me ditch Gabriel from my memory bank. "The problem is all inside your head," he said to me.

I rarely saw Delilah, but we spoke occasionally. She lived a good distance from me, and hadn't been introduced to any men I dated the past few years, including Aidan. For obvious reasons. Several summers back Nikki and I met her at a Mexican restaurant near her Cypress home, and I almost choked on a tortilla chip when she walked in wearing a bold print T-shirt that read: *Willow Should Take Her Stinky Pinky Back to the UK*. Willow Meath was a British neighbor who purportedly shagged several husbands in the hood, but when she snogged the spouse of a favorite neighbor, Delilah rendered her version of the Scarlet Letter by printing T-shirts. She distributed these throughout her neighborhood, and gave a buttload to homeless people who stood on nearby street corners. How she avoids lawsuits is beyond me.

May ninth unexpectedly hit me harder than usual, so when Aidan encouraged me to take an August break in Newport Beach, I accepted. Maybe my feelings might deepen, and with limited time left for basking in the sun why not end summer under California rays?

∽

Days after my ticket arrived, Nikki called, talking full tilt. "The Old Man asked me to have you call him. He's been trying to reach us for weeks and wants to know what's going on with you."

"And?"

"I wasn't sure what to tell him. He thinks you're moving to California."

"Is he okay? Health-wise?" I interrupted.

"Yes. He said he really needs to talk to you and you can reach him on his car phone, beeper or call his house collect. At any hour."

"Where's Fran?" I gulped.

"They're separated. He said they never married, but still have to get a divorce since they cohabited so long. I didn't know what to tell him about you, so I just kept quiet."

Life has no plot. I had a ticket for California, was contemplating marrying Aidan, and now Gabriel separates from Fran. Beau would've thumped my head had I phoned Carpenter Boy. Fran's departure simply meant one less female in the O'Quinn familial fortress, intent on keeping me out of Gabriel's life. "For improved mental health, I've got to rise above the O'Quinn quagmire, Nikki. Please don't relay any more personal messages from Gabriel. Emergencies only."

The time for me to detach and live life independent of Gabriel had commenced. Besides, this situation was a no brainer. Aidan was a wonderful guy who was offering me a life, far away from the heartbreak kid.

∽

"You're still heading West, aren't ya?" Aidan crooned into the phone.

"You betcha, cowboy. I've got a new bikini and know how to use it—so get ready to lose at beach volleyball. I've got a mean spike that's been looking for a victim since spring."

"Your spike can't trump my bump pass, so don't brag till we're off the sand. Besides, my penetration style has been touted in trade magazines and I know your weak side, so beware."

"Oh pleeease, Aidan. You better get used to eating sand 'cause that's what you'll be doing after my killer serves. Now, should I bring any formal threads or are we spending the week wearing slightly more than what Mother Nature gave us?"

"I'd love that, but we do have one event that'll require a cocktail dress. I bought you a little red number I saw in a shop window. You'll look spectacular in it."

"Ah, you California men think flattery and gifts like sexy red dresses will draw girls out of their g-strings and into your G-force."

"Speaking of G-force, don't forget to get flight insurance and list me as your beneficiary in case your plane crashes. This red dress had a hefty price tag and a no return policy," he joked.

"No can do, but I will bequeath my remains to you. I know how morbid you can be."

"You calling me a necrophiliac?"

"Without getting into semantics, let's just agree you're strange and let it go at that."

"We're both strange. Otherwise we wouldn't be together."

"Ditto," I agreed with his sentiment.

"And no pressure, but use the flight time to contemplate moving here permanently."

"No pressure?" I asked. Being strapped to a polygraph machine seemed less stressful.

"Just have a safe trip and know that I'm dying to see you!"

All I could say was "Ditto." The only person I would die to see at that moment was Beau. Over the past few months my desire to make my mentor proud had accelerated.

"See you soon, gorgeous." Aidan all but sang.

My week in California wasn't exactly pleasant. Health nut Aidan insisted I try a beach hut colonic. I'll spare you the details. But even a hose up my bum and a delightful, doting boyfriend couldn't hinder thoughts of Beau's whereabouts or Gabriel's decision to divorce Fran.

Aidan had Nikki's seal of approval, and she understood my reasons for not rushing forward with him. She seemed happy I was taking things slow for a change. Bless her heart. For years she listened to the repetitive rhythms of my breaking heart, and never once complained. Our bond has grown into a more special one than our previous link that entailed Nikki holding on while I shuffled her around more often than I switched lipstick shades. She cried for weeks when Mistletoe died, and cherishes Mistletoe *Deux*. Her genuine concern for others makes Nikki my reward in life. She received my dad's natural ebullience; my mother's forgiving attitude; Rachel's knack for making children feel important; Cousin Jim's tenacity; and Aunt Ellen's non-judgmental spirit. She's patient and calm like Gabriel, with an incredible fondness for nature, and like me, she's a bit sassy—and really loves her music.

Nikki's relentless encouragement kept me checking with the Galveston café owner. Before long we were in negotiation mode. I wasn't going to let that sweet shop slip by me, but had to be financially sensible in my endeavors. It would soon be mine, and I would follow Beau's suggestion of serving lunch. The café's small kitchen meant minimal remodeling. Filling it with antiques would be a breeze, since my house and two storage units were packed with countless items. No more storage fees and no need to purchase additional pieces for many months. If my house sold as quickly as anticipated, I could buy a home in Clear Lake, only thirty minutes away. Lots of cards on the table, but I was confident Beau's Lady Luck was on my side.

Nikki relayed messages about Gloria making grand strides with her heart treatment, but otherwise mentioned nothing personal about Gabriel O'Quinn. He had been the cynosure of my life for twenty-three years and forgetting him would not be easy. Still, I was determined to learn about life without him attached. How could I truly gauge my feelings for other men, while using Gabriel as a meter? But forgetting did not come easy. When May marked nine months of not hearing his voice, sharp memories began coursing through me like an inextinguishable fire. On May ninth,

I couldn't close my eyes without visualizing him. Sometimes I saw his face as it looked that night in '69 standing in the middle of the Jewel Box when I opened my eyes after our first kiss, and sometimes I saw his charming smile that cold December day when he pulled his T-shirt over his head and gave it to me. Those images might never fade, so I stayed super busy to help push them further to the back of my brain. Between traveling to California and busting my buns refurbishing furniture for the grand opening of my (and Beau's) shop, I spent time with Nikki. I couldn't track down Patrice for guidance, so I replayed Beau's tape on Risk, drawing inner strength not just from the words, but from hearing his soothing bass voice.

∽

"If I come to Houston next weekend, what are my chances of getting your hands out of paint thinner and into something more fun?" Aidan asked.

"You talking tanned flesh, cowboy?" My mind conjured images of his fab physique.

"That, plus a surprise."

"I love surprises, which is why I'll never install that new Caller ID technology."

"Well, I'd love to take you to a party at Roz and Roger's. Roz found some numerologist guy she confers with before making decisions."

"Are you saying I need help with decision making?"

"I'd never say such a thing," he answered in amused tone. "Just thought it would be a fun evening. Who knows what he might see in our future."

"Life is what you make it, Mr. Sculley. But I'll tag along and get a reading or two."

Aidan and I went to the party, and after barely greeting the host and hostess, he suggested I duck into the room for a psychic assessment. I was game for a hypothetical peek into my future—but not without a cocktail. I sent Aidan for my French martini as I entered the room where Roz stationed her guru, Mort Wiseman.

"So, you're a psychic," I said respectfully.

"Well, I enjoy sharing my metaphysical gift," said the short, russet haired man. "But I own an advertising agency, so I prefer the term businessman."

"Beg pardon." I reached for my martini from Aidan. "Nevertheless, a name like Wiseman could be a big hit on the psychic hot line."

His seraphic face remained unruffled as he stretched his plump hand forward, took mine and turned it palm up. I let him hold it until he rolled into details about my childhood, calling me a dreamer who'd left small town beginnings in search of a lavish lifestyle.

"What happened to the old tall, dark, stranger routine?" I frowned.

Mort didn't respond, but did ask Aidan to leave and return when he was ready for a reading. Apparently Mort was a one-on-one visionary. "I see a modest home, then larger ones, but much unhappiness." Mort scratched his chin. "Now I see an average home filled with happiness. Then anguish, confusion, sadness." His hazel eyes searched my face.

"I thought you did future readings, not past." I looked at the door, wondering whose ears were planted against the other side.

"We must review the past to predict the future," he said stoically. "And your fickle 'run away from problems' nature has influenced your former decisions."

I broke free of his grip.

"Care to discuss your guilt over your lost child?"

My distinct gulp filled the quiet room. How could he possibly know that secret? First I was stunned, and then weeping.

"Cherie, the spirit of your child is free, and you should be too. There was never malice in your actions—just a young, confused girl reacting rashly during an overwhelming time in her life. And never think the life you aborted caused the loss of your beloved young man. It was simply his time to fly among other guardian angels and spread his benevolence. He's with you often, but spends most of his time assisting lost souls. He says you're going to be fine."

"Sean." I wiped away tears. When Aidan tapped on the door again I reached over and gently kissed Mort's cheek. "Nice meeting you Mort, but my cola in transit and this martini are begging for liberation. Read someone else's palm. Mine's accompanying me to the ladies room." I motioned Aidan for his turn in the hot seat.

I felt comfort and relief over the unveiling of facts only Gabriel and Delilah knew. I'd been hiding my illegal abortion for so many years, I never dreamed a guy with a crystal ball would be the one to pry open my guilt-lined crypt. I'm sure Mort could have dredged up my sequined pasties and adulteress status too.

Aidan wandered out with a major grin on his face. Guru guy had predicted marriage and mega business success for him. How nice. I was sure Aidan's success would continue, but wasn't sure who his lucky bride might be.

After two martinis I decided to head back to clairvoyant corner. It seemed Mort anticipated my return. He handed me a stack of tarot cards to shuffle and cut. I obeyed, and then returned to him. Chewing the side of his mouth, he arranged and studied the cards before rolling into his spiel. "I'm seeing white go-go boots." He gave me a quick glance.

"My tribute to Nancy Sinatra." I shrugged. "Mort, I'm aware of my past. Can we move onto my future?"

Without hesitation, he studied the cards. "I see a blond man with blue eyes, surrounded by five women. Possibly a mother, a sibling, children, a green-eyed wife." Mort hesitated.

What did rehashing O'Quinn issues have to do with my future? Apparently Mort was in limbo, but I wanted to move ahead. "Mort," I said sweetly, "you've proven your ability, however you don't seem willing to discuss my future. But whatever it may be, it's my call. Your crystal ball failed to highlight a fabulous father figure. It's his advice that keeps me moving forward with gusto and I believe I can handle the trip without your direction. No offense."

"None taken," Mort replied. "But since the whereabouts of your dear friend greatly concerns you, I can tell you Mr. Jack of Clubs is alive but barely breathing air into his lungs."

"Omigod!" I felt faint as I grabbed Mort's arm. "Where's Beau?"

"In a place you can't reach him—due to family complications. But he's living his last days as comfortable as possible."

"Family complications?" I asked.

"Jealous ex-wife who won't let another female anywhere near him, especially one she remembers from some tiny little club."

My anxiety was accompanied by nausea, but I was ready to go find Beau. Mort offered an odd smile that seemed to be all-knowing yet cocky. My fanny bid farewell to his hot seat.

"Well?" Aidan questioned with raised eyebrow, eager to learn my future.

"Mort predicted we'd move to Tijuana and raise our tri-lingual triplets."

"You're not going to marry me, are you?" Aidan asked.

"Can we discuss this elsewhere? I don't do sensitive subjects in crowded places."

We found our hosts, and then said farewell to friends as Aidan escorted me outside. Several folks stopped him along the way wanting invites to sunny California, before we finally made it to the car and on the road. He patiently waited for me to continue our conversation.

"Aidan, I'm opening a business in a few weeks, and if you think I've been stressed thus far, just wait. This is the biggest risk I've ever taken and I'm a tad overwhelmed."

"But you don't have to take risks. I'm making enough money you never have to work. You can play at the ocean all day or do whatever you want. Or you can open the business in Newport Beach."

"I'm a Texas girl, Aidan. Galveston is rich with history, and when I saw the 'for sale' sign on the café where Beau and I shared our last lunch, I had to own it." My mind drifted to people I didn't know personally, but would miss. For twenty years I spent mornings watching perpetually happy Don Nelson do his thing on Channel 13, sports wouldn't be the same without humorous sportscaster Craig Roberts, I couldn't whip through traffic jams without Master Lanny Griffith, and I didn't want to sacrifice my Rock N Roll Army membership by parting with Col. St. James, who had DJ'd on almost every radio station in Texas since 1970.

"Still sounds like a big risk. What if you fail?"

Aidan was talking risk to the wrong person. I could've rattled off every line of the quote Beau recorded for me, but I barely got past "Risks must be taken, because the greater hazard in life is to risk nothing," when Aidan interrupted with some Dylan verse about letting go and moving on down the road. Our final goodbye—said via words of others.

284

29

For over a week I methodically called every hospital and nursing home in the Houston area, including River Oaks, where Beau's ex-wife Celeste owned a home. Nothing. I presumed Celeste acquired home care for her dying ex-husband, and I wasn't about to disturb that environment, even though I desperately wanted to see him one last time.

The shop opening was delayed three weeks, but I never missed Aidan and never once regretted my decision. I adored him—just wasn't in love with him. I'd hurt enough men by not fully reciprocating in the love department. Hopefully Aidan would find his dream woman and live happy ever after like Mr. Wiseman predicted.

Ellen and Charles went to Hawaii for two weeks to celebrate their thirty-fifth wedding anniversary, thus dropped Mother with me for a fourteen day visit. Boy did we ever connect! Years earlier Mother had dyed her graying champagne blonde hair a subtle scarlet shade, but over time her personality went fiery redhead. We sailed zingers back and forth, and indefatigable Lynn proved anything but uptight, arranging furniture and collectibles in perfect "show off" spots. Yes, she spouted quotes (less verbatim than in my youth), but my appreciation for her teaching method blossomed.

A jet-lagged Ellen collected Lynn the night before my grand opening, and our seventy-five-year-old mother insisted on driving home. I didn't fret as they handed her the keys. Lynn had more energy than all of us.

Nikki came to run the register and persuaded her friend Angela to waitress alongside two ladies I hired. Taking a risk, I made more specialty sandwiches than I ever dreamed would sell, and purchased several cakes from *Timtations*, a bakery owned by Nikki's friends Tim and Terri. I printed about a hundred copies of "Risk" onto parchment paper to place in all bags, hoping to hand out at least twenty bags to customers. And I played Beau's tape on Risk minutes before opening, soothed by the warmth of his voice.

Something magical happened that day. I sold all cucumber sandwiches, most of my spice tea, every slice of delicious cake, and seventy percent of my smaller furniture pieces for phenomenal profit. After everyone left and we locked the shop, I sat in my Queen Anne chair for a tiny breather. "Come relax a few minutes, Nikki," I urged.

"No thanks. I just wanna count this cash and get home to Tad."

I picked up a parchment paper copy of "Risk" from a table near my chair and although I knew it by heart, gave it another read. As I sadly recalled Beau's aging, weakened voice the night he read the quote to me, a vision appeared. A vision so real, I reached forward to the broadly smiling, impeccably dressed, forty-something Beau Duvalé who extended his hand and graciously said, "Welcome to the Jewel Box!" The image faded and a sensation of light snow drifted across my body bringing a chill unlike any I'd ever felt. I grabbed my cashmere throw and wrapped cocoon style, trying to regain normal temperature. Seconds later I was warm and cozy, ready to complete my moment of Zen. Nikki interrupted by summoning me to the counter.

"Mom, did you put this *Jack of Clubs* card under the tray for any special reason?"

"No. I cleared the register of everything but cash, long before we opened this morning."

"Weird," she said.

"No, lovey." I looked into the register at the card. "It's blessings from Beau."

Nikki worked several more weekends with me, even though I never asked. Things slowed down after the grand opening, but stayed respectfully steady. Long after I hired a lady to assist part time, Nikki frequently showed up to run the register or help rearrange things.

Then came the call.

"Hey, Mom," Nikki sang into the phone. "Can you handle this weekend without me?"

"Of course," I assured. "As much as I appreciate all your hard work, I don't expect you to be driving down here every weekend to play cashier."

"Well, I'll miss clipping fifties from the register when you're not looking, but I think you've got the hang of it now. Plus you said something about hiring full-time summer help."

"Not to worry, Nikki. I'll miss seeing you so often, but realize you have a busy life in Houston."

"Yeah," she responded casually. "I guess it's going to get much, much busier."

She was coy and enjoyed making me fish for answers to her clues.

"How so?" I nibbled her bait.

"Tad proposed!" She squealed excitedly into the phone.

"Omigod, Jacy Nicole!" I almost dropped the receiver. "What a thrilling surprise!"

"We wanted to drive down and tell you, but he just got off his knees and I couldn't contain my excitement for the hour drive to Galveston. You're the first to know."

"I'm over the moon." I wanted to hug her through the phone. Having witnessed my multiple marriages and failed relationships, I knew Nikki wouldn't commit unless she was one hundred percent sure. They had dated four years and knew each other well. "When's the big day?"

"Not to worry," she trilled. "We're waiting until Tad passes the bar, so it'll be another year. Does that give us enough time to put it all together?"

"Of course it does," I said, praying she'd keep it simple.

"Great, Mom. Well, we're off to hit a couple of jewelry stores and see if anything knocks my socks off. Tad knew better than to surprise me with a ring. Our jewelry taste is vastly different."

"Tad's a wise man. Congratulations, sweet girl!"

"Thanks, Mom. Why don't we meet next weekend? You can help me look at more rings and congratulate Tad. He has tons of studying, and you're a better shopping partner."

❧

I met Tad and Nikki at Bennigan's, so Tad could formally ask for her hand in marriage before she and I went looking at rings. Tad kissed my cheek, and then kissed her goodbye. Over and over. Looking at them, I remembered Mark Twain's quote in a letter about love and grief, in which Twain called marriage the supreme felicity. He said the deeper the love, the surer the tragedy and the more heartbreaking when it came. I wanted Twain to be totally incorrect in their case.

We shopped four straight hours before breaking for a bite to eat. Nikki slowly savored every bite while I rushed through the meal. Then we were off again, my feet begging for mercy worse than the day of my shop's grand opening. Finally just as stores were drawing shades, Nikki found the perfect ring—a brilliant square solitaire. Naturally, she would bring Tad to get his opinion, but we both knew this was the one.

I relished our time together as single women knowing things would change once she began life with her own family. Having been an only child, Nikki wanted lots of little McDougals. Tad agreed. They hired a wedding planner, bumping my involvement to minimal. Thank goodness! Melancholy interlaced my happiness as I dropped her off without lingering long, due to my feet threatening to mutiny.

After taking an extra long foot soak and relaxing bubble bath, I got a sudden urge to drive thirty minutes to Galveston to make sure my shop had been properly locked. I threw on my staples; a sundress and some va-va-voom lipstick.

The alarm was indeed set, so I disarmed it, turned on my stereo, and then sat in my Queen Anne armchair to enjoy the tranquility of my place. It was worth the drive to let my eyes drift over all the unusual pieces Beau salvaged and I refinished—items forever tagged "Display Only." The chime on my grandfather clock revealed midnight was about to arrive, bringing with it another May ninth. When would that date stop being so damn meaningful? "Let go, Cherie." I attempted to stop the storm of memories rushing through me. I changed mental subject by debating whether to drive home to Clear Lake or sleep upstairs on my twin bed in the room adjoining my office. Even with the shop's alarm system and the police station only blocks away, I never slept as well in the shop as I did at home. I stretched for a minute, trying to decide. That's when I heard a noise outside. I did a freeze frame and listened judiciously in case my hearing was playing tricks on me. Assuming it was only the wind, I relaxed somewhat while slowly walking across the hardwood floor toward my phone. Then came a loud tapping at my front door. The police station was on speed dial, but I was shaking too much to press a button.

"Got any Cokes in there, Blondie?" Gabriel yelled.

The sound of his voice ignited the slow burning fire he had lit inside me years earlier. A flame that time and distance hadn't been able to extinguish. My heart was racing wildly and my body was trembling, but I felt amazingly calm. I took several deep breaths, tried to brush goose bumps from my arms, and then walked to the door without stumbling. It had been four years since I last saw him, but besides gaining half a pound, he still looked the same as he stood smiling through his sexy moustache. He raked hair from his forehead while I punched in the security code and unlocked the dead bolt.

"I'm fresh out of your favorite beverage." I opened the door.

"Oh, but you're definitely the real thing." He reached to hug me.

It was our first awkward hug. What was he doing, waltzing back into my life after all these years?

He put his hand behind his neck, tugged at it as though he was trying to massage away stiffness. "Here." He handed me a piece of paper with a quote written on it.

I read it aloud. *"There is a great deal of pain in life, and perhaps the only pain that can be avoided is the pain that comes from trying to avoid pain."*

"By R.D. Laing," he finished.

"You getting poetic with old age?" I asked as tears welled in my eyes.

"Dammit, Cherie! I'll love you till I die," he loudly proclaimed. Then in a lower, unsteady voice he added, "I never married Fran, but had to get an official divorce. I want my one and only true love with me. Please come home."

I had to sit down on that one. "I am home, Gabriel." I dropped back into my armchair at the front entrance.

"Home can be where ever you want it to be." He looked at me. "The Friendswood's farm or your house in Clear Lake. I was wrong for not resolving the family issues, way back when."

"It wasn't your fault, Gabriel. Some issues simply can't be resolved. . ."

"Yes they can!" He interrupted and knelt beside my chair. "I realize it's difficult for you to believe I can exist without Gloria and Hope, but I have for almost three years. I should have stood up for you during our marriage, instead of pitying Gloria. She played her spousal abuse card for too many decades, and I finally had enough of her conniving. So did Ben, after he found out how nasty she'd been to Mei."

I could hardly believe my ears.

"I called Lauren and Skylar before heading here." He began to lightly stroke my hand. "They want me to be happy and sent me here with their blessings— but even without— nothing was stopping me tonight. Christ, I've driven by for months. I'm tired of feeling like a part of me is missing. I don't want to spend another day without you, Cherie. We're getting too old to waste precious minutes. I know you didn't stop loving me just because we weren't together."

KLDE had the knack. *Ain't Nothin' Like The Real Thing* by Marvin Gaye and Tammy Terrell flowed from my radio. Gabriel's eyes carefully scanned my face. "I can live without you Cherie, but I don't want to," he said quietly. "I can't erase my mistakes. Especially the one I made regarding the abortion. I'm sorry I didn't recognize your pain over that loss. I should've shown more love and emotional support. Can you ever forgive me?"

"Let's forgive each other. I hurt you by rushing away years ago. Neither of us behaved responsibly back then, but I think we've changed a bit." I stood from the chair and took a few steps toward the shop window.

"It's May ninth," he said, stopping me in my tracks and turning me around to face him.

"Really?" I grinned. "I hadn't noticed." With my green eyes softly locked on his baby blues, I leaned against him and reveled in the warmth of our gentle, guilt-free kiss.

"I love you," we said in unison. Gabriel pulled me against him and placed another delicious kiss on my mouth. Everything stood still as those old familiar feelings and years of history between us, melted together.

"Hey, I heard it through the grapevine that Vegas has round-the-clock wedding chapels."

"Beau's favorite city?" I rubbed my lipstick residue from his mouth. "What a perfect place to have my spiritual guide as our witness!"

"Yeah? Well, we'll buy clothes when we get there, so git in the truck, Blondie and let's head to the airport. I can't think of a better day for you to go from being Ms. O'Quinn back to being Mrs. O'Quinn."

"That's a fact and not a fiction!"

30

It's been nine and a half years since our May ninth Las Vegas wedding, and we're still celebrating marital bliss. No, it's not one hundred percent perfect, but close enough it's unlikely friends and family are still wagering on our survival rate. We sold both homes and moved to Tiki Island, a sleepy waterfront community closer to my shop. Gabriel watches Letterman with me, and I not only read Ken Hoffman's column, I occasionally write Ken about finding Houston's best French martini. I still don't give an embryotic rat's ass about fast food. Otherwise, when problems arise, no one clams up and no one runs away. We deal with issues like responsible, mature adults who know we're lucky to have a second chance.

Our relationship with Gabriel's daughters has flourished, and despite forgiving Gloria and Hope, we remain respectfully distant. Ellen and Mother often come to Houston where we attend Lynn's favorite, the *Deborah Duncan* TV show. If Deborah ever does a show about being thankful for family members who bail you out of jams without casting judgment, we'll be guests instead of audience members. My nephew Jim and his wife Roxanne are now parents of champagne blonde, future femme fatale, Alexis. Kent faded to black eons earlier, and due to their special bond built over decades, Gabriel walked Nikki down the aisle. They both grinned while making the short walk, like a duo with special secrets under their hats. Nikki and Tad are celebrating year eight and have given us three darling granddaughters and Luke married his longtime girlfriend, Chloé who blessed us with twin grandsons.

Ten years have brought countless familiar faces through my shop, including Patrice and her retired airline pilot husband, Art, Eduardo and his twenty year companion, Brian, Bianca and Brandon with their six (yes, six) children, babysitter extraordinaire Rachel, all the way from Florida, and even a recently divorced and still effervescent Katie, who lives in the area and stopped in solely due to my shop's name. Browsing with one of her two grown daughters, Kat recognized me immediately even though I was nowhere near the register. We've both changed since our youth, but our bond remains special. She drops by from time to time and once a year we trek to Houston for lunch at Brennan's. A trip filled with reminiscing about our mischievous teen years and sharing favorite memories of our beloved Beau.

Even with my business thriving, next year I'm selling to savor life on the bay. A former workaholic, Gabriel now rarely oversees his crews, much less works with them. Our pace has slowed as we focus on enjoying life to its fullest, which includes boating with Gabriel at the helm while I'm teaching little ones to water ski. We also spend time with recently adopted dogs: Beau—a debonair and gentle Airedale, and Jewel—a fearless and sassy Jack Russell Terrier. Thank goodness for an Internet website that helps find homes for unwanted newborn and adult pets. And thanks to another Internet website, I found a different kind of peace by learning Beau had passed away in '94, two years after our lunch in Galveston, and the exact day of our shop's grand opening. The sensation of light snow that evening had been Beau, swinging by with a sprinkling of unconditional love for me. His last residence reflected the same county as Celeste's home, so I felt relieved to know his final days were spent surrounded by loved ones.

Which brings me to the somewhat emotional, last antique shopping spree Nikki and I shared. I debated going since the shop will soon be closing, but Nikki seemed excited to be spending time with me. Or maybe getting time away from her brood.

The weather was unusually hot for late October and the crowd was larger than we'd imagined, with an assortment of people who looked like extras for a Quentin Tarantino film. When we passed an overweight woman in combat boots and bib overalls with a Lone Star beer hanging from her mouth and a kid who was way past weaning age fastened to her breast, Nikki piped up, "Someone should enforce a law against drinking while nursing."

"It's impossible to legislate morality, lovey." I pushed through the crowd.

"Well, witnessing brainless behavior like that makes me want to puke."

"You're such a poetic child." I put my arm around her shoulder. Her closeness to Gabriel still surfaces via quips and other idiosyncrasies imprinted by him.

"Look, Mom." She squinted into the sun and nodded her head forward. "There's a tent filled with furniture."

"Hmmm." I looked around. "I'm beginning to think our chances of finding anything decent, run along the same lines as finding Grandma at Chippendales tucking dollars into Fireman Fred's g-string. Let's call it a day if there's nothing worthwhile in this place."

"Oh Mom, the day is young!" Nikki locked her arm in mine and pulled me along.

As we entered the area filled with tables, chairs, and dressers—some of which had seen better days, we saw what looked like quality pieces inside a metal warehouse. Walking through the building, I touched a marble statue that seemed totally out of place, and leaned forward to take a better look at a bar in the far corner. I rushed ahead of Nikki, inching through the narrow path of tables and barstools stacked into a small mountain. A shriek of excitement escaped my mouth.

"Someone pour ice water down your back, Mom?" Nikki hurried to catch up.

"I'm not sure, but I think that's Beau's old bar." I kept walking. "From the Jewel Box."

Finally close enough to get a good look and put my hands on the elaborately crafted mahogany bar, I looked up and smiled, just about the time Nikki lifted its three thousand dollar price tag and gasped. A burly old man, sitting near a desk and sucking on the stub of a cigar, slowly got out of his overstuffed chair, and waddled over, digging his trousers out of his bum as he walked.

"That's a mighty fine piece you're lookin' at ma'am."

"It's awfully big." I tried to keep my composure as I walked around to the other side of the bar. If this was Beau's old bar, I wasn't about to leave without it. "Any idea where this came from or its chain of ownership?"

"Well, it's pretty old and a beautifully crafted piece."

I hate haggling. "If you can give me some background," I interrupted, "this might turn into a great day for both of us."

Chewing his cigar and scratching the nape of his neck under a fluff of thick gray hair, he grumbled about having to look in his files as he languidly drifted to his desk and pulled out a dilapidated manila folder. I followed and looked across the desk trying to read upside down writing on the worst record keeping register I'd ever seen. Flipping back and forth through the pages, the old man eyeballed papers with a slight grimace, obviously having a tough time deciphering his records. "Hmmm." He shifted his cigar to one side of his mouth. "I bought it from John Mueller of Austin in '98 when he sold his restaurant."

"Previous owners?" Nikki asked for me.

"Looks like a total of three. Mueller bought it from some Houston restaurateur—a Rob Rehill, who had bought it from another restaurateur, Beauregard Duval in '72."

He had mispronounced Duvalé, which wasn't unusual, but to my knowledge the Jewel Box never served food. Apparently trouser digger didn't want to admit this bar was actually used inside a watering hole. I asked if he had a flashlight. He offered his lighter. Nikki watched as I went to the right end of the bar, leaned down and sparked a flame underneath the middle shelf. Passage of time made it slightly difficult to read. I flicked off the lighter when it overheated my fingers, and then gently rubbed my hand over the engraved C/G, trying to conceal my smile.

"I'll give you your asking price plus whatever you charge for delivery, but I want it delivered as soon as possible."

"It's a deal, lady!" He spouted, almost choking on his cigar. "Name the date."

"Next Sunday, October 26th, 2003, six p.m. sharp." I wrote him a check.

"We'll have it there. Thank you very much, Ms. O'Quinn."

"That's Mrs. O'Quinn. And you're very welcome!"

He smiled and waddled away, tugging at his trousers.

"I still can't believe you found that bar!" Nikki smiled broadly as we left the area.

"Kismet my love, kismet. Now I have something that belonged to Beau other than the treasure chest, metal detector, books, and his tape about risk."

"You know the old man is going to claim this for sipping his evening beverage."

"Only when weather doesn't allow him to sit outdoors. But let's keep it a secret until it gets delivered. I want to surprise him and can't wait to see his face. 'Course Gabriel will have to figure out where the heck it's going to fit in our house eventually."

"Just promise you won't move again, Mom."

"I swear." I put my hand up, pledge fashion. "Unless, it's back to Houston near you. Now let's get on the road and take you home to your family."

"Yes, lets. I had a wonderful day Mom, but I do miss my girls and that man of mine."

"Likewise. And now I have a secret to keep from my man. But I think I can."

"Uh huh," Nikki mumbled as we headed for home.

❧

Delilah had been gone from the shop almost an hour and I was beginning to worry why perpetually punctual Gabriel hadn't arrived. Maybe I'd told him to arrive after eight, wanting to make sure the bar was actually delivered before he drove down. Delilah left her pack of cinnamon gum, so I popped a stick into my mouth and leisurely rested my head on Beau's bar. Soon I was running my fingertips lovingly along the mahogany surface and calling up some marvelous old memories. I never recall isolated bad moments at the Jewel Box—only wonderful times. Beau was a remarkable man, and it was a special force that situated his owning a bawdy business just when I needed him to enter my life. He believed in Lady Luck, but I was the lucky one to have known him.

I trashed my gum just as Gabriel drove up. Unable to contain my excitement, I rushed to greet him and kissed him more times than usual.

"Whoa, Cinnamon Girl! If you're going to get this excited every time I visit, I'll swing by this place every damn day from now on."

"Won't be here much longer, remember?"

"Oh I remember, Blondie. You'll be at home cooking, cleaning, and caring for me."

"You're taking hallucinogens again, aren't ya?"

"How else can I live with you?" He kissed my cheek. "Now what the hell was so important that you had me come down here with a cold front about to blow through the Gulf Coast?"

"Yeah, it may drop down to fifty tonight, my warm weather lover."

"I can handle that, but if it drops to forty, I'll be sportin' my ratty long johns you hate."

"I don't hate anything you wear. I just prefer you wearing nothing but your moustache." I grabbed his hand. "Close your eyes and let me lead the way."

"Blondie, if you say 'Turn left through the swinging doors to the kitchen corridor, Senator Kennedy,' I'm out of here."

"Not funny." I chastised. "That was a travesty and Bobby Kennedy was one of Sean's heroes."

"I'm sorry," he apologized with sincerity.

I guided him a few more steps, watching to make sure his eyes stayed shut.

"What's that God-awful perfume smell?" He stopped in his tracks and wrinkled his nose.

"Delilah came by and marked her territory while complaining about her life. But she's gone, so keep walking." I steered him to the bar. "Okay, you can look."

"Halle-fuckin-lujah." A smile streamed across his face. After all, he worked in wood, had a photographic memory, and apparently this bar had been almost as special to him as it was to me.

"Sooooooo. . . ." I cooed coyly.

"I can't believe it! Where the hell did you find Beau's old bar?"

"In Warrenton at the antique festival. And now it's all ours." I couldn't stop smiling.

"This'll make a great place for sipping my evening cocktail." He kissed my cheek.

"Nikki knows you too well." I grinned.

"Boy does this ever take me back." He walked around behind the bar and stuck his hand underneath to feel for our initials.

"Here's a flashlight."

"Kiss my ass and call me Elvis," Gabriel said in delicately soft tone, his eyes getting misty as he shook his head. "Talk about life coming full circle."

I looked toward the shop window at Beau's "original" Jewel Box treasure chest, now holding various antiques including the copy of Emerson's *Twelve Essential Essays* book he had given me so many years ago, and then glanced at the metal detector above the bar, beautifully encased in the box Gabriel constructed. Clinging to my latest *Jack of Clubs* card, I walked around to embrace the love of my life and felt tipsy as he pulled me to his chest.

Looking past his shoulder, I glanced toward the window and through glowing amber lighting, smiled as I read the subtle red inscription of my shop's white octagonal sign, *The Jewel Box.*

Michelle McCarty grew up as the youngest of five sisters in a small Texas town. Finding it difficult to be heard over older siblings, she began expressing herself through writing at an early age. Daydreaming and writing proved cathartic for teenage angst, but didn't do much in the way of enhancing her social skills. Not comfortable speaking in public, Michelle says writing stories opens a window in her heart where words swing dance into each other and fill her with joy, and sometimes great pride. Writing takes her to imaginary places filled with ordinary and extraordinary characters who offer intimate details of their humorous, eccentric, romantic, dramatic, and sometimes mundane lives. She writes to learn moral lessons by placing characters in a variety of situations, which in turn offers soul searching and sometimes personal resolutions. Michelle believes flawed characters reveal that everyone, no matter how imperfect or seemingly insignificant, offers something special in pretend worlds as well as in real life. When not writing, Michelle's time is filled with twin granddaughters, Annabella and Alexandria who zap her energy yet light up her life. She also works part-time as editor for an online newspaper.

The Jewel Box is Michelle's first published novel. To learn about her upcoming novel, *Beyond the Pale*, and more, please visit her website: http://cmichellemccarty-author.com or www.facebook.com/AuthorCMichelleMcCarty

Acknowledgements

My heartfelt thanks to family and friends whose encouragement kept me pounding on the keyboard. For those who read my first raw version; Kimberly Ryan McCarty Easdon, Joanne Leonard, Jim Leonard, Patrice Biskynis, Kathleen Nagy, and Martha Lindsey. Next up are editors Barbara Bamberger Scott of *A Woman's Write,* and Peggy Stautberg who I was guided to via benevolent Rita Mills, my friend and owner of *The Book Connection* and *The New Era Times*. For reading my "almost" final version, Yvonne Storrs, Scott Jones, Terri Porter Garcia, Lori Langland, Wanda Williams, Karen Lindsey, Shirley Hall, and Ray Cloninger, who photoshopped my jacket cover photograph to enhance the Jack of Clubs card held by model Leaann Haley Hoffman. Also appreciated are authors, Mark Richard Hunter and Lindy S. Hudis, and screenwriter, Wild Bill Hinckley who answered pesky questions during my stint with a traditional publisher. Not nearly enough can be said about the gracious kindness of author Terri Giuliano Long, whose invaluable insight and praise gave me hope as a writer. Enormous thanks to brilliant and enlightened publicist, Sarah Gish, and mammoth appreciation for Kathy Luersen's expertise on Houston's adult entertainment venues during the late Sixties. Extra hugs and kisses to my twin granddaughters, Annabella and Alexandria, for suffering neglect while I wrote, edited, edited, and edited. Last but by no means least, my deepest gratitude goes to beautiful soul, Michelle Mynier.

And thank you, readers! I feel humbled and honored that you took time to read this story.

19295169R00165

Made in the USA
Charleston, SC
16 May 2013